Dancing with Death

REG McKAY

DANCING WITH
DEATH

BLACK & WHITE PUBLISHING

First published 2007
by Black & White Publishing Ltd
99 Giles Street, Edinburgh, EH6 6BZ

ISBN 13: 978 1 84502 094 1
ISBN 10: 1 84502 094 4

A CIP catalogue record for this book is available from
The British Library.

Printed and bound by Creative Print and Design Group Ltd
Typeset by AJT

To all women –
may they always dance in safety

BOOK

of

RUTH

Monday, 15 January 1968

Let the people tremble.

For days, great winds have shaken the city by her roots, ripping off roofs and shaking foundations. The people squeal and the newspapers rant, 'WHY US? WHY NOW?' The heathens.

'My people have forgotten what it means to do right,' sayeth the Lord. So they will reap His wrath. First the walls will come tumbling down . . . then . . . ah, then . . .

Yesterday, a man was killed in Anderston when large chunks of masonry came smashing down on him. The people cried out in fear and prayed to their idols that the worst was over.

Now, I sit here under the flickering light bulb listening to God's rage. It is fiercer than ever. What do they expect when they do not believe? When they do not repent?

Tomorrow, they'll pick their way through the debris, pulling out corpses from the mess, and cry out in fear. Some will crawl back to the churches and get down on their knees and pray. All too late. The city will be ruined as She deserves. A home for sinners is a sinful place.

Don't they know this is the first sign? Only the first sign.

As they greeted the New Year with strong liquor and song, as they danced in the streets, their women showing no shame, as they worshipped false idols, I prayed. Prayers of the just. Prayers that are heard.

I am in preparation and my time is close.

Soon, I will walk among them, drink in their dives and dance in their dens. My face will be of the innocent, my dress of the clean. They will not know me as I am. Their harlots will take my hand, step to my step and trust in me, even in dark places.

Soon they will feel my presence.

They will know me as John and they will fear me.

Across the street, an old woman stooped and bent into the wind. Her cheap brown camel coat pressed against her body, flapping up now and then to reveal thick-soled, calf-length boots topped by dense brown stockings sagging at the knees of scrawny legs. The plastic of her see-through rainmate billowed and filled with the wind – the wind they hoped would die forever.

Ruth sheltered in a shop doorway, cupped her hands to shield the fluttering flame of a match and lit a cigarette. Dragging deeply, she wondered, not for the first time, why the taste of the tobacco fitted here, her adopted city of Glasgow, more than anywhere else she'd been. Something about the city suited smoke and addiction and the aroma of burning tobacco. Decadent? Wicked? Careless of life? All of that and more. Even after only a few months, she thought of Glasgow not as a place but as an old dame – sometimes deep bosomed and generous, sometimes stone faced and cruel but always worldly-wise and always 'She'.

A bluster of wind fired the tip of Ruth's cigarette angry red and long and she stepped farther back, nearer the shop door. Across the street, the flesh-and-blood old dame continued her struggle. With each step, her feet lifted higher and higher, pausing in mid movement before clamping down on the pavement.

'Stepping over gravestones,' Ruth muttered to herself and she smiled as she remembered an old boy in the village down south where she grew up – a strange lonesome man smelling of horse sweat and wearing layers of tweedy clothes and Wellington boots all year round. His hair was always cut tight to the skull and he had staring eyes that bore through you and followed you, no matter how fast you ran. All the kids were scared of the old boy, especially of his eyes, but it was his strange, high-stepping gait that worried Ruth most. 'Stepping over gravestones,' is what locals said since he could often be found at the cemetery, lurking behind the bushes, staring with those eyes.

For years, a man with that weird walk haunted Ruth's childhood nightmares till she was old enough to understand that he was a poor soul, abandoned to his own devices, gormless, harmless, no threat at all. She learned then that the greatest threats come in the most mundane packages – especially where people are concerned. The realisation was to shape her future career choice – psychology, criminal psychology. She had to find out what made the ordinary murderous and the murderous appear so ordinary.

A gust grabbed the old woman and spun her half round. She steadied herself, lifted her shopping bag high, grasped it to her stomach and then took another step. A bit of wind wasn't going to stop her.

WHACK. High above the street where there used to be roof slates, a tarpaulin lifted, whipped by the wind. WHACK. Then a rumble of canvas. Closing her eyes, Ruth heard boat sails grumbling in the breeze and imagined herself back then, back home, down south in the warm belly of Kent, in the little coastal village where she was raised. A little blonde girl sitting in the sun by the harbour wall, watching the moored yachts bob gently in the water, tasting ice cream and smelling Lux soap. WHACK. The tarpaulin thrashed again and reminded her where she was.

A bus crashed past, its sickly yellow lights showing a scattering of huddled, faceless passengers all wrapped up against the wind and the rain. It was early in the afternoon but already it was almost dark. It had been that way a lot lately – as if night had taken up permanent residence in the city.

3

Across the road, the old woman had made it to the crossing that split Byres Road. Holding on to a lamp post, her chest heaved in and out and her deep breathing was visible through the thick layers of her clothes. Looking up and down the street, Ruth realised there was no one else around – none of the usual students, shoppers or commuters or even drunks heading to and fro between the many pubs. A street that was always so full of life now seemed dead, apart from her and the old woman – always the women out braving the storm, always the women out alone.

Steadying herself with one hand grasping the lamp post, the old woman went to move off. Left for the university, right for the posh hinterlands of Hyndland or straight on for the cheap tenements of Partick where Ruth herself lived. Which way would the old woman go?

Edging up to the kerb, she bobbed her head right and left then stepped out on to the road. The car came out of the gloom at speed, headlights on full beam, wipers thrashing against the rain. In the moaning of the wind, the old woman hadn't heard the car as it rushed past, missing her by a few feet. Only then did she start and stagger back, glowering after it as it paused for a second at the junction before shooting off, heading to Hyndland. The old woman steadied herself and started off again, straight on for Partick.

'This city's a dangerous place,' thought Ruth, 'especially for women on their own and poor women more than most.'

Dropping her butt on the ground, she watched it skitter across the road with red sparks flowing behind it. A milk bottle chased after it, spitting shards of glass as it rolled faster and faster. She yanked up the hood of her duffel coat, hoisted her briefcase under one arm and headed out into the storm.

Wednesday, 17 January 1968

It is over – or so they think. When the wind stopped, they believed their troubles had ended too. That's not the way of life – the way of the Lord.

Every day the newspapers are filled with stories of deaths and destruction. 'The Great Glasgow Gale' they call it. A disaster. A catastrophe. A terrible start to the year, they say, as if God works to a calendar.

They have felt His force. All around the city, buildings lie damaged and wrecked. Roofs torn off. Cars overturned. Sewers burst. Windows smashed. Power cables snatched away like threads. Devastation and darkness. He has created my perfect place.

At night I walk among them. I wear my best suit and good coat against the wind. They pass me without a second look but I look at them and see them with mine eyes. In the city centre, I stroll into their pubs. The pubs never close while churches lie wrecked and ruined. That is the way of Man – careless with the Holy places, careful with the hovels. As they drink and joke and jostle, I stand among them drinking whisky, unseen. There but not there. It is to be my way and, every time I venture out, I get better – better at my calling.

Oh, they see me. See the me I want them to see – the polite me, the charming me, the me who takes a small whisky and wishes them good health – but to the real me they are blind. The fools have no idea – no idea of who I am.

They maybe take me for a military chap. Some do. If it's not my smart suit, polished shoes and neat hair, it's my watch or my manners which are beyond reproach. Ill manners are a sign of Satan and I do my Father's work.

Occasionally someone thinks me an off-duty copper. They never say but I can tell by their mood as they throw unsubtle but comically furtive and evil glances in my direction. What? Do they think their eyes fire arrows? Small men in small slovenly backwaters with such a great view of their own importance. Such a poor view of their reality.

A soldier or a policeman? Maybe they're not so wrong at that.

In the beginning, I would go to different pubs, busy pubs. For hours, I would stand among them as if I was one of them. Men whose bodies were unclean yet who walked with the air of nobility, their rank breath shouting out to others as if the world needed to listen to them or perish. And brazen women with their shrill laughter, beehive hairdos and heavy breasts pushed out into your face as gifts. As they sit, their short frocks ride above their knees and, crossing their legs, they know they're showing you the flesh that no one should see save their mother, husband or doctor. And toothless old fogeys devoid of the dignity of age. Their wisdom is to get drunk and stay drunk. Blotting out the world they inhabit? Not if God has anything to with it.

Dirty, filthy, unclean hovels, fouled by the massed rank breath of their worthless lives. I was pleased when that time came to an end and, the rite passed, I moved on.

For years, I had wondered where my next calling would take me. There was no need to be concerned. Damn me for my lack of faith. The path was clear – He showed me. The music called and I followed.

Forgive me, Lord, for I hath sinned.

The music took me. Transported me. My feet learned the steps and my hips the rhythm even as the band struck out into a new number. Dancing comes naturally to me. Who would have believed it? Me – I believed it.

Temptation I suffer as all good men do. Have suffered all my life or, at least, since my calling. The minute I was chosen for His work, the temptations rained upon my soul.

The seduction of boy love.

The excitement of a gamble.

Money and all its power.

Blooding the beast in the field.

I have succumbed every time. Yet, every time I have struck myself down and repented, leaving my fate in the hands of Him, the one true God. Every time my Father has found it in Himself to forgive me, His chosen one. Yet I pay the price. Pay it still.

In the ballrooms, my feet tap to the beat and I catch the scent of the young women swirling past. Dark pleasures stir in me to play their game. As a young man, before my calling, I ached for this company. I was tall, skinny, awkward. How would I ever succeed with the ladies? It drove me to a sadness that haunted my waking and sleeping. Loneliness was to be my adulthood as it had been my childhood. If only I'd known then that finding company was so easy, maybe my life would have taken a different turn. Thank God it remained a mystery and I stayed on the one true path.

The Locarno, Dennistoun Palais, Majestic and Astoria are the stuff made for adolescent dreams – bright lights, loud music and sweet females all in a row. But, of course, none are ladies. Sluts. Whores. Adulteresses all. Especially in one place. Especially on one night. Easy prey. That's where I'll go.

'Fancy a jig, hen?' The drunk swayed from side to side in front of Ruth, his booze-numbed legs struggling to keep him upright. She smiled and went to move past him, only to find him there right in front of her again, the sweet smell of fortified wine hovering around him like some cheap scent. 'Naw? No dancin'?'

'I've got work to go to,' Ruth replied, still smiling at him. So he was a drunk, down and out, sleeping rough somewhere – it wasn't in her nature or her beliefs to judge such people badly. They were victims of society – that's how she saw it.

'Work? A fine-looking young lassie like youse? What can you be off to do in your wee short frock and the lippy all on?' The drunk man was of an age somewhere between sodden maturity and liver-wrecked death. The skin of his face was brownish red, weather-beaten from too many hours outdoors with no place else to go, but with a grey sheen of a short beard betraying days away from a razor. Curious about everything to do with people, Ruth wondered where such a man could go for a shave and a wash and made a mental note to find out.

'Up at the university,' she answered, nodding in the direction of what locals still called Gilmorehill but its proper name was Glasgow University, 'I'm a postgrad student.' Even as the phrase left her lips, she cursed herself for saying 'postgrad'. It sounded prissy, snobby and would mean nothing to her newfound friend.

'A student!' The drunk didn't seem to have even heard the phrase that offended Ruth so much. 'A good-looking lassie like you? What are you studying for? Going to be a teachie?'

'No, I'm studying to be a psychologist.' She knew she was digging herself in deeper but what choice did she have? Lie to the man? That would be disrespectful. He bobbed back, bent at the waist, as if he was going to fall over, and then staggered back towards her fast, just stopping before he bumped into her.

'That would be a pure fuckin' waste.' He stopped and cleared his throat, phlegm rattling in his chest. 'You locked up in a school with they weans. A pure waste, hen.'

'I'm not going to be a teacher. I'm going to be a psych . . .'

'And another thing – the other teachers are women. Schools are stowed out with women so, so they are. You might as well get ye to a convent.'

Only in the west end of Glasgow would a down-and-out drunk paraphrase Shakespeare, Ruth thought, yet she couldn't help wondering about his life story. How had he ended up on the streets? That curiosity was her weakness or her strength, according to different folk.

'You know what curiosity did to the cat?' her mother used to warn her.

She fumbled in her shoulder bag for her purse, turned away from the man and opened it. A couple of pound notes, a ten-shilling note but the only change she had was two battered halfpennies. It wasn't enough really but the notes were far too much.

> Baybeee, now that I've found you,
> I can't let you go,
> I'll build my world around you,
> I need you so . . .

Arms outstretched, the drunk was now singing to her in a surprisingly youthful voice – almost as surprising as him choosing a recent hit pop song by The Foundations to serenade her.

Whatever he did with his life, he obviously spent some of it close to a transistor radio or maybe in some pub with a jukebox or maybe some homeless hostel with a TV and regular doses of *Top of the Pops*? Ruth pushed the two coins into his hand and headed away from him, up the crowded pavement, head down, walking fast.

> Even though you don't need me,
> You don't neeeed me . . .

Behind her, his voice trailed off into silence, much to Ruth's relief. People were beginning to stare – some trendy, long-haired young guys in their wide flared denims, tie-dyed T-shirts and faded ex-army combat jackets she recognised from the pubs and the live rock gigs she had been attending lately. Peace and love might be the message of this generation but being laid back was a necessary state of being. Chilled. Not exactly what she was achieving being embarrassed by a lone drunk in a busy street.

'HOI, HOI, YOU, TEACHIE!'

With dread Ruth stopped and turned to face the man.

'WHAT THE FUCK YOU CALL THIS THEN?' He was holding up the two halfpennies she'd given him. 'YOU SNOBBY BITCHES ARE AW THE SAME – MEAN BASTARDS.'

Ruth turned away and walked on, the heat of her blushes burning her cheeks.

'AND ME SINGING YOU A WEE SONG. AND ASKING YOU FOR A JIG.'

Ruth had almost reached the safety of the corner into Great George Street where she'd turn and be away from his shouts.

'A JIG,' he roared again and she glanced back just as she was about to head to safety. 'JIG-A-JIG MORE LIKE.' He was standing on the pavement, legs akimbo, slowly stroking his genitals with one hand, his grey-pink tongue licking his lips.

Climbing the hill of Great George Street, Ruth seethed with rage. It wasn't the man's poverty or even his ungratefulness. It was his belief he had the right to put her down, to embarrass her, to sexually threaten her – his confidence that he was more powerful than her and he'd use that power in whatever way he chose to because he was male and she was female. Were all men the same?

'Hello, darling!' A young man, standing with friends outside the rickety wooden structure of the George Snooker Hall, called out gently to her and followed it up with a low wolf whistle.

She could see he was handsome, clean, fresh-faced and well dressed.

Then he spoke out again. 'Fancy a drink sometime?'

Ruth stopped walking and turned to face him. 'Fuck off,' she spat. 'Just fuck off.' Then she stormed off on her way.

Outside the snooker hall, her young admirer was being insulted by his mates.

'Aw, you numpty.'

'She's far too good for you.'

'Imagine thinking a class bird like that would be interested in you.'

'Look, boys, he's blushing.'

''S a wee shame, so it is.'

All Ruth could hear was their raised voices and their laughter. Laughing at her was what she assumed.

'Men,' she muttered, as she continued on her way towards her class, 'bloody men are all the bloody same – bloody evil.'

'There is no such thing as a criminal type. No such thing as being born to do evil. No such singular pattern of humanity that is to be found in all criminals.' Ruth was in full swing, talking to her tutor, Professor Pickford, in his room off the quadrangle at the ancient university building. He had challenged her, saying that maybe her PhD doctorate was based on a false premise, that maybe she should change her approach to the more medical model and the search for a single, common essence of criminality that might be found in blood, semen or the pattern of the brain. In her case, as a psychologist, try to identify specific and certain behaviours linked to such physical patterns. His gentle doll-like face remained passive with its usual kind smile as he witnessed the impact of this challenge.

Ruth was explaining her views with passion and energy – just as he had hoped she would. 'Each human being is unique. All criminals are human beings. Therefore criminals are unique,' she continued. 'No two criminals are identical. In short, no two men are the same.'

It was less than twenty minutes since the scenes with the drunk and then the cute boy with the unimaginative chat-up line. Twenty minutes since she'd muttered, 'Bloody men are all the bloody same – bloody evil.' The scene was still raw on her nerves, her comment still ringing in her ears. Yet here she was contradicting herself. Or was she?

Ruth wasn't entirely convinced by the arguments of radical females raising the rights of women and raging around the university because too many of the women were straightforward man-haters. Too many of them needed therapy not politics, in her view, but the more sensible ones had a point. The power between men and women was too weighted towards the blokes – always had been. So, women were paid lower wages. So, they did the housework. So, their men beat them up. So, rape went largely unreported. So, so many things. But *were* all men the same? Ruth didn't think they were in the important things. They just covered their individuality behind the mentality of the tribe – the tribe of men. Acted tough. Swaggered through life. Treated women as second-class citizens. Men needed liberating from that as much as women needed liberating from their sexist shackles.

'Liberal bitch' she'd been called at the last women's meeting she had attended and expressed her views. Her detractor was one of the extremists who wore baggy clothes, smelled of wet dog, never shaved her legs, smoked endless roll-ups and had taken to sleeping with other women as a revolt against men – or so she said. Men were all women-bullies, women-haters, women-killers, women-slave-masters if you let them – so she said talking loudly over every other woman in the room. Till Ruth spoke up.

'Liberal bitch' was all hairy legs could say in reply but it seemed to be enough – as if that was the worst insult anyone could be given. Most of the other women nodded in pale-faced agreement and turned away from Ruth. She got the message, picked up her things and quietly left the room. She was sad to go since she enjoyed the group especially the company of two of the women. Not just as friends. More than that. They excited her the way an older girl at school used to excite her – excited her more than men. It was Ruth's uncomfortable secret and it was going to stay that way. Alone again. But that's how it was with her – always had been. Maybe it helped her to see the world more clearly. She hoped so.

'There is no commonality between, say, burglars, then?' Professor Pickford brought her back to the room with a gentle question.

'Only in what they do,' Ruth replied. 'Not as people.'

'Yet many crooks only break into houses,' he persisted. 'They wouldn't dream of robbing a bank or blackmail or assaulting anyone but they choose to burgle. Why would so many disparate individuals with separate lives and distinct experiences end up choosing to commit the same crimes?'

'Free choice,' Ruth responded. 'They have made the same choice but have arrived at similar destinations from different routes on the basis of their different experiences and they've made a choice that is, in each and every case, unique to them.'

The professor wasn't finished with the argument in any way but he decided to leave it for the moment and try another angle. 'And killers? Is it the same for them?'

'Even more so,' Ruth replied.

'And serial killers? Do they have the same freedom of choice?'

The phrase 'serial killers' had only been coined a few years before and was only used by those who studied human behaviour, like psychologists. The public were more likely to say something like 'thrill killers' or simply 'psychos'. Glasgow had played a part in the coining of the phrase 'serial killer' when Peter Manuel had been sentenced to death at the old North Court for seven murders. While he waited for the hangman in the condemned cell, he had confessed to more – fourteen in total. Killing not for gain, not for revenge, not through anger, just for the killing – motivated by his distinct, complex psychological make-up.

Ruth knew all of that, of course, and Professor Pickford had chosen serial killers deliberately. She proposed to specialise in criminal behaviour and, if she was to do that, she had to develop some knowledge, some science, some extraordinary understanding of the new horror, the beast of nightmares who was a reality – the man who killed for killing's sake.

Ruth picked up her cigarettes and set about choosing and lighting one as if it needed all her concentration. 'Professor, you know what worries me?' She dragged deep on the smoke, extinguishing the match with vigorous shakes of her wrist.

'Worries you, Ruth?' asked the wise old man, moving wisps of fine silver hair off his brow with one slow stroke of his fingers.

'We sit here in this lovely ancient building discussing human nature, psychology, motivation – yet the real world isn't here.'

'You think?'

'It's out there in the tenements and the slums and the factories and the shipyards. Where real people are.'

'Real people? Oh yes, them.' He meant his remark as a small joke.

'Ordinary people with ordinary lives – that's who we should be working with.'

'Ordinary lives – is there any such thing?'

'That's what I mean.' Ruth looked up from tapping the tip of her cigarette in the ashtray. Across the room the professor beamed back at her. He had such an innocent pixie face that would suit sitting above a dog collar or a monk's cassock – the type of face you could trust. 'By the time we study people, serious problems have already emerged. They have moved on in their life journey to some mental illness or aberrant behaviour. By then, it's too late.'

'Too late to stop the effects of that behaviour?'

'Yes and maybe to help them avoid their illness, avoid the troubles and pain.'

'Do you think it is possible to prevent depression rather than cure it after the event?'

'Yes, I believe that is possible.'

'To stop the schizophrenic believing he is Napoleon? To prevent murderers?'

'Wouldn't that be something worth aiming for?'

'And what about serial killers? Aren't they a bit complex? Other-worldly? And isn't their sickness hidden deep in their

15

every thought and act? Could we really identify serial killers out there among the butchers, bakers and candlestick makers?'

The term serial killer might have been defined only a few years ago but there had been enough studies carried out already in California, London and even Glasgow for Ruth to realise that, apart from the killing, the one thing they all had in common was the deep-rooted complexity of their psychological states. Wives, parents, lovers, they had all lived with serial killers for many years and been clueless about their loved one's lethal hobby.

'Isn't it at least worth trying,' she asked, looking the professor directly in the eye, 'for the sake of those other ordinary people?'

He raised his eyes in a quizzical manner, inviting her to explain.

'Those very ordinary people out there. The innocent ones – the ones who get killed.'

BOOK

of

PATRICIA

'TB?' The two letters still held the power to shock and terrify even in 1968 when it was no longer the mass killer it had once been.

'Aye, someone was telling me that's what the hospital had been built for – originally, like.' Pat Docker was chatting with her mother and father as the two women set the table for dinner.

'Oh, aye,' said her mother, without looking up from her task, 'I knew that. A sick kids' hospital. That was Mearnskirk.'

'Well, apparently, it was just for TB sufferers,' Pat continued. 'Children with TB and that was why it was built out in the country – for the fresh-air therapy.'

'Ha,' Pat's father laughed from his seat by the fireside, making Pat's four-year-old son, Sandy, look up from the floor at his feet where he played with a toy car. 'They were big on fresh air back then. Remember the Lawsons? The old man of the family? He had TB and was sent to Hairmyres Hospital just up the road. All the wards had these big glass doors and the nurses would wheel the patients out in their beds if need be – rain, hail or bloody shine.'

'Mind your language in front of you-know-who,' snapped Pat's mother, nodding in Sandy's direction. A good wee boy who loved his grandfather and with a well-developed habit of copying everything he did or said. He missed his dad or so his granny was fond of declaring, adding that he needed a man's influence in his life.

'Aye, aw right. Sorry,' apologised Pat's father and he was. He doted on the wee fellow. 'As I was saying, old man Lawson eventually got let back home and he was telling everybody

19

about they windows and lying there under the Lanarkshire clouds. "TB was never going to kill me," he used to say, "but see that bl . . . blo . . ."'

Pat's mother threw her man a sour look.

'"That blooming fresh air? I thought I'd never survive it."'

'Was that it?' asked Pat's mother. 'That's the story?'

'Aye, well,' said Pat's father, still chuckling, 'remember how terrified folk were of catching TB? But old man Lawson was more in fear of the Scottish weather, as well he might be – bloody freezing out that way, so it is.'

Another sour look is all he got for his efforts.

Pat smiled to herself, feeling the warm familiarity of her parents' banter. It was just their way of saying that they loved each other without saying they loved each other. They were happy together – her mother, father, her and four-year-old Sandy. She knew they would be even when things had gone wrong with her marriage.

She had been happy for the first few years when she met and married Alex. Even then she knew that his work in the RAF meant they would have to live apart from time to time but, with the confidence of youth, she believed that they would overcome those difficult periods.

'Absence makes the heart grow fonder,' she had reassured her mother and she had been right for a while. Maybe she had been right all along since it was when Alex was posted to Cyprus and she and Sandy had joined him there that the marriage became strained. Pat just couldn't settle in the warm, sunny climate of Cyprus and, worse, in a closed community made up entirely of servicemen and their families.

It was war but not as she'd ever thought of it. Cyprus had won its independence from Britain only a few years before in 1960. Trouble had festered on with sporadic bombings of cafés and drive-by shootings by those Greek Cypriots who wanted to chase the Turkish residents out – Cypriots who weren't too fond of the British either. In spite of UN troops being moved in, they failed to keep the peace and all service-men's families were kept strictly to compounds guarded by armed soldiers.

For Pat Docker, it was just too claustrophobic, too inward looking. She was a lively women, always had been, and she wanted to go out and work and meet people and socialise. Instead she was stuck with the same group of women and their children all the time. One or two of the women were OK but, like Pat, they felt trapped. It wasn't what she expected of a marriage.

She and Alex began to quarrel and she took her son and headed home to her parents' flat in Langside Place in the Battlefield area in Glasgow's southside. Her mother and father were saddened by their daughter's plight and hoped that she and Alex could sort out their difficulties. But the Wilsons were a caring couple who loved their daughter and their young grandson and, without hesitation, they welcomed her and Sandy into their home, as Pat knew they would.

Alex had been posted back to Digby in Lincolnshire – it was closer but not close enough. He and Pat had talked of divorce – after all, they were still only twenty-five years old and young enough to start over. There was no bad blood or ill feeling between them and neither were keen to rush into something so final – to give up on each other so easily. So, by February 1968, all they had done was talk.

Meantime, Pat got on with her life. She and her mother worked different shifts at Mearnskirk Hospital, ensuring there was always someone to care for Sandy – something her mother did without a grumble. It was almost an ideal situation for the young mother.

'Sandy?'

At his mother's quiet voice, her boy looked up from where he was playing.

'Want to watch the telly?'

'Aye,' he said enthusiastically.

21

'Aye? Aye?' asked his granny, opening her eyes widely in mock anger. 'Is that not something that you see with?'

Sandy had heard this before from his gran and he giggled.

'What's the word?'

'Yes,' he said with a grin.

'Yes what?'

'Yes, please.'

'Good boy,' answered his gran, happy that her grandson was taking in her wee lesson in talking politely. She then leaned over to switch on the TV.

'What's on? What's on?' Sandy asked with an excited shout as the grey screen turned to a murky white and then broke into a greyish fuzzy picture of man in a suit and wearing a bowtie who was making some announcement.

'I think . . .' said Pat, hesitating to create some drama, 'I think it's . . .' and she hummed a good effort at the opening theme tune.

'THUNDERBIRDS ARE GO!' Sandy shouted in a shrill, excited voice as he plonked himself down on the rug, a few feet from the small screen.

'What was it you were saying anyway, hen?' Pat's father asked her.

'When?'

'Before.'

'Aye, before he so rudely interrupted you with one of his daft stories,' Pat's mother butted in. Sandy was too pre-occupied by Lady Penelope and the other puppets acting out the drama on the screen to notice that his grandmother almost always said 'Aye' rather than the polite 'Yes'.

Pat's mind had been away somewhere else entirely. She was like that – active in body and thought, never stopping for a minute's rest or so it seemed sometimes.

'About the weans with TB?' her mother added helpfully.

'Oh, aye, the kids.' Pat smiled at her own forgetfulness. 'Well, you know how the taxi drivers take sick kids from

22

Glasgow away down to the coast for a day every year?' It wasn't so much a question as a statement. The Glasgow taxi drivers' annual act of generosity was well known to all Glaswegians. 'Well, apparently Mearnskirk Hospital was one of the first places that they went to when they were setting it up.'

'Aye, makes sense. All those poor kids with TB was no laughing matter,' her old man said with a straight face and in a serious tone.

'How would you know?' Pat's mother asked from the cooker where she was stirring the stew for that night's dinner. The way the women worked their shifts meant that although their paths crossed regularly throughout the week it was only briefly so, whenever they got the chance, they always tried to have a sit-down meal in the early evening. The stew, potatoes and cabbage would keep Pat's mum going on the long shift she faced that night. 'You and your stories.'

'On you go, hen,' Pat's father said, ignoring his wife's comments.

'Well, they were telling me that, when the taxi drivers started that, they got help from some local group.' Pat was busy setting the small table for dinner. As she did this, she kept an eye on Sandy, whose gaze was firmly focused on the box while his hands were acting out space rocket movements. She carried on talking to her father and mother. 'The Gayboys or something.'

'Gayboys! Ha.' Her father was laughing at her, with tears rolling down his cheeks, and, by the cooker, even her mother was smiling. 'Billy McGregor and the Gaybirds, ye daftie. And they weren't a group. They were band – a big band.'

'Who?'

'Just one of the biggest bands of their time.'

'Aye, so they were saying.'

'They were that good they used to pack The Barrowland Ballroom every night they played.'

23

'The Barrowland?' asked Pat, her curiosity fired by mention of one of Glasgow's favourite venues for dancing – the dancing she loved.

'Aye, you didnae think you youngsters discovered The Barrowland, did you? You and your long-haired laddies and their guitars, sounding and looking more like Jessies than Jims? Naw, naw. They've been jigging at The Barrowland for a long time.'

'I know, Dad, I know,' said Pat with a resigned sigh, knowing that her father was about to launch into one of his stories.

From her place at the cooker, her mother threw Pat a sympathetic glance, followed by a smile.

Oblivious as usual to the unspoken messages between the women, her father proved Pat right. 'Maggie McIver owned and ran The Barrowland Ballroom and the Barras themselves. One of the top dance venues in Britain and one of Europe's biggest flea markets – no' bad for a Glasgow woman, eh?'

'Aye, Dad, but . . .'

'Did you know that, during the war, it was so popular with soldiers on leave – I mean no' just Scots but Yanks, Poles, Frenchies and the rest – that Lord Haw-Haw included it regularly in his propaganda broadcasts?'

'Lord who?' asked Pat, immediately regretting asking a question that would be sure to prolong the tale.

'An English traitor working for the Nazis. Used the wireless to try and wind up our folk. Said that, when the Germans were victorious, The Barrowland would welcome their troops with open arms. The little Lord So-and-So didn't know Maggie McIver. No' half. If the Hun ever made it to Glasgow, she'd have . . .'

'Stew's ready,' Pat's mother shouted. 'Come on, Sandy, teatime.'

An obedient wee boy, Sandy got up immediately, somehow managing it without taking his eyes off the TV in spite of the fact that *Thunderbirds* had been replaced by the man with the bowtie once again. Still staring at the box, he backed towards the table till he found his chair and only then, and reluctantly at that, did he turn his gaze away from the grey images and clamber up on to his seat.

'Good boy, Sandy,' said Pat, stroking her son's hair as she pushed his chair closer to the table. Sitting down beside him, she began cutting up the vegetables and potatoes on his plate, making sure the food was cool enough.

'Was there something you wanted to ask, Pat?' asked her mother, taking advantage of her husband's silence as he shovelled beef and potatoes into his mouth.

'Aye, well, I was wondering if it would be OK . . .'

Pat's mother smiled at her, sending out the message that it was OK to ask – that she had a good idea what the question was going to be anyway.

'If maybe you'd babysit one night this week so I could go to the dancing?'

Pat's mother had guessed right. She knew her daughter loved dancing. She'd be out every night of the week if she didn't have young Sandy to care for. Pat doted on Sandy and hardly ever went out but she was young and needed more to life than work and childcare.

'Of course, Pat, no problem. What night were you thinking of?'

Glaswegians were dancing mad – always had been. It was possible to go dancing every night of the week in a range of different ballrooms, all with top bands – or groups as the young folk had taken to calling them.

'Well, I was thinking that you're no' working on Thursday,' replied Pat.

Thursday – not quite the weekend when the city venues became packed and rowdy with drunken young folk but almost the weekend and the evening when serious dancers, usually a slightly older crowd, would venture out. Thursday was a good night for a twenty-five-year-old single parent, who loved to dance, to get her glad rags on.

'Aye that should be OK,' replied her mother. 'You and me will be just fine, eh, Sandy?' she said, ruffling the boy's hair and setting him grinning. 'Where were you thinking of going? No' The Barrowland, surely?'

'It's no' the same Barrowland, of course,' butted in Pat's father. 'Did you know it was gutted by fire about ten year back, Pat? Word at the time was it was some business competitor up to some shenanigans but it was never proved. Maggie McIver had it totally rebuilt and . . .'

'Going to hold your tongue just for a wee minute about Maggie McIver, eh?' Pat's mother was beginning to get exasperated with her man's stories. She had serious business to discuss with her daughter.

'Why no' The Barrowland?' asked Pat.

'It's Thursday night,' said her mother. 'Palais Night at The Barrowland.'

'Oh, aye, so it is.'

'Palais Night?' Now Pat's father was listening to the women. 'Fancy name for a knocking shop.'

Thursday nights at The Barrowland Ballroom were renowned for married people going along to seek or continue affairs – a night when casual sex was a higher priority than dancing. Much as Pat's mother and father were all for her having a social life, they weren't going to support her going out to meet men. Not that she'd ever given them any suspicion or cause for concern on that matter but she was young and healthy, after all. However, they saw her still as a married woman.

'No, no,' said Pat with a smile, 'I was thinking of going to The Magic Stick.'

'The what?' asked her mother.

'The Majestic, hen,' her husband told her with a smirk.

'The Majestic is the place to be these days,' said Pat. 'Great music and a good crowd – dancers, you know.'

Her parents were nodding at her with a smile and some relief. The dancing – that's what their daughter loved.

26

'Grab-a-lumber Thursday night at The Barrowland? You wouldn't catch me dead at that.'

'Do you mind?'

'Pardon?' Ruth struggled to hear the young man over the loud music. She was sitting in The Curlers, a west-end pub popular with students, left-wing lecturers and the scores of media people who lived in the area or worked up at the BBC's Scottish headquarters in nearby Queen Margaret Drive.

The young bloke tried again. 'The ashtray, please,' he said as he pointed.

This time Ruth understood and she pulled the ashtray along the table to sit between them. It was a chipped blue metal affair and she knew that it carried the legend 'Senior Service'. She knew but couldn't see it for the mangled butts and pile of ash that filled the tray to overflowing – so full, it was of little use as an ashtray. Most of The Curlers' customers didn't hesitate to use the floor as an ashtray, downstairs in the bar at least. Upstairs was the lounge. Carpeted and with chintzy curtains and thick wallpaper with a velvet feel, it was strictly ashtray-using territory. Not that any switched-on customer ever ventured upstairs.

But the young guy proceeded to use the packed ashtray. Polite? Ruth wondered. Or a chat-up line?

'THE MUSIC IS HELLISH LOUD,' he said, roaring the obvious.

Someone had put The Love Affair's 'Everlasting Love' on the jukebox – a strange song for a pub known to attract radical left-wingers more into Bob Dylan or Pink Floyd than pop songs. Ruth was convinced that that record had somehow been made to play at many decibels louder than other records.

'IT ALWAYS IS,' she shouted back at the young bloke.

'WHAT?'

'THAT RECORD,' she tried again, 'ALWAYS PLAYS LOUD.' She motioned to put both hands over her ears.

He understood enough to nod and smile then turned to lift and sip his pint of lager. They sat looking straightforward into the crowded bar. Ruth smiled at herself. She had been travelling home on the underground and had decided not to get off at Partick, close to her flat, but at Hillhead to visit a pub for a quiet drink. There were plenty of pubs down in Partick but a woman alone wouldn't be allowed in or, if she was, everyone would assume she was a prostitute. It was different the short distance up Byres Road, nearer the university.

'Quiet drink,' she muttered to herself with a giggle that no one heard, not even her. At last The Love Affair's turn came to a close and the bar fell into the murmur of muted chat – or that's how Ruth heard it.

'Ciggie?' The young man on the bench beside her was proffering an open packet of Kensitas. Like her Embassy, they were a more expensive brand of cigarette than he need have bought unless, of course, he preferred the taste. Kensitas were stronger than her brand, but a good smoke, so she accepted one. It was only polite even though she'd noticed that the young man had stubbed out a cigarette just a minute before. He didn't look like a chain-smoker to her.

'Thank God that's over,' he said, leaning forward, cracking a match and shielding it with cupped hands in spite of them being in the breeze-free indoors.

She lit her cigarette, blew the smoke high into the air away from her companion and said, 'Yeah. What I was trying to tell you earlier was that I think they made that record so it would play much louder than others.'

'Why would they do that?' he asked, turning on his seat to face her.

29

'A lot of people like their music loud these days. It sounds good that way – if you don't want to chat.'

'Aye or hear yourself think.'

She smiled at his quip and went on, 'It sells more records.'

'Is that allowed?'

'I don't see why not.'

'It's a bit of a con, though.'

'I'm not sure about that.'

'No?'

'Well, it's less of a con than payola.' There was no response from the man so Ruth explained, 'Bribing radio stations to play a record.'

'Aye, right enough.'

'Or going to the right record shops – the ones they use for compiling the top ten – and buying a lot of your record.'

'That must cost a good few bob,' he offered.

'Yes but not nearly as much as what they'd earn with a top-ten hit.'

'That'll be the modern music industry for you,' he said. 'The musicians all talking peace and love but the real power behind them is in the hands of the captains of industry – the money men – as usual.'

'Yeah.' She nodded, feeling a little sad. He was right – absolutely right. 'But it's not just a modern-day crime, you know.'

'No?'

'It's been around for decades, longer – even from the times when musicians made most of their living from selling sheet music.'

'Really?'

'Oh, yeah.'

'Where there's cash, there's crime, eh?' he said.

She couldn't have put it better herself and his phrase stirred curiosity in her about this man with the bad chat-up opener. And she wasn't the only curious one.

The gentle whistle of the intro of Manfred Mann's version of 'The Mighty Quinn' struck up. That was more like The Curlers' crowd and, even better, you could listen and chat as well.

As usual, Ruth was watching the people around her, her eyes sweeping the room – a lifetime's habit that she was no longer conscious of. Across the bar, sitting in a corner, an old man was filling his pipe. With his thick coat buttoned and belted and his woollen muffler wrapped round his neck, his only concession to being indoors was his battered checked cap lying on the table beside his half-pint of stout and a small measure of golden-coloured whisky. Seeming so out of place in that bar full of denim-clad, long-haired types, he had probably been coming to the pub for years, sitting in that same corner, smoking his pipe, drinking his half and half. The world had changed around him. Ruth wondered if he felt left behind. Alone? Threatened?

'You seem to know a lot about crime,' the young guy observed. 'What are you? A law student?'

Ruth watched the old bloke tap the tobacco down in his pipe bowl, suck on the mouthpiece, clearing the stem, and strike a match. He could've been a pipe-smoker back at her home village or anywhere in the world really. They all followed the same rigmarole without ever having met each other or ever having been told how to smoke a pipe most likely. Did that make people predictable? Or was it just pipe-smoking that was predictable?

'A law student?' she turned and laughed at the young man's question. 'They don't know about crime.'

'No? But surely that's their business – or will be?'

'All they need to know about is the law and they learn that from books.'

The young man didn't know it but he had stumbled into one of Ruth's pet hates.

'Procedures. Rules. Precedents. That's what they learn.'

31

'So, are you saying they don't get taught about criminals, then, although most of them get paid to deal with criminals?'

'That's exactly what I'm saying.'

'Can't be right, that.' The young guy looked perturbed, puzzled. 'Is that where the saying comes from, then?'

'What saying?'

'The law's an ass.'

Ruth smiled broadly. He didn't know it but he had just moved a step closer to becoming her friend if he wanted to – crossed a line that suggested maybe they had some things in common.

'Ruth, by the way.' Still smiling, she held out her hand. She watched him blush and wondered if it was because she had taken the initiative to make introductions or if he was cursing himself for not doing so. She hoped it was the latter.

'Peter,' he said, taking her hand. 'Pleased to meet you, Ruth.'

'And me to meet you, Pete.'

'Peter,' he said, pleasantly though assertively, 'it's just Peter.'

'Peter. Sorry.'

'Would you like another, Ruth?'

As he held up his almost-empty glass, Ruth checked her watch. She had planned a quick drink to break the monotony of time spent on her own and she did have to work later. Fall behind her planned schedule and she'd end up in big trouble.

'Yes, please, but just one, Peter. I can't stay long.'

'What is it? Is Wednesday night hair-washing night?' He was grinning as he spoke, meaning to be cheeky but also telling her he was offering her a way out without him giving up on her.

'Something like that.' She smiled back and he was off, trying to make his way through the bodies to the bar. Why did she not tell him that she had to work? Not wanting to come across as boring and dull? A little part of her still playing to the traditional expectations of women being lovers, mothers and housewives? Ruth thought she was well beyond that but sat there and wondered as she watched Peter, looking at him properly for the first time.

She already knew he had a handsome, almost sweet, face and his black hair was cut short, unfashionable but neat. He was a worker not a student, for sure. Now she could see he was tall and slim with broad shoulders – athletic. He certainly looked fit enough. He wore a single-breasted suit of plain charcoal material, with sharp, narrow lapels and four or five buttons at the cuffs. A follower of fashion, he hadn't fallen for the checked suits older men were favouring but a classic style. A sign he knew his own mind? A sign of good taste?

At the bar, he signalled over the heads of the other drinkers and was getting served – jumping the queue. Maybe there was another more dominant side to Peter than the awkward, nervous man who had started chatting to her? As he waited for the barman to fetch his drinks, he turned and looked back at Ruth, catching her looking at him. Another blush from Peter and a wide grin.

A cold rush of air signalled that the pub door had opened. Across the way, the old boy, who had a clear view of the door, was struggling to get to his feet in the narrow space between his bench and the heavy metal table. Edging round the table, he lifted his battered cap, put it on and started for the door. Halfway there, he turned, went back to the table and lifted his still-smoking pipe from the ashtray. Ruth bet herself that the old guy could count on the fingers of one hand the number of times he had forgotten his pipe in many decades of contented smoking. Was there something up with him? Then she noticed that he hadn't finished either of his drinks. Something had definitely upset the old guy. Then it walked into her view.

Bright red knee-length draped jacket with black velvet collar and cuffs. Drainpipe trousers tight all the way down his legs and almost tucking into his shoes – bulky, thick, crêpe-soled creepers. A pink, open-necked bowling shirt and draped round the collar a black bootlace tie threaded through a silver buckle in the shape of a wolf head. His hair, glistening with Brylcreem, was combed in a perfect duck's arse and the look was finished off with thick sideburns running down his face and along either side of his chin.

The Teddy Boy just stood there a few feet from the door, sweeping the bar with his eyes. Knowing everyone in the bar was seeing him. Was scared of him. He stood there with his hands on his waist, his long jacket falling at the back like a peacock's tail, daring anyone in the pub to catch his eye. Just then, four other Teddy Boys strutted in and stood behind him in a V formation. It was as if they were about to burst into some old rock'n'roll number but it wasn't music that was on their minds – clearly not music. As a group, they moved to-wards the bar and grown men lifted their drinks and cleared the way. Ruth noticed a pale-faced young barman backing off and slipping out of a staff door. Were they after him?

Just then, Peter had paid for their drinks and turned to head back to their table but his way was blocked by the Teddy Boys. He went to move round them but one Teddy Boy stepped to the side and into his path. Ruth couldn't hear what he said but there was something about the way Peter moved, stretching to his full height, puffing out his chest, dropping his hands to waist height . . . It was all very subtle but she felt the difference. He spoke quietly to the Teddy Boy in his way who, in turn, looked at his friend in the bright red jacket. Peter turned and spoke to him. Without a word the Teddy Boy leader nodded his head and his mate stepped out of Peter's way.

Back at the table with the drinks, Peter behaved as if noth-ing had happened. Ruth knew better.

'Cheers,' Peter said, lifting his glass and clinking it against hers as Ruth did the same. 'So . . .'

'Yes?'

'What do you study?' he asked, with a relaxed grin. 'You never actually told me.'

Ruth laughed. 'Psychology.'

'Psych what?'

'Psychology – the study of human behaviour.'

'Like mad people?'

'Yeah but . . .'

'You give out pills and electric shocks then?'

'No, that's psychiatrists. They're medical doctors specialising in insanity.'

'And that's not what you do?'

'Nooo,' Ruth was laughing again. This man Peter made her laugh a lot.

'Thank the wee man for that,' he said, taking a big gulp of his drink, his face all feigned relief. 'Wouldn't want you sussing me out so soon.'

Smiling at his act, Ruth asked, 'And what do you do, Peter?'

'You're the psych-whatever, you tell me.'

'OK,' she said, playing along with the game. 'Well, you're not a school teacher.'

'Why not?' Disappointment stretched across his face.

'Too well dressed.'

Her reply pleased him.

'You're not a plumber, joiner or bricklayer.'

'Well?'

'Hands are too soft.'

Peter wasn't sure if he liked that comment and bent his arm, stretching his bicep, inviting her to feel it.

'You're not an actor. A twenty packet of Kensitas cigarettes, tailored suit, good shoes,' she said, bending to look under the table to check. 'Too much money.'

'So far, so right. So what am I then, Doctor?'

'I think . . .' She hesitated, putting her fingers to her temple,

35

a look of concentration on her face. 'I think . . .' Suddenly she noticed that he had stopped looking at her but was carefully looking into the body of the pub instead, as if he'd spotted something.

She followed his gaze but then he said, 'You know, I think it might be a good idea to drink up and leave now.'

Then she spotted them for herself. Five young guys, with short haircuts and wearing blouson jackets and Sta-press trousers, had been down the far end of the bar but had now moved up closer to the Teddy Boys and were staring at them. Mods had gained some notoriety in huge punch-ups against the leather-clad, motorbike-riding Rockers but, since they weren't in that pub that night, the Teddy Boys would do for a scrap.

Deep prickly heat crossed her body and her heart thumped in her chest. Ruth didn't need to be asked twice to leave.

Out on Byres Road, busy with folk out for the night, they walked towards Partick and her flat.

'I thought The Curlers was an intellectuals' pub – trendy, no trouble,' she said.

'It usually is,' Peter replied, 'but that's Glasgow for you. I mean it's 1968 – what other city still has Teddy Boys?'

'It's a city of many faces,' she offered.

'Aye, a city that can go from peace to bloody violence in a heartbeat.'

Behind them men's voices were shouting. Turning round, they could see the Teddy Boys and the Mods spilling on to the street and beginning to brawl outside the pub.

They quickened their pace. 'A place to expect the unexpected.'

'Hmm,' she murmured in agreement as they walked side by side. 'Not a banker either.'

'What?'

'You're not a banker either, are you, Peter?' She was looking up at him, smiling. 'And I'm a psychologist not a psychic.'

He laughed at her use of the words.

'So tell me.'

'Does it go with the job?'

'What?'

'Being a nosy so-and-so?' He smiled and turned to look back, checking the street fight wasn't heading their way.

'Yeah, so cough up,' she demanded.

He was nodding to himself and nibbling his lower lip, considering his next move. 'See before I do, promise me we can meet again.' His words hit the air with a nervous rush. 'Say Saturday? How's about a curry up at Gibson Street?'

'OK,' she replied immediately, surprising herself. Ruth had enjoyed Peter's company all right but usually she was more careful than that. She'd only ever had two boyfriends both while at university in London. Both relationships had ended badly when it became clear that the men wanted more from her than she was willing or able to give. The last thing Ruth wanted was for that history to repeat itself. But Peter *was* good company and his question had caught her off guard. 'On one condition – only if your occupation isn't hired killer!' She laughed but he didn't.

'Maybe worse,' he said tersely.

'Worse? What could be worse than . . .'

'I'm a policeman,' he blurted out, almost shouting the words. 'I'm a police constable based in The Marine – sorry, the Partick Police Station just down there.'

'Well . . . ' She hesitated, working out her reply. 'It's not worse but it is a surprise.'

'Some women would rather go out with a killer than a polis,' he said but his eyes were asking it as a question.

'I know,' she replied, grinning up at him. 'I know.'

Having agreed a time and meeting place for Saturday night, they parted at the bottom of Byres Road with big grins and waves.

As she walked towards her flat, Ruth mused on Peter the policeman. Then she thought of herself. Why hadn't she told him what type of psychologist she was and given him her usual mantra of 'if there can be forensic medicine why not forensic psychology'? Why had she not spoken about how she had spent that afternoon in High Burnside walking the streets and looking at a house? It looked like any other good house in a well-to-do area but it was more than that and had to do with another Peter. It was the Watts' house where Peter Manuel had killed three women in 1956. Why hadn't she said that she planned to visit all the scenes of Manuel's murders and not just his murders but other murders and atrocities? It wasn't policeman Peter she didn't tell but Peter the man. Why did she feel the need to keep all that secret?

Then again, why hadn't she let him walk her to her flat entrance, to her close? To avoid the embarrassment of the goodnight kiss expected in such rituals? Maybe but that wasn't the main reason – well, not the main reason anyway. She had just met the man and, as Ruth well knew, some people aren't what they seem – not what they seem at all.

Wednesday, 21 February 1968

Tonight I stay at home and pray. Tomorrow night I will kill.

The city is ready for me now. The fools who run this place can't even repair some minor damage. A few roofs and old buildings crumble and they sit on their hands, munching their gums. They bleat in the newspapers about how much it will cost and how long it will take. Idiots. These are the same men who would stand in judgement of me.

I remember them so well from school. You can tell a man by looking at the boy. These are the same ones who called me names.

CISSY.

MUMMY'S BOY.

SMELLY.

Just because I wore good hard-wearing clothes that were darned and repaired. Waste is sinful. Just because I was quiet, modest, a church-goer. Just because I didn't play football. They couldn't see that I didn't want to play football and thought I couldn't play football. In their eyes, that was a great weakness. Not like them. They were strong or so they thought.

I kept my thoughts to myself and God. Not like them, always shouting and boasting and pushing and fighting. Seeking out the ones they thought of as weak and tormenting them. Tormenting me. The same ones, who thought they were special as boys, think they are special as men. They were wrong then. They are wrong now as they'll soon learn.

They crucified me every day. Laughing at me. Calling me names. Worse. Beating me for no reason. Turn the other cheek, my mother taught me and I obeyed. It was a lesson I learned almost all of my childhood.

The pain I was able to endure. The humiliation was harder. A group of boys cornering me in the playground or on my way home and an audience would quickly gather, egging them on, laughing at me. Girls more than most. The girls.

One day, as I lay beaten and my face bloody, the boys held me there and pulled down my shorts and underwear. And held me there for all to see. The girls giggled. The janitor rescued me and took me to my teacher. She spoke sympathetic words then did nothing. What more should I have expected from a woman who wore her blouse buttons undone to show her breasts? High heels that click-clicked along the corridor and drew your eyes to her legs. Who left clouds of scent trailing behind her wherever she went. What else could I have expected from a whore who smoked?

In my teenage years, the beatings became less frequent but the torments were there all the same. From afar, I'd see the boys take a girl into some bomb-wrecked building and there, in the rubble, she'd expose herself – strip naked for their pleasure. I was never invited but sometimes I'd follow at a distance and find a secret place to watch them. Forgive me, Father.

One time, I was spotted and chased by the boys. Beaten when they caught me. Why? What had I stolen from them? What difference did one more pair of eyes make? The girl had already willingly sacrificed her dignity to many. Had done so before. Would do so again. What was so wrong with my gaze?

At home at night, I prayed to God to wreak vengeance on that girl. I prayed for Him to take her. She died two years later. Leukaemia, they said, but I know it was His will.

Yet I envied those boys. Father, forgive me.

It was a trial set by Him. I see that now. Evil lust would drive me. At home, life was orderly and chaste. My mother knew everything, ran everything the way it should be. Yet, during those years, I'd find myself a lonely boy drawn to lonesome places and there I'd let the lust rule victorious. Envy and lust. What a sinner I was. Father, forgive me.

Then Satan appeared in one of his many guises. But lust made me blind to his evil ways. I took him for a man who lived nearby. A strange man who lived on his own, smelled unclean and scared young children. A man taken to walking in lonesome places.

I had sought refuge in an old air-raid shelter. It stank of human filth but it was dark, secret, and I gave way to lust. Alone, I thought. But just as God sees everything, Satan finds all sin. He was upon me, his hand on my rod, shoving his into mine. And I let him. Forgive me, Father. I let him.

I stood there in the dark, wet with our filth, naked and cold, and howled. But by the time I left, I had seen the light. Devils had snared me. Those boys and their evil ways. Those girls and their whores' ways. I promised my Father I'd mend my ways and follow his message – His calling for me to punish them.

Punish the women for they are truly evil. Punish the men since the world will blame them all. Punish them all through a life of fear.

Tonight I fast and pray. Tomorrow I drink and kill.

Those boys, now men, who can't repair a city, they bleat so much the army has been sent in – the Argyll and Sutherland Highlanders. Fine men they are as they go about the business of clearing the city of the gales' debris. I see them also when I go out on my preparations. In the pubs and ballrooms. Neat appearance, short hair, polite in their manners – they could be my brothers. Now I will be more invisible than ever.

I have been to my favourite place many times on many nights and many women have taken to me and allowed me to escort them home. There in dark alleyways and broken-down buildings, they hold on to me and open themselves. Who needs the girls of my youth? I now have the beautiful women of my world. Open and exposed.

Only last week, I met a woman who told me to call her Mary but I'm sure that wasn't her real name. Her wedding ring may have been the reason for her lie. Dressed like a tart, she stank of whisky, cheap perfume and stale cigarettes. On our way to her home, she offered me a drink from a bottle hidden in her handbag. As she laughed and handed me the drink, I thought I saw it, the Fire in her eyes. The signal I've been waiting for.

Near her home, she led me through a close and down into the back green. There, outhouses faced all ways, creating a dark, secret square behind them. I was not the first John Mary had taken there.

She reached for me first with her painted lips and then with her hands. I saw the Fire in her eyes again and lifted her skirts, feeling her heat where no man should go save her husband. But there was something missing and I stopped. She asked me what was wrong and looked up into my face. The Fire was no longer in her eyes. The time had not been right.

Turning and walking away, behind me I heard her plead with me to stay then call out such names. Such filth. Taking His name in vain. Then I knew she wasn't the one but Satan tempting me. This time I didn't succumb. But it was a signal that the time was close. So close the Evil One tried to tempt me from my path.

Tonight I pray. Tomorrow I kill.

'Well, how does your mum look, Sandy?' Pat Docker was standing in her parents' living room showing off her outfit to her four-year-old son. 'Do I look nice?' She held the sides of her yellow crocheted dress and gave a little twirl, giggling as she did. Sandy was watching her with his big eyes and nodded slowly. The boy loved his mother and she doted on him.

It was early evening on Thursday, 22 February. After making sure the household had had an early dinner, Pat had helped wash the dishes and clear everything away. Then, and only then, did she get ready for her night at the dancing. She was a good mother and a good daughter who deserved a break, a night out.

Pat looked the picture of absolute modern fashion. Crochet dresses were very trendy, especially those in bright colours that came to just above the knee as hers did. The colour and style suited her pale complexion and her thick, dark brown, wavy hair, also cut trendily short. Brown shoes completed the ensemble perfectly.

Pat's mother and father had noticed their daughter's excitement rise as she had got changed and fussed over her make-up. Not too much as many of the young women did copying singers like Cilla Black and Dusty Springfield. Just enough lipstick to make her smile sparkle. Just enough eye-shadow to draw people to her rich, warm hazel eyes. With her tiny turned-up nose, she was a very attractive young woman indeed – a very good catch for any young man.

Her parents could see how Pat would attract the men. Not wanting their daughter to go from one relationship into another and, perhaps, end up in a worse situation, that worried them a little. But they trusted her, didn't lecture her. After all, this was the 1960s and she was a grown woman of twenty-five.

'Are you meeting up with any of the girls?' her mother asked Pat.

'No, I thought I'd just go along myself,' Pat replied, adjusting her lipstick in the mirror.

'Will that no' be a bit lonely?' asked her father. He couldn't understand a young person going out on the town on their own. Where was the fun in that?

'Oh, Dad, I'm just joking,' Pat laughed. 'I'm meeting up with a couple of the girls but you know you can have a good time one your own when you're . . .'

'Dancing,' her mother finished Pat's sentence with a chortle. She loved her daughter's enthusiasm for life, for dancing. It reminded her of when Pat was a wee lassie and all excited about Christmas or her birthday. Her happiness was so strong you could almost reach out and touch it. Her excitement so strong it infected people around her. Such an open wee girl and she had some of that innocence still. Or so her mother hoped.

Her daughter would take care though, wouldn't she? She was someone who didn't take risks and played things safe whenever she could. Though her parents weren't sure if that applied to birth control. That wasn't any of their business.

The pill had been introduced just a few years before but only for married women. Pat was married in the eyes of the law if not in day-to-day practice. Did that mean she qualified for the pill? Had she asked for it? If she was taking the pill, she would be safe from pregnancy and that was a good thing. But, if she'd asked for the pill, did that mean she was planning on having sex? Not with her husband who she hadn't seen in five months but with someone else. Someone they didn't know. Someone maybe even Pat hadn't met yet. An

44

unplanned baby wasn't the only thing to watch out for. A bad man was much more of a danger. Much more.

'You just catching the bus to Hope Street then, hen?' The question was one that everyone knew the answer to. Pat didn't have the spare cash for a taxi and was careful with her money, preferring to make little Sandy her top priority rather than easy travelling.

'Yes, Mum, I am going to The Majestic,' answered Pat, knowing the real question her mother had wanted to ask.

'That's good, hen, that's good,' Pat's mother said. 'You know quite a few of the crowd there, eh?'

'Aye, I do.'

'That'll be some company for you, then.'

'Some decent dancing partners – that's all I'm looking for.'

'You'll have a good time, then.'

'I always have a good time at The Majestic,' smiled Pat as she leaned over Sandy to give him a farewell kiss and cuddle. Putting on her grey hooded coat and lifting up her brown handbag, Pat headed for the door saying, 'Don't go sitting up for me, now.' It was a joke. She was long past the age when any parent would've stayed awake fretting about her return.

'We won't, hen.'

'I'll not be late,' Pat called as she stepped through the front door and out. Out for a night on the town, out dancing, out in a world where everyone seemed to be going in search of fun. But where everyone's idea of fun wasn't the same. Not the same at all.

With every step, billows of white breath streamed from his mouth and his feet crunched on the frost-hardened ground. The razor-cold air was still and sharp, burning his throat. A nearby chimney belched wood smoke as the householders set their fire, raising themselves for the day. The smoke smelled both sweet and lonely that early in the day when no one was about apart from him. The city seemed desolate and dangerous. Haunted.

It was a short walk for Maurice Goodman as he went to fetch his car. He lived at 27 Carmichael Place in the Battlefield area in the southside of Glasgow. A cabinetmaker by trade, Goodman was setting off for work as he did around 7.30 most days. He drove the route and was going to collect his car which was securely garaged nearby on Carmichael Lane. The familiar amble was less than a hundred yards door to door – the type of daily activity he undertook so often he could sleepwalk it. No need to think, no decisions to make, no need even to see what was around him. Most days.

Up the lonely lane, the morning got even quieter. The frost was nipping at Maurice Goodman's ears and nose and he couldn't wait to get in the car, get the engine running, choke out and the heater blowing full blast. Luckily for him his car was garaged. No scraping away ice from the windows for him. He'd be warm soon enough. Sooner than he thought.

A few paces from his garage, Goodman pulled out his keys. They jingled in the frozen still air as he got ready to open the door. He was almost there at the recess leading to the door. That's when he saw it. Lying near the garage door was a crumpled naked body. A fine silver frost covered the flesh, giving it a ghostly sheen in the weak light of early morning.

Maurice Goodman didn't hesitate. He turned on his heel and half ran, half walked straight back to his house and his telephone. 'There's a dead body in Carmichael Lane,' he blurted into the mouthpiece. 'A dead body.'

'Are you sure the person is dead?' the police operator asked.

Open staring eyes, tongue swollen on the lips, naked but covered in ice and frost – the whole snapshot would stay with Goodman forever and it screamed at him that the person was dead but all he could say was, 'Yes, of course I'm sure.'

'Is it a man or woman?' the policeman asked.

'Eh, I'm not sure,' replied Goodman. He hadn't looked. Of course, he hadn't taken the time to see if the body was a man or a woman. In his state of shock, who would? The image of the corpse floated into his consciousness again. 'I think it's a man. I think so.'

A naked corpse lying in a quiet lane meant only one thing – murder. The police immediately alerted the Flying Squad who initially investigated all such crimes in the city. In spite of them being based at the Central Police Office in the city centre, they were at the scene in no time. They weren't called the Flying Squad for nothing.

As with most cops, Detective Sergeant Andrew Johnstone and Detective Constable Norman MacDonald knew the city as well as they knew their own homes. They parked their unmarked car on Overdale Street, knowing that Carmichael Lane ran from there to Ledard Road. Leaving the motor, they walked down the lane looking for death.

They were two good and experienced cops. But good cops never get blasé about dead bodies. Somebody's son or daughter, father or mother had died before their time in a violent way. That's never something anyone should get used to, especially the police. They walked on without speaking, their footsteps crunching on the thick frost the only noise in the still air. Suddenly, they arrived at the corpse.

At first all they saw was a long, pale shape stretched out on the ground but, just as Maurice Goodman had done, the cops recognised the shape as undoubtedly human at a glance.

'It's a man,' one said to the other when they were still a few yards away. From the direction they had approached the body was lying with its head nearest them. Short brown hair, long slender limbs. 'A young bloke.' Within three steps they realised their mistake. 'Fuck sake!' The policeman pulled up sharp, drawing his breath in. 'It's a lassie.'

All dead bodies are difficult to deal with without feeling something but dead women are harder than men – especially young women. Almost as hard as some poor murdered child.

The cops were professional and stood over the sad sight, making specific, accurate observations of the corpse. She lay on her back, her head tilted to the right. She was stark naked and no clothes, no coat, no handbag, no shoes lay nearby. Nothing. It was as if her killer had stripped her, killed and left her there in all her naked shame for them to find. Maybe for the world to see. Being hard-headed cops, all they allowed themselves to think was that evidence had been removed from the scene of crime.

If they needed any convincing that they were dealing with a murder inquiry the proof lay below them on the hard, frozen ground. Promptly they called their office.

'It's a bad one,' they said down the line. 'A young woman. Naked. We've got a sex killer on the loose.'

A team of detectives and uniformed officers congregated in Carmichael Lane. Dressed in thick coats and wearing gloves against the winter cold, the plainclothes men looked like businessmen. Stamping their feet to keep their circulation going, most just stood around and smoked. If it hadn't been for the presence of the uniformed cops and the panda cars blocking both ends of the lane, the detectives wouldn't have attracted much attention which was just the way they preferred it.

Yet those who read the local newspapers or were avid followers of true crime would have recognised one of them. Detective Superintendent Elphinstone Dalglish had been put on the case – a sure sign that the police were taking this murder very seriously. Dalglish's unusual first name had long ago stopped being the butt of locker-room jokes. He was one of the best detectives of his generation at a time when there were many sleuths working in police uniform. Respect was what Dalglish got from his colleagues and, when he was allocated the investigation, the cops knew their boss, Detective Chief Superintendent Tom Goodall, wanted this case solved and quickly.

The first priority was to seal off the scene, making sure no one, not even police officers, touched the body or even trampled near her. A group of officers set about walking the lane, inch by inch, to see if they could find any of Jane Doe's belongings while two detectives sat down with Maurice Goodman in his home and interviewed him. Neither activity produced any clues that would help solve a murder.

As these initial inquiries went on, the most important person in the investigation at the time arrived. At both ends of the lane, some local folk had gathered, straining their necks to see what had happened. As the area awoke, word had circulated that there had been a murder – a woman, so someone said. As people do all over the world, curiosity about the macabre had got the better of otherwise decent people and they were braving the cold on the off chance of a glimpse of the body, a snippet of information from the police. But the police guarding the lane weren't saying anything or letting anyone through. Apart from one man.

With a slight nod to one of the uniformed police, a man in a heavy coat, carrying a black case, was allowed into the lane. With long strides, he headed towards the corpse, nodding to familiar faces among the police as he moved. No one stopped and chatted. No one made any flippant remarks. No one gave a warm greeting. That was the sombre protocol of their business. Besides, the investigation had just taken a step forward. The doctor had arrived.

The police surgeon, Dr James Imrie wasn't going to have an easy or pleasant task. The young woman's naked body seemed somehow obscene lying there in that lane surrounded by male cops but police surgeons have to get used to those kind of scenes and worse. The best Dr Imrie could do for that poor woman now was to help find her killer and the only way he could do that was to get on with his examination – whatever it took.

Covered in thick frost and stiff with rigor mortis, the cadaver was impossible to move or manipulate. Much of the examination would have to wait till she had thawed and the rigor had lifted. That would be later down at the city mortuary next to the High Court. But there was enough that could be seen for the doctor to be helpful – more than enough.

Her face and head had injuries of the type made by punching or kicking. Though nasty, none of them could have killed

50

the woman. Subdued her spirit, perhaps, but not ended her life. More interesting to the doctor was a thick line running across her neck. Deep purple and turning blue to black, a considerable force had been applied to make such bruising. By good luck, the woman's head lay at an angle that allowed the doctor to see the side of her neck without having to struggle with the stiffened muscles. Sure enough, the bruise ran along her neck and disappeared into her hairline at the back.

'Any joy, Doctor?' Elphinstone Dalglish asked.

'I think so,' replied Dr Imrie, rising to his feet and rubbing the cold and pain from his knees from kneeling on the ground. 'She's definitely been strangled and, as far as I can see, that's the most likely cause of death.'

'I thought so from . . .' Dalglish indicated his own neck to show that he had spotted the deep bruised line, as would any experienced detective who had seen many murder scenes.

'It's definitely murder,' continued the doctor, 'as if you needed to be told that. Something string-like but strong has been used – a belt, a piece of rope or even some nylons, I reckon.'

'The boys have walked the lane,' Dalglish went on, 'and found nothing.'

'Nothing at all?'

'Not a scrap – nothing belonging to her, never mind a murder weapon.' Dalglish looked up and down the lane as if checking that his team hadn't missed anything then continued, 'You know what I'm going to ask you now.'

The doctor smiled.

'Any idea? Even approximate?'

'If this had been summer and the night had been cool and dry, I'd have made a decent educated guess at time of death.'

Dalglish was nodding his head.

'But, with the freezing conditions and the onset of rigor mortis, there's no chance. No chance at all. Even the rigor will have developed at a different speed from normal because of the cold.'

He had given the response Elphinstone Dalglish had expected, though he'd had to ask just the same.

'We'll have to keep the boys off the scene till the forensic team get here,' declared Dalglish. 'This lane looks bare of any clues but they're the boys who see what we can't see, eh? Maybe the murder weapon is lying right under our noses.'

Just as he spoke, the forensic team arrived and, behind them, a van drew up. From the back of it, uniformed cops began unloading sheets and poles. As the cops erected a cover over the body, the forensic staff took over the lane. It was their territory now. Their turn to sift for clues that even the best of detectives wouldn't see. With no clothes or possessions belonging to the victim, the forensic team's work was more important than ever. That and old-fashioned police work.

The forensic team formed a line across Carmichael Lane and moved forward in a painful, slow progress. Now and then one would stop and stoop, scraping at some suspicious-looking substance on a stone, picking up a rusting tack, examining some shards of broken glass. It would take them some time to sift that short lane for evidence.

Meantime, the police officers set out on that tried-and-tested method that's as old as cop forces themselves – door-to-door inquiries. The words they used each time were different, more relaxed, natural as you do in conversation. These were good cops who knew how to get the best from wary members of the public but their questions always covered the same ground:

'Did you hear anything suspicious from the lane last night?'

'Any shouts or noises?'

'Did you see anyone in the lane? A courting couple, perhaps?'

'Has any of your family failed to return home?'

'Do you know anyone who's worried about a member of their family?'

The local citizens were being as helpful as they could be – most were even anxious to help. They lived in a quiet part of the city where trouble was rare. Even when there was a big football international match just over the hill in Hampden Park, they usually avoided any grief. Even when it was Scotland versus England and the streets nearby were mobbed with drunken partisans of either side intent on violence to settle ancient scores, watched over by policemen on horseback, their batons pulled ready for trouble. Even then their area remained quiet, trouble-free – just the way they liked it.

But, in spite of all the public-spirited nature of the locals, the cops weren't getting far. Then, down in the frozen lane of death, there was a breakthrough. A forensic officer called for his colleagues' attention. He stood just a few yards from the body, looking down at the ground, his face stained with a slight look of disgust. His boss and a detective joined him and followed his gaze. There on the ground, coiled like a sleeping serpent, lay a sanitary towel. One of the old-fashioned type, it was about a foot long and three inches wide with little cloth hooks and thin cotton tiers which formed a belt at the top. Made of cotton, it was chosen because it was absorbent rather than strong. It wasn't the murder weapon but it might be useful somehow in their investigation.

The sanitary towel was used and heavily soiled with blood. The victim's blood? If not, then whose? And how did it come to end up on the ground? And so close to the body? How long had it been lying there? The same length of time as the dead woman? Those and a hundred more questions rushed through the detective's mind. That used sanitary towel could prove to be a vital clue.

An hour later, the weak February sun had lifted in the sky, the melting frost had a watery sheen and the world seemed a brighter, more humane place – even in that lane. The detectives grouped together to apprise each other of their progress. Time and time again, they had learned that what they dis-

53

covered in the first few hours of an investigation came to be crucial.

From the far end of the lane, the onlookers saw only a group of men in coats, some in hats, most smoking cigarettes, a few passing round a steaming flask and pouring strong tea into cups. The more observant would've noticed them paying attention to one man in particular, Elphinstone Dalglish summing up the total of that morning's work. 'A young woman – early to mid twenties, the doctor reckons. Murdered – most likely cause of death, strangulation. Most likely murder weapon, a rope or something similar.'

'Can we be sure she wasn't killed with bare hands?' one of the detectives asked.

'Not entirely at this stage,' Dalglish replied, 'but the doctor's pretty sure and he knows his stuff. Now, what else have we got?'

Some of the detectives looked at their feet and others cleared their throats. They knew what was coming. It wasn't their fault but they still took it personally – always did in a murder case.

'A used sanitary towel.' Dalglish paused for dramatic effect. 'No clothes, no handbag, no coat, no way to identify the lassie.' He stopped and looked at the men around him. His expression could easily be mistaken for anger, disappointment in his team, but they knew better. What Dalglish was feeling angry about was an innocent woman being killed. 'We don't even know if that sanitary towel is the victim's and, even if it is, whether it's going to be of any value to the forensic boys. No local information of any use – yet.'

None of the cops said anything but most inwardly groaned. They knew that was a signal that the tedious door-to-door interviews were set to continue for some time.

'It's what?' Dalglish looked at his watch. 'Just coming up to eleven o'clock. Right. Are the newspaper folk here yet?'

'Oh, aye, most of them have been hanging around for a couple of hours,' replied one of the detectives.

'Bring them over, then – well, the ones from the Glasgow evening papers. I think we'll be in time to catch the early afternoon editions.'

A couple of his men looked at him, questions in their eyes.

· 'You have something to say?' asked their boss. 'Get it out.'

'Going to the newspapers so soon, Sir . . .' One had found his voice. 'With no name and no lines of inquiry . . . well, with so little . . . We wouldn't usually . . .'

The detective was absolutely right but this wasn't a usual situation, as Dalglish explained. 'See those hacks down there, son?' asked Dalglish, nodding his head towards the press people gathered at the end of the lane. 'They're not hacks as far as I'm concerned. Today they are colleagues.' He let the information sink in. 'They are going to help us crack the first problem of exactly who is it we have lying there under that cover.' This time he nodded in the other direction to where the victim lay. 'Look, lads, we're going to have to act quickly. There's a dangerous man roaming free in Glasgow.'

Some of his men looked him in the eye, nodding their heads.

'One of the *most* dangerous.'

Again that silence.

'A woman killer.' Dalglish turned and checked that the newspapermen moving up the lane weren't close enough to hear his words. He was going to be very careful, very limited in what he told them as he did not want to reveal any clues that might help the killer or, almost as bad, attract nutcases claiming to be the killer. Then he turned and finished his statement to his men. 'This one's a sadist – a strangler.'

Friday, 23 February 1968

I have cleansed her.

First, she took to me in the light.

Second, I took her into the dark.

Third, the light of my Father shone on us.

I have cleansed her. Now she is saved.

When she smiled at me in that ballroom, I knew right away that she was the one. I saw the Fire in her eyes and this time it didn't go out. I wasn't deceived. She was ready. Chosen. I knew that by the end of the night, I'd find that everything was as it should be. Everything in its place. That she would be in the state He called for. He guided me to her. He guided her to me.

I had been there an hour or so and danced with several women. They sent me the signals. Told me with their eyes and their hips that they would walk with me. But I knew it was a final test. That they were sent there to distract me from my purpose. That, if I walked with them, I would find out that all was not right – that they were not the chosen one. Find out too late that not everything was in place. Find out too late in the dark.

I left those women. Politely and cheerfully. Anger is beyond me now. Who needs anger when he has God?

Now and then I'd go down to the bar where they sold orange juice. Orange juice, not whisky, as if that was the saving of all those lost souls. Even the women smuggle in half- bottles of whisky in their handbags, sneaking to the toilets to touch up their make-up and take a few slugs. They emerge smelling of fresh cheap perfume and sour drink. It will take more than lukewarm diluted orange to bring them back from the gates of Hell.

The many are damned. I can only save the chosen few. The special ones. The ones with the Fire.

Back with the music, I saw her standing there alone. I had seen her before. Weeks before, she had caught my eye then. Beautiful, bright eyed, wide smile. She looked the part but she wasn't ready. I watched her that night with other men. Taking to the floor as if there were no other cares. As if she were sin-free. Brazen. She was brazen.

We danced for hours. We drank orange juice. Just orange juice. Was it my manners? My polite approach? My lack of swearing? My gentlemanliness? Did that put her off taking illicit swigs from her half-bottle? Or did she really carry no booze? What did it matter? She was the one.

As we danced I noticed she wore a wedding band. Not on her left hand as might be expected but on her right. What? Did she think that, by changing the ring from her wedding finger to another, she fooled anyone? But then maybe she wanted to fool no one. Isn't that the way of all whores?

When I told her my name was John she didn't laugh and joke like the others. Those who pointed out that all the men there that night claimed to be a John or a Jim. That the name was no more than a cover-up for some earthly lies. Deceits about wives and children at home. Lies those laughing women didn't mind. Lies most told themselves. Maybe she sensed my great secret. My purpose. And I wasn't lying.

At the close of play, I offered to see her home in a taxi. Immediately she agreed. Who are these women who walk with strangers? Who are these hussies who let you hold them and look up into your face so openly, pleading to be taken? The doomed – that's who.

She didn't want to go into the dark. Maybe then she sensed her fate. Work, she said, early in the morning. I promised I would take her home soon. A child, she said, waiting for her. I pretended to be interested and still led her by the arm. Married, she said, once we were down that lane in the pitch dark. We all have our secrets, I told her in my quiet way and felt her down there in the heat of her loins. Everything was in place. She was ready.

She called out loud. Did she think the world would hear her?

My secret, I said. Don't you want to know it? She struggled with my hands but the strength of the Lord was within me. My secret? Don't you want to know? She said yes in a whimper. Did she think there was time left for pity? Did she think forgiveness was still possible?

You know me as John, I said, but my real name is TERROR.

Then I cleansed her.

'Oh shit.' The ambulance man was bent over the young woman's body, ready to lift her on to a stretcher.

'What?' asked the uniformed cop standing nearby, noticing the bloke's face had gone pure white. Surely, in his kind of work, a dead body wouldn't cause that kind of upset – even if it was of a young woman, even if it was a murder victim.

'I know this lassie,' the ambulance driver gasped. 'I'm bloody sure I do.'

The policeman and the other ambulance man were by his side quickly, reaching to hold him up.

'No, I'm OK,' he insisted, shaking them off. 'It just got to me. No' expecting it, know? I mean her. No' expecting her.'

The policeman wasn't convinced the man was OK but, respecting his word, said, 'You'll have to talk with one of the plainclothes. You be OK here for a minute?'

'Aye, aye,' replied the ambulance man, sounding irritated by the concern of the cop and not noticing his own colleague nodding silently at the policeman, telling him in a glance that it would be OK and he'd look after his mate.

'There's some tea there, OK?' The policeman pointed at a box full of flasks, cups and the other tea-making paraphernalia lying on the ground close by. 'Maybe you should have a cup of sweet tea for . . .'

'Aye, aye. For the fucking shock.' The ambulance man was irritated by the cop's suggestion even if it had been offered kindly. What did he think ambulance men did for a living? Transport corpses?

When the policeman returned a few minutes later with two detectives, he noticed the ambulance men had ignored his offer of tea but had gone about their job and lifted the body into the back of their vehicle, ready to be transported for a post mortem.

'You think you know her, then?' one of the plainclothes cops asked.

'No' so much know as recognise,' replied the ambulance man.

'How?'

'I'm no' sure. It's just I'm certain I've seen her face a few times. I think around my work.'

'What do you mean?' asked the cop, careful not to put words in the man's mouth. This conversation could be crucial to the murder case or could be made into a big waste of precious time.

A cat, white with two or three black patches, had suddenly appeared at their feet rubbing herself against their legs, purring for attention, looking up into their faces, fearless. No one leaned down to stroke her fur but then neither did they chase her away. There was something reassuring in her presence. One of the cops thought to himself how strange that was. No beast of any kind had been seen in the lane that morning yet that kind of residential area must be heaving with pets and wildlife knowing that the living was easy and safer than in most places. He couldn't even remember hearing any birds. Now that the body had been lifted off the ground and safely ensconced in the back of an ambulance, a cat had appeared. Did the cat have some sense of death? Of evil? Did she know that was now gone? They were questions he kept strictly to himself.

'She might be a nurse,' the ambulance man replied. 'In this work, we see a lot of young nurses.'

'Lucky you!' A policeman tried to instil some humour into a tense situation.

'Aye, I wish.' The ambulance man wasn't so shaken he couldn't take the comment in good spirits. 'But we're in and out of hospitals all the time. This one, though, I remember her.'

'Well, she's a looker,' said a cop.

'It's no' just that,' the ambulance man went on, 'there was something special about her. A good personality. Kind, you know? At least, I think it's the same lassie.'

That group of men were used to seeing dead bodies and had long ago learned that death changes how some people look.

'I don't suppose you remember a name?' asked a policeman.

'No and, to be honest, I'm not even sure which hospital I might have seen her at. We just go to where we're told. Could be anywhere on this side of Glasgow.'

'I suppose the Victoria's the biggest by far, eh?' asked the policeman, referring to one of the largest hospitals in Glasgow.

'Oh, aye, and we'd get most calls to take patients there.'

'Aye and *from* there,' his mate added.

'You've been very helpful,' announced one of the detectives. 'Are you sure you're OK to go on working?'

'Och, aye, I'm fine,' replied the ambulance man. 'Like you, we learn to deal with all sorts in this job. Had to learn a long time ago that everybody's at risk of the worst things happening to them. Even good-looking young nurses.'

As the ambulance slowly edged out of the lane one of the watching cops muttered to himself, 'Especially good-looking young nurses.'

Two of the police team were immediately dispatched to the sprawling campus of the Victoria Infirmary. Built in the name of that queen almost a century before, the core of the hospital looked old, outdated and creepy even in daytime. Over the years, new laboratories and medical wings had been added till it became a major teaching hospital serving about half of the southside of Glasgow's huge, mainly poor, population – a population who were greatly in need of medical care. Most of that care was provided by nurses, the majority of whom were female and young.

The cops' question to the Victoria Infirmary's administrative staff was not an easy one. 'Is any nurse missing?' It would take hours of sifting records and checking. Then they asked their next questions. 'Is any nurse, who might be on holiday or even off sick, missing?' 'Are any of your staff worried about a pal who didn't come home last night?' Now, it could take days to find out the answers to such questions but, nevertheless, the clerical and management staff set about the task. When, later that day, they reported to the cops that, of the nurses due at work, none was missing, someone was about to save them further trouble – someone very close at hand.

'It's about that poor murdered lassie.' John Wilson looked wracked with worry, his face pale and drawn. 'My daughter, Pat, didn't come home last night – isn't back yet.'

The policeman nodded slowly. They had a few similar approaches that day but all had turned out as false alarms – mainly young daughters who'd been staying over at boyfriends' flats and were too scared to go home to face the parental music. One teenage woman had run away but, thankfully, she'd picked up the nerve and a phone to get a message to her folks. As soon as word got round that a young woman had been murdered, every family in the area with a young adult daughter saw such domestic difficulties as diabolical. The cops didn't mind that. These were just decent people who were concerned about their kin. But there was something about this man that worried the cop.

'Is she in the habit of staying out?'

'She's a good girl. She would've come home if she could.' Wilson hesitated, rubbing his face with both palms. 'But sometimes she stays with pals so I didn't worry at first. She was at the dancing and sometimes, if she's late and misses her last bus . . . You know . . . well, she's twenty-five – a grown woman really. I didn't worry when her bed was empty this morning. Didn't worry.' John Wilson was worrying now and the cop could sense the man was half blaming himself, half in dread that it was his daughter who they had found in the lane. 'But she's a good lassie. Never stayed out all night and all the next day. Never. And always gets in touch. No' just for us but for her wee boy.'

'Mr Wilson, I'm going to have to ask you a few questions.'

'Aye, anything – anything at all.' John Wilson looked down at his feet and wrung his hands together. There was a dull pressure deep in his chest. A pain of dread that he knew wouldn't shift till he saw his daughter alive and well. A pain of dread that wouldn't shift.

By early evening, the police had ascertained that twenty-five-year-old Pat Docker was slim, with short brown hair and hazel eyes, that she was the mother of one child and that she worked as an auxiliary nurse. Pat Docker met all the descriptions they had of the murdered woman. Even the ambulance man who thought he had recognised her might well have been right although the cops were looking for missing nurses from the Victoria Infirmary while Pat worked at Mearnskirk Hospital.

Carmichael Lane was a very short distance from Langside Place, where Pat lived with her son and her parents. What had her father John Wilson said? 'She's a good girl. She would've come home if she could.' Had she been on her way home when she was attacked? Murdered by someone she knew? Was the young woman being as good as her father said when evil pounced on her?

'Mr Wilson,' said the cop, 'I know this is a hard thing to do but would you mind viewing the woman's body? For identification purposes? I know it's not easy but it would be useful to us even if it isn't Pat. And . . .'

'I need to know,' butted in John Wilson, tears glistening in his eyes, 'need to know if it's our Patricia.'

The police mortuary lay in an old part of Glasgow next to the ancient High Court and across from Glasgow Green, where public hangings had taken place as thousands watched and cheered. The building itself was old, full of nooks and crannies, twists and turns. In that place, thousands of victims of bloody violence had lain, taken from life too early. Even in summer with the heating full on, chill blasts would float through rooms and doors would open without reason. Cupboards would spring open and slam shut again. Drawers would creak and crack as if there was someone trying to get out. No wonder, then, that the mortuary was believed to be haunted – so haunted that experienced attendants would flee in the middle of the night never to return, not even to collect wages they were due.

There, in that place, John Wilson took a walk that no parent should walk.

It was his daughter, Pat Docker.

When John Wilson went home and he and his wife collapsed with grief and tried to work out what to tell young Sandy, how to tell the wee boy, the murder investigation took a step forward.

'So what do we have?' Elphinstone Dalglish sat in the Central Police Office surrounded by the investigation team late on the Friday night. 'We know the murder victim was Pat Docker, a clean-living young woman by all accounts.'

Around him, heads nodded as Dalglish took his time as usual.

'We know she was at The Majestic Ballroom on the night of her death. So we'll target that for eyewitnesses.'

Next to him, a detective was taking notes for the group that they would turn into an action plan.

'Most important . . .'

All eyes were on Dalglish now.

'Most of all, we know she was married but separated, that her husband, Alex Docker, is in the RAF and stationed in Lincolnshire but not this week.' Dalglish stopped, that angry look in his eyes again, and took a long drink from his cup of tea which, while he was speaking, had gone cold. 'This week he's on leave – on leave in Scotland.'

He nodded his head at some of the police officers who were learning this for the first time. They understood what Dalglish was drawing from this information.

'Let's go and see Alex Docker. This could be our strangler.'

Hail, Hail, the Celts are here,
What the hell do we care
What the hell do we care . . .

Across the street a dozen or so young men, dressed in green-and-white hooped football tops and carrying green-and-white scarves at full stretch above their heads, marched down the pavement, forcing everyone and everything out of their way. Ruth watched them, noticing how they didn't so much walk as sway in time to the beat of their song – a battle song – the way she imagined some victorious band of warriors might after they'd faced the enemy and won. Adrenalin and beer buzzing through their bodies, the taste of blood in their mouths, the scent of their enemy's defeat in their noses – behaviour as old as war and just as dangerous.

'There's always trouble in Byres Road when you and I get together.' In spite of the racket coming from the young football supporters, Peter's presence suddenly beside her startled her.

She turned and smiled. 'Where did you creep up from?'

'Creep? Well, that beats accusations of crawling out from under some slimy stone that most folk accuse us of.'

'Surely pigs live in sties not under boulders,' Ruth laughed.

'Ouch.'

'Well, you started it.'

We don't care what the animals say
What the hell do we care . . .

Almost on cue, farther down the street, the football supporters had reached an appropriate part of their song. Ruth and Peter stood and watched for a minute as the group almost reached Partick Cross.

'Did they win?' asked Ruth.

'Celtic always win this weather,' replied Peter with a grin.

'A supporter, are we?'

'Well, if you're born on the wrong side of the tracks in this city, you have to be.'

'The wrong side?'

'Oh, you've got a lot to learn about Glasgow, Ruth. A lot. But that's for another time – a more serious time – though, eh? Tonight's strictly pleasure.'

'Agreed.'

'Drink before we eat?' Peter checked his watch. 'We've got plenty of time.'

'Never say no.'

They crossed the road and into the Rubáiyát. It was one of the newer, trendier pubs in the area and it showed. As Peter fetched the drinks, Ruth took in her surroundings. The crowd were the usual lot of academics and students she'd quickly got used to in the west end but the decor was a bit special. There were huge etched mirrors and ceramic tiles with some verses and scenes from the poems of Omar Khayyám that were collected in *The Rubáiyát* – hence the name of the pub.

'So you don't know the result then?' Ruth asked as Peter laid their drinks on the table.

'What? Oh, the game. No.' He shook his head with a smile and she noticed again his healthy overgrown-schoolboy good looks. Maybe he had been born on the wrong side of the tracks, as he'd put it, but he had been raised well.

'A man who doesn't know his own football team's result . . .' She pulled a shocked face. 'I knew there was something I liked about you.'

'Even like me as a copper?'

'That really bothers you, doesn't it?' Ruth's tone changed from teasing to genuine.

'Well, aye, it does. These days everybody seems to be set against authority. Anti-Vietnam war demos. Ban the Bomb. Free Ireland. And the polis? We're the worst – "Oink! Oink!"' He made a reasonable attempt at imitating a porker.

'So you think I'm just like everyone else, then?'

'Aye.' He was blushing but she wasn't sure why. 'No. I mean you're young and bright and beautiful.' Now she understood. 'And all people like you seem to be set on being . . . well . . . extreme. I've just met you, Ruth, and I like you very much but I can see that you're . . . eh . . . free. No, that's no' it.'

'Liberated?' she offered.

'Yeah, that's the word. You're liberated.'

Ruth took in what Peter was saying and, while considering her response, took in events around her. At the other side of the small bar, there was an older woman. Drunk, blousy and talkative, her hair was dyed too black and the seam of her skirt was trailing fine threads. Every time she crossed her legs, her skirt rode higher and higher up her full thighs. When she reached out her hand to pick up her glass or flick ash from her cigarette, her cleavage heaved into view and the top of a lacy bra became visible. She was in the company of a younger man. Smartly dressed and obviously well off, he was watching the leg-and-breast show with unsubtle and very sober sleazy intent. Around the bar, men looked over at the couple and grinned knowingly. The young man had plans for the woman – that much was obvious – and Ruth hoped that the woman was in on the plans, prayed that she was.

Then Ruth noticed that she was the only other woman in the place – and that included the staff – and a pang of anguish crossed her chest. Was she going to end up like that woman? Sitting prey for men to take at will? Or was she going to be stronger than that?

'I've not exactly been open with you, Peter,' she said, looking him in the face.

He looked back at her with an anxious expression. What did he think? That she was a journalist out to gain inside information? A card-carrying member of the International Marxist Group out to seduce him away from his fascist job?

'I'm not an ordinary psychologist.'

Peter's expression turned to puzzlement.

'I only study criminal cases.' Out of the side of her eye she saw the young man order another double Bacardi and Coke for his lady friend and a half-pint of lager for himself. 'I'm more like you than you think.'

Now he was smiling, relaxed but still curious.

'You find out who did what and try and arrest them. I find out why they did what they did and try and change them.'

Nodding, Peter said, 'Aye, no' so different after all.'

'See, so you're not a pig in my book,' Ruth smiled. 'Though I've yet to see your eating manners.'

'Oh, sod it!' Peter was looking at his watch. 'We need to go. I've booked a table at the Shish but, if we're late, they'll let it go. There's always a queue waiting on a Saturday night.' He was standing up, draining his drink.

'Popular place, is it?'

'The Shish Mahal? Aye, especially with all those long-haired student riff-raff.'

'Students – bloody nuisance, eh?'

They made it to their table at the Shish Mahal just in time. Ruth sat and took in her surroundings. Thick, velvety-feeling wallpaper in dark, blood-red patterns and a carpet to match. Crisp white tablecloth and waiters smartly dressed in what she took for native Indian or Pakistani costume. An older man in a turban and a smart tunic buttoned to his neck had the most luxurious white-silver beard she'd ever seen. The effect made him look stern, fierce even, but he turned out to be very welcoming. All of that seemed exotic to Ruth but the most

69

overpowering sensation was the blend of spices and scents that filled the air. It was almost overwhelming and it was a first for her. Even when she was studying in London for her degree, the most common restaurants were Italian or steak houses or American-style burger joints. Now here she was confronted by a menu she couldn't begin to understand. She had no option but to reveal to Peter that this was her first curry – ever.

'So you want me to order for you?' he asked with smile.

'Could you, please?'

'Well, one good turn deserves another,' he said with a suddenly serious expression she dreaded. Was this the come-on? The sexual play? Was he no different from the man with the drunk woman back at the Rubáiyát? 'I'll order your food *if* . . .' A pause for effect. 'you tell me all about your work.'

'You sure?'

'Aye.'

'It might put you off your dinner.'

'I'll take my chances.'

As Ruth discovered she loved poppadoms, spiced onions, lamb biriani and nan bread, she told Peter about her visits to the murder scenes in Glasgow and down in London. How she had visited several prisons and met with convicted killers as part of her final degree year. Her plans to set up similar arrangements as part of her PhD and how the governors of Peterhead and Barlinnie Prisons had already agreed. How she was particularly interested in sex killers and serial killers and had trailed Jack the Ripper's haunts and visited the Gorton area of Manchester tracing the actions of the Moors Murderers and how she had written to Myra Hindley three times asking for an interview and still not had a reply. She prattled on and on about Peter Manuel being sexually impotent and Londoner John Christie having sex with many of his victims after he had killed them and then she realised that a waiter was standing by their table.

'Pudding? Coffee?' Peter asked with smile.

Ruth suddenly realised she had worked her way through a mountain of delicious food and hardly drawn breath. She had been talking all night about her work and Peter had been listening quietly. 'I'm sorry, Peter,' she said, 'I must have bored you witless.'

'Not at all and, as you can see,' he said, pointing at the almost empty plates and dishes in front of them, 'you didn't put me off my grub either.'

'OK but it's your turn now. Tell me about your work.'

'You sure?'

'Of course – I'm interested.'

'Might seem a bit boring after your tales – writing to Myra Hindley, eh?'

'Peter!' Ruth was warning him to get on with it.

'Well, it has taken an interesting turn, as it happens, since we met the other night. Maybe you've brought me good luck because, as a new boy, I was getting all the boring stuff to do – serving warrants, walking the boozer beats at closing time . . .'

'Peter.'

'Did you hear about that young woman who was murdered in the southside? Found in a lane yesterday morning?' He picked up his fresh pint of lager. 'Well, I got drafted in to help the big boys – Flying Squad, no less.'

'Now you are impressing me,' she smiled.

'Just the legwork, you understand. The house-to-house interviews and that kind of stuff. But I get to be included in some of the briefings. Dead good, so it is.'

'Your first murder inquiry?' Ruth asked.

Peter nodded. 'It's what I went into this job to do, isn't it? Catching killers, making the world a bit safer for people. That's what cops should do.'

Ruth smiled to herself, noting that he was as idealistic as any campus radical she had met – maybe even more so,

71

depending on your view of police forces. She just hoped her new friend's innocent optimism wouldn't end in tears.

'But, in this job, I get to see guys like Elphinstone Dalglish and particularly Tom Goodall in action. Well, now and then I do but they're the real deal – proper detectives, no' interested in pen-pushing or politics. Maybe I'll even get a chance to see Joe Beattie at work. I reckon he's the best – the top man.' Peter caught Ruth's eye and gave her an embarrassed smirk, knowing he had gone off on one. He hoped, in his enthusiasm, he hadn't made a bad impression. After all, it was the 1960s and even cops were meant to be laid-back.

Over two slow pints of lager and watched by waiters throwing them dirty looks in the hope that they'd take the hint and leave to let some new, late-night customers get their table, Peter told Ruth all about Pat Docker. Eventually, they took the waiters' hints and, once out on Gibson Street, they discovered that the night had turned cold and crisp but with a clear sky dotted with winking stars – a perfect night for a walk home up University Avenue.

'The detectives suspected the husband at first,' Peter continued, as they walked close together, 'what with the separation and him just happening to be in Scotland that same night.'

'Yeah, it's amazing the number of people who get killed by someone really close to them,' said Ruth.

'But it turned out he had a solid alibi,' Peter went on, as they passed the Men's Union, which was all splendid architecture above ground but, from the basement, came the raucous shouts of boozed-up male students. No women were allowed in there – not even as staff. 'He was with relatives in Midlothian or some place miles away all the time. Poor guy was really upset about his wife – separated or no'.'

'So, have they hit a dead end, then?' Ruth asked, failing to spot the humour in the use of that particular phrase in connection with a murder.

'No, not at all,' replied Peter. 'They found out from her parents that Pat had been at The Majestic dance hall on the night she died so it's likely that that's where she would've been last seen alive – maybe in the company of her killer.' Peter stopped and shrugged. 'Who knows? But, last night, some of the team went there. They had the music stopped and asked to speak to anyone who had been there the night before.' He smiled broadly to himself.

'What's funny?' Ruth asked.

'Funny? Nothing really. But I was really disappointed when I wasn't asked to go along. Then, when the boys discovered there were hundreds there on the Friday who'd also been there on the Thursday . . .' Another big smile. 'They were there for hours interviewing them – bloody hours asking the same questions.'

'So did it help?' Ruth wondered if she was asking too many questions about a sensitive murder investigation but Peter didn't seem to be bothered.

'No, not much. But there's some interesting stuff from the post mortem. It was carried out by a top man, Professor Gilbert Forbes from . . .'

'The Department of Forensic Medicine at Glasgow University who is the latest in a long line of eminent forensic practitioners at the university . . .' Ruth was rattling out the words in a sing-song, heard-it-all-before manner. 'The most famous being Professor John Glaister who made many significant breakthroughs in forensic science, not least of which was his contribution to the case of Dr Buck Ruxton who . . .'

'All right, all right!' Peter held his hands up in the air in surrender. 'Teaching my granny to suck eggs. Sorry.'

Ruth smiled condescendingly and motioned for him to continue.

'The post mortem confirmed that Pat had been strangled,' Peter continued. 'The docs reckon he may have used her own stockings. How sick is that?'

'A sex killing,' said Ruth.

'You reckon?'

She nodded her head in reply.

'The gaffer seems really concerned that it was strangulation for some reason. Me, I'd have thought a knifer or a shooter would be worse.'

'Strangulation is always up close and personal – and slow. He's a sadist, in other words.'

Peter was listening to Ruth carefully, nodding his head.

'Also, especially with something like a stocking, it's more likely to be cold and premeditated. Planned.'

'Let's go this way,' said Peter, leading her through the hefty wrought-iron gates to the old university buildings. 'It's a short cut that avoids Byres Road – don't want us hexing it again, do we?'

Ruth followed his lead down the side of the main building with its gothic spires and turrets and then they were walking along Professors' Row, where the few lights shining from large bay windows indicated that only one or two of the learned ones were at home.

'That's bloody scary,' said Peter.

'What?' asked Ruth, feeling a little edgy because of the route they were taking. It was an ancient place full of ancient ghosts.

'The strangler. So if he didn't know Pat Docker or maybe had just met her that night at the dancing, his reason for killing her was what?'

'His own, very personal reasons,' replied Ruth, avoiding getting into the academic theories that would probably bore Peter. Besides, they were just theories and that was her purpose through her work – finding the theories that were capable of creating science, real knowledge.

'And those personal reasons might mean?'

'That he will kill again,' replied Ruth, sure in her knowledge on this occasion and keen to give something back to Peter. 'Tell me,' she said, 'had Pat been raped?'

'You know, now that you mention it, the gaffer didn't say. I had just assumed that, with her being naked, she had been.' He hesitated. 'Big mistake, eh?'

Ruth nodded but in a kindly way.

Just then, they came to the end of Professors' Row and the corner of the main university building. They looked out on to a steep but narrow valley and, at the other side, an angry, huge monolith of a building was scowling at them. It took her breath away.

Hearing her gasp, Peter said, 'They call that Kelvingrove Art Gallery. It's a museum really – full of dinosaurs and all sorts as well as wonderful works of art. Legend has it that it was accidentally built facing the wrong way and, when the architect realised his mistake, he took himself up to the roof, to that corner there,' he said, pointing, 'and threw himself off. Dead.'

'It's simply beautiful,' Ruth whispered.

'I know,' he replied. 'Imagine designing that and then killing yourself because your creation was looking the wrong way.'

'A waste – such a sheer bloody waste.'

They stood looking across the narrow glen for a while then Peter spoke up. 'Funny thing, though. Pat was stripped naked. I mean she wasn't even wearing her watch. Absolutely nothing of hers has been found. They are even dragging the River Cart to see if it was all dumped in there. But the one thing that *was* found . . .' He suddenly stopped in mid sentence.

'What?'

'I don't know any other way to say this.'

'Go on.'

Peter sighed loudly. 'It was a sanitary towel. A used sanitary towel.' He left those words, forbidden in polite company, to sink in then added, 'Pat Docker's used sanitary towel. It was the only thing of hers the killer left.'

They stood side by side in the dark, looking out on a vista they both knew would stay with them forever.

But Ruth had stopped thinking about the view. She was thinking about everything he had told her about Pat Docker – especially that used sanitary towel. Pat Docker's used sanitary towel – the one and only thing of hers the killer had left. Had left there deliberately.

They turned from the scowling museum and walked towards the steps that would eventually take them down to Dumbarton Road and their flats in Partick.

'Peter?' said Ruth, as they walked.

'Yes.'

'Can we see each other again?'

'Of course, of course,' he spluttered, not being used to a woman inviting him out. 'I was going to ask you. There's a new place in town with a disc jockey and dancing and the food's good.'

'No,' Ruth replied quietly, 'I mean, if you don't mind, I'd like to go to The Majestic Ballroom.'

'The Magic Stick?' asked Peter, baffled.

'Yeah,' Ruth replied quietly, 'I want to go dancing.'

Friday, 1 March 1968

Fools and charlatans. They accept the public purse and puff their chests out in pride. 'Trust us,' they say, 'we'll protect you.' Protect them? They don't even know where I am, never mind who I am.

The place where they are looking is full of empty-headed hairies and dirty-nailed louts from all over the city. They go there because it is in the city centre. The bright lights. The busy streets. The fancy pubs. The prostitutes lifting their skirts on street corners. The fast trains. The late-night buses. The chip shops open late at night, run by men and women in white overalls, using fancy greaseproof paper. George Square at one in the morning, passing each other, giving or receiving wolf whistles, telling them the party isn't over if they don't want it to be. The party need never end, so they think. They go there because they are fools and sinners only worthy of my contempt.

They are beneath me.

Yet the police think I go there. Do they think I am one of them?

My Father chose my favourite place with care. And He was right.

God kept His word and blinded their eyes to my Light. I am safe to do his bidding.

One week after the cleansing, I returned to my place. My sweet Patricia had Devils in her and they struggled and fought. She wanted to be saved, I know that, but the Devils wouldn't let her go and they scratched and kicked and hit out. I am stronger than I look. Many have learned that. With His power in me, that night I was as strong as Him.

After the cleansing I saw that my face was scratched. Devils always leave their marks in blood red for the world to see. Healing has never come fast to me. It is a price I pay for my fine pale skin. I feared I would have to stay hidden for weeks. Take to my shelter and pray. On the Sunday, I rose at dawn and fasted all day, paying homage to His Grace. Rising on Monday, the marks were gone. No trace. No sign.

In the New Book, they would call it a miracle. In my book, I know it is His way. His way for the chosen one. His way for me.

Without blemish or mark, I returned to my favourite place. I walked among them and looked them in the face. They saw nothing – not even John. Where I smiled at her and she smiled back, over by the stage, at the end of a dance, where I lifted her chin and saw the Fire in her eyes. His Fire showing me the way. By the cloakroom, where I stood waiting for her at the end of the night. The end of the night but the beginning of the future. On that night, I was calm, still, unmoved. But then, as I stood there again one week later, my heart swelled and filled my chest, heat filled my head till sweat ran down my nose and a great lust filled my loins. Gasping for air, I marched for the door, resisting the temptation in my legs to run. Outside, I walked quickly to the right then to the right again till I was on the great green. There, in the darkness, in the shelter of a tree, I loosened my clothes and praying to Him for forgiveness held my lust in both hands. All the while her words running through my mind. All the while her final call before she met her Maker. All the while feeling again her trembling flesh and the fear in her breath till I shouted out loud to Him. Those words of hers.

Her last words.

'LEAVE ME ALONE!'

'Is she sure it was a woman's voice she heard and that she heard those precise words?' Detective Superintendent Elphinstone Dalglish was sitting behind his desk listening to two of his team give a witness account in the Pat Docker murder investigation. Not an eyewitness but an ear witness yet the information could be important in identifying precisely the time of the murder.

For two weeks solid, policemen had been sent out to the Battlefield area interviewing locals in ever-widening circles from the murder scene and were making little progress. This witness lived close by and had just been out the first couple of times police had gone to her door.

One of the reporting detectives looked down at his notebook. 'Definitely a woman's voice and, when I pressed the witness, Sir, at first she said she was sure about the words. Then I left it a while and, when I raised it again later, she became a wee bit uncertain – said it might have been "LET ME GO!"'

Dalglish was slightly nodding his head. As an experienced cop, he knew that such witness statements were never as clear-cut as the Hollywood filmmakers and the TV boys conveyed. Real life was too imperfect and awkward for them. An honest witness almost always expressed some doubt, some vagueness, which reflects the true state of the human memory in such matters.

'How did this woman seem to you?' Dalglish asked.

'Sir?' asked one of the cops, uncertain what his boss meant.

'There's been a bit of publicity around this case,' Dalglish explained, 'and we've already had enough attention seekers claiming they witnessed something that simply didn't happen. So d'you think she's one of them?'

The two detectives looked at each other and without exchanging words turned to their boss and shook their heads.

'A very honest person, Sir,' said the reporting detective. 'You know, no' fanciful.'

'A good church-goer,' said his neighbour, trying to be helpful. 'Protestant, I think,' he added for reasons that needed no explanation in Glasgow.

Except that didn't wash with Elphinstone Dalglish the policeman. 'So, what?' He looked at the two men, anger firing in his eyes. 'Are all Proddies honest and all Catholics liars now, eh?' His angry stare stayed focused on the men. 'Ach, get back to your work.'

The two men stood up to go, one searching in his pocket for his cigarettes, nervous at having upset his gaffer.

'Eh, something else,' said the first detective, receiving an angry look from Dalglish. 'The witness said it could've been both.'

A furrowed brow and a puzzled stare from Dalglish.

'Both statements, Sir. She might've heard two shouts.'

Dalglish was giving short, dull-eyed nods.

'She just wasn't sure, Sir.'

'An honest Proddie, right enough,' announced Dalglish, knowing he was stinging the edgy, smoking cop but also meaning every word. He believed that witness. 'Tell you what,' he added, with the hint of a smile on his lips, 'as a reward, join the boys on the taxis. They need all the help they can get.'

Dalglish knew the two men would be heavy hearted. Who wouldn't be when assigned the thankless task of tracking down and interviewing all the taxi drivers on duty in Glasgow on the night of the murder who might have picked up Pat Docker and maybe a man in the city centre that night? In his early days, drivers of taxis, buses and trams were known as the Third Force and they were always happy to provide the police with information. Now, too many taxi drivers were working on the sly and feared the taxman or didn't have a licence to operate. Some of them were even in cahoots with the other side, with the gangsters, and would get their arms broken if they spoke to the cops. So finding the right taxi driver – if he existed – was like looking for a needle in a haystack and a lot of the hay was shuffling with the wind. Life was getting much messier than it used to be and Elphinstone Dalglish didn't see it as progress.

'You ready to go, Sir?' It was one of his detective sergeants, a good officer in Dalglish's reckoning.

'Aye, of course.' Dalglish beckoned him in with one hand then continued, 'Where is it we're heading again?' He had some paperwork to get through but that could wait if there was business to deal with in an active case, especially Pat Docker's murder.

'It's the Cart, Sir.'

'Aye, a dirty river than runs through Glasgow. Not as big as the Clyde – or as dirty, come to think of it – but dirty enough just the same.' It was as close as Dalglish came to cracking a joke.

The DS smiled. 'We said the other day we'd review progress this morning.'

'Aye, we did, didn't we? I really should put all this stuff in my diary.'

'Sir?'

'And read my bloody diary every day.'

'Sir.'

Elphinstone Dalglish was renowned for his skills of organisation but had a habit of immersing himself with his troops in the middle of a big investigation. Through them, he had the ability to see the case emerge, understand what was important and mark it for further action. Trouble was he was sometimes deep in another debate before he had planned and scheduled the first. Over a short campaign, he was as sharp as a scalpel. The longer it went on, the more his good officers had to guide him to what he told them had to be done. It was a weakness but a forgivable one.

The sound of the city dulled into peace and quiet as they drove off the main road down the quiet track. In that city, it didn't take long or any great distance to move from busy, buzzing streets to tranquil solitude. As the two cops stepped out of the car, the sound of lapping, laughing water filled their ears. They took the few steps to the riverbank and knew they couldn't feed the ducks even if they wanted to. A blind man would have known there would be no ducks in that rancid, stinking river.

Dalglish followed the rivulets of water as they got larger and faster, spreading out in a growing V shape, till a black-headed hunchback appeared slowly at first and then rose sharply, breaking the surface and the restful silence.

The diver cleared his goggles, disengaged his mouthpiece and then turned to the far bank where his watcher stood, dressed for water, dressed to give help if needed. The diver raised his arm in salute and the watcher replied in kind then jabbed his arm to the other bank. Shaking water from his head and filling his lungs with deep breaths, the diver looked again. The watcher repeated his actions and slowly the limb-weary diver turned, saw Dalglish and the detective sergeant and raised an open-handed salute.

'Them,' he muttered to himself, 'I really must keep a diary.'

Two minutes later on the bank of the Cart, the diver squatted, smoking, and spoke with his senior officers.

'We have no problem with this job, Sir, as you know.'

'Aye, you're a good team.' Dalglish nodded and meant every word he said.

'We always follow orders to the letter, as you know.'

Dalglish did know and could keep company enthralled by his tales of crime cracking that wouldn't have been possible if not for the police divers. That was from his career alone. Glasgow had been early in using divers in murder investigations – had broken new waters, as the crews themselves liked to say in a joke that had long lost its zest. But they didn't care. They were divers. They were different.

'In any job, you get to know your territory. We get to know water. And we know there's nothing left of Pat Docker down there.' The diver dragged on his fag and watched a water rat stare at him from a few feet away before turning and sliding seamlessly, noiselessly into the brown river. He had come to respect all rats but especially water rats. 'Don't ask me to explain it further – I'm no good with words. Water now . . . I know water.' He signalled with his thumb over his shoulder at the river. 'She's given up everything she has of Patricia Docker. She's a good girl, wants to help even more, but the old lady doesn't have any more to give.'

Dalglish looked down at the diver. A three-day-old growth of a beard, hair straggling in rat tails down his neck, smoking funny-smelling roll-ups, speaking like some weirdo about a wee bit of a polluted stream like it was human. If he had been one of his ordinary cops, Dalglish would have had him on the sick and out of the force and never looked back. But this was a diver and they were different. And this was a special sort of diver. Gifted. Maybe you had to be a wee bit crazy to be him.

Dalglish cleared his throat. 'She . . .' He cursed himself silently and started again. 'The Cart has produced what we think is Pat Docker's handbag?'

The diver nodded. 'We're pretty sure it is.' The diver shrugged and turned to watch the water rat easing his way through the water, trailing a gentle, practised wake.

'Now *that* is swimming,' he muttered.

Dalglish had followed his gaze and knew exactly what the diver had been looking at and admiring. He shook his head and rolled his eyes.

'But you found her watch case?' He left time for the comment to sink in as if his meaning should be obvious. 'We know it is her watch case?'

The diver looked up and simply nodded.

'Her tiny, fucking, cheap, bastarding watch case?'

The diver looked up again and stared.

'Down in those manky waters?'

The diver nodded, thinking he had been paid a compliment but at the same time unsure.

'And you say you can't find me nothing else? Fucking nothing?'

Now the diver understood. 'That's my point, Sir,' he said, clearing his throat and stubbing out his roll-up. 'We've been over this stretch of the river so often, so thoroughly, that we even managed to find her watch case. Since then, we've found nothing – just as we expected – and I believe there's nothing left to find.'

Dalglish kicked at a stone, sending it skipping across the ground and into the river.

'Sorry, Sir.'

'Ach, for what? Telling me bad news? Never apologise for that, son. Might make some folk think that you're more than the messenger. Know what I mean?'

The diver nodded his head.

'Right, finish up and get out of here. You'll no' miss the stench, eh?'

'Smell, Sir? What smell?' The diver was smiling broadly up at his boss who smiled back.

Dalglish and the detective sergeant started walking to their car when Dalglish stopped and called back, 'And well done, son. Pass my thanks on to your team.'

Later, in the police car, Dalglish spoke his thoughts out loud. 'A sex killer who takes all his victim's clothes away and doesn't just dump them in the nearest river . . . We've got a dangerous one here.'

As the unmarked police car headed away from the river Cart making its slow, painful journey through the streets of Glasgow's southside there was silence between the two cops. The detective sergeant knew Dalglish, his boss, would be feeling down, knowing that he had to accept that yet another angle of the investigation had produced little of value. Although they were sure the handbag and the watch case found in the Cart belonged to Pat Docker, they were of no use to the police in tracking down the killer.

It was worse than that. Days after the murder, they had issued one thousand posters asking for information. Then they issued another appeal, being specific about the injuries they thought the killer would have had to his knuckles through scraping them on a wall in the lane as Pat had struggled. Surely people would notice if someone they knew had suddenly got damaged hands? Yet all they had received were snippets and too many time-wasters. It was as if the killer didn't exist.

Under Dalglish's supervision, they had been very thorough and had thrown resources into the investigation. In spite of detailed searches of ever nook and cranny, every back alley, every stinking dump, every reeking bin all around Battlefield, not one stitch of Pat Docker's clothes had been found. Any decent cop knew that, the longer the search failed to turn up the missing items, the less likely it was that any would be found.

Whoever the killer was, he was careful – very careful.

'So what do we have now?' Dalglish suddenly spoke out as if he had been reading the sergeant's mind. 'One guy at

The Majestic Ballroom who swears he saw Pat that night . . . A neighbour who heard a woman call out . . .' Dalglish was counting the points off on his fingers. 'A Morris 1000 Traveller that stopped at the gates of Queen's Park to pick up a young woman waiting at a bus stop . . . and, more promising, a white Ford Consul 375 spotted in Overdale Street yards from the murder site.' Dalglish noisily sucked air in through his teeth. The list clearly wasn't making him a happy man. 'A bloody party happening in a flat overlooking the murder scene. A party full of journalists and photographers, for God's sake, and none of them saw or heard a thing.' Another noisy suck. 'Journalists? Some fucking journalists. The same guys queuing up now for a story on the killing and it happened right under their noses.'

The detective sergeant smiled to himself ruefully. Interviewing that mob of hacks had caused a right stooshie. It wasn't just that their editors were fuming that they'd been so close to a murder and hadn't see a thing but some of the guys were meant to be working that night – out on assignments – and, instead, they were boozing it up as yards away a strangler ended some lassie's life. The party had been so close to the murder scene that all one of the press photographers would have had to do was stick his camera out of a window to get a good shot.

When the police started interviewing the journalists, they had to contact their editors to confirm certain information – journalists, after all, are just as likely murderers as joiners. All hell broke loose in certain newspapers and a few were even given their jotters. That gave some of the media-hating cops a bit of a laugh. They had only been doing their job but sometimes there were perks. That's how some cops saw it.

'So . . .' Dalglish had done his thinking and was off again. 'where should our efforts go now? There's The Majestic for sure.'

'Sir, you might remember none of Pat's friends can confirm

86

she was there.' The detective sergeant was trying to be helpful. There was always too much information to manage in such an investigation. Even a top cop like Dalglish might let some slip his mind. 'None of them were.'

'Aye, true enough, but there's the eyewitness. The bloke who said he had seen her at the dancing before and danced with her that night.'

'It's just one man out of – what? – hundreds,' added the detective sergeant.

'This bloody traffic,' grumbled Dalglish, 'nose to tail. The sooner they get that new Kingston Bridge built the better. Aye, I know, but I think we're lucky to get even one positive sighting – at the dancing, I mean. Unless somebody lumbers somebody else or gets a knock-back from them, then they're no likely to remember faces, are they?'

'Or gets into a fight with them,' the detective sergeant added, smiling.

'Aye, that's more like the dancing in Glasgow, eh? Maybe it's a shame our Pat wasn't a fighter.'

'Aye, maybe the uniformed boys would have lifted her and saved her life.'

'Aye, maybe, but then again, maybe our killer would've gone after someone else.' Dalglish wasn't about to spell out his fears more than that. His officers were good men on the whole but there were a couple with loose tongues and another couple he knew had arrangements with some local journalists. Funny thing – some cops hated journalists while others traded information for cash with them. He didn't want any suggestion that Pat Docker's killer could kill again being leaked. No suggestion that might indicate he was probably mental. No public information that could spark fear or hysteria. 'No, Pat told her mother and father she was going to The Majestic. Why would she lie?' Dalglish didn't wait for an answer. 'No reason that we know of. Then there's the eyewitness. No, she was at The Majestic all right.'

The two men drove on in silence for a while and then Dalglish spoke up. 'Draft in a couple of female officers.'

'Sir?'

'Choose a couple of young ones with modern dress sense.'

'Sir?' Dalglish had given him a few strange orders in his time but this one had foxed the detective sergeant.

'We're going to bring Pat Docker back to life.'

Saturday, 9 March 1968

Step by step, Patricia comes to life in front of me. Not the old Patricia, the sinful Patricia, but the new Patricia, the saved Patricia.

We start with her underwear as all good girls would. New stockings I've bought since her other ones were damaged on the night of her cleansing. Suspender belt, pants and bra. Her crocheted dress still smelling of her perfume and the scent of her terror. Then her shoes.

If someone walked into my room, all they'd see was some woman's clothing lying out on my bed. All the world is blind. Only I can see her. And my Father.

Late at night, I sit and drink and talk with her as we did the night we met. She is coy but friendly just as she was then. I see her broad smile – so trusting. I hear her laugh with the girl's voice singing through. A woman's body but a girl still – a touch of innocence in a sinful world, in a sinful life.

Sometimes, as we talk, I look from the window of my room out on to the street. Now and then, someone will look up and see me but see nothing. They wave to their neighbour – the friendly man who keeps himself to himself, lives a regular life and goes to church each Sunday. They see the me who is a good neighbour. They can't see my secret. I look down at them and they look back just for an instant but, all the while, I talk to Patricia – tell her how the world is full of fools and she is in a better place.

Life inside my home was one of great solitude till Patricia arrived. It was part of my calling to cut myself off from others in the place I live. Secrecy has been a price I've paid for my calling and it has been a great burden. Even the company of fools would have cured the ache of the man in me. I'm only human after all and imperfect. Often the temptation got too great and I stood behind my door willing someone to knock so I could invite them in. Another trial set to tempt me but I resisted and was rewarded. Now I am not alone. With my Patricia by my side, all the while I watch the time. As that hour comes, not the witching hour, after then and later by minutes, I feel the seconds pass by. Feel them in my soul as others feel blood in their veins, their hearts beating in their chests. Long, painful seconds that will take me there.

Once again we are in that dark lane and she's calling out.

Once more I cleanse her.

Once more we dance.

'I'm sorry, Ruth, but I can't go.' Peter sat across from Ruth in the small bar of The Doublet on Park Road. They had decided to meet there as a good place to grab a taxi to take them to Hope Street and The Majestic Ballroom.

'But it's just a night at the dancing.' Ruth felt anger well up at the last-minute let-down. 'Not exactly breaking any rules, are you?'

'No.' He was flustered, embarrassed and was struggling to find the right words that would have Ruth judge him well not badly. 'But it is the centre of the investigation in Pat Docker's murder – the focal point.'

'Sure,' she nodded, 'but you knew that when you agreed to go. Said you'd take me, as I recall.' After Ruth had asked him to go with her to The Majestic, Peter had tried to recapture some of his male pride by insisting that the night would be on him. The pair of them had bickered in a good-natured way till Ruth decided to give in just so they could drop the subject and she could get off home to study.

'But it's even more the case now,' Peter said.

Ruth opened her eyes wide and tilted her head, demanding that he explain.

'Most of the other lines of inquiry have drawn a blank,' Peter continued. 'But there's an eyewitness who said he danced with Pat at The Majestic that night and that's where she told her parents she was going.'

'And?'

'And so we're concentrating our investigation on that ballroom.'

'Peter, all you're doing is giving the very reasons I want to go to The Majestic. Do you think I like getting dressed up like this?' Ruth favoured denim miniskirts and loose-fitting, brightly coloured flowery tops. Sometimes she'd wear bellbottom denims, knowing that her long legs and slim figure suited that style. Studying at home, she'd slip a couple of extra shillings in the meter and put the gas fire full up so she could feel warm and relaxed, wearing an oversized Levi denim shirt and not much else. Now here she was in the one dress she had for formal dos like weddings and the recent spate of christenings she'd been to lately as all her married cousins and old school friends seemed to produce yet another baby every month. She was even wearing her dress shoes – high-heeled stilettos, not her usual comfortable flat moccasins – and she'd put her long hair up with two jewelled combs at either side. It wasn't so much that she was all dressed up with no place to go, more that she resented having to dress up in the first place. And now here was Peter telling her she needn't have bothered.

'You look nice,' Peter said, meaning every word and not knowing Ruth hated the word 'nice' as much as she hated dressing that way. 'But that's kind of my point,' he went on, noticing a flicker of anger in her eyes, 'the squad have got a female polis who looks a bit like Pat. They're dressing her up in similar gear and taking her through what they think were Pat's last known movements – bringing her to life, as it were.'

'A re-enactment,' Ruth added, nodding. Her interest in the case was flaring and overpowering her irritation at Peter letting her down. 'The police don't carry out those very often.'

'That's what I'm saying.' He thought he was getting through to her. 'They want to stir up folks. See if they can get someone else to remember seeing Pat that night . . .'

'It's a good method.' Ruth had been involved as an observer in one such re-enactment when studying in London and afterwards she'd written a psychology paper on the impact of such visual scenes on memory. It was a method that was rarely used by the police but she had concluded that they should go further by filming the re-enactments and show them on the TV and even in the cinemas before big feature films started. 'They are pulling out all the stops in this case, eh?'

'Aye, they are,' replied Peter, relieved that they'd found some common ground. 'But that re-enactment is, of course, at The Majestic.' His sentence ended up sounding high pitched, reflecting how frustrated he felt as he tried again to get his point across.

'When? Tonight?'

Peter shrugged. 'Don't think so.'

'Well, then, surely you could go there and get a sense of the place?' Ruth was back on the main topic. 'Off-duty, just another face in the crowd, maybe you'll get a better feel of what happened that night – the night of the murder.' She had just summed up her own reasons for wanting to go to The Majestic in the first place. Surely they had that much in common?

'Aye, but . . .'

As Peter struggled for words, Ruth's attention drifted to the bar where two older men in donkey jackets, heavy-soled working boots and wide, straight-legged denims stained with what looked like dry plaster were drinking pints. The Doublet was an old traditional pub but it had been taken over by the students and lecturers of the west end. The men looked out of place but didn't seem to notice or care. Probably they had been working locally and decided to have a pint together before they headed home. They'd look out of place in any west end pub so The Doublet was as good a choice as any.

'How much?' asked one of the men as the barman set two pints in front of him.

The barman repeated the cost of the drinks.

'*How* much?' The workman wasn't used to west-end prices.

The barman mumbled something.

'You should be wearing a mask, pal,' said the customer counting out the cash on to the bar.

'Aye,' offered his mate in support, 'and a stripy jumper with a big sack on your back marked "SWAG".'

'What's so funny?'

Peter had caught Ruth smiling at the workmen's humour. Typical working-class Glasgow humour, she reckoned. How could she explain that she had been listening in to someone else when Peter obviously thought he should be getting all her attention? So she didn't even try. 'Nothing.'

'It's like this, Ruth.' Peter looked straight across at her, his eyes asking her to understand and believe him. 'I'm just a uniformed cop – the new boy, not long off probation, who, a few months ago, was wearing a blue band on my cap. I'm lucky to be involved in the Docker case in any way at all.'

Ruth was nodding her head, showing that she understood.

'But plainclothes don't exactly consult me or involve me in their plans.' He fidgeted with his packet of Kensitas, opened it, offered one to Ruth and then took one himself. Leaning over to light her cigarette, he went on, quietly but intently, 'The murder investigation team could be there tonight for all I know.' Then he stopped abruptly as if he had explained himself totally and no other words were required.

Ruth looked across at Peter and wondered how old he was. She hadn't felt the need to ask before but suddenly his uncertainty sounded like immaturity and he seemed younger than her. It wasn't so much what he was saying but the nervous manner in which he was struggling to explain himself. She noticed he had on a different suit, black and expensive looking as usual but with flared trousers – new, very new. His outfit was completed by a crisp white shirt, pencil-thin tie and the shiniest pair of shoes she'd seen since her grandfather died. Had he got rigged out for the dancing, making his mind up about The Majestic as he did so?

Then he explained the suit. 'We could go someplace else. For a meal. Maybe try one of the new Chinese restaurants along Sauchiehall Street, the Garnethill end. It's not far from here. I've never had Chinese food.' Somehow he understood from Ruth's uncharacteristic silence that food wasn't on her agenda. 'Or another dancing? Most folk these days go to The Barrowland Ballroom. It's the in place.'

'Peter,' she said, drawing in a big breath, 'it isn't the dancing I'm interested in.' She was also beginning to doubt she was interested in him. She could forgive most things but not a faint heart. 'It's The Majestic and the reasons you don't want to go . . . those are precisely my reasons for wanting to go.'

'I'm sorry,' he said quietly. She had just told him what he already knew.

'Me too,' she replied and gave him a little smile. 'But don't worry – I'll just go on my own.'

'You will not!' He almost barked the words at her but then, realising he'd gone too far, he added, 'I mean you can't . . . shouldn't.'

'Can't? Shouldn't? Why not?'

'Only women looking for one thing go to the jigging on their own.' He bit his lip and cursed himself. 'You're not like that. Of course you're not.'

Ruth wondered what gave him the right to think he knew anything about her sexually.

'What I mean is that some of the men who go there will think you are looking to be picked up.' He still hadn't finished. 'And a murderer hangs around The Majestic. It's fucking dangerous!' Peter, almost shouting now, caught himself and abruptly went silent.

If he was worried about other people paying him attention, he needn't have bothered because it was the two workmen at the bar who were attracting all eyes and ears.

'I'm telling you it is,' said one loudly.

'Naw, it's no',' said the other. 'How much? Two bob?'

'Naw, half a dollar.'

The two men spat on the palms of their right hands and shook on it, sealing the bet.

'Right, will this do you?'

The workman took a tightly wound ball of string out of his pocket. His mate took it from him, weighed it up and ran it up one forearm, flicking his bicep and sending the ball of string into a curve and catching it in his large hand. He then turned to the bar and rolled the ball along it from hand to hand, testing if it ran freely.

Satisfied, he turned and said, 'OK, prove it.'

'Naw,' replied his mate. 'You're going to prove it.'

All around the small pub, eyes were focused on the two men. Most folk weren't sure what the argument was about but were curious to learn.

'Put the ball carefully on the ground there,' the workman directed.

A few drinkers lifted their pints and made way for them.

'Carefully now. That's it. Now give it a gentle push this way – towards me. Gently.'

The second workman squatted, placed the ball of string on the floor and, with great ceremony, waited a few seconds before flicking it with the fingers of one hand and sending it trickling a few feet.

'Wait now.'

The ball stopped rolling and, a split second later, rolled back the way, past the still-squatting workman and kept rolling till it banged into someone's foot. 'See! Told you the floor had a bad slope. You need bloody glasses if you didn't see that.'

'Aye, aw right,' said the bet-losing workman, blushing.

Ruth wondered about strong, hardy men who could take all sorts of physical graft but still struggled with a bit of social embarrassment.

'Half a crown, please. Thank you. Now let that be a lesson to you!' The winning workman was talking loudly, his chest puffed out, happy he had come out on top. 'Some places aren't what they seem.'

Out on Park Road, Peter tried to talk Ruth out of her trip to The Majestic. 'It's dangerous,' he kept saying. 'There's a killer out there.'

'Have you not listened to a word I've told you about my work, Peter? I study criminals and believe the only way to do that is face-to-face.'

At that, she managed to hail a passing taxi and, with Peter still trying to persuade her otherwise, she was clambering into the back of the black hack. Slamming the door shut behind her, she saw Peter standing there staring at her, still mouthing something at her. Behind him the two workmen from the pub emerged, not so pally now. The two squared up to each other on the pavement. Ruth recognised their threatening postures. First one pushed the other hard on the shoulder. Then the other threw a punch and, within a couple of seconds, they were brawling. Hearing the noise behind him, Peter looked at the two street fighters. A policeman is never off duty – Ruth knew that. Peter moved towards the men, hesitated and then turned back again to stare at her and mouth more words she couldn't hear.

'Hope Street, please,' Ruth said to the taxi driver, 'The Majestic.'

As the diesel engine roared and farted and the taxi jolted forward, Ruth edged round in her seat to look back towards the pub. The two workmen were now wrestling on the pavement, arms and legs flailing everywhere. Peter was on the road, running after the cab waving and shouting after her – shouting words she couldn't hear.

Peter ignored the tooting of a car horn and kept running along Park Road.

'Don't go, Ruth. Don't go there,' he shouted. 'It's fucking dangerous.'

The tall man in the brown suit appeared again. All night, ever since he had asked Ruth to dance, he had never been more than a few feet from her, standing on his own, smiling at her when he caught her eye. There was something creepy about the man's persistence. Threatening even. Ruth regretted being so bloody-minded. Regretted going to the dancing on her own.

It had all started to plan. Paying off the taxi driver through the window of his cab, Ruth turned and walked the few steps towards The Majestic. At either side of the door were copies of the poster issued by the police, asking for help in the Pat Docker case. The posters were all over the city and hard to miss, even if some of the places they'd been pasted on looked like building sites as the work to repair damage from the gales dragged on. Yet there was something poignant about the posters here. It was the last place the police believed Pat Docker was seen alive – apart from her time with her killer.

The bright lights strained Ruth's eyes as she walked through The Majestic's front doors. She was there in work mode yet couldn't help feel the buzz of the others out to play. Men in sharp suits. Teddy Boys strutting in their finery. Off-duty soldiers with their close-cropped hair. Women with tall beehives and strings of fake pearls. More Beatle fringes than she could imagine. Cheap costume jewellery glittering on every dress. The smell of scent wafting by, competing with aftershave – Old Spice, most often. Men with their hair creamed and combed and stopping to comb it again, before they went through to the hall. Giggles and laughter. Pals cracking jokes with each other and moving on to get to the real action as soon as possible. Out in the foyer, the noise of music, sounding good, was already loud. The Majestic was buzzing and Ruth felt it.

She went to the cloakroom to drop her coat off and check her make-up. The place was heaving with women queuing up, two-by-two, for the cubicles. Others were edging their way to get in front of mirrors. Some dropped their headscarves to reveal big hair stacked with curlers. A few minutes later, there they stood, hair inch-perfect.

Two women in bus conductress uniforms peeled their clothes off where they stood – no inhibitions among the girls. From a tartan holdall, they pulled their outfits for the night and set about getting dressed. In what seemed like no time at all, one stood in front of the other and asked how she looked.

'A pure doll, so you are,' her pal said.

'You sure this frock's aw right, but?' the woman asked, seeking more reassurance.

'Cracking, so it is. If I was a bloke, I'd nip you myself.'

The comment set her friend grinning and preening herself in the mirror.

'But you're no' a bloke, though, eh?'

'How do you know I'm no' a lizzie?' her pal retorted, reaching out with two hands to squeeze her friend's backside, which sent the pair of them into cackles of laughter.

Next to Ruth, two other women watched the antics of the pair as they passed a half-bottle of vodka between them, drinking straight from the neck. Unlike most of the others within hearing distance, the two with the vodka weren't smiling but appeared sullen, angry.

'What are you looking at?' said one of the women fooling around in front of the mirror.

'I'll tell youse when I work it out,' replied the woman with the vodka bottle in her hand.

'Cheeky bitch.'

'Maybe but at least I don't go stealing other people's men.'

'What are you on about?'

'You.'

'Me?'

'Last week. I went for a pee and by the time I came back you were away with my man.'

'Your man?' The penny was dropping as she remembered the bloke who had escorted her home the week before.

'Aye. My man.'

'I don't see you wearing his ring.'

'No but I'll bet he wore yours, eh?' The woman handed the bottle of vodka to her mate so she had both hands free. With one hand she formed a circle and, through it, she slipped two fingers of the other in and out.

'You cheeky bitch.'

Ruth was out of that cloakroom and fast as the fight kicked off. Hanging around any longer would've been taking her approach to psychology too far. It was one thing to come face-to-face with those involved in crime but it was another to get injured in a catfight.

Out on the dance floor, the night was in full swing. Men stood round the outside of the hall watching the women dancing with their friends or standing and chatting. The Swinging Sixties might have been declared but some old rituals died hard.

Ruth walked slowly and casually around the room, stopping now and then to stand and watch the band, tapping her feet to the music, swaying her hips. Here and there, a man would look over and smile. She'd smile back and walk on. It was all about a balance of not appearing out of place but, at the same time, remembering she was there to see and learn.

Then she was tapped gently on the shoulder. A tall man in a brown suit stood smiling down at her. 'Would you like to dance?' he asked in a voice that sounded polite, proper, even in that short sentence.

It was all about fitting in, Ruth reminded herself. She was at the dancing. She had to dance.

As they moved across the floor in time to the music, she noticed how skilled her partner was in avoiding the other couples cramming the floor. He could dance all right and he knew it. Ruth wouldn't describe him as handsome but he wasn't unattractive either. His even features and smooth face seemed almost devoid of characteristics apart from a constant small smile. He would be a difficult man to read. A good poker player. A good detective. Was she on the floor with one of the murder investigation team?

At the end of the dance, he asked her to dance again. He hadn't been much company, saying nothing as they danced on the floor but then the music was so loud she would've struggled to hear him anyway. Maybe he was an experienced hand at Glasgow ballrooms and had learned long ago that trying to communicate while the music was playing was a waste of time – embarrassing even.

'You're a fab dancer,' he said, with that same smile still on his lips, 'and there aren't many in this place.'

She understood the compliment. There were some fantastic dancers in the hall and many of them were women – women who seemed to love the dancing. Compared to them, Ruth was just an awkward novice. So she understood the man's compliment, accepted it graciously and agreed to dance again. It was her big mistake.

The second dance over, Ruth went to move on with a smile and a nod. Of course, he'd asked her to dance again and she'd refused. But that second dance had sent him messages that she liked him. How was she to know there were unwritten rules and rule number one was never to dance twice with anyone you don't fancy? As she went to leave him he grabbed her arm, gripping it tightly enough to stop her in her tracks. Ruth turned and scowled at him, pushed his hand off her arm and walked away quickly.

Ruth went about her business – observing. As she walked past the main door to the hall that led out into the foyer, she saw the checked caps of Glasgow police. If required, she could've given a potted history of that check. How it was introduced first by Sir Percy Sillitoe, Glasgow's Chief Constable and the so-called Hammer of the Gangs. Chosen for its visibility, even at a distance, coppers called it the Sillitoe Tartan – not a bad compliment for an Englishman. After its successful introduction in Glasgow, many other forces had gone on to copy it. She could even have reeled off some of the forces that hadn't but that wasn't what she was about that night. She was more concerned by what the cops were up to. She wasn't going to be surprised.

The two battling women from the cloakroom stood in front of the cops, shamefaced and sullen. One of the policemen was speaking to a man in a flash evening suit and big bowtie. The manager? A bouncer? Whoever he was he was talking twenty to the dozen and occasionally pointing at one or other of the women. Ruth noticed scratch marks running down one woman's face while the other was dabbing at her nose with a tiny crimson-stained handkerchief and one of her eyes was puffed and bloodshot. The two combatants' friends stood a little distance off, watching the proceedings with worried looks. And there he was, the tall man in the brown suit, a few feet away, staring at Ruth with that smile.

She moved off, down towards the stage where the music was loudest. From there, she could see the women watching the band, all smiles and waves, more interested in their attention than the dancing. Occasionally, a band member would smile back or even move to the front of the stage between numbers, bending over to chat to one of his favourites. These women were more intent on getting off with one of the musicians than any of the paying customers. Yet, even here, Ruth saw that the women were in small groups or pairs. None had come alone.

A few songs later, Ruth had completed the circuit of the hall and concluded that, so far, she'd spotted just two other women at the dancing that night who appeared to be on their own. So three women, including her, out of how many? A hundred? More? Peter had revealed that Pat Docker's regular friends hadn't gone with her to the dancing on the night she was killed. The police were still looking for other friends, of course, but hadn't found any. Had she gone dancing on her own? Why would she have done that?

Then he turned up again, that tall man in the brown suit – still standing a few feet off, still smiling. Ruth threw him a glower and held his stare but he didn't blush and look away as she'd expected him to. He just stood there smiling at her. Enough was enough. She headed towards one of the bars, interested to see the mating rituals there and, of increasing importance, to check if there were any more unaccompanied women hanging around.

'Two by two,' Ruth muttered quietly to herself. 'The animals went into the ark two by two and the men and women here arrive and pair off two by two. If Pat was by herself, what the hell was she doing on her own? Unless, of course, she was meeting a man.'

Nearby, a young woman was having a giggle at the good-looking blonde who was talking to herself. Then she turned to her pal to share the joke with her. Ruth caught their actions and silently thanked them. Thanked the pair of them, yet another pair of women, and headed for the cloakroom to pick up her coat.

On the way back to the foyer, Ruth mused over the principles of what she was calling 'The Rule of Twos'. Most women went to the dancing in pairs. Would one woman get off with some man and leave her friend alone and stranded? Unlikely, unless she was a heartless sod and Pat Docker wasn't that, by all accounts. If three females went to the dancing together, would one leave the other two for preferred male company? Probably, because the two left were still company for each other. So . . .

'I'll take you home.' The tall man in the brown suit was right by her side and he stage-whispered the words in a suddenly gruff rasp of a voice close to her ear. His hand snaked out and gripped her by the wrist, this time a stage beyond firm. His grip twisted her skin and hurt like hell.

Ruth didn't even have to think. The heel of her right hand shot up and caught the man under his chin. He released his hold on her instantly and staggered back, almost tipping over.

'Fucking bitch!' the tall man in the brown suit shouted as blood began spilling from his mouth. He must have bitten his lip as she struck him but Ruth hoped his teeth had cut into his tongue too. That would be much more painful for much longer. She headed for the door and brown suit made another lunge at her but his time the man in the flash evening suit and bowtie grabbed him in a stranglehold around the neck.

'On ye go, hen,' evening suit shouted at her. 'Away home. We'll take care of this bastard.'

In the few steps it took for her to reach the main door, two other bouncers in black evening suits arrived and were manhandling brown suit, taking him someplace and not out to the main street. Ruth guessed they weren't going to have a chat or bother calling the cops. She was entirely on the bouncers' side.

Out on Hope Street, she headed towards Central Station where she knew there would be a queue of taxis waiting at the largest rank she had seen outside of London. People moved along the pavements heading to pubs, clubs or maybe one of the many cinemas. Maybe some were heading for The Majestic. Whatever they had in mind, they were also providing another service – valuable service. They made Ruth feel safe.

'Going my way?' The man's voice, close behind her, inches from her ear, made her jump. A shiver ran down her back, followed by heat searing through her legs. Had the bouncers let brown suit go?

'Where are the pigs when you need one?' Ruth reached out and thumped Peter on the shoulder. Then she managed to smile, turning it into a playful gesture but knowing some of her fear and anger from the scene with brown suit went into that blow.

'Pleased to see me, eh?' Peter smiled and rubbed his shoulder theatrically.

'What the hell are you doing here? Creeping up on me like that?' Ruth demanded.

'Just passing.'

'No you weren't.' She threw him a stern look.

'No, I wasn't,' he admitted. Then he shrugged. 'I couldn't let you go to The Majestic on your own. For . . . well, I've already said.'

Over a drink in the Central Hotel lounge bar, Peter confessed that he had hailed a taxi shortly after pleading with Ruth not to go to The Majestic and followed her there. By the time he arrived, she had already gone in so he decided to hang around, watching from across the street. His plan was to go into The Majestic if he was convinced that there was no police action there that night. But he had hesitated and that plan had turned into a two-hour vigil in a shop doorway, his eyes never leaving the ballroom's door so that he could make sure he didn't miss her, make sure she was OK.

'What if I'd stayed till the very end?' she asked.

Peter shrugged.

'Or worse – what if I'd left with a man?' She could see the traces of a blush cross his cheeks. 'What would you have

done? Confronted him? Ordered me to go home with you?'
She was laughing at him and his blush was in full blast.

'But . . .' He was stammering. 'Well . . . that wouldn't have happened, would it?'

'Why not? Are you saying I couldn't get a . . . what do you call it here again?'

'A lumber.'

'Yes, a lumber. That I'm too hackit to get a lumber?' Ruth was proud that she'd recalled one of the many Glasgow dialect words for ugly. She had gained the impression that, just as the Eskimos had with snow and ice, so the Glaswegians had many dialect words for violence and ugliness.

'No, no' that!' His face was bright now, thinking about the scene, wondering what he would have done. 'But it's just as you said. You were at The Majestic to work, not play.' He watched her carefully. 'Isn't that why you were so dead set on going there? Even on your own?' Game to Peter.

'Yeah, I was working,' Ruth conceded with a smile, 'and you were right.'

Peter raised his eyes in mock shock.

'At least about it being dangerous.'

The mock shock expression got even wider.

'For ordinary people, I mean – not for me.' There was no way she was going lose face by telling him about the tall man in the brown suit. 'But it is dangerous for ordinary women just out to have a good time.' She stopped and shook her head – serious now, looking worried. 'I couldn't believe how many young women were there – most of them drunk, most obviously looking for a man – and, if anything, they were outnumbered by men out hunting women.'

Peter shrugged. 'That's the dancing for you.'

'Sure but just a few weeks after the murder of a young woman? And at the place she was last seen alive where the police have made numerous public appeals for information about her? No one at The Majestic can claim not to have heard

107

of the murder yet the place is a pick-up joint. Right now, that makes it a sweet shop for sadists.'

Peter conceded that she had a point. 'But what can you do?' he asked. 'You can't stop people from going out, from getting on with their lives, from enjoying themselves.'

'No but you can educate them. Tell them the risks.'

'But we don't even know who the killer might be yet.'

'No but we do know a lot about him,' added Ruth. He had just wandered into her territory. 'The murderer is a strangler. From studies of serial killers in the past ten years . . . Do you know what I mean by serial killer?'

She was right to ask. At that stage, the phrase was a technical one that had recently been invented by psychiatrists and psychologists and not used by the public. Peter nodded his head. 'Well, since Manuel's trial, we know many serial killers are stranglers. That the slow face-to-face murder feeds whatever sadistic needs they have – often sexual needs. We know that stranglers tend to plan their murders – as serial killers do. That they are likely to be respectable citizens, holding down decent jobs and getting on OK with their neighbours. So, they aren't likely to feature anywhere on police files. We know that serial killers have to start somewhere and, once they start, they relive the murder over and over till they need to kill again. That could be years or months away. On the other hand, it could be weeks or days away. It might be tonight.' Ruth stopped to drink from her glass. 'Peter, we know all of this and Glasgow, right now, might have a serial killer stalking the streets. Stalking The Majestic. Because if he did meet Pat Docker there, he'll more than likely choose his next victim there.'

'That was some speech, Ruth.'

'Sorry,' she looked up and gave him a small smile, 'but watching those women tonight as if they didn't have a care in the world just made me feel so scared for them. And angry. And . . . and . . .'

'Aye?'

'Who do you think the public will blame?' Ruth suddenly seemed to change tack.

'What?'

'If another woman is killed by the same man?'

'They'll blame the killer, of course. Who else?'

'Not the police?'

'We're doing our best.'

'I'm sure you are but shouldn't you be warning the people? Warning the women?'

'Excuse me, Sir.' A waiter stood by their table looking smart and formal in his black trousers, crisp white shirt, bowtie and waistcoat. 'Are you guests, Sir?'

Peter looked up, flummoxed by the question coming out of the blue as they were discussing the dangers of sex killers.

'No,' replied Ruth, looking up at the waiter, 'we're not residents.' Then she smiled across at Peter who was flustered again, maybe by the very thought of them sharing a room, a bed. She looked down at his watch and, sure enough, it was ten o'clock, closing time.

'Could I ask you to finish your drinks then, please, Sir?' And, with that, the waiter slipped smoothly to the next table.

In the taxi heading back to the west end, Ruth looked out of the window. The night had turned from crisp cold to drizzle damp as fat rain fell and soaked the streets, setting night-time Glasgow sparkling. The whish-whish of the wind-screen wipers lulled her mood as they set a sad slow rhythm. Ruth felt overwhelmed by a feeling of melancholy – something she had never suffered from till she moved to her adopted city. Such a hard, lethal place also reached out and gently stroked her heartstrings.

'At The Majestic,' Ruth's voice was gruff, sleepy, 'have you still not got any more leads?'

Peter shook his head. 'Just the one man who said he had danced with her. Since none of her known pals admits to being with her that night, we're trying to track down others. Pat was a popular woman but, so far, no joy.'

'I reckon Pat went with two other women,' said Ruth. 'Either that or she went alone.'

'What? I mean why do you think that?'

Ruth explained her Rule of Twos to Peter's satisfaction then he added, '"Course, there's always another possibility.'

Ruth looked at him, wondering what this novice and ambitious young copper could've thought of that she hadn't.

'Our strangler might have a pal – an accomplice.'

'True.' She let the vowel trail long, as if giving great thought to his pearl of wisdom. 'But stranglers, like serial killers, rarely work in teams.' She noticed a slight downturn of disappointment in his lips. 'Mind you, we're only just learning about the psychology of all kinds of killers – just started unravelling the complex ones. So you never know, maybe you've hit on something.'

Geed up now, Peter added what he considered his main point. 'Just imagine . . .' He turned round fully on the taxi's bench seat to stare at her. 'Imagine two stranglers at large.'

She nodded her head, taking his remark seriously, before turning to stare out of the taxi window at the rain. 'Or, even worse,' she thought to herself, 'imagine Pat Docker wasn't at The Majestic on the night she was murdered. Imagine if it was some other place that she'd met the killer. Imagine if he's back there again tonight – watching and waiting for his next victim.'

Thursday, 14 March 1968

Once again I walked among them and took stock. They are my flock and I must watch over them.

Even as I make my way to my favourite place, I feel the Lord well up in me, His spirit fill me, and I know I am safe. Tonight I was distracted on my journey. As usual, I travelled to the city centre and walked the rest of the way. It is part of the ritual and I take pleasure in it.

Slow is my motto. Slow, slow, slow with the excitement building inside me. My every step takes me closer. My every delay postpones my passion. But I am in control like a lover slipping off his woman's clothes inch by inch – all the better to heighten her, prepare her for his needs. So I walk slow, slow, slow.

Tonight I took a detour. Along Argyle Street with its busy pavements. Staff, mainly attractive women, streamed out of Arnott's, heading for buses and trains. Some maybe had their good clothes in a bag and were going on to the dancing. How many, I wonder, have men and children at home? I went under the Heilanman's Umbrella which was stinking of oil from the trains on the bridge above and of exhaust fumes from the cars as they moved slowly past, nose to tail, taking office workers home. Who else can afford cars? There an old man stopped me, his cap in hand, asking for a few pennies for a cup of tea. His breath stank of meths and his body of human filth – more fit for the company of swine than decent people. Messengers of the Lord. His rheumy eyes held my gaze and he poked his cap at me. Then he asked me again for money for tea. I wanted to scream 'LIAR!' and 'SHITE CLARTED!' and 'STINKING!' and 'ALKY!' and 'LIAR!' and strike him down. Stamp on his pathetic face with the heel of my shoe. Kick him on to the road, feed him to the wheels of the traffic. Such an anger welled up in me. Such a fury. He had spoiled my ritual. My lonely time.

In my coat pockets, my hands gripped themselves in white tight fists, ready to pummel him to the earth. Instead, I let my anger flow to them and then out of them. Sweat dribbled down my back and electric heat burned in my forehead. My teeth clenched tight, wanting to bite his rotten flesh. A nerve twitched in my lip and a great faintness took me till I swooned. But I held myself upright and the Beast passed on, out of me. Another trial had been beaten. Another temptation refused.

My trouser pocket was full of change but I searched till I found a sixpence. A silver sixpence. A tanner. The tramp was there to see to my betrayal. One blow to his worthless body and my quest for God's will would have ended in an instant. That tramp might as well have kissed me in front of my enemies. He was my Judas and Judases always get paid in silver. A silver tanner.

Striding away, I left him there, no doubt speechless about my generosity or dumbfounded by his failure to tempt me from the one true way. Devils come in all sorts of guises. Turning right, I headed up Hope Street – a well-named road all in all.

> The hope which is laid up for you in heaven. The hope
> of the gospel. The hope of glory.

Hoping for glory. Glory – that's what they hope for. Glory in this world not the next. The hope of man. The hope of the police. The hope that they find me there in that Majestic place. Some hope. I walked past the doors of the ballroom and felt their frustration. It has been weeks now since I cleansed my Patricia yet still they search for me there in a place I will not go. I was tempted to turn and enter. Stand among the fools. Dance with the women. Maybe look for Fire in their eyes. But I knew the Fire would not be there.

The Fire is my purpose. My mission. My life. Why honour them with my presence?

I turned and walked away. Back to my place. My favourite place. Where the Fire will sparkle one day again and I will follow His will.

The Fire was not burning that night. Except in my Patricia who danced with me once more in my favourite place. My hunting ground. Dancing.

112

'When did you dance with Pat Docker?' Elphinstone Dalglish was in his usual direct mood – straightforward, straight talking, no tricks or complexities.

'But you've asked me that before.' The man's voice was high pitched, almost wailing. 'You and the other bobbies. Loads of times before.'

'Well, you'll know the answer, then.'

The man let out a huge, resigned sigh and repeated the answer he had given so many times before about the night he danced with Pat Docker at The Majestic – the night she was murdered.

'It was early in the night,' he said. 'I'd seen the lassie before at The Majestic. Danced with her before. She was a great dancer, so she was. So we had a couple of dances. Early in the night, as I've said.'

'Did you fancy her, then?' The questioner was the other half of Dalglish's double act for the night, his boss, Detective Chief Superintendent Tom Goodall, head of Glasgow's detectives. The witness had recognised Goodall. Who wouldn't? He was one of the best cops of his generation and he wasn't there to keep Elphinstone Dalglish company. They had a big decision to make that night.

'Fancy her? What are you getting at?' barked the witness as he glared at the cops with indignation blazing from his eyes. He should have guessed that he wasn't in for an easy ride when they asked him to go down to the police station – the HQ, in fact. He should have worried when he saw that two of the city's top cops were taking him over his statement again.

'You were at the dancing,' Tom Goodall went on, po-faced as usual. 'Unless things have changed since my day, most men go the dancing to meet women – to get off with a lassie.'

'Aye.'

'So isn't that why you were there?'

The witness shifted his seat and looked round the room. There wasn't much to look at since the detectives had led him into one of the sparsest interview rooms. Save for a metal-legged table, a tin ashtray and four chairs, the room was bare. The windowless walls were painted with gloss paint in an institutional green-grey colour – cold and unwelcoming but hard-wearing. A room smelling of stale cigarette smoke and bleach. A room for serious interviews. The witness should've noticed and worried.

'Aye but no' her. She was just someone that was good to dance with. Didn't fancy my chances. Besides, I had my eye on another wee bird that night.'

'Any luck?' It was a typical Tom Goodall question. Brief, to the point and seemingly harmless. Except cops who had worked with Goodall knew better. He did nothing by accident.

'Eh, no.'

'No? That's a shame.' Goodall stopped speaking and seemed to stare into the distance. It was as if he'd lost his train of thought or interest in the interview – as if he was struggling to think what to ask next. Many suspects, defence lawyers and new colleagues made the mistake of assuming that of Goodall to their great cost. He hadn't lost his way but was planning ahead, many questions further on from the one he was going to ask next.

'Aye, well, some nights you're lucky . . .' began the witness.

'So, what time did you reckon you danced with Pat Docker?' Goodall demanded again.

'I told ye – early.'

114

'Aye early but what does that mean to you? Seven o'clock? Eight o'clock? Nine o'clock?'

'I told you before, I can't remember.'

'But you were telling us before.' Goodall pulled over a buff-coloured file and opened it. 'Aye, says here you went to The Majestic a lot. Almost every week. In fact, every Thursday.'

'Aye, so?'

'So, did you not have a routine?' Goodall left the question hanging.

It was the witness's turn to stare into space and think how to answer.

'You know, you pick up your wages, bus home, some tea, change into your good gear, bus into town – that sort of routine.'

As he was speaking, Elphinstone Dalglish picked up the file in front of Goodall and flicked through it. Without waiting for the witness to reply, he said, 'Aye, I thought so.'

The witness turned to him.

'You told two of our officers on two different occasions that you went to the dancing round about the same time every Thursday. Is that right?'

'Aye but . . .'

'So what time did you usually get there at?' It was Tom Goodall again. 'And how long after that did you dance with Pat Docker?'

Silence.

'Come on, son, it's not a hard question.' Goodall wasn't taking time out to think now.

'About seven o'clock, I suppose,' the witness replied.

'Seven o'clock what? That you got there or you danced with her?'

'Eh . . . danced with her.'

The two detectives nodded their heads amiably as if they were now a bit happier about how the interview was progressing.

'Aye, it would've been about then,' the witness said, his confidence returning.

'So, how come . . .' Goodall closed the file. 'How come we calculate that Pat Docker couldn't even have arrived at The Majestic at that time?'

The witness's jaw fell slack and his mouth gaped open.

'And you have told us several times that she was with some friends – some women you'd seen her with before.' Goodall put his hand on the buff cardboard of the file cover. 'Several times yet not one of her friends were with her that night – not one.'

As Goodall spoke, Dalglish was tapping his fingers on the table, producing a hard, fast, impatient beat.

'Well?'

'I . . . I did. I mean she was so.'

'Did you actually see Patricia Docker that night?' It was Dalglish's turn.

'Now's the time to own up, son,' added Goodall, 'for your own good.'

The two detectives stayed silent for a while and waited. The witness's face was bright red, his forehead was damp with sweat and, on his lap, he was twisting and untwisting the fingers of both hands. No more outrage or angry indignation – he was feeling the heat. So the cops decided that he should be left to it for a while. 'You consider what we've been saying,' said Goodall, standing up, 'and we'll be back in a while.'

Out in the corridor, Dalglish and Goodall walked away from the closed door of the interview room in silence. Once they were in Dalglish's room, Dalglish was the first to speak up. 'The bastard's been lying to us all along, Tom.'

'Aye and wasted almost four weeks of a murder investigation. Four weeks for the killer to cover his tracks. Four weeks for folk who were in the right place who might have seen something to forget.'

'He might well have ruined our chances, you know.'

'Aye, in spite of us putting as many resources into this as we could muster. If only we'd been following the right leads, we might have cracked this case.'

'Aye and I hate to think how much money we've wasted. The overtime budget is well overspent now and for what? Nothing. We should throw the book at the bastard.' Dalglish was furious, as most cops would be. Some experienced detectives hated time-wasters even more than they hated the criminals themselves. 'And that bloody re-enactment,' Dalglish groaned, rubbing his forehead. 'No wonder we didn't getting any witnesses coming forward. All that bloody effort and we were in the wrong place! It's a bloody embarrassment, Tom.'

During Dalglish's rant, Goodall had been nodding his head in agreement. 'Aye, we should go public on it,' he said, 'hold him up as an example of what will happen to any future attention-seeking loonies.'

'Maybe – and we should make it plain that we hold him responsible for Pat Docker's murderer still being on the loose. Put flesh and bones on what he's done, give it a face and a name – for poor Patricia Docker's sake.'

'It's high time we did something like that,' Goodall said. 'For too long, these time-wasters have been let off scot-free and, it seems to me, there are more of them now than ever I can remember.'

'I think you're right there, Tom. Maybe it's because we're informing the public more. Using the press and the TV. We know that can be helpful in a case like this and maybe these nutters are just the price we pay.'

'Aye, so let's charge this one big time.'

'Charge him? I know what some of the boys will want to do to him when they find out.'

'I'm almost tempted to stand back and let them.'

'Aye, I know what you mean.' Dalglish turned in his chair and looked out his office window at the Glasgow sky turning from leaden grey of day to the charcoal of early evening. 'Know what you mean, all right.'

A knock on the door stirred Dalglish from his angry reverie. 'Come in,' he shouted.

'Sorry to interrupt you, Sir,' One of his detective sergeants looked round his office door. 'Could I have a quick word? It's about the Docker case.'

Down in the interview room, the witness had finally prised himself from his chair and was pacing the floor. Why had he done it? That was what he kept asking himself and he couldn't find an answer. To start with, the words had just come tumbling out of his mouth, as if of their own accord. He had told the police he had danced with Pat Docker even before he was aware of thinking it. All he could remember now was how good it had felt at the time. It felt good that the officers were so grateful for his information. It felt good that he was trying to help. And he felt important when they told him he was their main witness. He felt heroic when he told his family and friends. He'd felt all of that but he'd never felt like a liar – not till now.

'Sorry about the wait,' said Tom Goodall as he and Elphinstone Dalglish re-entered the room. 'Something came up but that means you'll have had plenty of time to think.'

The witness nodded his head and all three men remained standing, looking at each other.

'Well?' demanded Dalglish. 'Did you see Pat Docker that night?'

The witness looked at his shoes, his chin pressed into his chest, and shook his head. Tears filled his eyes with the shame of it. He had been caught out over something he had never planned to do but wasn't brave enough to confess of his own will. Caught out and now he'd be in trouble. He didn't know much about the law but he guessed he was going to be charged with something. Something serious. Now the whole city would know him for what he was. Know his weakness. His one weak moment. How could he go out in public again? What would his friends think? The newspapers would get a photograph of him and put him on the front pages. THE MAN WHO HELPED A KILLER. His life was finished. He would have to move. But how far? Start again. Get a new job. But could he? Would he be on the dole the rest of his life? A friendless soul in some strange city with no money. His life was ruined.

'You have wasted our time,' started Dalglish in a voice that quivered with fury. 'An innocent young woman was murdered by a sadist probably for kicks and you fucking well helped him.' Dalglish drew breath loudly, filling his chest, trying to calm down. 'You had the oldest police force in Britain, one of the largest in the whole of Europe, one of the best in the world, and you directed us to the wrong fucking scene.'

'Why?' Although Goodall's voice was low and calm, he was every bit as angry as Dalglish – maybe even angrier. The two cops, hard-eyed men, stood and stared at the wet-eyed witness, crying with self-pity. His chin was smeared with snot and tears and he was weeping as he had never done since he was a young child.

Catching his breath and wiping his face with his sleeve, he started to speak. 'I . . .'

'Don't fucking tell us!' Goodall's timing was perfect. 'We are not interested in your pathetic behaviour. As of now, we're not interested in you.'

'You can rot in hell as far as we're concerned,' added Dalglish.

'Probably will,' said Goodall.

'"Perverting the Course of Justice",' pronounced Dalglish.

'"Wasting Police Time",' added Goodall.

'And, who knows, maybe "Art and Part in a Murder".' Dalglish knew that the man wouldn't understand what he was saying but also knew the cops had no grounds for the Scottish equivalent of aiding and abetting. They had checked the man out early on. He was a time-waster, not a murderer's mate.

'"Breach of the Peace" for good measure.'

'"Farting in the Fucking Street".'

'We should hang you out to dry.'

'Or sling you in the cells.'

'And tell the boys you've wasted their time.'

'Don't think you'd get much sleep.'

'Till we get you to the Royal.'

'Eventually.'

The witness slumped in a chair, head in his hands, his chest heaving. The two cops stood and watched him for a long minute then Goodall rattled loudly on the door, startling the witness who looked up, fear etched across his face. Two uniformed policemen entered the room. The witness's face blanched.

'You did not see Pat Docker at The Majestic on the night she died, did you?' Dalglish demanded again.

'No,' croaked the witness.

'We . . . know . . . you . . . didn't . . .' Dalglish took his time. 'You are very lucky – this time.'

The witness looked at him, a glimmer of hope in his eyes.

'We're going to let you go,' said Goodall, nodding at the witness to go with the uniformed cops. 'No charge.'

The witness couldn't believe what he was hearing.

'Very lucky. In spite of you wasting our time, we've had a bit of a breakthrough.'

A uniformed cop had taken the witness by the arm and was leading him slowly out of the room.

'Pat Docker wasn't at The Majestic that night,' added Dalglish.

The witness was being led to his freedom but he was hesitating – looking back at the detectives, wanting to know more.

'And she wasn't dancing with you. We *know* where Pat Docker was.'

'The Barrowland Ballroom?' Ruth was surprised and exasperated and she was letting it show – unusual for her.

'Seems so.' Peter held his hands up, declaring that he was not to be blamed.

'The witness at The Majestic?'

'Seems he didn't see Pat Docker after all.' Peter sent dribbles of fried rice spilling over the tablecloth as he tried again to lift food to his mouth with the chopsticks.

Ruth had to hand it to him – he wasn't afraid to try something new.

'Ooh, he'll be in big trouble,' she said, knowing exactly how the majority of police forces would treat time-wasters in a big case like this.

Peter shook his head and held one hand up, asking her to wait till he had chewed a large prawn in batter. He had just managed to get it to his lips but it was too big to get it all into his mouth.

Ruth noticed red sauce was dribbling down his chin. She smiled and reached out with her napkin to wipe it away before it landed on his shirt collar.

'How the hell do you break food up with these things?' he finally asked when his mouth was clear.

'Just watch the experts,' suggested Ruth, 'they're all around you.'

They were sitting in the Loon Fung restaurant in Sauchiehall Street early one evening in April. All the other diners seemed to be Chinese and they were perfectly at home with the food and the tools. At the next table a boy, who Ruth guessed would be about five years old, held a bowl close to his chin in one hand and deftly fed rice and meat into his mouth with chopsticks in the other. Round-faced, his thick jet black hair was cut in a long fringe and he seemed to be managing very well with his little hands and short, podgy fingers.

'I keep telling you, Peter, watch the people – watch and learn.'

'Aye, well, we should've been watching The Majestic witness a bit more closely.'

'Oops, did he have previous form for telling the cops porkies? Did someone slip up?'

'No, that's just my point. The squad checked him out and he came up absolutely clean as a whistle. He seemed a decent bloke – steady, you know. How could we have known that he was telling us lies?'

'Hire a psychologist!' Ruth was smiling at him but she was also deadly serious.

'What? The cops hire a shrink? Aye, right.'

He'd given exactly the response Ruth expected and he was in line with most of the senior policemen in Britain. 'No, no, silly me!' She pretended to mock herself. 'You'll hire psychics to help crack murder cases. Get them examining ducks' entrails or whatever and then follow their advice. Bloody charlatans every one. Yet you wouldn't dream of hiring scientists who study human behaviour and could actually be of some practical help.'

'Well, we deal with criminals not madmen.'

'And members of the public make up evidence for what reasons, Peter? Do *you* know why? We do.'

'Fair point.' He lifted his chopsticks again, thinking that maybe he could shelter from her sarcasm behind some clown antics with rice and prawns.

'So what are the police going to do now about Pat Docker?' Ruth had returned to her main interest.

Peter could do nothing about the police attitude towards psychologists but he could tell her a few titbits about the investigation. 'We've run off more posters and we're having them plastered all over the east end near The Barrowland Ballroom and all over the Barras Market as well. That's a stroke of luck since people come from all over to browse the stalls at the weekends.'

'Posters? But haven't most people seen the appeal for information?'

'Aye, I agree. It feels a wee bit like clutching at straws.'

'Think the detectives are running out of leads?'

'It's no' looking good. One of them was telling me that they've now concluded that Pat Docker went to the jigging herself that night.'

'Just as a certain psychologist predicted – ermmm . . . weeks ago.'

'Point taken. So no pals with her and now eight weeks since the murder . . .'

'It's looking bleak, right?' Ruth knew that, with every passing week, the murder was becoming more and more unlikely to be solved. The fact that the police had been targeting the wrong ballroom for most of that time was a major blow.

Just then, a waiter appeared at their table. Without uttering a word, he carefully laid a knife, fork and spoon by Peter's plate, gave a curt nod and disappeared again.

'Think he's trying to tell me something?' Peter asked, laughing at himself with Ruth nodding and smiling along.

'Did you notice his tattoos?' Ruth asked.

Peter shook his head.

She gestured at her own wrist where the cuff of her shirt rose up a little as she bent her arm. 'Just saw a little bit here but, if I saw his whole arm, I'd be able to tell you a lot more about him.'

'Some of your psycho magic tricks?'

'No, just reading his tattoos. Triad, definitely.'

'In a restaurant in Glasgow?'

'Why not? Wherever Chinese folk or people from Hong Kong move in, most will be law-abiding but some will be organised gangsters, others crooked and yet others will turn out to be killers. That's the way it is with people.'

'Christ and we're struggling to deal with our own gangs,' confessed Peter, saying what everyone already knew. Glasgow's streets were rife with razor gangs feuding over nothing more important than territory. Frankie Vaughan, the singer, had made a highly publicised visit to the Easterhouse area in an effort to bring about peace. The police held an amnesty on knives, cleavers and other weapons and the gangs came together and agreed a truce. By night-time, it was broken and war raged again on Glasgow's streets – streets that were no-go areas for the police.

'Our own gangs?' asked Ruth. 'These *are* our own people now – as well as the Asians and the West Indians and the Africans who've moved here. Life's not going to be the same in the future, thank God, but neither will police work.' On moving north Ruth had noticed how much more a white city Glasgow was compared with London, Birmingham and Manchester. Change was heading north but could they handle it?

'Jeezo, Ruth, listening to you is enough to put a man off his work sometimes.' He smiled across at her. 'And it's hard enough as it is.'

'As with lying witnesses,' she grinned. 'So why was Mr Majestic not charged? What he did seriously jeopardised a murder investigation – as good as helping the killer escape, maybe.'

'I wondered about that and asked one of the friendlier plainclothes boys. He reckoned it was because they didn't want to put off potential witnesses in the future. They might get the idea that it was dangerous to speak to us about Pat Docker.'

'Fair enough.' Ruth was impressed with the Glasgow police's strategy of leniency – they were not a force normally known for their softly-softly approach.

'Especially given what was going on that night at The Barrowland.'

'What? Dancing and murder?' She made it plain she was joking.

'Aye, that all right and a bit more than that at the same time.' He drew in a breath. 'Shenanigans. Sexual shenanigans.'

Ruth watched the five-year-old boy at the next table nod politely and smile as his mother spooned more food out of a large platter into his bowl. She could swear he had eaten three or four times the amount that she and Peter had managed between them and in half the time. Occasionally, when she got so engrossed in her study of the criminal mind, it always did her good to watch kids. Where there were children there was hope and joy.

'But surely that's half the point at least of going dancing?'

'Aye but it was Thursday night when Pat Docker went to The Barrowland. That's a special night.' Peter then explained how The Barrowland's so-called Palais Nights mainly attracted the over-twenty-fives and how they had the reputation for married men and women going there in order to have some fun away from their partners – how these Thursday nights at The Barrowland were, in most people's minds, more about one-night sexual liaisons than anything to do with dancing. 'So, understandably, witnesses were a wee bit reluctant to come forward,' Peter explained. 'Most of them weren't meant to be at The Barrowland as far as their wives were concerned. So the squad wanted to reassure them it's safe to talk to us.'

'OK but how do you know that these witnesses are telling the truth?'

'Well, of those who did come forward, a couple were interesting. One was just an ordinary guy, apart from two-timing his wife, and he thought he'd seen Pat that night – recognised her from the posters. The other was playing the same game but he was the one who convinced plainclothes that she really was at The Barrowland.' Peter stopped and took a long gulp of his lager. He eyed the waiter at the far end of the room to see if he could make out those tattoos. At that distance, it looked like the tail of something slipping out from under his cuff – a crocodile maybe or a dragon?

'Peter?' Ruth was impatient to hear the whole story about the witness.

'Aye? Sorry. Seems he knew Pat Docker but through his wife. The same wife . . .'

'He was cheating on?'

'Aye. Awkward. They worked together and the families lived quite close by. He risked losing a hell of a lot coming to us.'

'Did he see Pat with anyone?'

'Said she was there on her own. They bumped into each other – embarrassed, like. He thought his game was up – that she'd tell his wife. Then she said that she was meant to be at The Majestic that night and had laughed. Said she wouldn't clype on him if he didn't clype on her.'

'Clype?' That was a new one on Ruth.

'Sorry, sorry,' Peter laughed. 'Grass. Inform. Tell.'

'Oh, OK.' Except it wasn't really OK to Ruth. She'd have investigated this witness big time but she decided to hold her tongue, fearing she was in danger of pushing Peter too far. 'But did he see her dancing with a particular man?'

'Said she'd danced with a few blokes but not with anyone for a long time. Then he lost his bottle and headed for home. Said he felt awkward chasing skirt with Pat in the hall so he left early. And, before you ask, his wife apparently confirmed he got home about ten o'clock – from the pub, of course,' and Peter winked.

'So Pat Docker was definitely at The Barrowland.' Ruth was thinking out loud. 'On Palais Night. That's every Thursday night. Peter? Only Thursday nights?'

'Aye, Thursdays.' He was paying the bill to the same waiter, distracted again by trying to catch a glimpse of the man's tattoos. With the bill paid, they walked slowly towards the door of the restaurant. The five-year-old boy and his family were still feasting.

'You haven't asked me yet,' Peter said suddenly.

'Asked you?'

'To take you to The Barrowland some Thursday.'

'I'm not going to,' Ruth replied.

'Thank Christ,' he sighed. 'I didn't want to go through that row again.'

'No, no row this time,' she said and she smiled as, in her head, she planned a trip alone to The Barrowland Ballroom. Pat Docker had gone alone and so must she. Peter was useful for information about the cops' case but, if Ruth was to find out more, work out what made this killer tick, she had to go it alone – but, this time, she'd watch out for tall men in brown suits.

'It's funny!' Peter laughed out loud.

'What?'

'One of those witnesses was actually called Jim.'

'So?'

'On Palais Nights at The Barrowland, no one uses their real name – none of the married ones anyway.' He laughed more loudly. 'Every second man you meet there on a Thursday is called Jim.'

'And the others?'

Peter hooted at her question. 'They're no better.' He held the restaurant door open for Ruth. 'They say their name is John.'

Thursday, 25 April 1968

Beware the serpent's tongue.

He speaks the truth, of course, this time. We ARE a nation 'busy building its own funeral pyre'. Too right – this nation will burn in Hell and soon. He blames the influx of black people and so he should. With them, they bring their morals of the sewers and our government traitors have opened the floodgates to their filth. Even his lot, the Opposition, have sacked him. Can't be seen to upset Rastus and his whores.

Consider a situation. A white man works hard and long to provide for his wife and children. He is a working man and decent but he isn't skilled, his wages aren't high. He votes Labour – the Party of the People – because he believes it will serve him and his best. When paid overtime is offered, he grabs it with both hands, not caring for his own health. Caring for his wife and children – that is his only ambition. Come the day, and it will come soon, our decent white man will come home from work to discover his wife astride Rastus. Or maybe his daughter kneeling in front of the black man with his filthy member in her mouth.

What will our decent white man say then? That he was right to care for others? To believe in equality? Or will he pick up a staff to smite the black man? Then what will we do? Throw him in jail as a violent racialist – that's what.

So Enoch Powell has spoken out on the truth as our shores flood with Black Devils – as all true Tories should. Like the Prophet in his own land, he has been cast out and pilloried and sinners line up to throw the first stone. Beware the Serpent who looks wounded for he will turn on you and poison you for sure.

We all know his story. Powell is a brilliant man. Too brilliant. The youngest professor in Britain by the age of twenty-five. Joining the army during the war, working his way up from private to the youngest-ever brigadier at thirty-two. We all know his tale and are meant to marvel at his ability. But who favours gain and office? Not Him. Not the Lord. Not my Father. He favours humility. The Devil

128

loves show and Powell has shown his colours.

Was it not Powell who introduced the contraceptive pill to Britain? Many voices called out against it. Dangerous hormones killing our women. Costs to the government's budgets as everyone would demand it. Even some of the churches railed against it, citing encouragement to immoral behaviour. The Catholic Church banned it but they would. They have other Devils to serve. All the Churches did was squeak a lip service to their real masters.

It was a whores' charter. A licence to fornicate. An encouragement to throw modesty to the wind. An adulteresses' manifesto. At least before the pill, their shame was exposed as bastard brats grew within them. Now they can wipe between their legs and go out and face the world with their dirty behaviour their dirty secrets.

All womankind has fallen to Satan. They have taken the power to corrupt all good men.

Now Powell tries to make amends by chasing the black man from our shores. It is all too little and too late. His aren't the tears of the confessional. He speaks out when he has no power. Useless. Flag waving. Simple show.

I know he is on the side of the black Devils. I know he has freed whores and bitches. I know he is truly evil. Now I must go out in the world and fight the Lord's fight.

Where Powell and his cohorts have created troughs of filth, I must walk among the swine. Where women lift their skirts in public, I must cleanse.

He sees 'the River Tiber foaming with blood'. It is much closer to home than that and not an ancient myth. It is here in my city. And it is now.

I will return once more to my favourite place. There I'll face the Devils and, once more, dance the dance of Death.

She could smell fear out there in the deepest dark of the park where anything could happen.

Ruth stood on the edge of Glasgow Green at night – a Thursday night. She had been there before during the day but this was different. The wide expanse of grass running down to the River Clyde looked harmless, welcoming, healthy when the sun was up. She had imagined the transformation after dusk and had seen the worst. What she couldn't imagine was how it made her feel – terrified. She knew he had been there – might be there still.

Through Peter, she knew that the police had more or less given up on the case – that poor Pat Docker's murder might never be solved. It had been months now and winter had turned into summer but, as the weather grew hotter, the murder case grew colder.

Ruth had different ideas. She believed that there were early signs that this strangler was driven by the need to kill. A need that would not die till he did or till it burned itself out following years of killing, lines of corpses. Just because there hadn't been another killing – well, not one that they knew of – soon after Pat Docker's death, it meant nothing. Each serial killer had their own way, their own pattern. Ruth was going to keep searching for it. Seeking him out.

For months, she had trawled the area round The Barrowland Ballroom – the Calton as some folk called it while others preferred the Gallowgate. The latter name was from the fact that, nearby, they used to hang convicted souls in public – just as, before that, there had been public hangings right there on the spot she was looking at on Glasgow Green. If ghosts existed, plenty of unhappy spirits would be roaming that ground but it wasn't ghosts Ruth worried about that night – it was living, human ghouls.

In the daytime, at weekends, the Barras Market is a lively, thriving place to be. The people thronging the streets all seem to be in good moods and the air smells of candyfloss, fresh doughnuts and toffee apples. When visiting the place, Ruth felt the only thing she'd have to worry about was getting her purse stolen by one of the many pickpockets who roamed the streets or falling for the patter of one of the callers on the stalls and truly believing he was giving valuable goods away almost gratis.

During the week, those same streets were empty and, even in daylight, seemed to be transformed into Dickensian decay. The buildings were small, with creaky thick doors in strange-shaped doorways that Ruth had to stoop to enter. Inside, floors ran at crazy angles or thick floorboards jutted up one from the other to trip the unwary. Sewage ran down the roadsides with no one bothering about the rats that scuttled here and there, raiding burst bags of rubbish.

Many of the people matched the buildings as far as Ruth could see. They were all small with oversized heads and many had legs that were bowed in the extreme, making them walk like upright apes. Ruth knew these were the symptoms of generations of harsh poverty and she had to muster all her self-control to avoid gaping at them. It was as if, years ago, a circus had stopped off there and moved on, leaving its midgets and curiosities behind. There was something rotten in that part of Glasgow – the gateway to the east end, the gateway to hell.

In the middle of all that squalor, like a king's palace in its size and modern grandeur, sat The Barrowland Ballroom. In any other place, it would have looked ordinary. Its concrete front and opaque grey windows gave it the look of classic make-do architecture. It had been damaged by bombs during the war and rebuilt again in a hurry and it showed. But business was business and they stayed open all hours. It was the type of building that most people in most places would want to be knocked down but not The Barrowland. That ballroom had a special place in the minds and souls of Glaswegians even if there was somebody hunting the innocent there.

All dressed up and on her own, Ruth went to The Barrowland at night – Thursday nights. It struck her that the scene there was the same as at The Majestic except bigger and more blatant and the sexual games were more obvious, matter-of-fact. Then there was the number of women there on their own. Ruth counted over forty on a quick walk round the main hall. That didn't include those drinking orange juice in the bar, the ones down in the toilets or those simply hanging around one of the sofa areas. It didn't include any women up dancing with men. It didn't include the ones draping the stage, ogling the band. It didn't include anyone who Ruth wasn't sure of. There were bound to be more than forty women at The Barrowland on their own that Thursday. How many? Fifty? Sixty? Seventy? All looking for a man. Most with secrets to keep from husbands at home if Peter was right and she had no reason to doubt him.

Then there were the men. Ruth hadn't really taken note at The Majestic – the tall man in the brown suit had distracted her too much and too early – but there were plenty of men on their own at The Barrowland that night, men looking for women.

It was the perfect playground for quick, no-strings-attached sex – the perfect setting for a strangler to choose his prey.

She had also gone to The Barrowland on other nights just to compare. At first, it seemed much the same as Thursdays till she took her time, opened her eyes and walked among the people. There were fewer women there on their own – hardly any as far as Ruth could make out – and fewer lone men too.

132

Then there were the gangs. 'TONGS!' was all she heard seconds before it kicked off. Two groups of young men, wearing ankle-length black leather coats, rushed at each other from two different sides of the hall. Behind them ran young women. Dressed to the nines like all the others, they were handing out knives, razors and machetes from their handbags. Other dancers screamed and ran and Ruth was carried away with them. Thank God for mob rule and hysteria, she concluded later, because, otherwise, she was sure her terror-stricken legs wouldn't have budged at all.

As quickly as the fight had started, groups of men in suits were in amongst the gangs and were soon joined by streams of uniformed cops. The police were there so fast that Ruth suspected they had been waiting outside, waiting for trouble. Later, she learned that they had been. They waited most nights for the gangs to do battle – every night apart from Thursday nights.

Violence on Thursdays tended to take the form of one-on-one squabbles that were easily dealt with by the bouncers so it was deemed that the police were not required. Their priority was to deal a blow against the mass street violence that had made Glasgow so infamous. Thursdays were Palais Nights – shagging nights – and usually the gangs didn't bother turning up so the cops didn't turn up either, not even after a strangler was known to be on the loose. So Thursday nights, Palais Nights, were perfect for a predatory killer.

Late one other night, Ruth had gone to the lane where Pat Docker's body had been found. As she walked along, the clip-clip of her shoes echoed on the hard ground. She looked up at the windows at the back of tenements and saw lights shining from many of them. Here and there, people moved about, maybe getting ready for bed. They were so close yet the strangler had taken Pat there – killed her there. Was he desperate? Bloodlust rushing in his brain, throwing caution to the wind? Did he attack and kill Pat on the spur of the moment?

Farther up the lane, Ruth came to the inshot in front of the garage where Pat's body had been found. She looked up and noticed how the light angled from the flats and cut across the top of the lane. She stepped into the inshot and into darkness. Total blackout. In there, he was near people but not seen. Pat had called out, of course, and she might have called out even more than she did, making it a risky spot to kill someone, all right. But the strangler wasn't desperate or in a hurry. He thought he was invincible, thought that the world couldn't touch him. So far, he was right.

Shivers ran down Ruth's back. If she thought the gang fight at The Barrowland had been scary, being in that lane beat it by a mile. Almost spooked, she quickly looked up and down the lane to where streetlights shone and cars occasionally passed, turned on her heel and started walking quickly. There was something about murder that clung to the scene long after the event.

Near the end of the lane, Ruth heard a baby howl or at least that's what it seemed to be at first. Out of the dark shadows at the base of one wall, a cat ambled out and put her head up to Ruth, looking for a stroke. Squatting down, Ruth put her hand out and gently shoosh-shooshed the cat to come. She was a white cat with two or three black patches and friendly, sociable, looking for company.

'Is this your territory, Toots?' Ruth spoke to the cat quietly. The cat rubbed her jaw gently against the back of Ruth's hand and purred. 'If only you could speak, what a story you'd have to tell.'

Weeks later, after a Thursday night at The Barrowland Ballroom, Ruth waited till that time when people seemed to be pairing up and, having danced, laughed and chatted, decided the other person was OK to leave with. As couples began to slope out of the dance hall, she put on her coat and walked round the block till she stood on the edge of Glasgow Green. There, in the dark, she almost felt it instantly. The fear.

The danger. Like she had sensed at the scene of Pat Docker's murder. Yet here it was different, less personal, and could come from any direction.

Down to her right she could see the grand front of Glasgow's High Court and next to it the police mortuary. To her left was the grey hulk of the People's Palace, with its huge, silvery-grey, transparent glass conservatory revealing its frames and beams like the skeleton of some massive insect. At the other side of the People's Palace, four folk paced up and down. Ruth knew they were prostitutes. They'd wait for a car to pull in so that they could do some trade with the driver or else their punters would arrive on foot and, having agreed a price, they'd go behind the People's Palace or farther down the Green, nearer the Clyde and away from prying eyes.

It was one of the darkest corners of the city to be worked by prostitutes. The better-off women worked in Blythswood Square. One of the most prestigious parts of the city, it had been built on tobacco, coffee and slave money during Victorian days. Now it was occupied by lawyers, accountancy firms and gentlemen's clubs. It was also well lit and near the social centre of Sauchiehall Street, Hope Street, Argyle Street. But there, on Glasgow Green, where the lights were poor, no law-abiding citizens ventured at night and these women were paid less money than their city-centre counterparts. They had to be some of the most vulnerable people in Glasgow.

Ruth watched as a man approached the prostitutes on foot. She couldn't hear what was being said at that distance but the dull streetlights on the main road threw the group into silhouette. It was her personal magic-lantern show except this was real. After a very short chat, one of the women went with the man round the back of the People's Palace. Although hidden from the road, they were still perfectly visible to Ruth. But then suddenly they were gone from Ruth's view. One second in sight, the next vanished into one of the darkest corners.

They were there all right, up against that wall, but they might as well not have been there.

At the front of the building, the other women walked up and down, stamping their feet on the ground against the chilly night air. Two decided they'd had enough and, with a wave, they walked off together, heading towards Bridgeton. That left one prostitute out front and the woman in the shadows with the man.

Ruth shivered and pulled her coat tighter to her body but she couldn't leave – not while that woman was out of sight with the man. Then suddenly a shape appeared – the man striding away from the People's Palace across the Green. Walking fast. Half running. No sign of the prostitute. Her pal out on the street still looking for business.

Panic and dread hit Ruth in the stomach and she started walking, heading off to skirt the Green, avoid the man but get to where that woman was still in the dark. Then she appeared, pulling her frock down, adjusting her top, strolling back to her friend. Ruth stopped abruptly, the breath whooshing from her lungs in one long sigh. All she'd probably witnessed was a man feeling sullied and ashamed after his time with the prostitute. The working girl probably felt dirty and used, as she did after all her tricks. All Ruth had witnessed was an everyday scene.

Searching in her handbag, Ruth found her cigarettes and matches. Lighting one up, she noticed across the Green the two prostitutes doing exactly the same. Down to her right, the man was now a black shadow. Walking as fast as ever, he was heading towards the bridge and the Gorbals.

The trouble with this murder business, Ruth acknowledged to herself, is you can start to see it everywhere. The other trouble is that it *is* everywhere – it's only a question of when and where.

If a man was compelled to kill, to strangle, he'd do worse than to choose this area. The Barrowland Ballroom, the Barras, the pubs, the prostitutes, the Green – they all made it a perfect hunting ground. And, on Thursday nights, he could have his choice of prey.

'You'll be back, won't you?' Ruth spoke the words out loud into the darkness of the Green. 'Maybe you've never left.'

Wednesday, 25 December 1968

I hate my mother.

I hate my mother.

I hate my mother.

I HATE MY MOTHER.

BOOK

of

JEMIMA

'I'm telling my mammy on youse!' The young boy stood on the waste ground, muddy water dripping down both bare legs, the bottom of his shorts darkening with dampness.

'Aye so ye will!' The older boy held another boulder above his head and grinned. He walked slowly away as if he had changed his mind before turning and lobbing the big stone and making a direct hit in the deep, dirty pool of water from a burst drain.

'Mammy! Mammy!' roared the younger boy, turning on his heels and running away across the rough ground towards the tenement where he and his tormentor lived. Well, brothers will be brothers.

Seven-year-old Alan McDonald sometimes found it hard being the youngest of three children, as many babies of the family do. Most of the time he got on well with his brother and sister – most of the time.

'GERONIMO!' The boulder-thrower, nine-year-old Andrew McDonald, was now a Red Indian warrior. Waving a branch spear in one hand and slapping his imaginary horse's rump with the other, he sped after the Pony Express rider, otherwise known as young Alan. 'WOW! WOW! WOW!' whooped Geronimo as he gained ground fast on his target, who had forgotten all about his mother and was scarpering for the cover of the wooden fort that looked remarkably like a rickety dovecot.

Geronimo was gaining fast and the Pony Express looked doomed till, 'PKOW! PKOW!' The Cavalry had suddenly appeared from the west and was heading straight for the

Indians. Although the Cavalry was comprised of only one Bluecoat, it should be enough, especially since she was older sister Elizabeth, aged twelve.

Geronimo didn't stand a chance and the Pony Express man knew it as he turned his steed to join the fray. 'PKOW! PKOW!' He had dropped the reins and was firing revolvers with both hands. They were off. Geronimo in the lead was turning in his saddle to fire over his shoulder. The Cavalry was closing in and the Pony Express man was trying to head the Indian off by skirting round a hillock of earth, boulders and chunks of sandstone.

'PKOW. PKOW. PKOW.' There hadn't been a gunfight like it since the shootout at the OK Corral the very day before.

'The mail must get through,' shouted the Cavalry as she launched herself at Geronimo. The pair landed on the dry ground with a thump and some loud squeals. They went tumbling over, wrestling and laughing. Seconds later, the Pony Express man dived on top of them and suddenly all three forgot who was friend or foe. It was every boy and girl for themselves. Geronimo grabbed the Cavalry's hands and pinned her on her back on the ground as the Pony Express man delivered expert tickles to her oxters.

Another battle of Bridgeton had just ended. But, compared with the real-life battles that happened in that poverty stricken, brutal area as gang massacred gang, the McDonald kids' battles rarely produced casualties.

The summer of 1969 has been sunny and warm in anybody's book, never mind the citizens of Glasgow who were more accustomed to rain, rain and more rain. The McDonald kids took full advantage of the weather and the school holidays by spending their time on the waste ground and demolition sites that scarred their home territory of Bridgeton. And it was an arrangement that suited their mother, Jemima McDonald, just fine.

'ELIZABETH! ANDREW! ALAN!'

The three children ignored the familiar voice and kept playing. Now they had moved on to tig and young Alan was 'het'. He was running around like crazy as his short legs tried to catch his older brother and sister. Life was too much fun to listen to their mother.

'ALAN! ANDREW! ELIZABETH!'

There she was again.

'PIECES!'

As one, the children turned and ran towards home. That simple word had reminded them all that they had been out playing in the sun for hours and hadn't eaten anything since some fried sausages and boiled potatoes around noon.

Elizabeth, in the lead, raised her arm and waved wildly at her mum who was standing on the edge of the waste ground. Her mother waved back and then turned and walked away towards their home. She'd be waiting for them there – they knew that, knew it from a routine they'd followed almost every day of their short lives. Their mammy loved them and every day was playtime so what did they have to worry about?

'Away ye go, ye wee bastards.' The man staggered towards them, a green bottle in one hand, a roll-up cigarette in the other.

'Leave them alone, Bert. They're only weans.' His pal didn't budge while he spoke but stood at the small bonfire they built and lit every day, whatever the weather. In winter, the fire kept the damp chill from their bones as they drank their way through their lives. Yet, that summer, it wasn't heat they were after and it wasn't a force of habit – they simply liked fire.

'They're cunts, so they are,' said Bert, still staggering in the direction of the McDonald kids. 'Wee evil cunts.'

'No, they're no',' said another pal, accepting a bottle of wine as it was passed to him. 'They're just kids. Wee, innocent fuckin' kids.'

'Aye, so they are.' Bert had stopped staggering now but stood waving a clenched fist after the McDonalds, who were

well on their way, running home for some food. 'Wee, innocent, evil pricks just like every fuckin' kid these days.'

'No, they're no'. They're . . .'

'Nae fuckin' standards,' Bert interrupted and then he
stopped to take a swig of his Buckfast fortified wine. 'Rob ye
as soon as look at ye.'

'Whit? You havin' us on? You? How much time ye done
for blagging?'

'No' the point.' Bert turned back to face his colleagues,
who were known locally as 'The Sunshine Boys' because of
their habit of being outside and drinking in all weathers. 'That
was honest robbing.'

His drinking partners started to cackle and laugh.

'Aye, it was.' Bert didn't like it when anyone laughed at
him – didn't like it at all. 'Robbing factories and shops and
banks and the like – that was my racket. No' stealing from ma
fuckin' neighbours.' Bert kicked out at a stone and his foot
stopped dead. 'Ooch, ya fucker.' He'd hit the corner of a sandstone block, most of which was buried under the ground.

The other Sunshine Boys didn't try to conceal their laughter. They could handle Bert – they'd handled him before.

'Hey, Bert,' said one, 'did you no' do extra time once
for rattling some old bloody caretaker on the napper with a
crowbar?'

'Aye,' grunted Bert, trying to find some place to sit so he
could examine his damaged foot. 'So whit?'

'So was he no' somebody's neighbour?'

'Somebody's daddy?'

'Somebody's man?'

'See you, ye cunts . . .' Bert growled. He was bent over,
looking like he was about to spring at them.

'Naw, see you, ye prick?' One of the Sunshine Boys stepped
forward. 'You just hate weans – that's your fuckin' problem.
Now do ye want to make something of it or sit on yer arse
and have a bevvy?'

Bert spat heavy, thick mucus, expertly missing his feet, then crouched down, sitting on an old tree trunk, black and charred from an earlier leading role in one of the Sunshine Boys' bonfires. Taking a swig from his bottle and laying it down carefully, he pulled up his injured foot and began working at the shoelaces with trembling fingers. The pal who had challenged him looked down at Bert, also spat on the ground, his face crumpled in disgust. 'Christ Almighty! As if life doesn't stink bad enough around here.'

Oblivious to Bert's ire and the potential battle brewing among the Sunshine Boys, the McDonald kids had arrived at their home, a tenement flat at 15 Mackeith Street. They arrived as they had set off – running.

'Aw, what a bloody mess you are!' said their mother in a stern, angry tone that was belied by her warm smile. 'What have you been doing? Rolling on the ground?' Precisely what they had been doing. 'You better no' have ripped nothing, though.' That was a different, more serious matter. Clothes and bodies could be washed but clothes cost money and there wasn't much of that going around the McDonald household.

Their mother's name was Jemima but the children had hardly ever heard her called that. Mima was how she was known – Jemima was too old-fashioned, too much like a granny. Mima McDonald was no grandmother figure. She was a thirty-two-year-old mother of three children. Many women in areas like Bridgeton were burned out by that age and had taken to wearing cardigans, long skirts and comfortable shoes as they stayed in every night in front of the fire and the TV but not Mima. She was attractive, vibrant and fun loving, especially since she and her husband had split up years before.

At five foot seven inches, she was tall compared with most women. Slim but with a good figure, she wore her dark brown hair shoulder length. Her facial features were strong but not big – they made her look attractive in what some folk considered a Mediterranean way. Her kids thought their mammy was beautiful and they weren't alone.

Mima McDonald was popular with men and she was a free woman who knew what she wanted. If she was going to be anyone's sexual playmate, it was because she'd decided she'd be a sexual playmate. She had never heard of the women's lib or bothered herself much with reading long articles about emancipation or equal rights – if asked, she probably wouldn't know what those words meant – but Mima McDonald didn't need all that politicising and theorising. She lived free – well, as free she could with three kids to care for and not much money.

Mima loved life. Her children and family knew that. She loved men, as her list of boyfriends knew. And she loved one more thing.

'Now take your time,' Mima advised her kids as they sat in their Mackeith Street home with hands full of big wedges of white bread spread thick with margarine and jam – pieces. They were cramming them into their mouths like small, ravenous animals. 'If you eat too fast, you'll get sore bellies.' Cups of diluted orange drink placed on the table were being ignored for the moment.

'Mammy,' asked Alan, the youngest, 'can we go out and play again after this?'

'Aye,' replied their mother. She was busy at the ironing board where her best dress, a black pinafore, was getting her closest attention. 'But just for a wee while.'

'Aw, Mammy,' complained Andrew through a mouthful of bread and jam.

'Are you going out, Mammy?' asked Elizabeth. She was eating her piece in a slower, more grown-up – more ladylike – way than her brothers and she was also paying attention to what her mother was doing.

'Please, Mammy,' Andrew piped up, supporting his younger brother.

'Well, it'll no' be up to me,' said their mother.

'How no'?' demanded Andrew.

'Mammy?' Elizabeth's tone was exasperated, still seeking an answer to her question.

'Your Auntie Margaret will be looking after you the-night,' Mima answered Andrew.

'Mammy?' It was Elizabeth again. '*Are* you going out?'

She had noticed that her mother was ironing her best dress and a freshly washed and ironed blouse was on a hanger hooked on to the top of a door. And, if Elizabeth needed any more evidence of her mother's intentions for the evening, it was there. She knew that the dead giveaway was that her mother's long brown hair had been washed and dried and was now set in big, tight rollers. Elizabeth watched her mother. She noted how she applied her lipstick and put on her face powder with that little pink puff she kept in her compact. It smelled so sweet – special. It smelled like a night out. Elizabeth knew her mother would wrap a headscarf round her curlers and, when she got to the place, she would go straight to the bathroom where she'd take the curlers out and, looking in the mirror, she'd tease her hair into a perfect style. Elizabeth watched and learned these things from her mum. It wouldn't be too long before she was a young woman, getting dolled up and going out to meet boys.

'Are you, Mum?' Andrew had cottoned on to Elizabeth's question.

'TIG!' Wee Alan had just remembered he was still het and decided to pass that on to Andrew.

His older brother turned to him and grinned a threat that said, 'Get you later!'

'You'll be all right with Auntie Margaret, though,' Mima affirmed, knowing that the three kids had often stayed with her sister, Margaret O'Brien, who lived just across the landing. It was a home from home with a friendly, caring face.

The three children all nodded. Their mother was going out just to her local, among many people she knew, and on to the dancing at The Barrowland Ballroom. After all, it was one of her favourite nights when the crowd would be older, calmer and there'd be little danger of fights – Thursday night.

'Away out ye go and play for a while then.' Mima smiled at her children who she loved dearly.

'TIG!' Andrew had caught Alan unawares and made him het again.

'Aw no,' the wee boy complained but with laughter in his voice and ran after his older brother and sister as they dashed out of the flat.

'Remember now and don't go far,' Mima shouted after them from the door of her home. 'And be good for Auntie Margaret.'

The three children ignored her and were heading back to the waste ground.

'I'll see you later,' she shouted. 'See you later, alligators!'

'In a while, crocodile!' the kids shouted as one. And they rushed back to their game of tig, not a care in the world.

Thursday, 24 July 1969

Change has been my downfall. I know that to break from the familiar is to risk disappointment yet I strayed.

The warm weather was my undoing. The parks of Glasgow were filled with people all day. I preferred to go there in the evenings and catch the young women home from working in the factories and desperate to sit in the last rays of the sun. They unbutton their blouses, strip their stockings off and pull their skirts up high on their thighs – right there in broad daylight, in public. They are asking for it.

Others in the parks seem too concerned with other business. Most of the men play football. What a waste of life. Some hang around in their short sleeves, drinking from screw-tops of beer, acting tough. If some girls pass by, they whistle and call out. Showing off for their pals in the most part. Yet the women are there for the taking. My taking.

The Lord sent me a message. That the Fire would be some time in coming. After my Patricia was cleansed, I kept expecting to be sent my next soul every week, every day. I grew impatient. Weakness. Forgive me, Lord.

One night, I got drunk and went to my favourite place. Yet again there were hints of what might be but yet again no Fire. Later, I walked the streets of the city, anger burning in me. With every step, I hoped that someone might get in my way. Someone I could hurt. No one did.

Round George Square, packed with people looking for late-night buses. Three times I walked round that place and three times no one crossed my path.

When I went down the steps under the pavement that is the dungeon they call St Vincent Street toilets, I had no plan. My bladder ached with the beer and whisky. All I was searching for was relief. All I found was torment.

As I stood at the urinal, a young man stepped beside me. He undid himself but didn't urinate. Instead he waved his thing at me.

Long and swollen and he waved it at me. It was the whisky and my anger and frustration of time past and no soul to cleanse. God forgive me.

I followed him out and he glanced behind him as he walked. He smiled and his eyes glittered like light shone from them. Like there was fire in those eyes. The Fire?

In a dark lane close to the toilets, he unzipped himself and me. I held him and did his bidding. He grew large and thick in my hand but, in his, I did not. He laughed at me and stepped back. Pointing and laughing saying I wasn't a real man. Roaring inside my head. Disgust welling in my guts. I reached for him again with two hands – one on his prodding member, one on his sacks below. Gripped firmly then twisted and twisted and twisted. Father, forgive me.

I walked away, leaving him there groaning on the ground. Walking fast, panic in my chest, heading for home. In the back of the taxi, I noticed it. He'd spilled his filth all over my sleeve. That night I had surely walked with the Devil. Forgive me, Father.

For three days and nights, I fasted and prayed. I had sinned and I wasn't a real man. Was that my punishment? Had He deserted me? On the third night, He forgave me and told me I must be patient. Must wait. Cleansing souls was my purpose. The Fire made me whole. Only with the Fire and the cleansing would I be a full man. The Fire would not come till the Fire was ready. Every soul has its season.

So I was patient and visited new places. A new nurses' home at Yorkhill Hospital. Women from all over the world, none too fussy about closing her curtains. A show for free for anyone who cared. Parading their paps for all to see. True harlots every one.

To get close to those bitches, I took to going to the local bars. They arrived in groups with their scent and low-cut tops and short skirts and drank like men who had practised all their lives. No dancing in pubs, of course, but there was no need. They made it plain that they were available and to whom.

Twice I thought I saw the Fire. Twice I was wrong. Twice I left to their curses and blaspheming. Then I took to the parks – Queen's

Park, Elder Park, Pollok Park, Bellahouston Park and, my favourite, Victoria Park. Victoria Park is gentle and intimate. In one corner, there are fossils of trees many thousands of years old. The world marvelled at the science of unearthing and ageing those lumps of stone. I didn't. I knew He made them and He was more ancient than the trees and wiser still than any scientist.

Then there's the pond where rich wee boys from the fancy old houses nearby go to sail model yachts – tall-sailed ornate yachts. Some are as long as the boys themselves. Those toys must have cost a fortune. Spoiled young boys who did me a favour. Reminded me of my childhood and the hand-knitted woollen jumpers worn and repaired till they fell apart on my body. How games were seen as the work of the Devil and Christmas as a pagan rite. A joyless, colourless, toyless childhood. My childhood.

Mothers came along with some of the boys. They'd sit on a bench nearby and knit or read or smoke or talk to some other women. Well dressed and well behaved but I knew what they were really like. They were just women after all. With the lusts of women. A better class of fanny is all they were. The parks showed promise but that is all.

Looking is not cleansing.

A come-on wink is not the Fire.

I like Victoria Park. I'll go back there sometime.

But the parks kept me from my main place, my main task, and I returned there again. Tonight was Palais Night and I saw the Fire in her eye even as we danced. No matter that she had promised to meet someone. No matter that he turned up and excused himself to take her away from me. No matter. The Lord has taught me patience. She is the chosen one. Her time will come.

Soon.

Two long-haired, fluffy-bearded youths stood huddled against a wall, passing a joint between them. Ruth noticed how, in almost a year in Glasgow, the whole hippy movement had caught on and fast. Yet these two young guys weren't arranging a love-in – they were up to no good. Ruth slowed her pace to watch. Their antics would provide some light relief.

She had just come from the Mitchell Library where she'd had her head buried in newspaper reports from the USA about the Boston Strangler, Albert DeSalvo. DeSalvo had been convicted two years before and was believed to be responsible for thirteen murders and more – all young women, all strangled. DeSalvo had confessed voluntarily in the hope that he could claim a reward that would be passed to his family. If this worked out, he'd be happy with the prospect of spending the rest of his life in a psychiatric institution. Because of this, his attorney had argued insanity, an argument that failed. Now controversy raged about whether or not DeSalvo even was the Boston Strangler. The man intrigued Ruth not least because he was alive, in prison and available to learn from. A self-confessed serial killer who could answer questions was a rare opportunity. Yet, without leaving Glasgow, the only way to get decent information was to use the Mitchell's access to international newspapers – it was a slow, eye-boggling process.

To clear her head she had jumped on a bus that took her near Kelvin Way. A walk down that leafy boulevard and up through the university would be just the trick to blow the library dust from her mind and eyes.

'Go on, Jack,' said one long-haired young man, 'you said you would.'

'I said I'd start, Lewis. You said you would finish.'

'Well, man, I can't finish till you start – ipso facto.'

Ruth smiled to herself. They may believe in free love and that all property is theft but a classic education will always come out and, in the case of these two upper-class Glaswegians, she heard it in an accent that was halfway between sing-song polite Scottish society and the clear vowels of public school education. It was an accent all of its own – one that conveyed privilege and rank – and it grated on Ruth's nerves.

'*Audere est facere*,' said his friend, probably not wanting to be outdone. And then he added, somewhat unnecessarily no doubt, given his company, 'To dare is to do.'

Ruth wondered if he knew that he was quoting the motto of that most conservative of institutions, Tottenham Hotspur Football Club, a fact she'd gleaned from a football-daft friend while she was studying in London. Whatever the pair were up to, it was hardly going to be daring. It was August and the university term didn't start till October. Most of the buildings were closed and the staff off sunning themselves.

The long-haired guy called Jack now took a can of spray paint out of his pocket and shook it vigorously. Ruth stopped to watch as he turned to the wall and began to write. Slowly awkward, large, black letters appeared:

Y O U A R E

W H

At that, he stopped and passed the spray can to his friend who in turn passed him the spliff. The new possessor of the can sprayed:

A T

Jack and Lewis had obviously not misspent their youths. Their efforts at graffiti were pathetic and childish compared to some around the city. Ruth admired the way the gangs designed and drew their symbols on walls. Her favourite was how the Govan Young Team displayed the letters GYT – so simple, so clear and so skilled. That was art as far as she was concerned but what she had witnessed was clumsy posturing.

YOU ARE
WHAT
YOU EAT

And they had written it on the wall of what the university called The Refectory, a fancy name for a subsidised canteen that sold cheap and very filling food with as much mashed potatoes or as many chips as you could stomach. Not exactly the vanguard of revolutionary politics yet Ruth thought the two overeducated vandals had a point even if they did have enough money from their mummies and daddies to eat elsewhere.

'I should lift those two numpties!' The man's voice was right beside her.

Ruth turned to see a familiar face. 'It's my favourite copper!' She smiled at Peter. 'Imagine bumping into you here.'

Ruth moved to kiss Peter on the cheek. The move caught him unawares and he awkwardly bumped his lips against her chin. They hadn't seen each other for months. At first, it was due to his shift pattern. Peter blamed this on a new sergeant, who didn't like him for some reason, putting him on almost constant nights. Then it was her work regime. As she started making more and more contacts locally, she was spending more time out and about in the prisons and at murder scenes. And this, coupled with the fact that she still had to make the time to keep up with her studies, did mean that there were fewer opportunities for them to meet. But the most important reason was never expressed – the words neither had spoken but both had silently acknowledged. There was never going to be any real romance between them. Good friends? Yes but sexually there was no spark.

'I was just passing,' said Peter. And then he added, with a smile, 'Really! I'm just going to start my shift.' To demonstrate, he held up a tartan holdall. It was unnecessary since she'd already clocked that, under a casual waterproof jacket with a trendy round collar, he was wearing his uniform shirt, trousers and a pair of highly polished black shoes. Also there was that tie – the one that came already knotted and slipped under his collar. It was quick to put on and with a half-decent knot – the same knot every time – but, like all cops, he wore it for protection. Anyone attacking him would be out of luck if they tried to throttle him with his own tie.

'Ashamed to be a cop now, are we?' Ruth asked, knowing that most Glasgow policemen wore their uniforms to and from work – especially if they were travelling by bus or the underground where an unofficial policy let them travel for free.

'Ashamed?' Peter's face reddened. 'No, no. I just like to travel incognito these days. That way you can sneak up on the unsuspecting culprits.'

'Do you mean Fidel Castro and Che Guevara,' she said, nodding in the direction of the two graffiti artists, 'or me?' Ruth smiled.

'Well, who am I talking to?'

His reply reminded Ruth of how much she liked Peter's company – something that didn't happen often for her. For a long time, she'd known that she didn't need friends the way other people did but now she was also coming to realise something else about herself – she wasn't sexually attracted to men.

She sometimes felt a buzz of excitement when she was near certain women and she found this upsetting, disturbing even. She was a qualified psychologist so she knew she had to deal with this and accept herself whatever her sexuality. She also knew that the world might think it was modern and trendy and that barriers of all kinds were tumbling down all the time but people still had their prejudices – and being a lesbian was something that attracted a great deal of hostility. She promised herself that she would take time out to deal with all of that as soon as she had the time. Meantime, she was always finding more and more work to do. One day, though, one day.

'I'll walk with you a bit,' Ruth said to Peter.

'That was some shooting the other week, eh?' said Peter and they both knew what he was referring to.

Career criminal James Griffiths had gone ballistic when he was approached by the police. Arming himself with a stack of guns and a bandolier of bullets, he commandeered various cars and drove through the city streets firing at anyone he saw. The battle had started at Holyrood Crescent about half a mile from where Ruth and Peter were walking through the university grounds. After a raging battle and a siege, it ended in Springburn with Griffiths shot dead.

'You're telling me,' replied Ruth. 'Who needs Al Capone and Chicago when you have modern-day Glasgow, eh?'

'And it wasn't even Valentine's Day!' joked Peter, referring to Capone's notorious massacre of six rivals that had spawned as many Hollywood movies.

'St Swithin's Day,' Ruth replied.

'What?'

'It was St Swithin's Day – July the fifteenth – when Griffiths went on his rampage.'

Peter threw her a sour look.

'I know, I know,' she conceded, 'I'm full of—'

'Bloody useless information,' he finished her sentence with a laugh while Ruth held her hands up in submission.

'You know the saying about St Swithin's Day, don't you?'

He shook his head.

'If it's sunny, it will be sunny for forty days. If it rains, it will rain for forty days.'

'But that day it rained bullets so what the hell are we in for?'

The pair of them were enjoying their trivial train of conversation. 'More of the same, I reckon.'

With this, Peter had stopped laughing – violence in Glasgow wasn't funny.

They opted to take a short cut through the grounds of the Western Infirmary, cutting out a section of Byres Road with its crowded pavements and lines of traffic. The buildings loomed high above them, crooked and large. Ruth marvelled at how all the hospitals of that era looked menacing – more like Dracula's Castle than a place to receive care and life-saving treatment. There were hospitals like that in every city she had visited but the difference between them and Glasgow's hospitals was that Glasgow's all seemed to be of that same period and of that same style. It was as if, one hundred years ago, they stopped caring, stopped modernising, stopped building new medical units – or maybe they just liked their hospitals to be frightening.

'I'm glad I bumped into you, Ruth,' said Peter. 'I've missed our chats.'

'Me too, Peter,' she found herself saying. Was now the time to explain there could be no romance? Did he still think there might be a chance? Was he, like a lot of men, blind to the emotional side of life?

'As pals, like,' he added. A slight blush rose high on both cheeks and his eyes stayed focused on the ground in front of him and not looking at her.

'Sure,' she said, reaching out and taking his arm. Relief seeped through her and she added, 'Just as pals.'

Peter turned slightly and gave her a small crooked grin. 'There's another reason, come to think of it,' said Peter, stopping now to face Ruth. Somewhere high above them, the strains of Pink Floyd's 'See Emily Play' were wafting through an open window.

'Haunting music for a haunted place,' Ruth thought.

'What you talked about when we first met last year,' said Peter, as if that was enough information.

Ruth's screwed-up expression gave him a clue that an explanation was required.

'About the Pat Docker murder,' he went on, 'how there were signs that her killer might attack other women.'

'Yeah.' Ruth decided not to say that that wasn't exactly what she had said. She was spending too much time with academics who demanded precision in conversation and, as they had just agreed, they were pals.

'Well, I haven't forgotten it, you know. And I got thinking about it again.'

Over Peter's shoulder, Ruth watched as two women came out one of the doors that seemed to pepper the back of the hospital. One, a nurse in uniform, was talking in serious tones to the other. Dressed in a white coat and with stethoscope dangling from her pocket, Ruth took this second woman to be a doctor. The female doctor took long, confident strides and looked straight ahead while the nurse struggled to keep up with her. The nurse seemed to be trying to brief the doctor about something Ruth couldn't make out but, whatever it was, it seemed very important to the nurse. As they walked, the doctor fished a packet of cigarettes and a silver Ronson lighter out of one of the pockets of her white coat and, without missing a beat, she lit a cigarette. She looked important – a woman in control, a woman others needed – but she also looked familiar. And then it clicked – she was the woman in the Rubáiyát pub last year. The one Ruth had watched with the younger man who was deliberately getting her drunk and touching her thigh under her skirt. The one she worried about. Not a sad and weak

158

individual but a bright, intelligent professional. But was she all that and more?

Oblivious to Ruth's watching eye, Peter continued, 'It's just that there have been these rapes – bloody terrible rapes in the southside, city centre and around here.'

'That's awful!' Ruth returned her full attention to Peter as the doctor and nurse disappeared through another door.

'Aye, bloody terrible and the women weren't just raped.' Peter brought out his cigarettes and handed one to Ruth.

Using the small insignificant actions of choosing and lighting a cigarette to give him breathing space was a habit of his she still remembered.

'They were all badly assaulted – really nasty.' He dragged on his smoke. 'But here's the thing – plainclothes think they might all be related.' Peter stopped talking abruptly to let that information sink in. 'Think it's the same man.'

'That's not uncommon, Peter.' He nodded at her in agreement and waited till a group of men passed by, hospital workers, porters by the look of them, talking loudly about the football season that would soon kick off.

'Thing is – could it be your strangler?'

'MAMMY! MAMMY! MAMMY!' The child's voice was riddled with fear. 'WHERE'S MA MAMMY?'

It took young Alan McDonald no time at all to search the few rooms of the tenement flat in Mackeith Street and, sure enough, his mother wasn't there. He was only seven years old – just young, maybe too young to understand, to expect anything other than eternal security. Young enough to believe that no one would leave – to trust that entirely. To see nothing but comfort and happiness especially from one person – his mother.

Alan needed his mother, Mima, now more than ever. He was hurt, scared and needed to sit on her lap, to get a magic cuddle and for her to kiss his pain all better. But she wasn't there and his life plummeted to the depths of misery. Alan McDonald sat on the floor and howled.

'What's all this noise?' He looked up, his eyes soaked with tears. 'That's not my big boy crying like a baby, is it?' Mima McDonald helped Alan to his feet and then on to her knee. She hadn't been there at home but she wasn't far – just across the landing having a cup of tea with her sister, Margaret. Her three children knew that's where they'd find her when she wasn't at home – unless she was going to the shops or farther afield. In that case, she'd tell them and they'd know to go see their Auntie Margaret.

'Thought you'd gone forever, Mammy,' sniffled Alan.

'Don't be silly,' said Mima, giving him a warm cuddle, pulling him against her bosom and rocking her legs gently to and fro. 'I'll never leave my wee boy. You hear?'

Alan sniffed and nodded.

'Never.'

'Hurted my leg, Mammy,' Alan said, drawing his knee up to show her a small bloody wound.

'Oh, so you have. That must have been a sore one.'

'Aye, it was stingy.'

'It must've made you cry when it happened.'

Alan shook his head.

'No?'

'No, I just gave it a rub and came back here so's you could bandage it.'

'Did you?'

'Aye.' Alan was nodding his head, his eyes still swollen and glistening from the tears.

'You're a brave wee soldier for yer mammy, so you are.'

Alan nodded his head, wiped snot from his nose on his sleeve and stayed quite calm as his mother washed his cut knee with hot water mixed with Dettol. All the time he watched the water, intrigued how it turned milky white when Dettol was put in it.

'Thought the bad man got ye, Mammy,' he volunteered after a while.

'Bad man? What bad man?' Mima McDonald was alarmed.

Rumours were circulating that some man had been approaching young kids in the Bridgeton area, trying to tempt them away from home – trying to tempt them into some of the semi-derelict buildings, the numbers of which multiplied in the area every week. A young girl had been found in one, naked and crying. She had been sexually interfered with and Mima and her neighbours all agreed it could've been worse, much worse – rape at least and maybe even murder.

'You've no' met a bad man, have you, Alan?'

He shook his head from side to side.

'Are you sure?'

Alan gave an even more emphatic shaking of his head.

161

'Well, what bad man do you mean?'

Alan hesitated, scared that maybe he was going to get into some sort of trouble. He wasn't sure why – it was the type of thing he was still learning just because he was young. Sometimes, it was best to proceed with caution.

'The bad man that'll come and get you,' he eventually said.

'Come and get you?'

'Aye, when you're bad.'

'Bad?'

'When Andrew or me don't go to sleep at night or . . .'

'Oh, *that* bad man!' Mima sighed with relief that was tinged with a little bit of guilt.

Before she and her husband split, if the kids were particularly badly behaved, she'd warn them to wait till their father got home but, since she'd been on her own, her ultimate caution was that 'a bad man' would come and get them. As every mother knows, the use of the bogeyman as a disciplinary threat is simply meant to get the kids to behave, not terrify them into thinking that their mother might be abducted.

'That bad man doesn't come after mothers,' Mima reassured her son. 'Just weans when they aren't doing what they're told.'

'But I'm a good boy, Mammy.'

'You are, son. You are – a very good boy.' Mima decided to take full advantage of this little chat with her youngest. 'And you'll be good when yer mum's no' here, won't you?'

He nodded his head uncertainly.

'When she leaves you for a wee while with your Auntie Margaret?'

More nods.

'Like I will on Saturday night.'

'When's that, Mum?'

'That's tomorrow night. Your mammy's going out just for a wee while.'

Slower nods from Alan.

'Your mammy's going to get all dressed up. She's going to the dancing.'

Friday, 15 August 1969

You can't escape me.

I know where you will be and when.

The Lord is my shepherd.

You try and trick me but you can't. I listen and learn. I remember. I can still smell your flesh and hear your words and see the Fire in your eyes. So you don't always go on my favourite nights, the chosen nights. Do you think that can fool my Father? He created the days as he did the universe and all that lies within it. He created you, you whore. Now, through me, he will reclaim you.

Your time has come.

I am coming for you.

'Did you really go there tonight looking for me?' Mima was flattered. She was well used to attracting men but this one was younger than most, better looking, well dressed, clean, a good dancer, had money and polite manners. She was happy if her men had one or two of those attributes but this one seemed to have them all. She wasn't going to let him get away from her.

It was late on the Saturday night but not as late as usual for Mima. Her man had said he had to get up early the next day so they left a bit earlier than most folk. She didn't mind. He said he had to do so every Sunday and that was why he usually went to The Barrowland during the week.

That's when they had first met – the last time Mima had gone dancing one Thursday night. They'd had two dances but she had told him that she had promised to meet someone there that night. What she didn't tell him was that he was a married man or that she knew his wife or he had only one thing on his mind and it wasn't dancing. Not that she minded that too much. Well, it was the 1960s – everyone was having sex.

When her date had turned up, the ignorant pig just barged in and interrupted them. Mima had considered telling him to go away but she knew he'd create a scene, maybe get violent. He was well known in Bridgeton for throwing his weight around and for carrying a razor too. So she'd just gone with him and left the other guy, the one she really fancied. She'd thought that would be the end of it and she'd never see him again. After all, what did she know about him? Nothing really except that he'd said his name was John – John, like half the men at The Barrowland Ballroom most nights and especially Thursday nights.

They'd only had a couple of dances that first night and he'd come out with the 'Do you come here often?' line or something like that. She'd replied that she liked Thursday nights but her favourite was Saturday when The Barrowland was full to the gunnels and the dance floor was jumping. He'd remembered that and had come back on the Saturday just on the off chance that he'd meet her again. It was almost romantic. Mima liked that.

Now here they were strolling towards her place. She could tell he was the kind of bloke that could afford a taxi. He even carried a packet of cigarettes and didn't smoke. They were just to give to other people. That was money for you and real class. Yet there he was walking her home. Romantic.

When he'd asked her where she lived she'd been a bit embarrassed to say. Bridgeton wasn't even called that by the locals. The pronounced it Brigton and too many of them were proud of its bad reputation as a poor place and rough, brutal. She wasn't proud of it and she didn't want to put him off by giving him the impression she was a scruff. But he'd smiled and seemed quite pleased. Said that was close by and they could take a wee stroll if that was OK by her. It was very OK by Mima.

London Road had never looked so good. The pavements were still crowded with noisy drunks but she didn't mind them that night – not even when a guy had turned and spewed right at their feet. Her John had just taken her by the arm and guided her round the foul-smelling pool.

When they walked down Landressy Street and got close to Bridgeton Cross, Mima knew that, as usual, there would be gangs hanging around, all tooled up with no one to fight – but they would fight at the least excuse. In fact they didn't need an excuse most of the time.

One of the local heavies shouted out to her by name. Mima and him had had a fling a few months before. It was just sex.

166

The closest he got to taking her out was buying her a fish supper and sharing his cider with her – last of the big spenders. But she just waved back, friendly like, and he had nodded and shouted, 'You all right, hen?' What did he think? That the good-looking, well-dressed young guy beside her was some sort of threat?

'Doing great,' she'd answered and threw a big grin. 'How's yersel', Malky?'

She never found out how he was because she and John turned a corner and into Mackeith Street a few seconds later. Now she had a problem – a light was still on in her own flat. The kids must be in there watching TV or maybe Margaret was in there with them. She wasn't happy about taking him into her flat anyway – not a classy guy like that. She'd rushed out that night and left the place like a tip. Mima didn't have much, she knew that, but, if she'd known this man was going to be visiting, she'd have made sure her home was tidy and clean.

What a gentleman. There was no problem. He didn't seem let down or upset about her not inviting him up and saying she knew a wee place they could get some privacy. A place very close by where no one else went. Where no one would see them. No one hear them.

As she led him by the hand, Mima knew she had another problem and thought that maybe she should tell him before he found out for himself. Some men were disgusted by it – especially on the first date. Maybe she should tell him but that might put him off forever.

Warning him to watch his feet, Mima led him by the hand into the darkness. She wasn't going to tell him just yet and would give him a good time anyway. Mima knew how. There was no way she was letting him go. Not her John.

'Ssshh. They'll no' find us in here.' The small boy led his platoon into the empty house. They were hiding from another group, the way they did. When there was no other game going on, hide-and-seek was always fun.

The ground floor flat was empty but it wasn't too long ago that a family had lived there. Almost as soon as the tenants had moved out, someone had kicked the door in and converted the dilapidated flat into a communal resource for wine-guzzling alcoholics, homeless down-and-outs, young couples snatching a quick grope and fumble and children playing games. No one knew what to expect when they entered that place. They just knew to watch out.

The kids moved slowly, letting their eyes adjust to the darkness caused by the thick boards the local council had fixed over all the windows. They also had to watch their feet for rusty nails, broken glass and the worst – large turds of human shite.

Here and there floorboards had been yanked up and burned in the grate. In the middle of what used to be the living room some previous occupant had set a bonfire on the floor and it had left a charred gaping booby trap of a hole there. Silver-grey ash and lumps of scorched wood were scattered all over. One wall had a rough jagged hole where someone had tried to break through for reasons only known to themselves. Ragged flaps of wallpapered plaster hung loose and a thick electric cable was dangling down, its bare wires curling like fish hooks. Just going into that derelict flat in Mackeith Street would involve a series of dangers – just what bored kids enjoyed.

A big black bag tied at the top lay in one room. It must have been put there recently. The kids were frequent visitors to that place and they knew they hadn't seen it there before. Two of them set about trying to undo the bag without much success as someone with strong hands had wound the plastic into a treble knot so tightly and they had to give up. One found a long shard of glass and set about the plastic. After two quick stabs the bag fell apart and rotten food, wet newspapers and what looked and smelled like a lot of cat dirt spilled out of it. No one had ever found hidden treasure in that place but that didn't stop the youngsters from dreaming and looking.

'Ssshh! What's that?' The leader jabbed his hand in the air, palm open, and quickly dropped down on to his haunches.

His platoon copied him as fast as they could. They were a mixed bunch – both boys and girls, whose ages ranged from those nudging into their teenage years to the youngest at four years old. No one stopped to wonder why the shortest was always the slowest to get down. They had more pressing concerns than taking care of their youngest member.

'Ssshh. Listen.'

They squatted in total silence and listened. Somewhere close by they could hear big, slow drops dripping into water. Outside, in the distance, two of the multitude of wild dogs that roamed the scheme were having a barking contest. Something creaked and they all ducked down, holding their breath. Nothing. It was just the kind of noise all old buildings make.

'It's all clear,' said one to the leader.

'No, it's no',' he said.

'How?'

'Look there!' And he pointed at the corner of a recess.

At one time, a bed had probably been there, giving rest and comfort to people every night. Now the wallpaper peeled from the walls and the recess was dark and empty – almost empty.

'Nothing there,' said the lippy one who considered himself the deputy leader – even believed he could challenge for the leadership.

'Aye there is,' whispered the top man.

'No, there's no',' argued the deputy, still whispering in a coarse voice that was going through the process of breaking as puberty approached.

'Fucking is.'

'Fucking is no'.'

'What's fucking there then?' piped up a third, in a voice that was squeaky.

'Show youse, so I will,' said the leader, edging up to his full height. Slowly, cautiously, he stepped forward and moved towards the bed recess.

All of his group were straining their eyes, trying to see if they could make out anything but with no luck. Still a few feet from the recess, the leader wiped sweat from his hands on to his hips. From behind, his group thought he looked defiant and bold but he was really nervous and scared. Not that he would ever admit that – ever.

'Hey, Mister!' When he spoke out, his voice was cracking with dryness.

No reply.

'MISTER!'

His group had slowly risen to their feet and moved up behind hind him.

'Fuck sake, so there is!' conceded the deputy, seeing the shape for the first time.

'It's a fucking man, man,' muttered one of the group.

'It's a fucking man, aw right,' said the deputy, 'but is he alive?'

Everyone knew whose job it was to find the answer.

Slowly, the leader crouched down and picked up a piece of brick lying near his feet. 'OI!' he shouted.

No response.

'OI, YOU!'

Still nothing so he lobbed his missile at the shape, not hard enough to hurt anyone but enough to draw their attention – or so he hoped. Nothing. Picking up a long piece of wood that had once been part of a door frame, the leader crept forward. This time, his platoon stayed right where they were. When he was a couple of feet away from the human shape, he stopped and looked back at his friends. They looked back at him. This was why he was the leader. Slowly he reached out with the piece of wood at full stretch and prodded the shape. No movement, no noise, nothing. The leader took one small step closer and prodded again. Nothing.

'HE'S FUCKING DEAD!' he roared, turning and taking to his heels.

This time, his platoon were quickly up on their feet and even the youngest made it through the door before him. Out in the sunlight, they kept running till they were two tenements away – tenements that were occupied, tenements where people milled around the street.

'Hello, boys,' said a passing adult, a friendly face. 'What you been up to?'

'We've been in number twenty-three,' said the leader, still out of breath, half from his sprint and half from the fear gripping his chest. 'There's a body in there!'

'A body?' asked the adult. 'Naw.'

'Aye, so there is,' insisted the platoon's leader and the other kids joined in with excited support.

'Aye.'

'A dead body.'

'Just lying there, Mister.'

'A man, so it is.'

'Och, it'll no' be a man,' said the adult neighbour. 'It'll be a jakey and only half dead.' With that, he walked away, grinning to himself and listening to the kids behind him protesting with each other that it was a man and arguing whether it was

171

possible for anyone to be half dead. The passing neighbour had made a fair assumption. The many deserted and semi-derelict buildings in the area were most often used by home-less folk with booze problems. To keep warm, they dressed in as many layers of thick clothes as they could. They often had long straggly hair and they washed so seldom that their skin became the colour of dirt and dust. They were mainly men but, because of their appearance, it could be hard to tell which sex they were. To the locals, they were a breed apart – just jakeys, that's all.

The jakeys had fallen as low as most folk thought pos-sible. Cheap fortified wine was popular among the poor who wanted or needed to get drunk but even that was beyond the means of the jakeys. They would use meths or white spirits as stiffeners to their cheap wine, cider or lager, usually Special Brew, mixing up their poisons into some dangerous concoc-tions. Or they'd buzz lighter gas through the alcohol, adding butane to their brew. Glaswegians called their drink 'electric soup' and would argue as to the exact ingredients. What wasn't in debate was that, after a drinking session, the jakeys would often collapse unconscious and the odds were even as to whether they woke up or died where they lay.

'Half dead' the man had said and he knew what he was talking about. The kids weren't convinced.

All day in that part of Bridgeton, troops of children would hear about the body in the derelict flat and go round there to see for themselves. The band that had found the body dis-missed the first adult's half-dead theory and shared the news with other grown-ups, hoping to generate some interest but they were to be disappointed. Local people were all too used to jakeys and tramps dying in those buildings so, even if the kids were right, they really didn't care that much. If he was dead, he was dead. What did they want with all the hassle reporting it to the police would involve? It might have been Sunday, the so-called day of rest, but they had things to do, families to care for, meals to cook, pints to drink down at the local Orange social clubs.

By night-time, the excitement of the body in the house had evaporated for most of the kids. They sat themselves in front of TVs, had their weekly baths and sat back down again to watch some other programme. It was still the school holidays and they could stay up late. The following day, they would be out playing again in the sun. What did they have to worry about?

Nearby someone was beginning to worry and fret. Something was wrong big time and she feared the worst. It was going to be a long night for Margaret O'Brien.

'We're away out to play, Auntie Margaret,' Andrew McDonald called a second before he slammed the front door. It wasn't a question or something that was in any doubt – no school for them in the summer holidays so they'd go out and play.

'All right,' Margaret O'Brien shouted after them, 'but no' far and no' near the empty houses.' She received no acknowledgement and had no idea if they'd even heard her but she'd more important things on her mind that Monday morning – their mother, Mima.

As Margaret cleared away some of the dishes from breakfast time and tried her best to tidy up the chaos the three McDonald children added to her daily routine, she worked things over in her mind. Arnold the Dog barked a warning from the transistor radio in the corner and Tony Blackburn's all too chirpy tones announced the next record. 'Something in the Air' by Thunderclap Newman eased itself into the room. In spite of it having been in the charts for weeks, she loved that song and usually stopped what she was doing to listen but not that day.

The next thing she knew, Desmond Dekker was just finishing 'The Israelites' and Arnold the Dog was barking again before Blackburn announced, 'Sensational!' He then introduced his 'School Salute'. Margaret always listened to 'School Salute' in spite of there being no chance of her old school ever featuring. It always seemed to be well-off, blazer-wearing, toffee-nosed folk who appeared on 'School Salute'. Blackburn didn't make it sound that way but, compared with her life, she just knew they were better off. Who would pay any attention to her old school? It produced chib merchants, drunks and prostitutes as well as decent folk like her, who had a lifetime of drudgery and keeping house on next to no money to look forward to. But, for some reason, she still enjoyed that part of Tony Blackburn's show but not that morning.

Margaret hadn't been surprised on Sunday morning to discover that her sister, Mima, hadn't come home. It wasn't unusual for Mima to stay out all night after going to the dancing at The Barrowland Ballroom. Margaret wasn't daft. She knew what kept Mima away all night – men – but she was a big girl who could take care of herself and, besides, everyone deserved a life.

Ten years before, Mima might have got herself a reputation as being a bit easy but not now – everyone had a sex life now. Why not? As long as she didn't get pregnant and with the pill there was no excuse, no need to take risks.

Mima wasn't just out for a good time and Margaret knew that. She was always hopeful she'd meet her Mr Perfect – some guy who'd be happy to take on her three kids as well as her. It was asking a great deal, hoping against hope, but that was Mima. She always expected things to work out – never gave up on finding the right guy.

Whatever her hopes for finding a new relationship, first and foremost, Mima loved her three children. That was one of the reasons she never stayed out for more than one night. Not that the kids were too bothered. That Monday morning, as Margaret worried, they went about life in their normal, carefree way. Kids were kids and they were with someone they knew and trusted – they'd stayed with their auntie plenty of times when their mother hadn't come back at night but she always did come back. Always had until that morning. Two nights away was a first for Mima. Margaret was worried.

As the morning wore on, Margaret worried more and more. Mima could be anywhere and anything could have happened to her. Then Margaret remembered overhearing some children talking in loud and excited voices the day before. They were claiming they had found a body lying in one of the old derelict flats. That couldn't be Mima, could it? Margaret put the thought from her mind. The kids were probably just imagining it. If there was anything, it would be yet another bag of rubbish someone had dumped or, at worst, a big stray dog that had crawled in there to die. It would be nothing.

As the time passed and there was still no sign of Mima, Margaret could think of nothing else. She tried having cups of tea and turning the radio up but she just couldn't relax. More and more the body that the kids claimed to have seen in the flat at number twenty-three plagued her thoughts. It drove her crazy with worry.

Eventually, around 10 a.m., she decided there was only one way to put her mind at rest. Pushing open the door that hung lopsided on its hinges, Margaret stepped into the darkness. The rank stink of rotten food, old fires and human waste stuck to her teeth and filled her nose. Slowly, as she walked through the flat, step by careful step, her eyes began to adjust to the poor light. The place was a dump, an absolute mess. She couldn't believe any right-minded adult would go in there voluntarily. Somehow instinctively her steps led her towards the bed recess. Margaret was almost at the corner when she saw her, lying in a crumpled heap. Her body was bare for all to see, her eyes were wide open and her life had been snuffed out. It was her beautiful sister. Mima McDonald was dead.

'You can't go farther, hen,' the policeman, portly with wrinkles and grey sideburns, said when Ruth approached.

'Is that the murder scene?' she asked, smiling warmly at him and hoping to win him over. The answer to her question was somewhat obvious by virtue of the police cordon stopping people from getting near the flat and the number of uniforms and plainclothes men buzzing in and out of the close. But starting with the obvious was no bad thing. She was giving the man his place.

'Aye, it is, hen. A sad place to breathe your last, eh? But you're no' from round here, are you?'

The policeman had spent most of the day in Mackeith Street, stopping the locals from setting up camp at the scene, keeping an eye on unauthorised journalists and watching all the police activity in and out of the flat and out in the back close. He understood the locals' mentality of coming out to watch. Even in Bridgeton, a murder on your street was a bit of an event – especially when it was a neighbour, someone you all knew. A bit like the old public hangings, the cop thought, people were fascinated by the gory side of life.

'You're no' a reporter, are you?'

'No but I read about the murder in the papers,' she replied honestly.

'So you just thought you'd come and slum it in Brigton and see where a poor lassie met her end, eh?' His tone was sarcastic. 'Bad enough that the scum all turn up,' he said, nodding towards a group of adults nearby who all seemed relaxed – excited, even. Some were drinking from mugs of tea, a few of the women were still in gaudy-coloured house-coats and slippers and a couple of men were passing a bottle of beer between them. Ruth noticed how almost all of them were smoking. 'They've been hanging about there ever since that poor lassie was found but at least this is their street – know what I mean? You've a right to know what's going on in your backyard but you, hen, where have you travelled in from? Newton Bloody Mearns?' He had suggested one of the most expensive areas in Glasgow, one of the city's most well-to-do suburbs, and yet again Ruth cursed her accent.

'No,' she smiled. 'Partick.'

He nodded his head in approval at the mention of that working-class part of the west end. If, when Ruth had moved to Glasgow, she had happened to find a flat not in Partick but a hundred yards closer to the university in Hillhead or Hyndland, she reckoned the cop would have written her off as a toff or as the journalist she had denied being.

'Partick, aye,' he said, a note of approval in his voice. 'You'll be at the university, then, eh?'

'Yeah, I am. Just moved up last year.' She held out her open cigarette packet to him and he took one.

'What are you hoping to be? A teacher?' He flared up his fag with satisfaction. He didn't get many chances for a smoke on these boring watches with so many bosses about. Much easier when he was out on the beat.

'Eh, no.' Ruth quickly decided to miss out all the detail of her studying for a PhD and being interested in criminology. 'A psychologist.' She cringed and waited for the usual remarks about 'nutters' and 'funny farms' but none came.

'Good for you,' said the old cop. 'I have a lassie about your age up at Jordanhill College. She's going to be a teacher.' The pride in his voice was evident, unashamed.

'I'm just curious, you know, to get some idea of the type of person who does this sort of thing.'

'Aye, aye, I can see how that would be useful . . . for your studies, right? Like my lassie has to sit in classes with other teachers.'

Ruth nodded. 'It's a terrible thing to happen to a woman.'

'Aye and young as well – only thirty-two.'

Ruth had struck it lucky. The old cop had spent too many years standing around like this, a witness to what he considered real police work. He had tried to move up the promotion ladder and failed every time so was now condemned to work for his pension doing precisely what he had been doing since his first year in the job. His career had disappointed him but at least he had one consolation – he liked to talk.

'She goes for a wee night out to the dancing – just down there at The Barrowland so her sister says – a wee night out and ends up in that fucking dump.' The policeman nodded at 23 Mackeith Street and threw his cigarette butt on the ground, grinding it out harder than necessary with the sole of his black boot. 'There are some sick bastards about – if you'll pardon my French.'

'No offence taken!' She smiled and thought of adding a few curses as a joke but reckoned he wouldn't see the funny side. She marked him down as a man who thought men and women were different, had different tasks in life, different approaches and standards. Becoming a teacher or psychologist was fine but swearing wouldn't be ladylike behaviour in his book. As they spoke, Ruth watched four men in heavy donkey jackets and working boots go into the flat.

'Workmen?' she said. 'What are they doing here?'

'Naw, no' just workmen, hen – binmen. Excuse me a minute.'

The policeman stepped forward quickly to where a large group of children were hanging around, joking, laughing, playing pranks on each other and making a racket. 'Hey, you weans, I've told you before, beat it!'

None of them moved.

'Go on or I'll lift youse.'

A sea of small dirty faces with innocent angel eyes stared back at him.

'Get the fuck out of here or I'll boot yer arses for you.'

Now they shifted. Moving fast, the girls were squealing and the boys were laughing. They thought it was all a great lark but they also knew the threat was real. Coppers kicked kids up the arse or cuffed their lugs or worse whenever they thought they deserved it. They'd get no sympathy if they ran home to complain to their parents who would just tell them they must have deserved it and then they'd give them another slap for their trouble.

'Fucking weans around here,' puffed the policeman, going back to his position beside Ruth, 'wild as animals, so they are.'

'They seem full of mischief,' said Ruth, thinking that she was agreeing with the policeman, showing solidarity.

'Mischief? Bloody mischief?' He sounded insulted. 'That lot would rob ye as soon as look at ye. Do you know local weans found the body on Sunday morning? Fucking unbelievable. They all traipsed in to have a gander – even told some grown-ups but they're worse than the kids. Nobody did nothing till the next day when the lassie's sister found her. Thirty hours she lay there, they reckon. Fucking disgrace, so it is.'

'Poor woman,' said Ruth. 'The sister, I mean – she must have taken that badly.'

'Badly? Aye, you could say that. She's a mess of nerves. Keeps weeping and can't sleep. Says when she shuts her eyes all she can see is her sister, Mima, lying there. Think the doctor's had to give her something.'

'What about the kids?'

'Whose kids?'

'The dead woman's. I read in the paper she had three kids.'

'Aye, she did – oldest's only twelve.'

'What's going to happen to them?'

'Ach, I think the welfare's going to take them – end up in a bloody orphanage. Fucking shame, so it is.'

As he was speaking, two binmen emerged carrying a canvas sheet. It was stretched open and in the centre was a pile of what, to Ruth, looked like rubbish.

'Have they run out of bins?' said Ruth, trying to make a small joke out of it.

'Bins? Oh, you mean you think that's rubbish they're lifting? That's no' rubbish, hen,' the policeman said. He then turned to show her his profile and spoke quietly out of the side of his mouth. 'That's evidence.' And, obviously enjoying the melodrama, he followed this information up with a slow, conspiratorial wink. The policeman turned away to face the building again so that his back was towards Ruth.

Was he signalling the end of the discussion or showing her who was in charge by making her ask the next question? She had nothing to lose. 'How is that evidence? It just looks like . . . well, rubbish to me.'

Slowly the cop returned to his profile pose. 'They're having to sift through all the crap in there,' he said, nodding in the direction of the flat. 'And, believe me, it's a lot – the place is a fucking midden. And they're having to take the stuff out in the back green. Loads of the shite, so there is. We're going to be stuck here for bloody days.'

'Is it the murder weapon they're hoping to get?'

'No, no, hen, they've got that. It wasn't anything fancy.' And he illustrated his meaning by putting his own hands round his neck in a throttling action. 'With her own fucking tights, the bastard.'

'She was strangled with her own—' Ruth wasn't allowed to finish her question.

'CRAIG!' The shout came from over near the flat. Two men in lounge suits were standing there but they didn't have to be at a crime scene to look like detectives. Something about the

181

way they wore their civvies meant that they might as well have been uniforms. Did they all buy their clothes from the same shop? But identifying them was even easier than that. Ruth recognised the one who hadn't shouted – most Glaswegians would have. It was Detective Chief Superintendent Tom Goodall, one of the best-known detectives in the city.

In charge of the CID, Goodall had been involved in many high-profile cases. He'd arrested Peter Manuel, he'd been shot by an armed jeweller and he'd arrested John Duddy who, along with Harry Roberts, was involved in shooting three cops dead in London. But those few events didn't even scratch at the surface of the man's success as a detective. His portraits in the newspapers didn't show that he was a tall man with a stoop, who looked more university professor than top cop. But a top cop he was and Ruth knew that, if he was leading the investigation, Glasgow City Police were out to crack the case and fast.

'Craig, I've told you,' the plainclothes man with Goodall continued, 'keep the public back. That includes good-looking young women.'

Ruth didn't recognise the detective giving the uniformed cop the orders. It was former wartime fighter pilot Detective Superintendent Joe Beattie, a man with a huge reputation himself and one that was going to be tested to the full on the Mima McDonald murder.

'THIS IS NO PLACE FOR A FINE-LOOKING LASSIE LIKE YOURSELF,' the uniformed cop said to Ruth, loudly enough for the detectives to hear. Then he whispered to her, 'They didn't find a lot of the poor woman's things – that's why they're searching the rubbish.' Clearing his voice again he barked out, 'STAND BACK NOW, PLEASE.' Holding his arms out wide and moving towards her as if he was on crowd control. 'Some of her stuff's missing.'

'What?' Ruth said quietly.

'Her handbag, for one thing.' He looked to the side, noticing that Goodall and Beattie had moved farther back and were talking to some guy in a white coat. 'Another thing,' he said quietly, his lips hardly moving, 'they think it was her dabs.' From her eyes he could see his words hadn't registered with Ruth. 'The curse?' he said. He tried again. 'She was menstruating. The filthy, murdering bastard, eh?' Then he roared at her again, 'AWAY HOME TO YOUR MAN AND COOK HIS TEA.'

Ruth turned to leave. She was going away but it wasn't to cook anyone's tea. A young woman goes to The Barrowland, ends up strangled with her own tights, her handbag missing and she was having her period – almost a copycat of Pat Docker. There was more than a strangler on the loose. A serial killer was stalking Glasgow and Ruth was on his trail.

Wednesday, 20 August 1969

She showed me the way. In every way. She must have known it was her time.

Such a sweet thing. Trusting. Open. Ready for me. Worth waiting for and no question. Worth saving.

I knew she'd be there on the Saturday. She more or less told me so when we met that first time. She was sending me a message. COME AND GET ME.

So I did. Life changes so fast. It's a sign we are spinning to an end, to the Second Coming of Him. And He will Come Soon.

Only a year ago, the debauchery was worst on a Thursday night. Now it doesn't matter what night it is. It is debauchery. An orgy. Depravity every night.

I went there and waited and she came to me. To Me. Stepped right up in front of me and smiled. She might as well have asked me to cleanse her right there and then. But all in good time.

We danced. We talked. She laughed at my ways. I smelled poverty and children on her. She mentioned none of them.

I felt the men who had crawled over her flesh. She had eyes for only me. ME.

But I was impatient and had a problem. The Sabbath was coming. I like to be on my own on the Sabbath. It is a day of no work and I was doing the Lord's bidding. The Lord's work here on earth.

I told her I had to get up early. In truth I don't sleep. She was very understanding and happy that I walk her home early.

'Early enough for a wee time alone,' she said and smiled at me. A sweet smile, right enough. But I could see her. See her dirty fair hair dyed brown. See her lying alone in her bed at night, her mind full of filth, frigging herself as her children slept nearby. See her thinking that maybe I would rescue her. She wasn't wrong there.

Mima, she said her name was, and I asked what it was short for. Jemima is what I called her then and what I will call her always. She liked it. Said it sounded good in my voice, my accent. After all, mine isn't the voice of the gutter.

I only thought it right that she be given her christened name, her Sunday name, on that night of all nights.

Jemima and I walked to her home. A short stroll though the streets of the east end. Threatening is how some people see them. Not me. What do I have to fear? The Lord is My Shepherd.

Twice people nodded hello to her. At Bridgeton Cross a man called out. Fuck their interfering ways. Fuck them all. I knew that night they could not touch me. Could not save her. She was mine.

For a minute I thought she would invite me into her hovel but no. With an apology she said something about a babysitter and I smiled. The stupid cunt thought I was being kind.

The babysitter was her first hint that she had children at home. I didn't bite the bait. Nor did I run. A mother abandoning her children to lift her skirts for a stranger. She was perfect. She was the one. She had the Fire.

The area was wrecked – like the Luftwaffe had just paid a visit. Barren land and smashed houses everywhere. Not the work of any storm but the work of man. The bloody fools. Worse than beasts, they make hovels of homes and wade in their own shit. Bloody men.

She led me by the hand into one dilapidated building. Even in the dark she slid through the splintered wood, broken glass, dark piles of anonymous refuge effortlessly. Not one booby trap did she hit. She had been there before – with other men.

She opened her coat, her arms and her lips to me. There in the dark I could see the Fire in her eyes so bright I thought I would be blinded. But I've been fooled before and moved to discover it there in the depths of her folds. Just then she pulled her mouth close to my ear and whispered, 'Need to tell you I'm on the rag.'

She had the Fire. She told me she had the Fire. She was surely chosen by Him. She was ready to be Saved.

I cleansed her.

'We can't prove the murders are linked.' Detective Superintendent Joe Beattie was adamant, holding his ground. 'The possible ID we have is only going to be useful in the Mima McDonald case.'

Two nights after Mima McDonald's body was found, the police had gone to The Barrowland Ballroom and appealed for information from anyone who may have seen her there on the previous Saturday, 16 August.

'ID? It's not exactly enough for an identity parade, Joe.' Beattie's boss, Detective Chief Superintendent Tom Goodall, sat in the passenger seat, in the front of the car, while they were being driven to a meeting. As ever, the two detectives talked shop not soccer.

'Aye, well, that's The Barrowland crowd for you. Used to be Thursday nights was for the married cheaters. Now? It's any night of the week.'

In spite of the police efforts and Mima McDonald being a popular regular at The Barrowland, only a slow trickle of witnesses had come forward and most of them only gave statements when they were guaranteed they could do so in confidence. Many of the dancers who recognised Mima were cheating on their husbands or wives.

'Are you sure we can't make an identikit out of the descriptions so far?' Tom Goodall was frustrated that the system Glasgow Police used – which was based on an American system – wasn't up to the task. The method allowed various facial features to be grouped together, according to witnesses' descriptions, and, when it had been introduced a few years before, it was seen as a massive advance that was going to nail a lot of criminals. In spite of having a wide range of human features, hair types and head shapes available, the system was just too limited when witnesses gave sparse details. Rarely were there so few descriptions of a suspect as there were in the Mima McDonald murder case.

'I'm absolutely certain. When we try, it just looks like Mr Nobody.' Beattie was just as unhappy as his boss. 'But some of the boys are working on it. Maybe we can come up with something else.'

Tom Goodall was in charge of the case but Joe Beattie managed the day-to-day investigation. Beattie kept his gaffer well informed but had to make sure he didn't pass on every consideration before some action was being proposed. His job was to deal with the mechanics of the investigation while Goodall's was to take an overall view. Getting some likeness of a man that had been seen with Mima McDonald on the night she was murdered was subject to a lot of debate among the police squad. Even a vague likeness distributed among the police and shown to witnesses, neighbours and people at the dancing that night would surely progress the investigation big time. But not yet.

'Even if we did manage it, I believe all we have is some description of the man who may have killed Mima McDonald but not Pat Docker.'

'I know what you're saying, Joe, and that's how we'll present it to the boys. But you and I know that, if we can get a suspect for Mima, then we can work on him – check him out on what we know about Pat. Remember Manuel, Joe?'

'How could I forget?'

Joe Beattie had been key in charging Scotland's most lethal killer of modern times. They had worked on him to prove one case, then another and another. The ploy worked and Manuel was found guilty and sentenced to death. As he waited for the hangman and with nothing left to lose, he confessed to many other murders.

187

'That's all I mean here, Joe. Brick by brick – that's how we'll get success in these cases. We'll start with Mima but we both need to keep the links between the Pat Docker and Mima McDonald cases in mind.' In his usual quiet, almost distracted tone DCS Tom Goodall had returned to their earlier debate – one they'd been having for days. Those who didn't know him sometimes assumed his quiet approach and thoughtful stares betrayed a lack of intelligence, the absence of an answer. If they did, they paid the price.

'Links? As I say, Tom, I'm not so sure. Similarities, maybe.'

'Let's go over them again.' Goodall was a perfectionist. Some of his troops said he worried cases to death like a terrier at some bigger dog's throat. He went on to list the links, pausing after each one to allow dispute or disagreement.

'Good-looking young women. Married but separated. Both mothers. Strangled with their own stockings or tights. Murdered yards from their homes. Killed late at night. Possessions missing – presumed taken. Both menstruating. And last but certainly not least – The Barrowland Ballroom.'

Joe Beattie was nodding his head at the list they had run over countless times. Sighing quietly he said, 'The city is full of young women separated from their husbands, catching a night out on the town and, these days, even nice girls expect a bit of bodily comfort. Maybe Pat Docker and Mima McDonald are just two of a very large and vulnerable group.'

'Fair point,' Goodall replied while keeping his eyes on the road. Neither he nor Beattie was driving the car but Goodall always watched out, always liked to see what was coming his way. 'You mean like prostitutes are vulnerable to violent perverts just because they are there doing their trade in dark places and are, by definition, selling sex.'

'Aye, so these are modern times with ordinary, young women out there just getting on with their lives but their attitude to men makes them easy targets.' Beattie paused and followed his boss's gaze, trying to work out what he was watching, but he could see nothing except queues of slowly moving cars and pavements filled with pedestrians. 'That's one of my points.'

'Yet the things these cases have in common . . . maybe it's not the victims' circumstances that they define, Joe, but the killer's MO.'

'Of course but a lot of the so-called links are such ordinary thing – late at night, sexual contact, dark places, near the victims' homes but also out of the way, in the dark. Even the strangling – strong man, weaker women. Tighten her throat, kill her and stop her screaming at the same time. Hands – the most convenient murder weapons there are and totally legal to carry in public.'

'Aye,' Goodall agreed, knowing only too well, from dealing with so many murders on the streets of Glasgow, that what Beattie was saying was true. 'But usually the hands are used as fists to batter the victims. Strangling them and with their stockings on both occasions?'

'The tights were off anyway, making them useful weapons that leave no prints.'

'So two separate men would think about that while killing two separate women in the same city in just over a year apart.'

'Maybe . . . aye. Maybe . . . fair enough. Though the bit that bothers me is the women menstruating.'

'I think that's the key.' Goodall was keen on this link and Beattie knew it.

'But how did the killer know? And what sort of woman goes for some sex with a man she's probably just met when she's got her period?'

'Like you say, Joe, these are modern times so . . . modern women?'

'OK but some of our men are starting to see something spooky here. A killer who senses his victims are bleeding.'

189

'And?'

'And it's not helping them to keep clear heads. Polis are just as superstitious as everyone else – but they shouldn't be. If our lads start imagining a blood-sniffing ogre's out there, it's not going to help the investigation. And, if the public get hold of that notion, there'll be panic everywhere.'

'And what if we have?' asked Goodall.

'Have what?'

'A blood-sniffing ogre out there – the same blood-sniffing ogre who's killed Pat Docker and Mima McDonald.'

Tom Goodall watched pedestrians moving in and out of shops as the police car slowly crawled up Sauchiehall Street. Joe Beattie decided his boss had gone off on one of his dwams as the boys called them – one of those blank staring-at-nothing phases that you interrupted at your own risk and that was if he heard you – though usually he didn't. Usually he was too far away in his own thoughts. As Beattie watched the wise old detective in silence, he made a bet with himself about what he was going to say next.

'I've got a hunch about this one, Joe.'

There it was. Beattie knew it. You ignored a Tom Goodall hunch at your peril. Too often his hunches had been so right.

'I think we're dealing with a sexual sadist – a serial killer.'

Curves appeared as the pencil flitted and scraped over the paper. Then the curves began to merge into the shape of a jawbone, a fine unblemished jaw line but it wasn't yet clear whether it was that of a man or woman.

Lennox Paterson sat in his room at the Glasgow School of Art. As befitted the Registrar and Deputy Director of the School, it was a very fine room in a very fine building. In 1896, Charles Rennie Mackintosh, a Glasgow architect, who gave full vent to his unique style which would later evolve into art nouveau, had designed the city's art school building. Although that was the history, even to the untutored eye, the Glasgow School of Art was a very special building indeed. Everywhere there were arches, nooks and crannies, oddly shaped wooden carvings and elongated roses. And there were halls and doors leading nowhere. The building was at once beautiful and un-nerving. It was as if some danger lurked within – some ogre, some magical beast.

As Lennox Paterson's pencil continued to flit across the page, a nose slowly emerged. He was bringing back conversations to guide his muse. Vague, emotional, weightedconversations with two people he had never met before. Two people who never met each other. Two people unaccustomed to art and the way of artists.

The woman was a young redhead. She had seen the man sitting on a couch just for a minute but she had paid attention. 'He was that handsome,' she had said. 'Expensive suit – smart.'

Not useful – Paterson needed to know what the man looked like, not his taste in clothes. He didn't press the young

191

woman. The police had already done that and had not got very far. He chatted, just chatted, and let her take her time.

'Short hair, a nice reddish colour,' she added, stroking her own red locks as she did so. 'Tall – I like tall men. And slim, you know, but no' skinny.' She crossed and uncrossed her legs, smiling as she did so. 'Nice face – an, eh, even face. Does that make sense? No. Like he didn't have a big nose or ears and his lips were full but no' fat and no' skinny – a wee grin on them most of the time. Nice, you know.' She crossed her legs again and started to rub one stockinged knee with a hand, slowly. 'He was a good looker, all right. Maybe about twenty-five years old. A catch for any lassie.'

Lennox Paterson had learned a lot from that young woman. 'Sexual attraction has its benefits in more ways than one,' he muttered to himself as his pencil drew the hairline. A full head of hair parted at the left but with short sides – most uncommon in 1969. Except in the forces or the police, of course.

On a later day, the young man had gone to Paterson's room to describe the same man who he thought he'd seen in a pub. At least the police thought it was the same man.

'Right full of himself, so he was,' the young man had said. 'A show-off, eh? A bum.' He cupped the cigarette between the fingers of one hand, dragging hard and fast as if he was angry. 'Fucking swanning around like everybody should be watching him. A smile on his gob for no fucking reason. Fucking tosser.'

Within a short while Lennox Paterson was wondering if jealousy made as good a witness as lust.

'A fucking ginger minger he was and old-fashioned – short haircut like my da's and wearing a suit and a tie. Does he no' know it's the 1960s, man?'

Paterson didn't judge the young man – that wasn't his job. Instead, he sympathised and listened and tried to then tease more information from him – useful information about how the man looked.

'Lanky bastard – skinny as fuck and well over six foot. But nothing tae him. Fucking gust a wind would've done for him.'

Another hour of anger and an occasional description and the young man had served his purpose. In a sarcastic tone, he had confirmed certain aspects of the man's looks – the same ones that the girl had waxed lyrical over, almost wet herself over.

Then, when Lennox Patterson's pencil shaped out two eyes, the sketch came alive. Was that the man? He couldn't be sure. Was it the young woman's idea of the man? Now that he was confident of.

He picked up the phone and dialled the number. 'Detective Superintendent James Binnie, please,' he said.

Binnie had had the idea. It took him a little while to persuade Joe Beattie it was worth a go. If Lennox Paterson hadn't volunteered on the first asking, Binnie's proposal would have been dropped but Paterson had agreed right away. Now, as he sat in his office looking at the result on the pad on his knee, he wondered if it had been worthwhile. There was a man there, right enough. But what man? Was it *the* man?

'DS Binnie, here.'

'James, it's Lennox Paterson at the School of Art.'

'How are you, Lennox?'

'Good, thanks. How's life with you?'

'Same as usual – working every hour and not making much progress with this case. Too many people with too many secrets.'

'Maybe I can help you.'

'Oh, fantastic! Did you get anywhere?'

'Well, I've got a portrait for you.'

'Brilliant.'

'It isn't great, mind.'

'Anything will be of help, Lennox – anything.'

'Well, you never know – right now, I might be looking at your strangler.'

The group of young men swaggered towards her through the dark shadows of the ill-lit street, swords and bayonets in their hands. Shoulder-length hair flowed out behind them. Long straggly beards made some look ancient, brutal, fierce. Others, clean-shaven with smooth complexions, seemed young, innocent, safe. Crimson, livid scars were worn on all their faces, warrior make-up for the streets of Glasgow. Still they moved towards her, silent and stern-faced.

Ruth wanted to flee – take to her heels, cross the street and dive into the nearest shop doorway, the darkest tenement close. Yet she needed to stay, needed to keep walking on this side of the road, on this stretch of the pavement – the way Mima and her killer would have come the night she died. Ruth had to, no matter who was heading her way.

Still they strode on – one big stride after another. No one talking, no one smiling, no one looking away. Heading her way.

A panda car appeared in the sparse, swiftly moving queue of traffic. It slowed down and its occupants, two uniformed cops, eyed the group. Safety at last or was it? A second later, the car took off again, heading away at speed.

'Gone to fetch back-up,' Ruth reassured herself. 'The place will be crawling with cops soon.'

Still the team swaggered towards her. Most were wearing black leather coats. Some were three-quarter length, fitted at the waist – latter-day dandies spoiling for a fight. The rest wore ankle-length coats, tight at the shoulders, wide lapels, splaying full and wide near the ground. Sword carriers and maybe worse, she reckoned. One stood out. Younger than the others yet he was taller, his strides longer, his face more set, his eyes dead eyes. The leader, for sure.

She wanted to pee. Needed to pee. If she tried to run she would pee but she couldn't run. Couldn't break her plan. If they had come this way at this time, so would she. That's what Ruth had promised herself. Nothing the killer had done was by accident. At no time was he out of control. Ruth knew she had to retrace his steps, walk the walk he walked with her.

If she ran she would have to start again – wait a week till the next Saturday. Yet, with every passing week, the trail got colder, his scent weaker. It had already been a month and more. She couldn't abandon her mission. She might as well abandon her career. What would be left of her if she did? Ruth asked the question but feared the answer. This wasn't professional any more. This was personal.

They were so close she could hear their big boots clump-clump on the pavement. Then she could smell them – all leather and sweat and stale tobacco and beer. She held her head high and walked on, down the middle of the pavement as they closed in on her and parted, passing by effortlessly, silently.

Brazier heat flushed through Ruth's body, her legs felt both light and heavy at the same time. She was high – she knew that. The rush of fear had caused a state of euphoria that would pass soon if the east-end Glasgow street dwellers allowed it to. But it was late on a Saturday night in one of the roughest patches in one of the world's most violent cities. What else was going to happen?

Thirty or forty yards up London Road, she spotted the panda car again. The two coppers were sitting looking down London Road with interest. They hadn't gone to fetch help but had retreated in fear. Now they were just sitting watching a spectator sport that was better than any Saturday night TV.

Ruth heard shouting behind her and, a split second later, she watched as one policeman pointed and nudged his neighbour. The gang were coming her way again and, this time, they were running and screaming and waving their blades in the air. Ruth quickly staggered two steps forward and then she saw him – the young guy they were chasing.

They caught him easily and were on him, kicking and stamping him as he writhed on the pavement. Then, for her, it all turned from fast to slow, slow motion.

Two of the gang grabbed his arms and hoisted him to his knees.

Holding him by the wrists, they suspended him.

His head was bowed and blood dripped from his face.

The young leader nodded to one of his team who stepped in front of their catch and raised his bayonet high.

His arms came down and he stuck the long-bladed weapon into the young man's stomach and twisted it and then stood back.

Howls of agony filled the air.

Blood and blue-black tubes spilled on the ground.

Acid vomit burned Ruth's throat and she gagged.

The cops stayed where they were.

Slowly, slowly, slowly, the leader raised a long-handled, heavy-headed axe behind his writhing captive and brought it down into the back of his skull.

The howling stopped.

As his insides slowly seeped on to the pavement, they left him lying there. The cops didn't move. They watched as the gang got back in line and headed off again back down London Road, their blades and swords still in their hands, shouting, 'GOUCHOS, YA BASS! GOUCHOS!'

Ruth turned away and staggered on her route as she knew she had to. Numb, exhausted, nauseous, her night had hardly begun. She knew the worst was yet to come.

'Ho, darling, give us a smile.'

Ruth walked on, eyes to the front, looking down at the ground.

'What's wrong, hen? Boyfriend give you a dizzy?'

The man had moved away from the group of men hanging around Bridgeton Cross at what locals called The Umbrella, a cast-iron pagoda-shaped structure with a clock tower on top. In daylight, Ruth thought it looked eccentric – a strange folly that had landed slap bang in the centre of tenements, factories and pubs – a little bit of beauty in the middle of poverty. But, at night, it served a sinister purpose – drunk young men, looking for trouble, used it as a meeting a place.

'Give us a smile – go on.'

The man's voice had moved closer but she daren't look up. After witnessing the gang gutting that young guy, her nerves were frayed. If there was more trouble, she really didn't think she could handle it but the problem was that she was now in bandit territory – Bridgeton late on a Saturday night where no taxi strayed, buses rarely ran and even the police steered clear. Even if she wanted to leave fast, there was no hope. If she was looking for help she was on her own. Ruth had no option but to keep her eyes to the front and keep walking.

'LEAVE HER ALONE, YOU ARSEHOLE!' It was a different man's voice.

'What the fuck's it got to do with you?' Her admirer wasn't happy.

'Anything I fucking decide.'

197

Ruth started walking faster. She didn't want to get caught up in any street fight even if one of the protagonists seemed to be coming to her defence.

'Question is what do you want to make of it, ya bampot?'

'Who's a fuckin' bampot?'

'You. Scaring the lassie just weeks after that woman was murdered a street away. What are you? Fucking mental?'

'Ah didnae mean tae scare her,' her admirer protested in a voice that now dripped with his own fear. Who had challenged him in a way that had scared him so much?

'Maybe no' but ye did.'

'Did Ah, hen?' her admirer was shouting at her.

Ruth slowed and looked back at the two young men.

'Ah'm sorry, so Ah'm are.' Her admirer had his hands up in the air, palms to the front. 'No offence meant, hen.' He was backing off. 'Sorry.' He turned and walked back to join the men hanging around The Umbrella.

'Are you OK?' asked her protector.

'I'm fine, thanks,' she replied. She was surprised that there was no quiver in her voice betraying her real state.

'Aye, you sound it, right enough.'

He was moving closer into the yellow glow from a nearby street light, smiling at her, a warm smile.

'Did he put the creeps up ye?'

His dark hair was cropped into a crew cut and his skin looked sallow, tanned. He was dressed in a short denim jacket, polo shirt and straight-legged denims with huge turn-ups, below which were high-cut, thick-soled Doc Marten boots that shone even under the dull lights. The man wore one of the uniforms favoured by a certain kind of Glasgow street fighter – the kind who didn't follow trends, hated hippies and still followed traditional pursuits such as working in the shipyards, watching football and drinking in the old bars. To anyone who understood the dress code of Glasgow's streets, he was a frightening picture. Yet there was something about

198

his gallantry in coming to her rescue, something about the way he understood the impact of Mima McDonald's murder on all women in that area, something about his warm smile . . .

Ruth found herself rabbiting on about the gang on London Road and how she thought they'd harm her and seeing them do such terrible things to that man and the cops preferring to watch rather than intervene. 'It's been a bad night,' she said finally.

'That's the east end of Glasgow for you,' he said, still smiling. 'Life's cheap here. As cheap as chips. It doesn't explain something else though.' He stopped there as he lifted a cigarette he had been rolling to his lips and swiftly licked the gummed paper edge. Nipping stray tobacco from either end, he tapped the cigarette against the back of his hand, rolled it lightly between two fingers and passed it to Ruth. 'What's a lassie like you doing in a hellhole like this? Are you lost or something?'

Without knowing why, Ruth decided to take a risk on the man. 'Investigating a murder.'

'Aw, fuck! You're no' polis, are you?'

'No, no,' she giggled. It was a funny thought but that wasn't why she giggled. Her nerves were still jangling.

'Thank fuck, man, or I'd have to shout Baw Jaws there back,' he said, nodding at The Umbrella, 'and leave you to him.' Then he smiled wider, his eyes crinkling at the edges. 'Naw, I couldn't do that – no' even if you were the filth.'

'It's not the murder I'm investigating – more like the murderer,' Ruth said, somehow trusting this young guy she'd just met. But what else was she going to do? Lie? Why would she do that?

'Sounds a bit like the same thing to me, man. Like the polis, right enough. They say they're investigating a murder but really they're trying to nab somebody for it. Sometimes it's even the murderer they jail.'

'That's the difference,' said Ruth. 'I'm not out to jail anyone. Just to understand why.' She explained her studies as a psychologist specialising on criminals, especially killers, and how she had been to The Barrowland Ballroom several nights, chatting to people who might have seen Mima and the man. Once the people had decided she wasn't an undercover cop, they'd talk to her. She thought they were relaxed, chatty and telling her more than they were telling the police. 'I'm building up a profile of the predatory male.'

'The what?'

'Sorry, the men who go there on their own with the intention of snaring some female to have sex with – and worse.'

'Oh, aye, they sad bastards.'

'Except this one's not just sad – he's lethal.'

'Dead right he is.' There was no smile this time.

Ruth went on to explain how she had worked out Mima's likely route back to Mackeith Street. 'Along Bain Street, up London Road, turn into Landressy Street . . .'

'Good choice,' he interrupted. 'You could've gone through the Cross and down Main Street but that's dangerous as fuck at night. Landressy Street's safer. Mima would've come down that way.'

'Through the Cross then on into Mackeith Street.'

He was nodding his head. 'Then what?'

'Then see what he would see. Then go into number twenty-three.'

'Christ, you've got balls.'

'Thanks!' It was Ruth's turn to laugh. 'I think.'

'Aye, sorry, I mean are you no' feart? That place spooks the hell out of me.'

In truth, she had been frightened even before she set off, even before the gruesome events of the night.

'Want me to go with you?' Her jaw dropped and he noticed. 'Christ, no. Sorry, I see what you're thinking.' Ruth started to say something but he interrupted, 'No, no. I wasn't thinking. No' bloody thinking.' Then he looked away, spat a little blob of foamy white spittle through his teeth, kicked the ground with the toe of one of his big boots and turned back to her. 'Look, I'll tell you some things then you can decide if you want me riding shotgun or no'. If it's no, I'm out of here and no offence taken. Deal?'

'OK.'

'First things first, they call me Malky,' he said, holding out his hand.

'Ruth,' she replied, shaking his fist. The skin felt rough and calloused. A worker's hand. An honest hand?

'Second thing is,' he hesitated, 'I knew Mima. Knew her quite well. Went out with her a few times – you know, just for fun. She was a lot of fun was Mima – a lot of fun. Warm and kind, you know.'

'I'm sorry, Malky. Sorry she's dead.'

'So am I. Sorrier still I couldn't've maybe stopped her getting killed. Except I didn't, did I? Nice bloke Malky just let her walk on by.'

'I don't understand. How could you . . .'

'That's coming to the last thing I've got to say.'

'Hey, Malky, got yersel' a wee lumber, eh? Nice one!'

Across the street two old men were walking two old dogs. All four were scruffy, slow and of dubious origins – mongrels all. With no leads, the dogs walked ahead, stopping now and then to look back at the men, pleading with them to hurry up – like two grannies out with infants who were dragging their heels. The dogs were walking the men – making sure they got home.

'Airchie! Shuggie! You behaving, you two?' Malky called over with a wave.

Hearing his voice, both of the dogs stopped in their tracks and scarpered over to him, their big bellies wobbling as they moved, ears pinned back, excited, happy. As he bent down to pat and stroke the two dogs, both began yelping, pushing and vying for his undivided attention.

Malky spoke to the two men. 'You been out for your usual then?'

'Aye, a couple of hauf and haufs and then up the road. See you've been busy like?' the one called Airchie said.

'Aye and better looking than yer usual company,' added Shuggie.

'She's no' a Brigton lass then,' Airchie added as a statement but meant it as a question.

'No, she's no' local and, aye, she's a looker and no, she's no' a lumber and her name is Ruth,' Malky rattled it all off rapid style. 'That you two satisfied now then?'

'Pleased to meet you, Ruth,' announced Airchie. 'You could do worse than that one, hen – much as it pains me to say it.'

'Aye and you could do a lot better as well,' added Shuggie.

'How's that then?' Airchie asked his mate.

'Well, he supports the Hun, doesn't he?'

'Aye, right enough. I'd forgotten. Ye cannae see his spiked tail frae here.'

The dogs had found their way back to the men and were standing yards away on the pavement, willing them to follow. The men obeyed, shouting farewells to Malky and Ruth.

'There goes the two bravest men in Brigton,' Malky spoke quietly to Ruth.

'How?' asked Ruth, expecting some comment about army service or street warfare.

'Two homos living together openly. Takes some bottle in an area like this.'

She knew what Malky meant.

'And, almost worse, they're both Celtic-supporting Catholics.' Malky shook his head. 'This place is full of bitter Rangers-supporting Protestants.' Malky shook his head again. 'Most folk would've moved away but no' those two. They're Brigton men and in Brigton they've stayed.'

'Pals of yours, obviously,' said Ruth, watching the two old men and two old dogs slowly walk off.

'Aye, they are that. But that's what it's like round here

when you're local. Everybody knows you.' Malky laughed. 'No hiding place. No secrets.'

It wasn't just Malky who would have no secrets, Ruth was thinking, but Mima McDonald as well.

As if reading her mind, Malky went on, 'What were we saying before Nancy and Betty interrupted us?' There was no malice in his use of women's names for the old boys, just warmth and fondness and a bit of a slag-off – the Glasgow way of saying he cared for them without ever saying he cared for them. 'Aye, I saw Mima that night. Saw her with some bloke as they passed by back at the Cross – just where I saw you, actually.'

'The night she was killed?'

Malky nodded silently in response and Ruth noticed his eyes were moist.

'The guy she was with wasn't from hereabouts. Nothing unusual in that – Mima liked to meet new people, new faces. She was a warm woman.'

'So why do you say you could've stopped it happening?'

'The man – I didn't like the look of him.'

'Why?' Ruth was going slowly, trying to decide how best to get Malky to continue talking about the man who could be the killer. 'Was he, eh, rough looking?'

'You mean like me?' Malky smiled at her. 'No, no. Exactly the opposite. Big smooth prick – tall, good looking with no facial tattoos.' He drew his finger down his right cheek and for the first time she noticed a long curved scar. 'And he was wearing a fancy suit and a collar and tie. Stuck out like a skelped arse around here. But that wasn't it. He'd kind of fairish hair, cut short in a side parting like some fucking snobby, overgrown schoolkid. That's it. He looked like a kid dressed up in a man's suit. But that wasn't it entirely either. It was his smile. No, no' a smile – a smirk. That's it – like he was dead fucking pleased with himself, like he thought the rest of the world was shite. I just worried he thought that of Mima as well.'

'So what did you do?'

Malky was rolling another cigarette but looked up. 'Next to nothing.' His voice cracked. 'I shouted across to Mima, asked if she was all right. She said she was great and gave me a wave as she walked off with him down this way. Hand in hand they were and I'm watching them, but. Doing fucking nothing. Just watching. Then he did it.' He stopped to light his cigarette.

'Did what, Malky? What did he do?'

He picked a shred of tobacco from the tip of his tongue and said, 'He looked back at me over his shoulder – straight at me with that stupid smirk on his mug and gave a wee wave.'

Ruth looked at The Umbrella where Malky would've been standing that night and tried to bring the image to life in her mind. She could feel how that would haunt someone, someone with feelings – someone like Malky.

'OK,' she said to him.

'OK?'

'OK, you can come with me to Mackeith Street – into the murder house . . . if you want?'

'You sure?' he asked.

She smiled, took him by the arm and started leading him on the short walk to the scene of Mima McDonald's death.

'I'd be honoured,' she replied. As they walked, Ruth prayed she wasn't wrong.

Saturday, 6 September 1969

I love an anniversary.

Birthdays? I forget mine. I know why – misery and disappointment as a child. I'd listen to other boys talk about their presents or hear them invite lads to their homes for a party. Some would be so pleased they would even come and show me what their parents had bought them – even me. Then my birthday would come around and nothing. Nothing. Each year I'd pray that she would change. But she didn't. Every night before my day of birth, I'd lie in my bed and dream that the next day would be different from all the others. It wasn't. After a while it was easier just to forget that I was born. Forget when I was born.

Disappointment rots the soul and makes man weak. Best not to expect anything.

Don't wait to be given. Take.

Thursday, 25 May 1967. Now that was a day to remember. Most Scots were sitting in front of their goggle box watching Celtic become the first British football club to win the European Cup. But I have no interest in football. I have more serious callings.

The stroke had left her unable to move – apart from her eyes. She could see and hear and eat and drink and piss and shit. That's all she could do.

For a year, I fed her, bathed her filth, turned her in the bed, read her Bible, kept her alive. She couldn't speak but that didn't stop her from ruling me. They say humans adapt to compensate for a loss of a sense. So blind people hear more acutely. Deaf people see every detail. She spoke through her eyes. Not emotions. Not looking angry or upset or scolding. WHOLE FUCKING SENTENCES. SENTENCE AFTER FUCKING SENTENCE. WITHOUT FUCKING CEASE.

I heard her all day and it didn't matter if I left her room and went downstairs or outside next to the bushes or in the far corner of the garden – I still heard her. She spoke to me – all day, every day, every minute.

I would abandon her and take a taxi into the city but she spoke to me still.

In Church I'd kneel and pray and my own message to Him would be drowned out by her words.

At home at night, as I sat in the living room praying to the Lord to make her still, make her quiet, her words drowned out my prayers to Him.

Night after night, I couldn't sleep. I took to going to the pubs and drinking whisky. At home, exhausted and drunk, I'd check on her. And there she'd be, lying just as I left her – perfectly still and eyes wide open – but her voice stilled, silent at last. Downstairs I'd collapse on the sofa and sleep, deep, dark, warm sleep. Then she'd call to me again and I'd awake. Only minutes had passed.

My wits were deserting me. Then He sent me the passage to Salvation.

That night, Thursday, 25 May 1967, at thirteen minutes before midnight, I sat on her bed, lifted a pillow and cleansed her.

My mother is silent now.

I love an anniversary.

But now, tonight it's another I celebrate. My Jemima. Patricia is already laid out and waiting. My Jemima's handbag is on my knee and I hold it to me with one hand as I write. Soon I will open it and lay out her things – carefully, piece by piece. A purse with a few coins I know she has touched. A comb with a long thin handle that she has held tight many times. A bus ticket that took her on a journey. Hair rollers. My favourite. Those rollers that smell of her scalp. Smell of her musk. Smell of her sex. Smell of her soul.

It is nearing thirteen minutes to midnight. Soon I will see my Jemima again. See her as I did that night in our place. The place where I cleansed her.

I wish I was there.

The flat was in darkness. No one was at home. Ruth stood in front of 15 Mackeith Street and felt sad. Just a few weeks before it had been a family home and now it was dead – dead like the mother. Dead like Mima.

Questions flooded her mind. Questions that only became clear now that she was standing there where it had all happened.

Had they stopped on their way? Did Mima look at her home? Did he? Did he know that was where she lived? Why would they come here otherwise? What would she have told him? He must have known and didn't care. Or did he care? Did he want to kill her on her own doorstep?

Why didn't they go into her house? Did he think there was a man at home? Why would she tell him that? Some men would run a mile at the prospect of being tackled by an angry husband. Besides, there was no man at home for Mima – just her two wee men and her wee girl. He would've known about the children. That's why they wouldn't have gone into her place. Maybe she even told him that her sister lived across the landing. But her sister is a grown-up and probably knew Mima's ways. No, it was the children. She didn't take him into her place for fear that the children might hear and want to see their mother. Or was killing her in her home against his rules? So he knew about her children and still he killed her.

Even in the night, the murder house seemed so close to Mima's home – almost next door. With its empty houses and boarded-up windows and stretches of waste ground, the area was frightening to an outsider like Ruth. But this was Mima's backyard – the place where she went about her everyday life. Here, she felt safe, secure. Is that how he wanted her to feel?

Malky went on ahead and quietly cleared a way into the murder house at 23 Mackeith Street. Ruth waited, watching. Nearby house lights were on. Accordions and fiddles beat out old Scottish country dance music through some window – fast music, happy music. A family get-together maybe or some old couple reliving happier times? The music wasn't a lullaby. They'd be awake for some time as would many of their neighbours. He had stood here on this very spot and learned he wasn't alone. People were close by who might hear a scream or shout. Still he walked on into the flat to kill her.

'Psst, Ruth!' Malky was at the close mouth of number twenty-three calling her in a coarse whisper, waving her to follow him. 'You know the cops won't like you going in there?' he asked in the same whisper. He knew that they could easily be heard on that street.

'Yeah, I know but, if I want to do my research right, I have to take some risks.'

He nodded.

'But you don't have to, Malky.' She suddenly realised he wouldn't want to get lifted by the police. He was no doubt known to them and, while they might give her a bad time, they would probably give him hell.

'Me?' he whispered. 'Too late for me to worry about a couple of polis – I was thinking of you.'

'Why? I mean thank you but why?' After all, she'd got him into this situation.

'Well, you'll be a good girl, eh?'

Even in the dark she could see him wink.

'Ever been arrested before?'

'No.'

'If you were, what would happen to your studies? The university, would they chuck you out?'

It was a good question and one Ruth hadn't considered. That had been sloppy of her but, then, she didn't break into crime scenes every day. 'I don't know.' She was standing there at the entrance to 23 Mackeith Street, in view of any passing beat bobby and thinking. She had to decide fast. 'I have to take risks sometimes in this business, Malky. It's going to be the only way to get to some truth.'

'Fair dos but how's about I act as lookout? The cops have been coming round here several times a night since Mima . . .'

'But I thought you wanted to see inside?'

'To tell you the truth, when I got that door open, I felt like . . . I don't know . . . Like I was being disrespectful. Like I was standing on Mima's grave or something.'

Hardman Malky was possibly one of the most sensitive people Ruth had ever met – another lesson to her that appearances can be deceptive. Not always but sometimes. She nodded her head in agreement.

'Right, watch your feet in there, OK? It's dangerous.'

Ruth stood inside the doorway of the murder flat, letting her eyes adjust to the darkness and working out how it would have happened on the night. To help her understand, she began talking to the man, the killer, in her thoughts. 'You would've let her lead you, wouldn't you? Did she take you by the hand and guide you over the floor, apologising for the stench and telling you to take care?'

Ruth felt her way carefully across the floor, imagining the pair of them doing just that. Was Mima happy? Was she giggling? Excited about her new man and what was about to come?

'She stood with her back against this wall, didn't she? Here inside the recess so no one could see her nakedness even if they came through that door with a torch. Was she coy with you? Or happy and eager? Did she reach up to put her arms around your neck?'

Ruth stood looking at the spot in the recess where she thought Mima would've stood, imagining her face smiling up through the dark. She was a warm woman, Malky had said, with a warm smile. Ruth closed her eyes and saw Mima smiling up at him. A smile that said, 'Love me.'

'Did you take your time? Are you a considerate lover? Even with blood lust pumping through you? Or did you rush her, stripping her quickly, pushing aside her hands if she complained or told you to slow down?

'Did she tell you that she was menstruating or did you feel her sanitary towel through her pants? Is that what made you kill her or is that what you wanted of her?

'Do you need the blood?

'Do you need the blood to get hard? To feel a man?'

Voices drifted in from the street. Ruth could make out men's and women's voices, happy and friendly. They'd be strolling home after a Saturday night out, she reckoned. Friends – familiar with each other so no effort at show or showing off, just calm chat as they strolled home. Yet, in that murder flat, she could hear every word and, if she could hear them out there, they would be able to hear her from in there too – maybe not so clearly as she could hear them but . . . screams? They'd surely be able to hear that?

Making her way out, Ruth stood at the doorway and looked back. Did he do that too or did he hurry out, panic in his legs, sated now. She didn't think so. 'You walked out calmly, didn't you? You think you're safe. You think that you're protected. Invincible.'

In the close, Malky was waiting for her. Checking left and right down Mackeith Street, they stepped out and slowly waked away from the murder house.

'Did you get what you need?' he asked.

'Yeah, oh yes.' Her mind was still back there in that corner recess where he had killed Mima.

'So, what did you find out?' he asked.

'A few things about him and how he killed Mima,' she replied, suddenly feeling drained, exhausted.

'Anything really important?'

'Yes, the cops had better catch this man and quick. Before he kills again.'

'He doesn't look human.'

'So what are you? Some Hollywood heart-throb?'

'I mean you can't be sure if he's an ugly bugger or what.'

'Beauty is in the eye of the beholder. That's why only blind women go out with you.'

'Ach, it's just no' right.' The detective held up a piece of paper and looked at it again.

'It's a sketch, man, no' a photo – just a pencil sketch,' said his detective neighbour or what some other police forces would call his partner.

'Aye and the artist has done OK given they two numpties we sent him. But people don't think in sketches. I'm no' sure this is going to be any good.'

'Well, it's all we've got.'

'And it's too bloody late for debate.' Detective Superintendent Joe Beattie's voice took them both by surprise. They were in the middle of a big murder investigation and their boss had just walked in on them arguing about a drawing. That didn't look too good but at least it wasn't just any drawing but the sketch by Lennox Paterson from the Glasgow School of Art. The sketch of the man they believed had been seen with Mima McDonald on the night she was killed.

'Sorry, Sir,' barked one detective. Just because he was out of uniform and into a suit, it didn't mean he didn't need to show respect to authority, especially when the boss might think he was slacking.

'I should think so. Have you two nothing better to be getting on with?'

They knew what he meant. The squad had been carrying out more door-to-door interviews than the older cops could ever recall being carried out in any murder case before. They had thought that line of investigation had more or less been completed, their options exhausted. They were in for a shock.

'This,' said Joe Beattie, holding up a copy of Paterson's sketch, 'this is legal history.'

Around the room, he was being met with blank stares. They had seen sketches of suspects before. What was their boss talking about?

'This is going with you on door-to-door interviews. We're going to do them all again.'

Groans of complaint from somewhere in the room got a swift scowl from Beattie. 'Just remember there's a killer out there and the boss reckons he'll kill again.' He meant Detective Chief Superintendent Tom Goodall. 'He has a hunch and this,' he held the sketch up again, 'might just prevent us having to find out if his hunch is right.'

At the back of the murder investigation room, out of hearing, one detective quietly mumbled, out of the side of his mouth, 'Then again, it might no'.'

When Lennox Paterson had completed the sketch of the suspected killer, Goodall and Beattie decided they should use it as widely as possible. They had made some progress with witnesses but not nearly enough – too many were hiding too many secrets from wives and husbands about being at The Barrowland Ballroom. Goodall thought that being confronted with a drawing of the suspected killer might stir people's consciences as well as their memories. There was just one catch – they weren't sure it was legal.

In Scotland, pictures and drawings of suspects had been used among police officers but never publicly. Wanted posters, such as they were, or notices to the press were little more than written descriptions. Goodall reasoned that a picture, even a rough pencil sketch, would be much more effective. But Goodall was a top cop, not a lawyer.

He had gone to Glasgow's Procurator Fiscal, the man in charge of legal matters relating to the prosecution of crime in that city. He didn't know if it was legal in Scotland either. So he went to the Crown Office in Edinburgh with that same remit but for the whole of Scotland. There was a tense wait while the Crown Office lawyers considered the matter. Days and weeks ticked past – days and weeks of precious time in the murder investigation.

At one point, Goodall feared that the Crown wouldn't make a decision and the matter would be referred to the very top man, Henry Wilson, the Lord Advocate. He had a reputation of taking months on a judgement as he worried away over every small detail. That might ensure he arrived at the best legal decision but it would be a disaster for this investigation. Goodall didn't like it one bit. He had a killer to catch. But the Crown saved Goodall more anxiety and declared that distributing the sketch of the suspect was legal. So distribute it they did – using every means possible.

Glasgow citizens were shocked to find themselves looking at the front pages of their newspapers or watching the news on TV and being shown the face of a killer. They were becoming used to seeing pictures of killers on TV and in the press but they were always of convicted murderers who'd be locked up and out of harm's way. Now they were seeing the face of a man who was still free, still out there, still among them – a man who might kill again. Panic kicked in.

Had the cops' decision to circulate the picture been the right one? Had that sketch done more harm than good?

'I appreciate what you're saying, Mr McIver.' DCS Tom Goodall was talking quietly into the phone in his office dealing with a complaint. 'Yes, you have been cooperative in every way.'

The person on the other end of the line wasn't just an ordinary member of the public but one of the McIver family who owned the Barras flea market and, more importantly, The Barrowland Ballroom. The members of the McIver family weren't happy.

'I appreciate that police presence at the ballroom must have an effect on the public. I do. And I'm really sorry that your attendance figures are down.'

The Barrowland was only three quarters full even on the busiest nights. The McIver family blamed the cops' presence and their frequent appeals for information on Mima McDonald. They had cooperated fully so far even with the most detailed re-enactment Glasgow Police had ever carried out. A WPC, who looked very much like Mima McDonald, got rigged up in similar clothes and posed at the ballroom and walked what the cops thought had been her route to her death. In spite of two months having passed, the murder hunt was still front-page news and the papers played their part by publishing pictures of the look-a-like in several editions, over several days. Now the public had images of both the victim and the suspected killer. Surely that would stir some new leads?

'You've lost how much?' asked Goodall into the phone, hardly able to believe his ears.

It was well known that, when The Barrowland founder, Maggie McIver, died in 1958, she was a multimillionaire

215

– not bad for the daughter of an Ayrshire bobby. So there was money to be made, he knew that, but he still couldn't quite grasp how much he was being told – unless, of course, the businessman on the other end of the line was exaggerating?

'That's a great deal of money,' admitted Goodall, 'but how much more would you lose if there was another murder in your dance hall? If the next victim was also picked up at The Barrowland Ballroom?' He let that prospect sink in, knowing that it could have a disastrous impact on the ballroom.

'You don't think that's likely, do you?' asked the business-man at the other end of the phone.

'Oh, yes,' replied Goodall, 'I have a hunch that it will – if we don't catch him first.' Goodall deliberately played up to the public's image of him as a detective and his hunches. He also believed every word he had said.

'That would be terrible.'

'Yes, it would.'

Both men were in agreement but, for one, it meant a ter-rible loss of profits and, for the other, it meant a terrible loss for the next victim and her family.

'We must do everything we can to catch this murderer.'

'So, we can be assured of your full cooperation?'

'Of course – as always.'

Goodall put down the phone with a loud sigh. He had joined the police to catch crooks. He was good at that – en-joyed it even – and, when he left work at the end of the day, he felt he had contributed something to the city he lived in. Now the job had become part-diplomat, part-cop and, if you didn't succeed in the former, all too often you couldn't get on with the latter.

He had spent half an hour on the phone calming The Barrowland owners down and trying to get them to see the point of having a continued police presence there every night. Cops would stand by the door and take an occasional tour inside hoping that someone would want to tell them something, anything, about Mima or the man she was seen with.

There were side effects, of course, like the reduced attendance. The Barrowland owners had got that spot on. It was the cops many people were avoiding, not the prospect of meeting a killer. Some people would rather run the risk of being killed by some mad strangler than have the cops find out their business and risk it being revealed to their wives and husbands.

'That's Scotland for you,' muttered Goodall. 'Moral shame is a bigger threat than a killer.'

Tom Goodall knew the police presence meant other things too – like the fact that gang fights at The Barrowland had reduced to almost zero. As soon as the cops left, the gangs would be back but the management didn't mind that – after all, the street fighters had paid their entrance money before they hacked each other to pieces. If police work had taught him anything it was there was nothing so strange as folk. Nothing.

It was early evening and he was tired. It wasn't the hard work – he had never shirked that in his entire life – it was the lack of success in the Mima McDonald investigation and the Pat Docker one as well. He had tried everything he could think of in these cases – everything – but nothing had worked.

Mima's family had also clubbed together and offered a reward of £100. 'Bless them,' Goodall muttered out loud and he meant it. They had little money. They must have robbed every kitty they had put aside to pay every bill coming their way in order to raise that kind of money. It was a tidy sum but not huge. The grieving family took the view that they should try everything they could. It was an act of love for Mima and Tom Goodall felt for them. Good people – people on his side. But he also knew that £100 wouldn't be enough to tempt the terrified to share some crucial information and there were a lot of terrified people out there. It seemed to him that Glasgow was crawling with scared people.

It was October 1969. Mima had been dead for two months and Pat for twenty months and Tom Goodall couldn't see what to do next. The Barrowland had agreed to cooperate with one more public appeal on the following Saturday night. What he didn't tell them was that it was likely to be the last. Nothing much had come of all that police presence and, after all, they were right – why should their business suffer if the presence of the cops wasn't helping the investigation to move forward?

Goodall knew the cop presence was having another effect. It was keeping someone else away – the killer. That suited him just dandy. He might want to nail this man more than anything else right at that moment but he wasn't willing to risk any more young women's lives. They'd catch that killer without any more victims if Tom Goodall had anything to do with it.

Goodall sat at his desk, stretched and rubbed his face. He was tired – exhausted. The day had been long and it wasn't over yet. He had some meeting to attend to talk up the work of Glasgow Police to concerned local councillors – an example of the diplomacy part of the job. But something was bothering him. In spite of working it all through in his mind and having to concede the murder investigation wasn't going anywhere, he had that old feeling. I was hard to explain but there was a buzz like excitement beating in his chest – a fluttering feeling that he recognised so well. Tom Goodall had a hunch that something important was about to happen.

'Tom Goodall died last night.'

'Pardon?'

As Peter had spoken, the loudest cappuccino machine in the city had farted and fizzed, drowning out his words.

'Tom Goodall died last night,' he repeated.

He was sitting across from Ruth in a booth of the University Café near the bottom of Byres Road. He had phoned her early that morning, apologetic and breathless, asking if they could meet face to face for a short time. Like many other people, Peter had just had a telephone installed for the first time and he became nervous, chatting rapidly, when using the handset. So, when he'd said that he had something to tell her and it needed to be in person, she just put it down to his telephone awkwardness. How wrong she was.

'My God! The poor man.' Ruth felt as if she had known Tom Goodall through Peter and her study of Glasgow crime cases – known him and grown fond of him like other folk did with characters on the TV or some singer. She had hoped to meet him at some time but now that was never going to happen.

'Wasn't ill that we knew of.' Peter started to answer the usual questions when two friends talk about a sudden death.

'A heart attack?'

He shook his head. 'We don't know yet. Must have been something like that.'

'He'll be a big loss to the police.' Ruth meant it. You couldn't replace men like Tom Goodall with all their years of experience as well as their skill. Cops like him weren't simply recruited. They made themselves – on the job, on the street – and it might be some years before another emerged.

'Aye and going sudden like that means he was in the middle of some big cases – Mima McDonald being number one.'

'Excuse me. Sausage, bacon and egg here, was it?' A middle-aged, wiry-thin waitress stood at the end of their bench, balancing a plate full of food and a smaller of plate of white bread in one hand and two cups of steaming coffee in the other.

Ruth had arrived before Peter and ordered herself a fried breakfast and coffee for them both. She now regretted the food. It didn't seem right somehow. The waitress laid the food and cutlery out on the bench, pushed back strands of her greying hair, damp and straggly from the heat of the kitchen, and was off again.

'Still no breakthrough then?' Ruth asked, contemplating the food in front of her and trying to decide whether to eat it or leave it.

Peter shook his head as he took a sip of his coffee, grimacing from the scalding hot liquid. He laid his cup down and pulled his cigarettes and a lighter out of his pocket. He looked pale and shaken.

People reacted to death in different ways, Ruth knew that, and she guessed that Peter still had his parents and even his grandparents. Unlike her, the young cop was a stranger to death. She pushed her fry-up to one side.

'Tom wouldn't have been happy,' he said, blowing out a cloud of blue smoke and aiming it high over her head. 'He hated failing on a case. Saw it as a competition between him and the crook – in this case, the killer. He wouldn't have liked going with such unfinished business.'

Ruth noticed how Peter called Goodall 'Tom' and talked about his reputation as if he had deep personal knowledge of the man instead of only being involved in a few briefings with him. That was another way of dealing with death when you were struggling. The young policeman had a lot of life experience to catch up on – a lot.

'But he had a good team with him,' Ruth offered. 'Surely they'll carry on with his work.'

Peter shook his head and blew more smoke out, smoking faster than usual. 'In truth, the case was being wound down. Seems Tom had acknowledged that they'd tried everything and achieved next to bugger all.'

'Well, they . . . you have done a great deal. The re-enactments, the posters, the drawing of the suspect and the pictures of that WPC dressed up as Mima – difficult to see what else to do.' She knew she was comforting Peter in choosing that tack. What she really wanted to say was that they could bring in someone like her – someone who read the murder scene differently, someone who might give them an idea of who they were looking for and what he might do next. She had hinted to Peter that she would like to meet Goodall as part of her studies. But he was a lowly beat bobby and Goodall was head of the CID and a very busy man. She had held out no hope of the meeting happening that way. Maybe a letter from her on Glasgow University's Department of Psychology headed notepaper – just as Professor Pickford had allowed her to do before in requesting visits to prisons and some convicted men – would have done the trick. She had been biding her time till Goodall wasn't too busy with a case like Mima McDonald's. Ruth had waited too long.

'Aye and to make matters worse the press seem to have got fed up with the case.'

'Yeah.' Ruth nodded and tried to stop her attention wandering to the congealing sausage, bacon and egg by her elbow. She was hungry. 'Two months isn't bad to hold the media's attention – without some fresh blood being spilled, that is.'

'Aye and nobody wants that.'

'They'll move on though – probably to the Paddy Meehan trial.'

221

'Is that soon?' Peter asked, knowing she was referring to the bloke who stood charged with the murder of elderly Rachel Ross in Ayrshire. The same man who said he had an alibi in the form of his partner in crime, James Griffiths – the same Griffiths who led the cops on a shoot-out on the Glasgow streets. The same cops who eventually shot him dead though all they wanted in the first place was a statement about being Meehan's witness. All that and more made it a racing certainty that the Paddy Meehan murder trial would preoccupy the press and poor Mima McDonald would be forgotten.

'Yeah – in a couple of days in Edinburgh High Court. I was thinking of going through to watch some of it. That Meehan's an interesting character.' Ruth wasn't wrong about that and nor was she wrong to suspect that Paddy Meehan's story was about to become even more interesting. 'Come to think of it, Goodall would've been down as witness.' She wondered how many other trials would now be denied his expert evidence. 'What'll happen to Mima's investigation now, then?'

'The central CID boys and Flying Squad will withdraw.' Peter was lighting another cigarette and slurping at his cooled coffee, a faint white froth moustache clinging to his upper lip. 'It's already been placed under the full control of Eastern Division, under DS Jim Binnie – a good detective but he'll not get any extra manpower or anything.'

'And The Barrowland? Will the work there continue?'

Peter shook his head. 'No. Goodall had already decided that would end. Was getting us nowhere and having a bad effect on their business.' He shrugged.

'That means our strangler might get busy again,' said Ruth, 'at his favourite hunting ground.'

'Aye,' replied Peter, 'and you know what worries me as well?'

'Tell me.'

'Tom Goodall had a hunch about this case.'

'One of his famous hunches, yeah?'

'His hunch was that the same man killed Pat Docker and Mima McDonald.'

'He'd have had no argument from me there,' said Ruth, nodding her head vigorously.

'But it seems not everybody in the murder squad shared Goodall's views. And there's worse. His hunch also said that the murderer wasn't finished.'

Ruth was nodding her head in agreement again as Peter knew she would, her own views being supported by one of the best detectives of that era.

'With Goodall away, there's nothing and no one to stop the strangler killing again.'

'Sooner rather than later,' thought Ruth. 'Sooner rather than later.'

BOOK

of

HELEN

'It's such a shame you can't get longer off, George.' Helen Puttock was sitting in the front room of her house at 129 Earl Street, Scotstoun, talking to her husband over a cup of tea.

'I know but I take every chance I get for leave,' he replied. 'You know that, Helen.'

'Aye, I know but the boys miss you.'

On cue their sons, David and Michael, came in from playing together, hungry as usual.

'You do, don't you, my wee darlings?'

The boys looked at their mother, smiles and puzzlement written all over their faces.

'Miss your daddy?'

Of course they did. They readily agreed and with good reason. George doted on his boys but he didn't get the chance to spend time with them too often – the British Government and the Cold War with Russia saw to that.

Helen Gowans, as she was, had been down south in Wokingham visiting her brother, Sam, a few years before when she met George Puttock. It had been attraction at first sight. She was a slim, bright-eyed brunette and he was a tall, ruggedly handsome squaddie. By the time she returned to her mother's house, she and George were together and, a short while later, they were married in Glasgow. It was a love story but one with a problem – George's work.

Before they'd met, George had signed up for eleven years' service in the British Army serving in the Royal Electrical and Mechanical Engineers, the REME. He enjoyed his work and he was good at it – plus the money was steady and more than most working-class jobs on Civvy Street paid. But they were young and in love – what could get between them?

And then he was posted abroad. Bad Godesburg in what they called West Germany wasn't the most exotic of locations to be based but that's where British and other western forces were required in case of attack by the USSR. The USA's failed attempt, using CIA-trained Cuban exiles, to invade Cuba that culminated in disaster at the Bay of Pigs had only occurred in 1961. Worse had followed, in October 1962, when the USSR had installed missile bases out there. The crisis saw Presidents Khrushchev and Kennedy at loggerheads and brought the world to the brink of nuclear war.

All that might have seemed a world away from the lives of Helen and George Puttock but seven years was a very short time in international diplomacy and British troops remained stationed near the USSR border in numbers. So, a strategy to avoid another world war was what almost ruined their marriage.

At first, Helen and the two boys stayed at home with her mother, Jean Gowans, in Earl Street, Scotstoun. Jean had separated from Helen's father some years before and Helen was returning to the home her mother had made for her, her two sisters and her brother. It was like a home from home. Yet it wasn't her home.

Helen was a young, passionate woman in love with her husband. Soon she had upped sticks and gone to join him in Germany. What had started as an act of devotion ended up as a big mistake.

Helen hated Germany. She couldn't pick up the language and it seemed to her none of the locals could or would speak English. With two young children and no readily available babysitter in the garrison, she had no social life. Helen loved to socialise – always had – but now she was just a housewife and a mother. She felt old before her time and she didn't like it. When she and George starting rowing, she decided there was only one course of action that could save her marriage – returning home.

Friends and family were concerned that Helen and George had separated but she reassured them that was not the case. And, when Helen went back to her old ways of going out to pubs and clubs when money would allow, they became even more concerned. But their worries were knocked on the head when George turned up in Glasgow to stay with his wife and sons every time he had leave.

These were very happy times for the family – everyone could see that. Helen had managed to get her own place, a council house, along the road from her mother's, at 129 Earl Street, Scotstoun, in the west end of Glasgow. It was a good working-class area where people were friendly and everyone knew everyone else. It bordered on upper-class areas like Jordanhill and that brought benefits like the well-kept Victoria Park with its pond, swings and chute and, best of all, wide spaces of grass for Michael and David to play. As well as being close to her mother's, her new home was not far from her older sister Jeannie's home. Jeannie lived in Yoker, the neighbouring area to Scotstoun.

Money was tight. Caring for two young boys on her own was a challenge but with her mother and sister living nearby she always had support. Also, her man might have lived in another country but that wouldn't last forever and, in the meantime, he came to stay every chance he got. And so, with Helen now having got her pals and social life back, the world wasn't too bad a place for her – not too bad at all.

'Oh God, look at the time!' Helen was up and rushing to her bedroom. 'Here's me sitting blethering to you three when I should've got ready ages ago.'

George just shook his head and laughed. Noticing their father smiling, the two boys joined in.

'After your mum goes, we'll have something to eat and watch a bit of telly. OK with you two?'

The two lads nodded at their father, knowing he'd let them stay up a little later than their mother would – not too late, though.

'Oh, damn! Damn, damn, damn!' Helen's voice floated through from the bedroom.

'What's wrong?' George shouted.

'I've dropped my perfume,' she replied. He could tell as the smell of flowery scent came wafting through the house.

'Is anything broken?'

'No, no – just spilled. My good perfume – what a waste!'

A short while later, Helen's sister, Jeannie Williams, arrived looking all dolled up. The mother of three young children, Jeannie'd had bad luck in relationships. She'd been married twice – the first marriage ended in divorce and she'd separated from her second husband just a short time ago. Good looks certainly ran in the Gowans family – like Helen, Jeannie was very attractive.

Relaxed and vibrant, she shouted through to her sister Helen, 'What? No' ready?'

'Just about there,' came the reply, 'I spent too much time gabbing to George and the boys.' It wasn't like Helen to be running late. She always liked to be in control. She also liked her clothes and make-up to be perfect and would spend however long was necessary to get herself ready and looking her best.

'We've plenty of time,' said Jeannie. 'Just relax.'

When Helen appeared in a short, sleeveless black dress and black shoes, she looked beautiful. Her thick brunette hair was sitting just so and she was wearing her favourite bright red lipstick that showed off her pretty smile to good effect.

George Puttock must have felt very proud of his beautiful young wife. Helen was the type of woman most men would've been proud to be seen out and about in the town with – except he wouldn't be seen with her that night. He expected as much and had got used to it and accepted it. That night, he would be staying in looking after his sons and, when

230

they went to bed, he might have a beer and watch some TV. It would be a pleasant night, a relaxed night but one not spent with his wife.

'Ready?' Helen asked her sister as she put on her fake ocelot fur coat, the absolute height of fashion and admired by everyone. 'We'd better go.' Helen bent down to kiss her sons.

'Take it easy, Helen,' said Jeannie, picking up her handbag and heading to the door. 'No matter how long we take, it'll still be there waiting for us.'

With a final wave and cheerio, Jeannie and Helen left the house to go out for the night. It was Thursday night, a special night – it was Palais Night at The Barrowland Ballroom.

Thursday, 30 October 1969

Idiots. What do they take me for? Just another fool like them? Do they think I'm not in this world? Do they think I know nothing? See nothing?

At first they flooded my place with police. So what did they expect me to do? Walk in with my hands in the air? Surrender to those thick pricks of flat-footed bobbies? I might but only when my time is right. When He tells me I am ready. If He tells me I am ready.

Surrender? Why? That they don't understand my calling by Him is no surprise. At first I didn't understand it myself and struggled with what He was telling me to do. I understand it now.

Their game of cops and robbers doesn't upset me at all. Did they think I would become a hermit? The city and I are old friends. She sees me as Her saviour, as well She might. I went out and about and She sheltered me. I just avoided the uniforms at my favourite place. I may be chosen but that does not make me stupid.

The drawing they issued of me is a farce. Who combs their hair that way and the scowl – what a scowl. Mine is a face at peace with my Lord. A comforting face. A pleasant face. A face people trust. Why did they draw a man tormented?

My age is right but then they have used a whole decade. I am at the young end of their guess but appear ageless since the power of my Father is within me and His light shines through me.

Red hair? Do people only see what they know themselves? My guess is that some carrot-top gave the police a description. A girl in a bar once told me my hair was fair with auburn streaks – streaks that seemed like gold to her or so the slut said. She was drunk but still saw more clearly than those who would judge and jail me.

Do they think I am not of this world? Locked in some coffin like some cheap Hammer-House-of-Horror Dracula and only coming out at night?

Even as it pains me, I live in the world. Yes, He has shown me the Light but He has also shown me the Way. Their plans are known to me not through Him but through men. The idiots have let me know their thoughts and read their plans. I am within them but they do not see.

Another chosen one said, 'Render therefore unto Caesar the things that are Caesar's.' For once I believe he is right. Tonight I will give Caesar and his legions their just rewards. Tonight I will go dancing.

'Look, there's Marion and Jean,' said Helen, nudging her sister Jeannie.

'So it is,' replied Jeannie, waving at their two friends. 'That was well spotted in this crowd.'

The two sisters had arrived in the city centre at nine o'clock and decided it was too early to go into the dancing. Most people didn't arrive there till about ten o'clock when the pubs closed and they were no different. The Traders Tavern in Kent Street, close to The Barrowland, would do them nicely as it had many times before. When their two friends, Marion Cadder and Jean O'Donnell, joined them, they ordered whiskies and started gossiping about the week gone past.

The two women were particularly keen to hear about Jeannie's week and how her separation was going. Jeannie was a regular at The Barrowland but on Thursday nights only. Helen, on the other hand, went dancing at least twice a week, sometimes at the Albert Ballroom, a higher-class sort of place in Bath Street, but most often at The Barrowland. Sometimes she went with her other sister, Patsy, sometimes she didn't.

Because Helen was the sister who socialised more, Marion and Jean saw her more often than they saw Jeannie or Patsy. When they heard that Helen's husband George had arrived back from Germany after several months' absence, neither of them was surprised that she was out at the pub and heading for the dancing, leaving her man at home with the kids. This often happened and sometimes Helen even stayed out all night, saying she was staying with a girlfriend. No matter what other folk might think about this seemingly unusual relationship, George and Helen appeared quite content and at ease with the set-up.

The Traders Tavern was heaving with its usual locals and, that night, the number of drinkers was swollen by the older crowd heading to The Barrowland. Men and women eyed each other up across the crowded bar, making mental markers on those they fancied so that they could try to get a dance with them later. With so many people in their best clothes, all of them excited about the night to come, it was party time already.

'Aw for Christ's sake!' roared a man in a good suit, reeling back from his position at the bar. 'You bogging bastard.'

Around the room, people were craning their necks to see what the problem was. It wasn't just that they were nosy – they were on the alert for a fight kicking off, as they often did. At the first sign of that kind of grief, they'd be out of there fast.

'Sorry, pal,' said a small, thin man, his wizened face topped by a red tartan bonnet that matched his red tartan jacket. A lot of Glaswegians would recognise the man as the busker who played a double tin whistle. He targeted queues for cinemas and ballrooms all over the city.

'Should fucking think so. Look at my good dancing suit.'

'Aye, sorry about that, Jimmy.' And just to prove he was genuine, he stuck out a mitt and started rubbing the offended drinker's jacket. A sour smell wafted through the pub as he wiped off the vomit he had just spewed over his neighbour.

'Fucking leave it, man, you're just gonnae make it worse.'

'Aye, he'll leave it aw right,' announced the barman who had been serving the offender drinks for hours but somehow failed to notice his state of inebriation. 'He'll leave the fucking pub. Come here, you.' And he hiked the wiry man up by his jacket shoulders from the rear and marched him to the door as his booze-sodden legs struggled to place his feet on the floor. Before they reached it another pool of sick splattered over the floor. It didn't look as if any tin whistle would be getting played that night.

It was just another busy night in the Traders Tavern. Thursday nights always were but Helen and the other women liked it there.

After three or four whiskies and just before the bar staff rang the bell for closing time, the women agreed it was time for the big event – the dancing. In only a few minutes, the group of young women were there under the bright lights that declared 'The Barrowland'. They chatted away, feeling excited and buzzing with the prospect of what was to come as they patiently queued to go in. They had left the pub a few minutes early hoping to beat the rush but too many dancers had tried the same tactic. The friends didn't mind. It was all part of a night out. They stood with their four shillings in their hands ready to pay and get in as soon as possible and find the fun. Nearby a wobbly-legged man in matching red tartan bonnet and jacket was playing a tin whistle none too musically. Not many pennies were going his way that night.

Inside, the four women rushed to the cloakroom to leave their coats, check their hair, touch up their lipstick and apply a spray of perfume. Now they were ready for the action. They split up, with Helen and Jeannie pairing up which allowed Marion and Jean to go their own way. It was easier to hook a man when you were in a pair.

Helen and Jeannie first went to a room downstairs called Geordie's Byre. It was a small dance hall where records were played. It was always great fun there but it was just a warm-up for the real deal upstairs. The Barrowland closed at midnight. With their drinking time, the two women had to pack a lot of enjoyment into two hours but, then, so did most other people there that night and upstairs it showed.

The live music flooded their ears and made their hearts pound even before they entered the bigger hall. Walking through those doors seemed like walking into a sea of music, light and bodies, all moving, jigging, celebrating life.

Almost immediately, Helen and Jeanie were asked to dance

and dance they did. A few partners later and they were asked to dance again – this time by men who weren't together but that was OK. The two women were experienced enough at the dancing to know that, all too often, they wouldn't both fancy a couple of male friends who came to ask them for a dance. Besides, they were both old enough to look after themselves – and they were popular enough never to be without a dance.

Jeannie's partner turned out to be a good dancer – something she really appreciated, being swift and smooth on her own pins. She preferred the older style of music so she could jive and twist – proper dancing – and so did her partner. He was good looking enough but just not her style. Jeannie was a free agent again but in no hurry to get landed with another man. A night just dancing would do her fine and there would be nothing more apart from maybe a wee kiss and cuddle if he asked to see her home.

She checked round the hall to see how her sister Helen was doing. The two of them always kept an eye out for each other – they always had but more so since poor Mima McDonald was murdered a couple of months before. Jeannie had no need to worry. There, not far across the hall, was Helen in the arms of a tall, good-looking man and she seemed happy and relaxed. She would be fine so Jeannie turned back to her own dance partner.

'I'm Jeannie,' she said.

He cocked his hand behind his ear, struggling to hear her as the band struck up their next number.

'I'm Jeannie,' she repeated. 'What's your name?'

'Me?' The man smiled and laughed. 'My name is John.'

'I made a fortune last year.'

'Pardon?'

'After the big gale – I had so much work that people were willing to pay over the odds to have it done quicker.'

'I'm sorry, I can't hear you,' said Jeannie, struggling against the loud music and the raucous verbal pleasure of the hall full of folk.

'Roofer,' he pointed above his head, 'fixing the slates.'

Jeannie nodded but she wasn't hearing all he was saying and wasn't too interested anyway. She was soaking up the atmosphere, enjoying the night. Yet the guy was trying his best and being polite.

'Where are you from?' she asked, not being that interested but thinking it was nice to be nice.

'Eh, Castlemilk,' he answered, after what should've been a needless hesitation – unless he was lying, of course. In saying Castlemilk, he'd named one of the largest housing schemes in Glasgow. It was so big that Jeannie was none the wiser as to where he came from. It reminded her of the joke about the American and the Scot talking and, when the former found out where the latter was from, he asked if the Scot knew so-and-so since he also lived in Scotland. Then there was his name – John. Half the men in The Barrowland were pretending their names were John. He was married, for sure, Jeannie concluded – married and lying but that was OK by her. She had already decided she wanted nothing from the man apart from a few hours' dancing.

'Hiya!' Helen arrived by her sister's side in a flurry of energy and excitement. In tow was the tall good-looking man she had been dancing with for most of the night. 'You having a good time?' she asked Jeannie.

'Aye, great,' Jeannie replied. 'You seemed to be enjoying yourself.' She nodded behind Helen to her smiling escort and Helen giggled.

'This is John,' Helen said.

'Funny that,' said Jeannie, 'this is John too.'

The two women laughed while Jeannie's John looked on, seemingly unsure of himself, tongue-tied. Helen's John was an entirely different matter. He didn't say anything either but he smiled and somehow seemed confident and sophisticated. Right away, Jeannie could tell that he looked the part.

Helen's John was tall and slim, aged around twenty-five with short fairish-red hair in a side parting and pale skin with ruddy cheeks – handsome in anyone's book. His single-breasted, brown suit hung just right and its style was Italian. A light blue shirt with a dark striped tie and short suede boots completed his outfit. The total effect was chic and he knew it.

As they chatted between numbers Helen's John was relaxed, humorous and spoke with an educated, polite Glasgow accent that Jeannie had only heard before up the west end near the university or from a doctor, priest, teacher or the like. Helen was hanging on her John's every word.

Moving closer and looking up to hear what he was saying, Jeannie noticed some imperfections. Two of his front teeth overlapped slightly and he had a tooth missing at the side though far enough back not to be disfiguring. His dental flaws were only minor imperfections – after all, at that time in Glasgow, many people had had all their teeth removed by early adulthood. But they were imperfections, as was his constant fidgeting with a small badge he had on his lapel. Any time he was talking to someone, his hand would automatically go up and he'd finger the badge as if he didn't want anyone to see what it was. Why didn't he just take it off? Wasn't he allowed to remove it? What sort of badge must a man wear all the time?

'Jeannie Williams, by the way,' Jeannie had said as a way of declaring that she and Helen had no secrets.

He smiled and replied, 'John Temp . . .'

The band had started playing again.

He rolled his eyes and smiled. 'John Temp . . . n.'

But she still couldn't catch his surname. It didn't matter – he had done enough to convince her that he wasn't married.

As the dance drew to a close, Helen and Jeannie went to the cloakroom to collect their coats and the two Johns headed off to get their coats from the gents. The women went to the toilet, sorted their hair and touched up their make-up. Jeannie also changed from her dancing shoes into her boots.

'Where are they?' asked Helen as they emerged into the foyer.

Even though they would have had a great deal less to do than the women, the two Johns were nowhere to be seen. Eventually, the men appeared and Helen's John was in the throes of putting on his scarf. He placed it carefully round his neck, smoothed it flat against his body, neatly crossed the ends over each other and then put his coat on. He was like a small, fussy child repeating the rigmarole a parent had taught him.

'What a mammy's boy your John is, Helen,' Jeannie said.

Her sister just smiled.

John might have been a better class of bloke than the usual rough-and-ready types who frequented The Barrowland but was he cosseted, too soft? Jeannie wondered if he still lived with his mother.

In the light of the foyer, Jeannie noticed that Helen's John wore suede boots that were out of the ordinary. They were boots, all right, but cut away to give them an unusual shape. Very trendy – Italian probably – and they would've been expensive.

Having just changed into her own boots in the cloakroom, Jeannie decided to tease Helen's John. 'You're not the only one with kinky boots on,' she said to him, pointing to his feet. 'I've got my kinky boots on too.' She lifted one foot coquettishly.

It was meant as a playful remark but Helen's John didn't see the funny side. His face fell into a scowl, like a small boy taking the huff. This was clearly a man who couldn't take criticism.

Jeannie had run out of cigarettes. All night she had passed hers around and the others had accepted them with little in return. So she went to one of the cigarette dispensers in the foyer and put her money in but, no matter how she tried, she couldn't get any cigarettes out of it or her money refunded.

When Helen's John discovered what had happened, he said he'd sort it out.

'I demand to see the manager,' he said in a loud though polite voice. 'There is a problem. I wish to see the manager NOW or there will be trouble.'

'Just leave it, John,' said Jeannie.

'I will not.'

'John, we don't want any trouble,' pleaded Helen.

'There will be no trouble,' he said, 'for us.' His smile had gone. Now he looked cold and determined, detached and dangerous.

A thickset man with a scarred face, bulky biceps, a wide neck and a barrel chest turned up. The manger looked as if he could break a polite man like Helen's John without losing sweat. Instead he tried to reason.

But Helen's John was having none of it. 'Do you know who I am?' he said, almost frothing at the mouth. 'I have influence and I know my rights. With one phone call, I could have this place shut down like that.' He snapped his fingers to make his point.

'John, please don't,' said Helen. 'Look, I'm sorry,' she said to the manager, realising that this scene was in danger of getting out of hand and it was all over the price of a packet of cigarettes.

John brought something out of his inside pocket and showed it to Helen as he whispered in her ear. Her eyes opened wide, then she smiled. She didn't try and stop John from arguing with the manager after that.

From where Jeannie stood, she thought it looked like an official ID card and moved closer to see better. John quickly put the card away and went back to haranguing the manager.

'Who is the MP for this area?' demanded Helen's John. 'Who is he? I will personally write to him to make sure he's aware that this ballroom steals from its patrons. Deliberately runs cigarette machines that takes their money.'

'Calm down, please, Sir,' said the manager. 'These things happen. They're nobody's fault. See the assistant manager downstairs. He's in charge of the machines.'

With that, the manager stormed off, having had enough of what appeared to everyone, apart from John, to be a pointless overreaction.

'Dens of iniquity,' John blurted, 'my Father says all these places are dens of iniquity and He is right.' John stormed off to find the assistant manager, leaving Helen and Jeannie flummoxed. Had he just quoted the Bible or something? They weren't sure.

Helen's John never did find the assistant manager and Jeannie never got her cigarettes. Instead, the foursome went out into the night to walk the few hundred yards to the taxi rank at Glasgow Cross.

'Look at they fucking boots, man!' laughed one young man pointing at Helen's John's suede boots as they headed for Glasgow Cross. All the young guy's mates turned to look.

'Fucking brothel creepers, right enough, eh?' said another.

'Pervo's shoes,' laughed a third. 'You a fucking pervo, man?'

Helen's John said nothing. He just ignored the young men and kept walking with his eyes to the front as if he didn't care. But the fury in his stare and his tightly clenched white fists told a different tale.

'What are you doing now?' Helen's John suddenly demanded of the other John, Castlemilk John.

'Eh, it's OK,' he stuttered, 'I'll just catch a bus at George Square.'

Jeannie didn't mind him going off home. She wasn't surprised as she'd paid him little enough attention all night. Helen's John's behaviour had demanded her eyes and ears. She was beginning to think of him as Strange John. Yet her John, Castlemilk John, had suddenly changed his mind about seeing her home and she didn't know why. He had been very quiet for the last part of the evening – ever since he and the other John had come out of the gents. What had they been doing there that took so long? Had the other John said something to him?

'I'll maybe see you sometime.' Jeannie waved after Castlemilk John who gave a curt wave back and hurried on his way. Somehow she sensed she'd never see him again. Or would she?

'What are you doing now?' Helen's John demanded of Jeannie. 'Are you going home?'

'She lives close to me, John,' said Helen. 'She's coming along with me.' What Helen didn't say was that her own husband, George, had given her money for their taxi fare home just before they had left so of course she'd be travelling home with her sister.

John wasn't pleased about this arrangement and he didn't try to hide it.

The big diesel engine of the Hackney cab growled and roared and, in the back, John struggled to make himself heard above the noise. Despite this, he was talking a great deal as if holding court. Maybe he was just nervous but he didn't seem

243

that way. What was plain was that he was angry that Jeannie was there with them.

'Where do you live again, John?' asked Jeannie.

'Not far from you,' he replied and offered no more information.

Later she asked, 'What do you do for a living?'

'I work for my Father,' he replied, again offering nothing else.

And so it went on for some time with John never answering a question fully apart from saying he had a holiday caravan in Irvine and he played golf but he wasn't too good at it. The conversation was stilted, the atmosphere bad. At one point he started on about loose women who went to the dancing, leaving their men behind. He didn't approve and the two women didn't know why he had started on that topic. Then someone mentioned Rangers versus Celtic football matches.

'Heathens,' he spat. 'They are all heathens to a man. Parading a sport as representing the way of the Lord. Arguing that one group is right and the other wrong. How would they know God's way? It's only a game. A stupid game.'

'Are you not interested in the football then?' Helen innocently asked, worried about his sudden serious tone. 'Not even the New Year Old Firm match?'

He shook his head.

'What do you do at Hogmanay then?'

'Others drink,' he replied. 'I pray.' And then he began what was obviously a quote, 'And when she could no longer hide him, she took for him an ark of bulrushes . . .'

It seemed to Jeannie that the quote went on forever. She wasn't sure what it meant but she thought it was from the Bible – the language sounded biblical. All in all, she thought it was a very strange conversation piece to come out with after a night out at the dancing.

As the taxi wound its way into Scotstoun, John attracted the driver's attention and told him to drive on to Yoker where they'd drop Jeannie off first. Jeannie thought nothing of it. Having got on so well with Helen all night, the man obviously wanted some time alone with her – what man wouldn't?

As the taxi headed towards Yoker, John suddenly produced a packet of Embassy cigarettes, Jeannie's favourite brand. After all the fuss he had made about her losing her money in the cigarette machine at The Barrowland, he'd had cigarettes on him all the time. John offered Helen a cigarette but Jeannie was forced to ask for one. She hadn't had a smoke in a long while and was gasping. He would have known that – anyone would – yet he had forced her to ask for a fag.

John ignored her but as he turned away Jeannie reached out and grabbed a handful of his cigarettes. That wasn't her usual style but she couldn't understand why he was treating her so badly. John looked across at her and, with no emotion showing, he put the cigarette packet away. He didn't even smoke yet he carried cigarettes. What was that about?

As the taxi reached her street, Jeannie found herself calling to the taxi driver to let her off at the bottom of Kelso Street and not at her front door, fifty yards or so away. It was the type of thing she'd do if she didn't want someone to know exactly where she lived but that thought hadn't occurred to her that night. She just found herself doing it. After all, it had been a pleasant night at the dancing so what was there to worry about?

Out on the street, Jeannie stood and waved a warm cheerio to her sister and Helen waved back, all smiles. John just sat there staring to the front, his face stern, unmoving. Jeannie turned and headed towards her home. Behind her, in the taxi John finally looked out of the window to watch her go, giving her back his special smile and a wave of his hand. His night was just beginning.

Friday, 31 October 1969

The bitch. Why did she have to do that?

Wasn't she ready? Had she found no Grace?

She had the Fire. Why didn't she embrace the flames? Be swallowed by their cleansing power. My cleansing power. Why fight? Why struggle? Why resist?

The bitch.

As black as the devil is how some folk used to describe him but it was a compliment not a curse. He was a handsome boy, a good boy and no doubt.

'Smokey, be careful now,' Archie McIntyre called out through the cold morning air. A light mist had risen from the River Clyde only yards away and was drifting between the tenements as night slowly woke into day. If he had been a superstitious man, if he had been on unfamiliar territory, if it had been night, then he might have felt a little scared. But, in his own back close in the early morning, he was hard headed. All Archie was doing was taking his dog, a jet black Labrador called Smokey, for a walk.

Archie had to take care. The back close was bordered by a railway embankment and, beyond that, ran the deep waters of the Clyde. Smokey was a good dog, well behaved, but, like most dogs, he just couldn't help following his nose. Sometimes this took him on a trail that led to the railway track but not this time – this time it was going to lead him to other dangers.

'What have you got there?' Archie McIntyre called out. Smokey had his nose deep in some bundle lying just beside a close mouth. Some people from neighbouring streets wouldn't think twice of taking some particularly nasty rubbish and dumping it in other folks' back greens. Archie didn't want his dog getting sick.

Then Smokey started to whine. 'Come away from that rubbish, you,' he ordered in the friendly but firm tone that Smokey was well used to and usually obeyed. However, this time he just sat there and whined. 'What've you got there?'

he asked, moving quickly to where the dog sat. All he was expecting to see was a bundle of rags. He approached, thinking one of them had been used to cover something with a strong scent – a scent that was making Smokey whine. Rags were all he'd find, he reckoned, but, instead, he was staring down at a dead body.

The corpse was lying against the wall, towards the left side of the close, at the bottom of some drainpipes. Its skin was a pale shade of greenish-cream – a colour he'd never seen before – and, under the surface of the cheeks and forehead, he could make out navy-blue shadows. The eyes looked up at him, accusing yet lifeless. Archie McIntyre turned and ran.

'Come on! Come on, damn you!' He cursed the dial of the public phone box as it slowly, so slowly, revolved from nine and nine and nine. If only some of his neighbours had wakened when he had banged their doors – the neighbours he knew had telephones . . . They were all old-age pensioners, he knew that, and most were hard of hearing so he had no choice but to dash to the nearest phone box. 'Whiteinch Police,' he shouted into the mouthpiece when the emergency services answered. 'There's a dead body in the back close.'

Having told the police as much as he knew, Archie was still buzzing, still frightened. Forty years old and a labourer on the roads for Glasgow Corporation, he was just an ordinary citizen and ill prepared for finding dead bodies. What should he do while waiting for the police? The last thing he wanted to do was to go back there near the corpse with the staring eyes.

Archie and Smokey wandered aimlessly, automatically back to their own close. There they found their neighbour, Tommy Cummings, standing on the landing. It was a welcome friendly face at a time when Archie McIntyre needed company. Tommy had been on the bash the night before and was suffering the mother of all hangovers. What he needed was a gentle awakening, an easy start to the day, but, instead, he got a murder story.

Hardly believing his ears, Tommy staggered out to the neighbouring back close with Archie to see the corpse for himself. The conversation on the landing had taken less than five minutes yet, by the time they reached the body, two ambulance men and two policemen had beaten them to it.

'She's dead,' one ambulance man announced as Archie and Tommy arrived, telling them what was obvious.

'And no accident either,' said one of the bobbies, 'but murder.'

The two men looked down at the corpse. It was a young woman. Her clothes were in a mess and parts of her naked body were on display. One leg was entirely bare while the other wore a stocking. Then they looked up at her face. The missing stocking was wound tightly round her neck. It wouldn't need a doctor to confirm it was murder.

Immediately the police called in to their head office, B Division HQ at Partick Police Station, otherwise known as The Marine. In charge of CID there was Detective Chief Inspector Tom Valentine, one of Glasgow Police's top cops who had often been Joe Beattie's partner in their early days. That day, Valentine was due to be promoted to detective superintendent and, as he lifted the phone, he wasn't exactly sure what rank he was. He didn't much care either. Valentine only needed to hear the cursory details of the dead woman to know what to do next.

Calls went out to Detective Chief Superintendent Elphinstone Dalglish who, since the sudden death of Tom Goodall, was now head of Glasgow CID. Other calls were put out to Detective Superintendent Joe Beattie and, most telling of all, Detective Superintendent James Binnie. It was Binnie who had been left to investigate the murder of Mima McDonald and Valentine's intuition was screaming out that there was a link between her death and the murder that had just been reported.

Within an hour of Archie McIntyre discovering the dead woman, a collection of Glasgow's finest detectives had gathered in the back close and medics and forensic teams were busy beavering away.

'Do you walk your dog this way every morning?' Joe Beattie had immediately been allocated the case and he was questioning Archie McIntyre. The person who finds the body in a murder case is always the subject of major suspicion and, where possible, the first to be grilled. McIntyre had been the one to discover the corpse so grilled first he would be.

The police had set themselves up for a major investigation and a murder trailer, a fancy name for a caravan, had been rolled into the street.

Sitting in the trailer, McIntyre was still shaking from his grisly find. 'Aye, this way every morning.'

'Along the back of the tenements?'

'No, no, Smokey usually runs ahead – likes to stretch his legs – but no' . . . no' this morning.'

'So what made him change his ways this morning?'

'I don't know. Must've been the smell from the poor lassie. Smokey's a Lab, for Christ's sake – they've got sensitive noses.'

'Aye and this one's got a sensitive owner,' thought Beattie, having quickly come to the conclusion that Archie McIntyre was just the poor unfortunate soul who'd stumbled across the body.

'One more thing, Mr McIntyre,' said Beattie, 'could you come with me, please?'

Out in the back close, Archie McIntyre stood and stared down at the woman one more time, hoping it would be the last.

'I'm sorry,' he said, 'I don't recognise her.'

'Are you positive?'

'Absolutely certain.'

The police went to fetch Tommy Cummings, who was still suffering from his hangover, and they asked him if he recognised the dead woman but got the same negative response.

'Naw, she's no' local,' said Cummings. 'Archie and I would've clocked her if she was.'

It was some early bad news for the police. The dead woman was carrying no identification and they had no leads as to who she was. A local connection always offered up the opportunity to glean more information and often led to theories on motive and a possible culprit.

However, although that was a worrying dead end for Beattie, the body itself had thrown up a lot of information. There were bruises on her face in a pattern suggesting she had been punched repeatedly. Curiously, under the stocking that was wrapped tightly round her neck, some docken leaves were trapped and grass was stuck between the one shoe that she was still wearing and her foot. Had there been a struggle? Over at the end of the back green, where the embankment rose towards the railway track maybe?

She wasn't naked but her clothing was pulled up and apart and her pants were missing. Even without disturbing the body the policemen could see blood smearing her pubic hair and the top of her thighs. Had she been injured there? Or was she menstruating? Whatever the answer, this was more than murder.

Then Joe Beattie spotted the sanitary towel – not lying close by where her attacker had thrown it, not lying carelessly discarded but placed neatly under one of her arms. Was this more than an isolated murder? Was the strangler at it again?

'Are you all right, son?' Beattie was concerned for a young uniformed policeman nearby whose gaze had followed Joe Beattie's to where the woman bled and then up to that sanitary towel. The poor young cop looked a bit familiar to Joe Beattie but he also looked like he was going to faint.

'Sir? Yes, Sir.' Peter pulled himself up, straightened his back, and puffed out his chest in the hope of making himself look more alert and in control but he couldn't get that puce colour from his face.

'First body?' asked Beattie gently, quietly so the other cops wouldn't hear.

'Yes, Sir.'

'You should've seen me with mine,' Beattie continued, moving closer to the bobby so they could talk privately.

Men from the council were cutting the long grass at the back of the green. Beattie had ordered it so the cops could look for clues. He was sure he was right but, in the meantime, had to put up with workmen who weren't used to murder scenes but were intrigued by everything that was going on and seemed intent on listening in to every conversation.

'I'd seen dead servicemen before, in the war,' Beattie went on. 'Some were even my friends but it was my first civilian that got to me – my first woman.' Beattie shook his head. 'If you're lucky, son, you'll never get used to it but you'll learn to cope. You've started off better than I did. Well done.' He slapped the policeman lightly on the shoulder.

Peter turned to his boss, that famous detective, and smiled as best he could. 'Thank you, Sir.'

'No, thank you for being here. This is dirty work, son.' Beattie turned and looked down at the dead woman. 'And this is one of the dirtiest. But what's lying down there isn't a sickening mess, isn't a corpse – that's somebody's daughter, sister, maybe somebody's wife, somebody's mother. It's our privilege to do our best for her, eh?'

'Excuse me, Sir.' A uniformed sergeant had appeared by their side. 'There's a man out front saying he lives nearby and he's looking for his wife.'

'Right, come on, son,' Beattie nodded to Peter, 'you come with me. Our girl might just be about to find her family.'

It was the longest walk George Puttock ever took. It was only from the front of 97 Earl Street and through the close – twenty yards or thereabouts but it felt like a mile. He had told the cops all he knew. He lived at 129 Earl Street just two tenements away. His wife, Helen, had gone out to the dancing at The Barrowland with her sister Jeannie and hadn't come home. He didn't worry about that since she'd done it before. Then he'd woken up to the police cars and wagons on the street. Neighbours were talking about some young woman being found dead in a back green. He got to worrying – worrying so much he just had to come and see for himself so he'd know that it wasn't his Helen, that she'd be back later in the day, with that big smile of hers, full of her usual energy and chat. He had to see for himself.

When the medic pulled back the sheet, George Puttock gagged and his knees buckled. There she was, his beautiful Helen, looking all bruised and battered, limp and lifeless. Her hair was messed up and her lips seemed pale, so pale. Where was her favourite red lipstick? She used to say she wouldn't be seen dead going out without that lippy. Seen dead? The squaddie's heart was breaking. Then he saw her coat – her fake ocelot fur coat that she was so proud of and she was still wearing it, lying down there on the dirt near those filthy drains. She wouldn't like that. George wanted to pick her up, clean her down and carry her home – home to their two wee boys. He wanted to kiss her better but he couldn't, could he? His Helen was dead.

Two hours later, a car wound its way through the streets of Yoker, moving slowly as the driver looked out for a house number. It pulled in at the kerb and a thickset man wearing a suit, collar and tie and coat got out.

The RAP-rap-RAP on the door had something special to it, an air of authority that demanded a response no matter who you were or what you were doing. This householder was no exception.

'Jeannie Williams?' The man on the doorstep looked powerful, intelligent, but also sad. She nodded a response. 'I've got some bad news about your sister, Helen.'

An hour later, Joe Beattie left Jeannie Williams' house. She had been distraught, weeping, but she had managed to tell him a great deal of what had happened the night before. She was a useful witness and he knew that they'd meet many times in the future. Out of everything she had told him, there was one thing that kept ringing in his ears. 'I know who killed her,' she had said. 'It was a man called John.'

The Bible?' The man who couldn't help uttering that question was a journalist. Police press conferences were usually dry, formal affairs where he was used to hearing the strangest, most gruesome details and, normally, he'd manage to hold his tongue. But, at the police press conference held on the very day Helen Puttock's body had been discovered, he found himself uttering those words.

'Yes,' replied newly promoted Detective Chief Superintendent Elphinstone Dalglish, from the front of the room, 'as I said, he quoted the Bible.'

'Do we have any more details on that?' The question came from another journalist.

'Not at this time,' Dalglish replied, not wanting to reveal that his main witness, Jeannie Williams, was struggling to remember much of one long quote. Maybe she would one day and it would turn out to be a clue so there was no way Dalglish was going to tell that to the press. It would be like telling the killer how to evade capture.

'Could you be more precise on the murder weapon?' asked another reporter.

'In what sense?'

'You say he used one of her undergarments to strangle her but exactly which undergarment?' He knew his editor would love to make a front-page headline with some saucy detail. That's what their readers loved.

'Gentlemen . . .'

'Are there any other leads at this stage? Any suspects?'

255

'GENTLEMEN!' Dalglish spoke loudly, his voice booming out across the room. It had the desired effect – silence. 'Gentlemen, I did explain that I'm happy to give you information regularly, frequently even, but only if you meet me halfway – only if you agree to stay out of the case. Any interference could be disastrous in catching Helen Puttock's killer.' He wasn't going to tell them that, even as he spoke, Joe Beattie was grilling her husband, George Puttock, and other detectives were speaking to the manager of The Barrowland and the taxi driver who they had tracked down in double quick time. None of that was their business now. Maybe it would never be their business.

'We understand, Mr Dalglish,' said another reporter from one of the broadsheets, the serious papers, 'but, taking into account what you've said, would it be possible to give any indication of any lines of inquiry being pursued by you?'

Dalglish thought carefully. 'Tonight officers will be appealing for information at The Barrowland Ballroom where Helen Puttock was last night. Anyone who remembers seeing her there, especially if she was in the company of a man, should approach a police officer.' He hesitated then charged ahead, 'I guarantee that anyone who approaches us will be treated with total discretion – *total* discretion.' Dalglish was only too aware of The Barrowland's reputation for extramarital sexual liaisons and the difficulties Glasgow Police had faced in seeking witnesses in the Mima McDonald investigation. He'd guarantee confidentiality early on and keep guaranteeing it. What did he care about the sex shenanigans of grown adults? He had a killer to catch.

'Mr Dalglish, Mr Dalglish!' A hand was up from the back of the room. 'One final question, please. Do you think the killer might strike again?'

'One never knows with such dangerous men, of course,' Dalglish replied, having anticipated this query, 'but, at this stage, we have no reason to believe that this is anything other than a one-off murder. Nevertheless, the public should take great care till this man is caught.'

The reporters were well used to official police-speak and what they heard was the real message – there was a dangerous man out there who could strike again – and that's what they'd write and that's what folk would read in their papers the following day. And, what's more, Dalglish knew they would. He was just relieved that someone hadn't done their homework thoroughly and asked if the case was linked to others, like Pat Docker and Mima McDonald, given there were so many similarities. If they did make the connection, he would lie, of course, and say no. Yet, if they had done their research properly, they'd write the tale anyway. That's how the media worked so the longer the police could keep those fears out of the public's mind the better.

The next morning at his desk, Elphinstone Dalglish did his usual and flicked through the newspapers waiting there for him, looking for any reports on the work of Glasgow Police. He didn't have to flick for long. There it was in black and white in a big headline. A new monster had been born – 'BIBLE JOHN'.

Sunday, 2 November 1969

They know me as John.

Bible John – I like that. It has a ring to it. An air of importance. A certain air of mystery. Yet I have told the fools so much. Told them part of my story though they didn't listen, of course, and those who did listen didn't hear.

All they heard were words from the Bible:

> And when she could no longer hide him, she took for
> him an ark of bulrushes, and daubed it with slime and
> with pitch, and put the child therein; and she laid it in
> the flags by the river's brink;
> And his sister stood afar off, to wit what would be
> done to him.

My mother, my own mother placed me in the river of blood. My own sister looked over me, protected me till she was taken too young. My father, from whose seed I was created, left me too. Taken from us in the last days of the war – or so she said, my mother, my tormentor.

I have had three lives and I have told them the beginning. My earliest memories were of my sister. Warm, fair-haired, blue eyes. She loved me. It is her girlish bosom I remember lying against as she lifted me from my cot. It is she who took me out to the park. It is she who comforted me when I was frightened of the dark. Who sat with me in the sunshine and talked to me of fun and games and told me stories with happy endings.

Then she was gone and so was the light in my life.

TB, they said when I was old enough to understand. TB stole my sister. But my mother cursed her and killed her. My cold-hearted mother who put me in the hands of another cause. Who sold me into slavery. Who stayed with me and made sure I didn't escape. Who sacrificed the child in me to something I didn't understand. My mother, my jailer.

TB stole my sister but she didn't leave. She watched over me from afar and was my light through my trials. She watches me still.

I told them all that and more. But what do they hear? The Bible, that's all. What more can you expect when the world is full of heathens? Papists no doubt.

I told them my story and all they came up with was a name.

They know me as John and they will fear me.

'Funny polisman. Funny polisman.'

'Think they're from the wrong side of the track?' Ruth looked at Peter and smiled.

'The wrong side of the park, probably. That side privileged,' he said, nodding towards the large red sandstone houses of Victoria Park Drive, 'and that side no-hopers.' He turned and pointed in the opposite direction, where the smoke-stained tenements of Dumbarton Road ran through Whiteinch and into Scotstoun.

'Funny polisman. Funny polisman.' The two kids stood thirty yards away waving their arms in the air, egging Peter on to give chase.

'Do you always get this reaction in your uniform?' Ruth asked.

'No,' he replied, 'sometimes it's worse. Sometimes their big brothers want to slash me rather than slag me.'

'So was it the uniform that attracted you to the police force?' she said, holding out her hand as an imaginary mic.

'No, actually, it was the prospect of meeting journalists who have a never-ending list of bloody daft questions.'

'You'll have seen a bit of that lately, Peter?'

'Enough hot air to last me a lifetime.'

As soon as Peter had come off that first shift when they had found Helen Puttock's body, he had telephoned Ruth to tell her about the death and he had met up with her in Earl Street. Ruth had come to have a look at the murder scene. There, she'd joined the crowds still gathering to watch the cops as they searched the area, moving from close to close, carried out interviews. The trouble was that Peter and every other cop in the division plus scores of others drafted in from elsewhere in the city had been told that they'd be working long hours – round the clock if necessary – so he didn't know when he'd be free to speak to Ruth. But, when he'd spotted her in the crowd at Earl Street, he asked her to hang on for an hour or so when he was due a break.

The streets around Earl Street were heaving with cops, journalists and nosy members of the public so, instead of the rest and food he needed, he decided to walk in Victoria Park with Ruth, where their only audience was the two impudent teenagers.

'Do they bother you much?' asked Ruth.

'Nah, they're just kids.'

'Not those two ragamuffins,' Ruth laughed, wondering where that old-fashioned word had come from. 'The press – do *they* bother you much?'

'Me? No. Other uniformed cops? No. But some of the folk who live in Earl Street? Definitely. The guy who found the body and his dog have been interviewed and photographed by every paper. Poor guy is in a right state too – he's taken to his bed.'

'Finding a body, any body, is traumatic – never mind a murder victim. He should be given counselling.'

Peter looked at her as if she had two heads.

'If you talk these things through with a properly trained expert, it can help,' Ruth went on. 'Otherwise you're likely to be ill. Not ill in the head – physically ill.' She could see by Peter's expression that he wasn't convinced.

'The press have been right bastards, though,' he said, returning to that topic. 'Some of them are offering money for any tittle-tattle about Helen. Don't be surprised if she gets written up as some sort of floozy. And they call us the pigs.'

'How's her husband taking it all?'

'Not good – not good at all.'

261

Peter looked across the park into the distance where the two teenagers, bored now with calling him names, had decided to see if they could wrap the metal chains of the swings round the supporting poles. By rights, he should go over and stop them but he had more serious matters on his mind.

'But at least Joe Beattie doesn't think he's a suspect.'

'No?' said Ruth. 'That was quick.'

'Aye, I know what you mean but seems he and Helen had a strange kind of relationship – like he really didn't mind it when she went out to the dancing without him or even when she stayed out all night.'

'Who says? Him?'

'No. I mean aye but also Helen's sister Jeannie who was with her at the dancing. The way she describes him, George is the least likely killer in the world – especially of his wife.'

'So why does your Joe Beattie believe Jeannie?'

'She's our main witness.'

'Witness?'

'No, she didn't see the murder but believes she met the murderer. Look at those fucking kids.'

Up ahead, the two teenagers were playing ducks and drakes but they were deliberately aiming the stones they were skimming across the pond at real ducks.

'HOI. YOU TWO. FUCK OFF.'

'Funny polisman. Funny polisman,' sneered the kids as both of them gave Peter slow exaggerated V-signs.

'Let's walk towards the pond,' he suggested to Ruth. 'That should sort them out.'

'Sure but Jeannie?' she reminded him.

'Jeannie Williams, Helen's sister, has given a very good description of the man. We've also had a few reports from people at The Barrowland. Seems Helen was a regular and loads of people knew her. They've named a man they saw her with that night.'

262

Ruth stopped abruptly and put a hand on Peter's arm, turning him around to face her.

'No, before you ask, Joe Beattie hasn't told any of us the name. All we know is that he's from out in Lanarkshire someplace. They're trying to track him down.'

As they got nearer the pond, the two teenagers were walking slowly away, looking over their shoulders now and then but trying to look casual with their hands in their pockets. Peter bet himself they were actually poised to run. Fishing in a breast pocket of his jacket, he took out a stainless-steel whistle and let off a blast. Instantly the two boys took to their heels and sprinted off as fast as they could. Peter stood and laughed after them.

'The old jokes are always the best.'

'So this could be a shorter investigation?' said Ruth, bringing him back to what concerned her.

'Aye, with a bit of luck. When we get the bloke and Jeannie IDs him, then we're cooking with gas.'

'Even then, you'll have to tie him to the murder though. That might not be easy. He could just be somebody who fancies Helen – sorry, fancied her.'

'Aye but one of the plainclothes was telling me that they have something a bit special. He didn't say what but he reckons it's enough to catch the killer.'

'Lanarkshire seems a bit far out, Peter.'

'What do you mean?'

'If – and I'm just saying *if* – this strangler is the same one who killed Pat and Mima . . .'

'That's not the official line, though.'

'So what's the unofficial line?'

His face reddened into a slight blush and he sucked on his lower lip. 'Well, some of the guys are talking about that being the case – that there's one killer and three victims that we know of.'

'So let's just say *if* for the moment – for the sake of discussion, OK?'

He nodded his head.

'What this shrink would say,' she stopped to grin back at Peter, 'is that he is from Glasgow. Knows the city well – very well. Has probably been to Earl Street before – as well as the other murder scenes. Might well have been in here in this park.'

'How do you . . .'

'The city is one of his comfort zones. He feels secure, safe, believes that no one will catch him *if* he stays in this city.'

'How?'

'He plucks his victims from the dancing, from The Barrowland. It's very public. He could just as easily take out prostitutes in the darkness of Glasgow Green. That would be safer. That would make more sense . . . unless, of course, you don't *need* to take care.'

'But that's just madness.'

'Have the police caught him yet?'

'Well, no.'

'So who is crazy?'

Peter shrugged.

'Especially when you have *God* on your side.'

'God? God? Who needs that religious nonsense when you have good cops and forensic evidence, eh? What good will God do him then, eh, when we bring him in?'

'We'll see, Peter,' said Ruth. 'We'll see.'

It had been a long day and a long wait for Jeannie Williams at
The Marine police station in Partick. It was Sunday and meant
to be a day of rest but who could rest? Her sister had been
murdered only three days before and now she was about to
meet the killer for the second time. Or was she?

Jeannie's description of John had been so good and the
information from people who had been at The Barrowland
had come in so fast and free that the police had a suspect.
They even had a name and an address – John McInnes of 26
Queen Street, Stonehouse – and they were bringing him in for
identification.

It hadn't been difficult for the cops to get some background
on McInnes. He was seen as a bit of a strange fish. His stern
mother had brought him up in the strict Brethren faith and,
although he outwardly continued to follow that religion, he
was well known as a drinker, a womaniser and someone who
disappeared into Glasgow to go to the dancing on a regular
basis.

McInnes also dressed smartly in expensive suits, favouring Italian styles cut in expensive brown cloth. He had done
his national service in the army but had left in mysterious
circumstances, according to the locals. They weren't sure what
had happened but no one was surprised when he suddenly
appeared back at home. One hangover from that time was
his hair which he kept short, neat and with a perfect side
parting.

Then there were his moods. Most of the time, he would
be polite and sociable but then he'd become morose and de-

pressed for no reason anyone could fathom and he'd come out with statements that people found bizarre, puzzling.

The cops were sure they had their man.

'He's not there,' declared Jeannie Williams, having just looked up and down the ID parade twice.

'Are you sure, Jeannie?' asked Joe Beattie. 'Look again.'

Ever willing to help, Jeannie Williams did just that,

'I can see why people thought it was that man,' she said, pointing at McInnes, 'but it isn't. It's a good likeness – maybe sixty per cent – but no' quite there.'

Joe Beattie was struggling to hide his disappointment. Nailing the man last seen with Helen would've been a major step forward. The experienced detective also knew that, in the majority of solved cases, the cops interviewed the killer within forty-eight hours of the murder. With every day that passed, the case would become more difficult and less likely to be solved.

'I'm sorry,' Jeannie said.

'Sorry? For what, Jeannie? You've nothing to be sorry for. It's us who've brought you the wrong man. We owe you an apology.'

He was escorting Jeannie out of the police station to a car that would take her back to her home in Kelso Street, Yoker – back to her three children and the memories of seeing her sister Helen for the last time there on the corner of the street. Maybe if they had brought in the right man she would've rested more easily, believing the killer was in custody and going to be punished. She would have had some hope. Now what did she have?

'That looks dead like him!'

Jeannie had stopped by a noticeboard and was pointing at a wanted poster. It was the sketch by Lennox Paterson of Glasgow School of Art – the sketch of the man wanted for the murder of Mima McDonald.

Joe Beattie stood there stunned. He knew fine well the similarities between Mima and Helen's murders but hadn't revealed those to the public, not even a key witness like Jeannie Williams.

'It's a man wanted in another murder, Jeannie,' he said. 'A drawing by an artist.'

'Well, it's him, all right – that's Bible John.'

'It's been a long day, eh?' Beattie said as they headed outside towards the car.

He wasn't wrong. Jeannie had been in attendance at the police station since 11 a.m. but there had been some difficulty in tracking down McInnes and he hadn't been brought in till 5 p.m. Cops spent a lot of their lives hanging around waiting for the action and they knew how exhausting that could be.

Jeannie nodded.

'See in a couple of days, would you be willing to sit down with our Identification Branch? Try and get a picture of this killer.'

'Aye, of course.'

The police went about their business of conducting countless interviews and answering telephone calls – most were from well-meaning citizens but, as usual, they got their fair share of time-wasting cranks. As this mundane side of detective work went on, Jeannie Williams sat down with Osborne Butler, one of the top men in Glasgow Police's Identification Branch. Joe Beattie had faith in Jeannie Williams. Observant and with a good memory for detail, she would give a full description of the wanted man and, if anyone could use the identikit system to best effect, it was Butler.

Meanwhile, Beattie had other matters to be getting on with – matters that hadn't been revealed to the public for fear of jeopardising the case, matters that might prove crucial in convicting the killer.

The medics and forensic team had been busy. Helen Puttock had died of strangulation for sure but she had put up a struggle, a vicious fight for her life. At some point, she had been aware that something bad was going to happen and

267

had made a run for it, up the grass embankment. The killer had caught her, beat her about the face and pulled her back down the wet grass. The poor woman had dug her heels in – literally – thus the blades of grass caught between her shoes and her feet. She had fallen on the ground and docken leaves had caught on her stockings, one of which he'd used to kill her. The killer had overpowered her but had she damaged him? The police thought so and were looking for some man with scratches to his face and hands. Had anyone's man, anyone's son, anyone's brother come home that night all bloody, their clothes all muddy? Had anyone in that state caught a bus or hailed a taxi anywhere in Scotstoun late that night?

During the attack, as she tried to get free, would Helen have called out? If she had, why had no one heard her? The house-to-house interviews by the police had revealed the answer. Most of the residents were elderly, early-bedders, and many were hard of hearing. They were used to trouble in and around the street – nothing serious, just husbands and wives arguing, drunken rows, that kind of thing. A scream or shout they would have ignored – if they had even heard it. Husbands and wives arguing were none of their business.

Or was Helen too scared to call out so close to her home? Scared that someone she knew would come to her assistance? Scared to be faced with answering the question – what was she doing in that back green in the dark with a man while her husband was looking after their children? Or was her killer too strong for her? Did he simply overpower her too quickly? The signs of a struggle said otherwise. So did he know how to keep her quiet? A special grip that blocked her airways and suffocated her voice before it reached the night air? The kind of hold a judo expert might know . . . or even a soldier? There were plenty of former squaddies in the police. The cops rarely suspected a cop. Was that how they had failed to collar their man?

Joe Beattie did as all good cops do and worked with what and whom he could investigate. Officers had been dispatched to check with the drivers of taxis and buses who'd been in the Scotstoun area late on the night of the murder. Soon they became aware that the killer only had to walk a short distance to reach other areas, other bus routes. The task turned from large to enormous but not too big for Glasgow cops – or the public who were now keen to help track the killer.

'He's been fighting,' the man whispered to his mate as the late-night bus chugged along Dumbarton Road.

'What a bloody mess, eh?' his pal agreed. 'The state some people get into . . .'

The man they were talking about had just got on the night bus near the junction with Gardner Street. It was about 2 a.m. on Friday, 31 October 1969. Some of the other few passengers had been out on the town spending their week's wages. Others were heading to start early shifts in bakeries and factories. They knew to look out for trouble on those buses but the new arrival just sat down and minded his own business, speaking to no one. His brown suit was a mess of mud and what looked like grass stains. His blue shirt tail flapped loose over the waistband of his trousers which were all muddied at the knees. Most worrying of all was a long red weal that ran down one cheek. He looked like he had been fighting all right and too drunk or distressed to bother tidying himself up. Drunk, the other passengers assumed and held their breath waiting for trouble.

No trouble came. The man got off the bus a short while later on the west end of Sauchiehall Street outside the Lorne Hotel. The other passengers sighed with relief and watched the man in the brown suit walk off into the darkness.

Was that the killer? The cops thought so. Where did he go? The other passengers recalled him getting off at the Lorne Hotel but the driver thought it was near the junction with Gray Street in an area packed with tenements, small hotels and guesthouses. Was he heading for one of those? Or did he walk the short distance to Kelvin Way and stroll down the wide boulevard in the night from the Kelvingrove Art Museum towards the university and on to bedsit land, lost among the students?

The cops' trail ran cold but it was a start – a good start and there was more to come.

'Has she been raped?' Joe Beattie had put the question to the attending police surgeon as he bent over Helen Puttock's body. It was an obvious question given the state of her clothing and that bloody sanitary towel stuck under her arm – an obvious question but an important one. Beattie knew there was a strangler on the rampage but did he have a rapist too? A sexual sadist? He needed to know all he could about the killer.

'Impossible to tell at this stage,' the doctor said, giving Beattie the answer he'd expected. 'Probably but we'll find out more later.'

At the post mortem, they found out that Helen's body was seriously damaged with every sign that she'd been brutally raped. The injuries might well have been caused in other ways – maybe by an object – but a finding back at the scene of the murder persuaded them otherwise. The forensic team found something else at the scene – semen on Helen's clothes. With those injuries to her genitals and the semen she surely had been raped. They did have a sexual sadist on the loose.

There was another reason that the semen was an important find. The cops and the medics knew that work was going on developing something called DNA fingerprinting. It wouldn't be long, they hoped, before the scientists managed to develop a system that they would be able to use for matching DNA from a semen sample to the man who produced it. They had no doubt that the semen they had belonged to their killer so the semen sample was carefully sealed in a jar and preserved.

The teams at the scene of crime had discovered one more crucial piece of evidence – a deep bite mark on Helen's body.

Never a slouch to explore any avenue of investigation, Joe Beattie immediately made plans to have a plaster cast made of that bite and circulate it round dentists and the Glasgow School of Dentistry. Only two years before in Biggar, a young man named Gordon Hay had become the first person in the UK to be brought to justice because of bite-mark evidence. The cops had matched a bite mark he'd left on the body of young Linda Peacock to him and he was convicted of her murder. Beattie was up to date on such cases, especially ones that were so close to home. Colleagues from the Regional Crime Squad based in Glasgow had helped in the Linda Peacock case and the main expert witness was Dr Warren Harvey, a forensic orthodontist at Glasgow University. Beattie knew that a bite mark would be just as unique as any fingerprint.

Rape, a bite mark, the sighting on the bus, the description by Jeannie Williams, witnesses from The Barrowland Ballroom – crucial evidence was mounting day by day. A room in The Marine police station was rapidly filling to the gunnels with reports, witness statements, medical reports, witness sightings, forensic evidence and so on. There was a real danger that the essential clue that would finger the killer could get lost right there, buried under a weight of paperwork. The cops knew that had happened before too many times but Joe Beattie had just the man to deal with that problem.

Although a different style of investigator from Beattie and the late Tom Goodall, Detective Superintendent Tom Valentine was a top cop in Beattie's view. The murder cases Valentine had been involved in were generally the less high-profile ones and so he didn't appear in the public spotlight as often as some of his colleagues. Other detectives might have resented that but not Tom Valentine. His style was to be thorough and patient. He was skilled in cases like fraud where he embarked on the necessary paper chase with relish while most other cops groaned and struggled. He had waited years to nab certain cons – never forgetting, never letting go and, just when they thought they were safe, up he'd pop. Other cops would've lost interest years before. Thoroughness, organisation and patience were his trademarks – just the man for the job of organising and coordinating all the case material that would catch Bible John.

Tom Valentine was excused other duties and moved into the room full of evidence in The Marine on a full-time basis. While hundreds of police were scouring the streets and dealing with the public, he'd rarely leave that room. Working long shifts, he'd rarely see daylight. Tom Valentine would make sure that all the crucial evidence they were collecting was used to the best effect. Surely they were closing in on the killer?

'That man should get a medal.' Jeannie Williams was sitting in The Marine police station across from Joe Beattie.

'Aye, he's good, eh?' replied Beattie, passing her a cigarette to go with the mug of tea a uniformed officer had just brought in.

'It's so like him, it's scary.' She shivered involuntarily.

'It's all thanks to you, Jeannie.'

'Me? No, I just told him what Strange John looked like.' She tended to stick to her original term for the man called John, leaving the others to think of him as Bible John. Joe Beattie also preferred Jeannie's name for the hunted killer.

'Well, our ID Branch guys say you are the best witness they've ever had.'

Jeannie had spent days with the police Identification Branch working through hundreds of facial features till she was satisfied that they had caught the likeness of the man they called Bible John. Even then, Beattie hadn't been satisfied with the joining lines left by the identikit. He'd asked Osborne Butler to try and have those removed and Butler had succeeded. The result was a lot better but still Joe Beattie wasn't satisfied. He wanted a picture so good it might as well be a photograph. That's where his prime witness, Jeannie Williams, came in again.

'And Lennox Paterson agrees,' he added.

'Aw, he's such a nice man,' she replied, thinking of the three days she spent with Paterson at the School of Art, drinking tea and chatting as he drew. With Paterson, it didn't feel like work, didn't feel like police work. It was just pleasant chatting and she'd blethered nineteen to the dozen.

'I thought his sketch was spot on,' Jeannie continued, 'but this? This is *so* good.'

Paterson had been happy with his sketch but then he'd decided to try his hand at adding colour. Colour brought life to a drawing. Jeannie had been very good on that, especially the hair colour. Fairish-red. Dirty fair with red streaks. Not ginger. Definitely not ginger.

The police were relieved at the last comment. For weeks, they had been receiving sightings of Bible John – all tall, red-headed men, all wrong. In a city full of redheaded people, they were in for a long list of false trails, unless they could be more specific. To help Lennox check out the colour, they had gone to extraordinary lengths, going round hairdressers, picking up samples from the floors, and sending cops with fairish hair to him and Jeannie to see if they could find a match.

'MISSUS! MISSUS!' The man in the suit was running down the pavement shouting at a woman many yards in front. 'CAN I HAVE A WEE WORD?'

She was startled, uncertain. She'd heard the brakes of the man's car screeching to a halt and turned to see what was going on. Then the man had jumped out and sprinted after her, leaving his car in the middle of the road with its driver's door wide open.

'I'M FROM THE POLIS, MISSUS!' he shouted. 'HONEST!'

Right enough, he looked like a cop to her so she decided to take a chance.

'It's your dog,' he said, panting for breath as he caught up with her. 'It's got a lovely coat. Do you think I could cut a wee bit off? I'll no' hurt the dog. Honest. I like dogs.' To prove he was genuine, he was stroking and petting the friendly pooch.

The alert detective had to do a lot more explaining than that but, eventually, he left with a lock of the dog's hair – the dog's fairish-red hair. It was as close a match as they'd found and Lennox Paterson had used it to produce the coloured drawing that was impressing Jeannie Williams so much.

Joe Beattie walked her out of The Marine police station and to a car where a driver was waiting to drive her home. As Jeannie disappeared into the Partick streets, her last words were ringing in his ears, 'That'll get him no bother. That's *him.*'

As Beattie walked back towards his office, Paterson's coloured drawing still in his hand, he stopped at a noticeboard. There was the other drawing Paterson had done – the one of the man wanted for the murder of Mima McDonald. Beattie held the new drawing up and looked at the two side by side. 'You're the same bloody man, aren't you? There's no hiding it now. Bible John *has* killed before.'

Monday, 5 January 1970

Thank God my prayers are over. For five days, I've fasted and prayed. Five long days I've paid a special homage to my Father. I asked Him to see me through this trial. Prayed for Him to be my Saviour as I feel the devils closing in. They get so close. I feel them.

Ever since I cleansed my Helen, I have felt their eyes turn my way. Not since the boyhood of my torment have I felt their heat so, smelled their rank breaths moving closer, their sulphur farts fill the air. Now I do.

Something went wrong that night. Something so bad I cannot bring myself to write about it yet. When the memories float back into my mind, I grab the soft flesh under my arm or the back of my thigh and grip it tightly and twist till my blood smears my fingers and the devils have gone. If it continues like this, soon it may be time to go back to that place, my sanctuary. A safe place only flooded by memories of her.

The bitch had money. All that poverty, all that despair, all that childhood ridicule I suffered and she had money. The bitch.

At her funeral, her fellow crows turned out – the women dressed as dead grandmothers, the men in black suits and hats smelling of mothballs and carbolic. Among them I could see he was different. Grey suit, colour to his face, luxurious white hair well cut and a nose showing early signs of too much red wine. As he approached, I smelled flowers and not from the grave. A solicitor who was most saddened and so forth. Then he told me she has worldly goods to pass on and I was her sole heir. And I thought all mother had left me was nightmares.

The cunt had been holding out on me all my life.

In her death, I became alive. My life truly began.

I closed up the hovel that was our home and moved up here to the city, the big She. The big fertile She where my work was to be done. Then I thought my trials were over. All I had to do was prepare to see the Fire. Now this. First, a shadow in the night and now my face staring out at me from the newspapers.

Is this how You repay Your one true and loyal servant?

I buy all the newspapers. There I was in the *Daily Express* staring out. Then later in the *Evening Citizen*. No one in Glasgow could have missed that picture. Hardly anyone in Scotland and probably damned few in Britain. Just as well I have prepared.

Beards are everywhere these days. Before my fast and prayers, I read in a magazine of some music festival in America in a place called Woodstock. A farm in the middle of nowhere but all these hippies flocked there to listen to music. It amused me that the festival took place over the weekend in the middle of August and the Saturday was the day my Jemima was cleansed. As all the Children of Love were meeting, the real act of true Love was happening right here. Those men hippies wore long hair and beards and now every young man is copying them. But not me.

My moustache is fine. Full, drooping round my mouth but well trimmed, it suits my style and changes my face. My hair is grown a little as every other man seems to be growing theirs. It is combed in the other direction and parted on the right – a gift of being double crowned. Barbers always say to me it's the devil itself to cut. That still makes me laugh especially now when it has made a cloak for this child of the Lord. One small flick of the comb, then a touch of Brylcreem – the grease darkens my locks – and I push it farther back, off my forehead, pull it farther behind my ears. My own mother wouldn't recognise me. My own mother didn't recognise me.

Two weeks after my Helen was cleansed, I was stopped by the police – two uniformed officers who were very polite. I gave them my given name, not my chosen title. They asked their questions as if they were singing songs and looked drawn, tired. I answered politely – always willing to help the police – and they sent me on my way after ten minutes, thanking me for my cooperation.

I had been on my way to my favourite place but I knew the Lord had sent me a message so, instead, I had a few drinks. I went to the Traders Tavern where my Helen had been before we met. It was as disgusting as I had imagined but it's good to pay homage to those you have saved, those you love. Then I headed towards the Green but there were too many policemen on the way so I turned around and came home. That night I started to grow my moustache.

The ways of my Father are a mystery to behold. A fair-haired man with a dark moustache. I am gifted. Protected by Him. Soon I will move back to my refuge. A little time away from my city will be no burden. I need a rest after my efforts. But only for a short while. This storm will soon blow over.

Silence and darkness. Ruth stood among the shuttered and locked warehouses wondering why the lack of things could be so terrifying. No sound, no light, no people. Had she been let down? Or set up?

It had started easily enough. After their visit to Mima McDonald's death scene, Malky from Bridgeton had given her a phone number, saying she could contact him on it any evening. 'It's no' my house, mind,' he had warned. 'Just ask for me – say that it's Ruth who wants me.'

When Ruth did ring the number, it turned out to be a pub – a noisy pub and she wasn't even sure where it was. Competing with some Johnny Cash song and the rumble of male voices, the barman roared down the phone, 'Malky, hen? This place is stowed out with Malkies.'

She thought that would be the end of that but then he added, 'And who wants him?'

'Ruth. My name's Ruth.'

'Aw, *that* Malky. Hang on a minute.'

The receiver clattered down on some hard surface and Ruth waited.

'Ho, Malky, it's yer fancy woman – Ruth.'

Seconds later Malky's laughing voice was greeting her on the other end of the line. 'You've got these guys bursting tae find out about ye. I'm telling them nothing.'

'Hope I haven't caused you any trouble?'

'Nah, they're just threatening tae grass me tae the wife about my posh bird.'

'Your wife?' Malky seemed too young, too free to be married.

'Aye,' he replied. 'Oh, I see what you're thinking. We're no' hitched or that – just going steady. Anyway, she knows about you.'

'What? Knows about the crazy posh bird that goes hunting killers?' Ruth laughed.

'She thinks ye're mental, right enough, but hopes you catch the evil bastard.'

'Malky, that's why I'm phoning.'

'Didn't think it was tae tell me my football coupon had come up. Fire away.'

In the background, Johnny Cash gave way to Jim Reeves hearing the sound of 'Distant Drums' as Ruth explained why she was phoning. 'Do you know anyone I can trust in Scotstoun or Whiteinch?'

'Now why doesn't that question surprise me?'

Ruth wanted to get near the scene of Helen Puttock's murder. She wanted to go there at night, around the time it had happened, without prying eyes, just as she had done with Pat Docker and Mima McDonald but she had to bide her time. The police had hung around in Earl Street for a long time. Within a few months of Helen's murder, there was the picture of the man they called Bible John in every newspaper and the journalists had sussed that the killings of the three women might well be linked. The public were worried, twitchy, and nowhere more so than in Scotstoun.

The police, under Joe Beattie, had continued a very active investigation. The Barrowland had been plagued by cops for weeks. That had produced many descriptions of the man with Helen – of Bible John – but not much more. So they appeared to back off but, through Peter, she knew much better – she knew they had set a trap. Every night half a dozen couples dancing at The Barrowland were undercover cops. As Peter said, 'It's the first time I've gone to the dancing looking for a man.' It was a great strategy, Ruth thought, but one the public couldn't know about, one they didn't see. All they saw was the posters of Bible John on every flat surface in the city. In addition to the official ones, the *Daily Record* had several thousand run off with the police number to call on them for anybody who had information.

Even if she included cases she'd come across during her studies, this was the biggest manhunt Ruth had ever encountered. That had to make it one of the biggest police operations – if not *the* biggest – in modern times in the UK. The coordinated effort and the public willingness to help were remarkable, she thought, and, in the meantime, the public worried and fretted. People had stopped venturing out at night and the reports to the police of suspicious noises in their homes or strange men in their street had zoomed up.

Helen Puttock had been dead almost five months but, even now, Ruth had to be careful in approaching the scene of her murder. If she was spotted, the neighbours would call the cops for sure. She needed some help getting there without being eyeballed. That's where Malky came in and why she found herself standing among some warehouses in Scotstoun late at night.

'So you turned up, eh?' The voice was behind Ruth but close and sent an electric jolt of fear up her legs and back. 'We thought you'd bottle it.'

'Senga?'

'Aye.'

'Where did you spring from?' The question was out of Ruth's mouth before she thought about it.

'Spring? Fucking good one that. We've been standing here watching youse for five minutes.' Two young women walked out of the dark shelter of a warehouse wall and over to Ruth. 'Malky said you were all right but ye cannae be too safe, eh?'

'I'm Ruth.' She held her hand out.

'Aye – Senga and this is Maggie.' Senga nodded at the woman beside her but ignored Ruth's outstretched hand.

'Thanks for doing this,' said Ruth.

'Aye, no bother, anything for my cousin Malky,' said Senga. 'I owe him big time.'

Ruth didn't ask for details of the debt although she guessed it wasn't money but some other kind of favour. Malky looked like he lived week to week financially but, in other ways, the ways of the street, he was rich.

'And anything to get the evil prick, eh?'

Beside her Maggie nodded her head enthusiastically.

Senga continued, 'Don't go worrying about Maggie, Ruth, she's a bit shy round new faces, know? She'll no' say much.'

Without any warning, Senga walked away, with Maggie in tow, and went in the direction of Earl Street. Suddenly realising they were heading off, Ruth followed.

They walked quietly though the warehouses and factories towards a black looming mass Ruth knew would be the railway embankment and, on the other side, Earl Street. When trying to work out a way to visit the murder scene on her own, she'd considered this as the best approach yet, even in daylight, she couldn't find a route through that wouldn't create too much noise or result in her getting snagged on barbed-wire fences and covered with mud. There was also the problem of how she could get to the top of that embankment without being spotted by some soul concerned for her safety. Senga would know a way, Malky had said, and she prayed he was right.

'It's so dark down here,' Ruth said.

'That's the way we like it sometimes, hen,' replied Senga, 'when we're busy.' She turned to Ruth and winked a conspirator's wink.

Malky had explained to Ruth that his cousin was a member of the YY Posse, a long-established all-girl gang in Scotstoun, and he'd warned her that female gang members got up to fighting and robbing, just like their male counterparts.

'Is this a common route for you then?' asked Ruth.

'Aye and no,' said Senga. 'As kids, we'd come here to play, but. Now it's more needs must, like, if we're wanting to get on that section of Dumbarton Road without anybody noticing. A wee hairy ambush maybe.'

She was smiling and beside her Maggie was laughing, the only noise Ruth had heard come from her lips so far.

'Did Malky say we came this way that night?'

'What night?' Ruth asked.

'The night that Helen got it,' replied Senga.

Ruth felt foolish but she was paying more attention to their route than anything else. At the foot of the embankment, they had turned right, walked down fifty yards and now they were climbing up, their feet slipping on a well-worn path that was busy turning to mud in the rain.

'THAT night!' Ruth stopped suddenly.

Senga held her finger to her lips. 'Ssshh.'

'Sorry,' Ruth whispered, 'but you were here the night Helen was murdered?'

'Aye, we'd done a warehouse.' Senga continued walking ahead while she spoke. 'Broke into the office and blagged a few quid – no' much but no' bad either.'

Maggie was nodding her head.

'We'd set some alarm off in the bloody warehouse so we came this way to avoid the bizzies.'

They had reached the top of the embankment but two blocks down from the house in question and exactly where there was a big gap between two tenements. On Senga's unspoken command, Ruth ducked and the three women slipped over the side and all the way down. Ruth followed as they ran with their heads down for the gap between the tenements.

'We saw two men as well,' Senga continued, as they leaned against a gable wall to catch their breath.

'Saw two men here?' Ruth wasn't believing her ears. She hadn't heard of any other people being in the vicinity on that night Helen was killed. Now it seemed that area was crowded.

'Fag time, eh?' announced Senga.

Maggie nodded her head and started hunting in her coat pockets. Ruth beat her to it and passed round her packet of Embassy. As they lit and dragged on their cigarettes, a faint yellow glow from the nearby streetlights allowed Ruth to see her companions for the first time.

Senga had the same dark good looks as her cousin Malky. She wore her hair short, giving her a hard, boyish look, and her sallow skin made her teeth sparkle white. Bright eyes and high cheekbones gave her a face shining with life and intelligence. Athletic and the picture of health, she was attractive but only the blind would fail to see the devilment in her eyes. Senga was a handful.

Maggie had even longer hair than Ruth and it was blonder – an unusual feature in Glaswegians, as far as Ruth had noticed, except where telltale mousy brown roots were also on display. Maggie's roots were as blonde as the rest of her hair. Her curvy figure and large breasts were accentuated by the tight cut of her cheap, short, black leather coat. Voluptuous was a word that suited her. Her eyes were ponds of so fine a blue that they were almost transparent. With her full lips curled into a constant smile, Maggie was beautiful but silent.

'We was standing here divvying up the takings from the warehouse,' Senga explained, 'and we clocked them up there.' With the tip of her cigarette cupped in a hand, she pointed farther up the embankment, close to the back green where Helen had been killed. 'One was on the embankment, like, ducking down and staring at the tenements. Now and then he'd scarper up a bit probably to get a better view – the pervo. The other one was down, right at the back of the tenement – along the wall there. Hugging the bloody wall.'

'Did you see them clearly? I mean what they looked like?' Ruth asked trying to figure out how to encourage this young woman to talk detail.

'Aye and no,' she replied. 'The one against the wall – no chance. But up there on the embankment, even on a dark night, you're exposed but just your shape, right, your sil . . . sil . . .'

'Silhouette?'

'Aye, right, like you're playing shadows against the bedroom wall at night with your hands. Here, Maggie, I could do a rare wolf, so I could.'

Maggie grinned wider.

It was then Ruth realised that Senga and Maggie looked like adult women but were probably only fourteen or fifteen.

'So, you didn't see his face?'

'Naw, no way, man, but he was a skinny git – wearing dead tight drainpipe trousers and what looked like maybe a leather jacket. A biker's jacket – know?'

'Yeah, I know what you mean. What about his hair?'

'Long hair – shoulder length. And he seemed young, but.' Senga shrugged. 'A young shape – know?'

As Senga dragged on her cigarette, Ruth noticed two thick, dark tattoos on the back of her right hand, both home-made, both crude, both blue. One declared 'RFC', the other 'LOYAL'.

'We just thought they were peeping Toms, didn't we, Maggie?'

Maggie nodded her head and pursed her lips – the smiles and grins had disappeared from her face.

'Some of the old women up here are a bit careless in shutting their curtains. I was all for going up and giving them a kicking, eh?'

Maggie, still serious faced, nodded again.

Ruth noticed that down the peachy skin of one of Maggie's otherwise perfect cheeks ran a long scar, ragged and badly stitched.

'So what did you do?' Ruth asked.

'Fucking nothing,' Senga said, flipping her butt away into the night. 'Fucking nothing. What stupid bastards, eh?'

Senga walked off a couple of paces and stared up at where she'd seen the man that night. Maggie was tearful and looked frightened but she stood stock-still.

285

'We were hot – with the money from the warehouse – and I thought the wankers were only looking. So I said, "Let's split." And we did.'

Slowly, oh, so slowly, Maggie reached out one hand and placed it on Senga's shoulder.

'We were pure selfish bastards, Maggie, hen. I was a pure selfish bastard and all for a couple of quid.'

Maggie's eyes said 'No' but her lips said nothing.

'You did a logical thing, Senga – made a logical decision.' Ruth was trying to leave the young woman feeling as good about herself when they parted as she had done when they met.

'How's that then, Miss University?' Her tone was challenging.

'You only acted on the basis of what you knew. What you knew then.'

'Is that right?'

'They were peeping Toms – that's what you saw. You had to get out of there and fast. So what if they flashed their bits at some woman? She'd probably not even notice. That was the logic at the time and it was right.'

'See your logic? See shite. That was the killers we saw. That woman would've still been alive if we'd given they fuckers a good kicking.'

'The killers?'

'Well, who else was at that back green at that time on that fucking night?'

'Did you see anyone else here that night?' Ruth asked.

'Just a couple,' Senga replied, 'an older couple walking hand in hand. We turned our faces away though. Case they were local. Case the cops came asking them questions about the warehouse.'

'Maybe not the killers.' Ruth muttered the words.

'What's that?'

'I think we should maybe be calling it a night,' Ruth said loudly and clearly.

'D'you no' want to go up there? Up where Helen was found then?'

'No, I've seen enough,' she replied. 'You two have been very helpful.' Senga looked at her with a puzzled expression while, next to her, Maggie just grinned.

'Some folk are easy pleased, eh, Maggie?' Senga nudged her pal. 'Our night's just starting, eh?'

Big smiles from Maggie.

Ruth followed Senga and Maggie as they led the way out of Earl Street into the bright lights of Dumbarton Road. They stopped and said their farewells and Ruth thanked the two teenagers yet again.

'No problem,' said Senga, walking away.

'One more thing,' Ruth called out. Senga and Maggie turned and looked at her. 'Did you tell the cops about the men in the back green?'

Senga looked at Maggie and the two shook their heads sadly.

'The fuzz? Tell the fucking fuzz? We never do that.'

Now alone, Ruth walked slowly down Dumbarton Road with a lot on her mind. The man on the embankment and the one hugging the wall caused her a problem. Were they together? Just peeping Toms or worse? Did they see the murder? Should she tell the police? Did they already know?

'You aw right, hen?' A taxi had pulled in to the kerb and the driver was talking at her from his cab.

'Yeah, thanks,' she stammered, having been caught unawares, lost in her thoughts.

'You shouldn't be out on your own, love, at this time of night – especially no' down here. Where you heading?'

'Partick. Near Partick Cross – it's just a short walk.'

'Aye, past aw they tenements and dark closes. Jump in. I'm going back to the rank there anyway. This one's on me. I've got granddaughters your age.'

Without leaving his seat, he reached out and opened the back door. There was something kindly in the man's eyes, something reassuring in his grey hair, his well-worn face and gravel-filtered voice that she found reassuring. Ruth climbed into the back of the taxi.

'This is a dangerous part of town, love,' he said, manoeuvring his vehicle out on to Dumbarton Road. 'There's a killer out there – Bible John.'

'I know,' said Ruth, 'I know.' The question was – was there just one killer?

BOOK

of

JOHN

Wednesday, 13 May 1970

The fools. What do they take me for? Some animal? Some devil?

Bad enough that they spread my image all over the world. Bad enough that they call me names such as mad and sadist. Bad enough but now they try to besmirch my quest. They call me a sex beast.

I did not defile my Helen. I cleansed her. Took her into the light. Now they claim I left my filth on her. Like they would leave their filth.

That night things did not go to plan. First she took fright and struggled. Fear of the Lord is to be expected. Then I saw the shadows. Manly shapes moving around close by. I had to hurry. Of course, I didn't abandon my Helen with the Fire in her. I cleansed her and left her as I should but the devils were closing in. I had to flee.

Those devils must have used her. My poor Helen. But they were too late. She was saved. I had taken her from their Hell. Cleansed her of the pain of this existence. Still they used her.

Cleansing makes me feel whole. It is my Father's work I do after all and I feel the power of Him in me. He rewards me with that strength that lasts forever. I'm potent in this world. But I did not defile Helen. That is not my calling. Not what He asks of me.

Now the others blame me.

The fools.

The morning air was chilly and clear – ice clear, the way it can be on spring mornings in Scotland. It was a good sign that the day was going to warm up – eventually. But first the gaffer needed to get on with his work and count his men on shift. They were all there, bright and breezy, but he was worried.

'McSorley,' he shouted into the yard.

'Aye.' A small, wiry man with a beard edged forward and looked up, with an angry, challenging expression on his face. It was how he always looked at work.

'Did that wife of yours kick you out of bed this morning?'

'Of course she did,' McSorley replied, 'like every morning.'

'Wise woman. Weren't you on call-out last night?'

They worked for the Gas Board and there had been a mains leak. Why did that always seem to happen in the middle of the night?

'Aye.' McSorley knew the gaffer knew. He had the report right in front of him.

'And you still made it in early? Well, fuck me!'

There was a queue among the men to give the gaffer, Jimmy Phimister, a seeing-to. McSorley wasn't first in the queue or even in the queue, he was just in the bad books.

It was because of a small matter of driving a Gas Board van home for the night the week before but being diverted to a few pubs on the way. The boys had managed to recover a large amount of lead and copper and they'd got top dollar from the scrap merchant for it so a celebration was well in order. The trouble was that, when McSorley awoke the next morning, the van wasn't outside his front door where he usually parked it. He always drove home but had to admit he couldn't remember getting home that time. It was a puzzle and there was nothing else for it but to catch the bus to work and face the smelly stuff that would undoubtedly fly his way. On the way there, the puzzle was solved. There was the Gas Board van parked at a crazy angle on the central reservation of the busiest road in the north of Glasgow. It really had been some celebration.

The gaffers had found out about the escapade and it was up to Jimmy Phimister to discipline McSorley, who thought he was in for the sack or a final warning at the very least. Instead, Phimister took him with him on his work for the day – a day peppered with frequent stops at pubs and clubs where, more often than not, the two men were given drinks for nothing. On the odd occasion when they had to buy the drinks, it was the gaffer, Phimister, who carried the cost. He made a point of not letting McSorley pay for anything. Phimister was renowned for being the hardest of a bunch of hard gaffers. Surely all he was doing was punishing McSorley by making him wait for the discipline? A kind of mental torture. At the end of the day, a by now half-sozzled McSorley held his breath and waited for the axe to fall.

'Now,' said Phimister, 'let that be a lesson to you.'

End of disciplinary action? McSorley couldn't believe his luck. The toughest gaffer had let him off with a serious offence. More than that, he'd fed him free booze all day. Maybe it was because McSorley was one of the few Roman Catholics in the Gas Board at that time. The place was full of Protestants, members of the Orange Lodge and Freemasons. Phimister himself was a proud member of a Masonic Lodge and wore a badge to prove it. Maybe he had been told to go easy on the Gas Board's one Catholic. Maybe he had a soft spot for drinkers.

Either way, Phimister was OK by McSorley. He knew he was getting the edge of his sarcastic tongue as added punishment for misplacing that van but there were others who hadn't had an easy time from Jimmy Phimister – others who would see him dead or worse.

'Right enough though,' McSorley said to one of his workmates, 'Phimister's spot on. Everybody's in this morning and in early as well.'

His workmate just grinned a little knowing grin at him.

When the police panda car drove into the yard, an audience was waiting. Every workman turned and watched and smiled. McSorley was getting the message. There was some game afoot.

'Mr James Phimister?' asked the police sergeant.

'Aye. I mean yes, Sergeant, how can I help you?' Phimister was his usual gruff, businesslike self.

'Mr Phimister, we have reason to believe you can help us with our inquiries.'

'Me? What inquiries?'

'We'd like you to accompany us to the station, Sir.'

'But I've my work to do. I cannae just leave my work.'

'Either you come voluntarily, Sir, or I'll be obliged to arrest you.'

Being arrested anywhere by the cops wouldn't do Phimister's career any good – let alone being arrested at his place of work. 'Naw, naw, there's no need for that. Just tell me what inquiries.'

'It's in connection with the murder of Helen Puttock, Sir.'

'Murder?'

'We just have some questions to put to you.'

'Murder?' Phimister muttered again, shaking his head, already moving towards the panda car.

'WE'LL SEE YOU LATER, BIBLE JOHN!' shouted one of the workmen, raising laughter from the rest of the crew.

Three days later Jimmy Phimister returned to work, having been held and grilled by the police in the meantime. He sussed that one of his staff had phoned the cops but he knew there was a long line of suspects to choose from.

Phimister was tall and slim, his red hair was parted on the left, he liked to wear lounge suits and he often sneaked away without his wife to the dancing at The Barrowland Ballroom on Thursday nights. All the men knew that but, with the arrival of Bible John, his style and habits became a liability.

Phimister was cleared of any involvement in the Helen Puttock case but that wouldn't stop many more anonymous calls to the police that would lead to him being pulled in time and time again. He wasn't alone in this. By the summer of 1970, so many men had been repeatedly accused of being Bible John, so many assaulted in the street, so many referred to the cops, so many refused board and lodgings or service in a pub that it was becoming a big problem. Red-haired men were getting wives and girlfriends to dye their locks at home – willing to put up with the slagging from their friends as long as no one thought they were Bible John. Others bought hats or had crew cuts in spite of the fashion for long hair. More often than not, none of that worked since they were reported anyway with the added suspicion that they had recently tried to alter their appearance.

All of that amounted to a great deal of personal grief for the men – no young redheaded male could get a lumber, especially at the dancing. It also meant a great deal of wasted time for a police force who had been working all hours for the previous eight months. They were close to exhaustion and needed to do something. Yet the mistaken identities weren't always bad news for the police.

One of the men repeatedly accused of being Bible John and a serious suspect at one time was used in a re-enactment of Helen's last hours at The Barrowland. With careful choosing of the WPC playing Helen, the police stage-managed an extremely accurate portrayal of events. It was so accurate that some women who had been there the night Helen was killed broke down in tears and needed medical help. The whole show was captured by the BBC and screened across Britain.

'It's the way of the future,' Joe Beattie predicted. 'The TV will become a major crime-fighting tool.'

One man who was frequently reported to the police as Bible John was himself a serving police officer. This worried Joe Beattie. Jeannie Williams had said that, at one point in The Barrowland, Bible John had shown Helen what looked like some official documentation in a smart, black leather card holder. Helen had nodded and gone quiet and, after that, no matter how her strange partner had behaved, she seemed more relaxed. Bible John had refused to show the card holder to Jeannie. Had it been a police warrant card?

The police officer was placed on the official list of suspects for some time while the murder team quietly investigated him. Their initial inquiries didn't clear him so he too was dragged in and grilled for days. However, his answers satisfied Joe Beattie. The man was released and his name removed from the suspects' list but that didn't stop other members of the public fingering him as Bible John in the future.

Glasgow Police needed to protect the innocent and stop the repeated false accusations against the same men from wasting their resources and sapping their dwindling energy. For the first time ever, they had official ID cards made out and issued to scores of male members of the public. ID cards with a difference – they were proof of who the men weren't. With an official stamp and signature of authority the cards simply said:

I AM NOT BIBLE JOHN.

But the question still remained – who was? What length would the cops go to to find the answer?

'A clairvoyant, Joe? Are we really *that* desperate?' Detective Chief Superintendent Elphinstone Dalglish wasn't impressed with Joe Beattie's proposal.

'Aye, I know what it sounds like but this isn't just any clairvoyant.'

Beattie wasn't joking. Dutchman Gerard Croiset had a worldwide reputation as a clairvoyant and had helped to crack many crime cases. Just the year before, he had helped the police down south to work out what had happened to Muriel McKay. Alick McKay was *News of the World* owner Rupert Murdoch's deputy chairman and his wife, Muriel, had been held to ransom after the kidnappers had mistaken her for Murdoch's wife. Because of Croiset's information, two brothers called Hosein had been found guilty of killing her and feeding her body to some pigs. The case had been big news and Joe Beattie had no doubts that Croiset had played a crucial role in the conviction.

'But how will it look publicly? We'll be a laughing stock.' Beattie knew exactly what the boss meant but he had a plan.

'The *Daily Record* have brought him over here to help in the McAdam case.'

Three years before, seventeen-year-old Patricia McAdam had gone shopping in Glasgow and then set off to hitchhike back to her home in Dumfries. She was never seen again.

'So maybe the *Record* could bring him in on the Bible John hunt.'

'OK, I catch your drift,' said Dalglish. 'It would be the *Record* who'll be seen as bringing in the spook hunter, no' us.'

297

'Aye and they get the publicity from it and we get the clues.'

'Aye, *if* there are any.'

Joe Beattie spared Dalglish the arguments such as Croiset's track record and his insistence that he be told no background detail about any case and the missing people he had found and the fact that he was sanctioned by the Parapsychology Institute at the University of Utrecht, a group of academics who were sceptical about claims to such powers and tested them rigorously. Croiset was so impressive they called him paragnost, meaning 'a person beyond knowledge'. He could even have gone on about other clairvoyants' involvements in murder cases, not least of whom was Croiset's compatriot, Peter Hurkos, who had helped to crack the Boston Strangler murders. Joe Beattie spared his senior officer all those arguments and, instead, phoned Arnot McWhinnie, the crime reporter at the *Daily Record*.

Within two days, Gerard Croiset was sitting in a room in the *Daily Record*'s offices. As usual, he insisted on being given no background detail. He drew an urban area of streets and big buildings that he claimed was the part of Glasgow where Bible John could be found. When shown a street map of Glasgow, he pointed to the Govan area on the south-west side. According to Croiset, the area would have factories, shops, second-hand cars and a large, old rusting engine. Key to Bible John's whereabouts were two shopkeepers and a customer – one of the three was an elderly man who knew everything.

When McWhinnie tracked down an area that fitted Croiset's description perfectly, the cops were there within an hour and they began carrying out door-to-door interviews, flashing their pictures of Bible John and keeping a close eye out for two shopkeepers and an elderly customer who might fit the bill.

Far from keeping a low profile on using a clairvoyant, Joe Beattie went public and gave a press statement. 'We are following Mr Croiset's leads very carefully – very carefully indeed.' He then went on to give the massed ranks of the media a potted history on why Croiset should be taken seriously.

Some of the cops grumbled about this information going out publicly as a few other police forces in England had ended up being ridiculed in the media for similar moves. Joe Beattie was no one's fool and he had very good reasons for his public statement – not the least of which was the idea that it would quell the increasing public hysteria and fear over Bible John being on the loose. At least folk would see that the cops were doing something to try to track the killer down. Also, the *Daily Record* was going to publish reports on Croiset anyway – that was part of the deal. To be fair to the *Record*, they had played a very prominent role in trying to get information from the public on Bible John – in fact, they were the most active campaigners of all the newspapers.

However, Beattie could also have admitted to Elphinstone Dalglish that getting Croiset on board was something of an act of desperation. Six months had passed since Helen Puttock's murder and Beattie knew they were no further on than they had been after the first month.

'A cold case is a dead case,' he would say to his detectives. 'Let's keep it warm.' That's what Croiset the clairvoyant did – he kept the Bible John case warm.

But Croiset's involvement was also to lead Joe Beattie on a strange chase.

'Well maybes aye and maybes no, you see . . . ' The man took a sip from his mug of tea. 'That'll be my difficulty.'

'It would be a terrible injustice if we said aye,' agreed his mate, 'and the wrong man got into trouble.'

'A terrible injustice.'

'Aye, terrible.'

Overhead, gulls squawked and glided gently from side to side over the vessel, their eyes constantly peeled for the first sign of edibles.

'I couldna live with myself if that happened.'

'No, Sir, you're right. That would be a terrible weight for a man to hold in his conscience.'

The two men's accents, the gulls, the boat and the water spelled Western Isles fishermen. The surrounding scene, however, was as urban as you'd find. Beattie was interviewing the crew of the Govan Ferry on the River Clyde, almost slap bang in the middle of Glasgow.

The cops were sure that the sighting of the man in a dishevelled state on the bus the night Helen Puttock was murdered was Bible John. Up to then, they had assumed he had got off because he lived nearby in the tenements of the west end of Glasgow, north of the River Clyde. After Croiset's findings they realised that the bus had stopped just a short walk from the northern terminal of the Govan Ferry – a service that ran all night – and could have carried him to the south of the Clyde.

The ferrymen were being asked to think back six months. Yet at night the service wasn't exactly oversubscribed and, when it was used, it was mainly by groups returning home from a night out or cars and vans travelling for work reasons. Seldom would a lone man get on and even less often would it be a man whose suit was a mess and who had a bloody scrape on his face – both of which were signs that he'd been in a fight. Surely they'd remember someone like that?

No matter how much he encouraged or cajoled them, Joe Beattie couldn't get the two ferrymen to say they had seen such a man. On the other hand, they wouldn't say that they hadn't seen such a man. Eventually he gave up in frustration.

Though the cops were convinced that they'd identified the area Croiset had sketched – they even found an old rusty vehicle he'd drawn – the search of Govan had proven fruitless too. Gerard Croiset, his work done, had returned to Holland, no doubt to tackle other cases and no doubt with more success. An increasing number of Glasgow cops began to think that they should be following his example. It was time to move on.

Joe Beattie was now admitting to his trusted colleagues that the Helen Puttock case was going nowhere and it therefore followed that the investigations into the murders of Pat Docker and Mima McDonald would go nowhere. Joe Beattie hated failure – he saw it as failing the victims and failing their families. In this case, he also worried that, if they didn't stop Bible John, he'd be failing the next victim and the victim after that. He'd try anything rather than give up – absolutely anything . . . Like hypnotism?

Jeannie Williams had always said that Helen had told her something that night about Bible John – about what he did for a living or something – but, try as she might, Jeannie couldn't remember the details. If she was hypnotised, maybe the details would be recalled? There were plenty of trustworthy, serious practitioners about whose methods had been shown to give results. The problem was with the law. Was information obtained through hypnotism admissible in a trial? There were no legal precedents in Scotland or England. Was the witness conscious during hypnotism? Were they behaving with all their wits? What sort of state is induced that makes memories return? Could any of these questions be used by defence lawyers to have charges thrown out? The cops and the Crown had to get the legal answer. If they pressed ahead and the results of the hypnotism led to them getting their man, they ran the risk of it all being for nothing if the law stood against them – ran the risk of a sadistic strangler being set free, never to be tried for the murders of three women.

Finally, the legal judgement arrived – evidence obtained under hypnotism was legally inadmissible. Another door had slammed shut in the police's face. Joe Beattie promptly opened another one – the Freemasons.

Beattie thought back to the black leather card holder that Bible John had shown to Helen but wouldn't show to Jeannie.

They had considered the possibility that it was a police warrant card holder and feared one of their own could be involved but maybe it held a Freemasons' Lodge membership card. Also Jeannie had recalled how Bible John kept covering a badge on his lapel. Was that a Freemasons' badge? There were plenty of card-carrying Freemasons among the police but none of them gave Beattie any arguments when he proposed this theory.

'Right,' he said, 'let's start again.' He looked round at the pale faces and bleary eyes. He knew he had been working his team hard. They'd all been doing fifteen- to eighteen-hour days for months and now here he was piling more pressure on them. 'Contact all the Lodges and see if anyone recognises our man.' That was no mean feat in the west of Scotland. 'Go through all the suspects we've had in so far. Any Masons among them, I want them back in.'

Proud Freemason Jimmy Phimister was at his work at the Gas Board when they arrived for him yet again.

'What the fuck?' he grumbled. 'Look, you gave me a card to prove it's no' me.' He was waving the official police card declaring 'I AM NOT BIBLE JOHN'.

'Sorry, Jimmy,' said the arresting officer, 'it's no' that card we're interested in this time.'

Later that night, Jimmy Phimister was released with no charge.

Over the next fortnight, all other Freemasons so arrested were also released with no charge. It had been yet another good theory that had led to yet another dead end.

The murder investigation team then turned to science. The plaster cast Joe Beattie had of the deep bite mark on Helen's body had been sent to every dentist and related hospital service in the west of Scotland. It had taken months of tireless work which had been coordinated, as usual, by Detective Superintendent Tom Valentine. By the summer of 1970, the final dentist returned a negative result. It was a big disappointment for the team.

Along with all the other things they tried, old-fashioned police work was always on their agenda. So, armed with the colour drawings of Bible John, they set off to visit all the city's barbers and unisex hairdressers to see if anyone recognised the style and colour of the hair. Nobody did.

Meanwhile, every gent's outfitters and the hundreds of tailors in the area were approached. Had any man by this description bought any suit at any time? Probably an Italian style, single breasted, brown or blue? No. The cops were running out of options.

'This has got to be the biggest investigation I've ever seen, Joe,' said Detective Superintendent Tom Valentine, sitting in his room at The Marine – his big room packed with evidence on the Bible John case.

'You've done a great job in organising all this lot, Tom.' Beattie swung his arm out to show he meant all the files and reports filling every filing cabinet, covering every surface and spilling on to the floor in rickety tall columns.

'But a fat lot of good it's done us, eh?'

'A fucking mess we'd be in if you hadn't, though.'

'But we're getting nowhere fast, though, are we, Joe?'

'I'm not finished yet.'

'What? We bringing in a snake charmer next?' It was a friendly dig at the use of Croiset the clairvoyant.

'You're no' far off at that,' smiled Beattie, 'well, some people think so.'

'Christ, as useless as a snake charmer!' said Valentine. 'What could be more desperate than that?'

'I'm going to meet with a young lassie.' Valentine raised his eyebrows. 'Worse than that, she's a psychologist.'

'Brady and Hindley. Haigh – the Acid Bath Murderer.'

Ruth was pausing between each announcement.

'Jack the Ripper. Jack the Stripper. Burke and Hare. Albert Fish. John Christie. Ed Gein. Mary Ann Cotton. Peter Manuel, of course.'

'I get your point, Ruth,' said Joe Beattie, who was facing her across a table in the Glasgow Police Central office in St Andrew's Square.

He had thought it better to meet with her there than in the hurly-burly of The Marine. Besides, someone had whispered to him that she was pally with one of their young coppers and he didn't want either of them to be compromised.

'I'm familiar with what criminologists call serial killers.'

'Of course you are – I'm sorry.' She had never made such a report before to the police and wasn't sure on the protocol. Typically, she'd fallen into what she was used to – the style of academic lecturers. She took a deep breath and told herself to relax. 'My point is this – I believe Bible John killed Pat Docker, Mima McDonald and Helen Puttock. If that is the case – if you accept that is the case – then we can see patterns to his behaviour and, from that, we can understand what type of person he is.' She stopped and fiddled with the bundle of papers in her hand. 'What I have to say is only of value to you *if* you also believe he killed all three women.'

Beattie played with a paperclip, tapping it against the table, turning it over and tapping the other end against the table.

Ruth knew he was thinking.

'Go on,' was all he said.

'I'm happy to leave this with you.' She was indicating the neatly typed papers in her hands. 'But it might be useful if I summarise some points?' It was a question. 'So you can see what's in the box of chocolates?'

Joe Beattie smiled. 'Give me a flavour, you mean? A very good idea. You talk and I'll listen.'

A uniformed cop knocked and entered the room, carrying a tray that he set down on the table. Tea in china cups with saucers and a plate of Rich Tea biscuits – Joe Beattie had pushed the boat out for her.

Ruth knew that the usual standards were a bit lower and, with renewed confidence, she sipped her tea, put her lit cigarette in an ashtray and started.

'Law-abiding in every other way, he's not on your books. A loner from childhood. Has a dominant mother figure but also an unloving mother figure. Could be adopted. Bullied and isolated as a child – never learned how to make friends. Oppressed as a child – possibly strict religious upbringing or mother with a strong world view.'

Joe Beattie edged towards the front of his seat and looked puzzled. 'World view?' he asked.

Ruth apologised and explained, 'Could be she was fanatical about something like politics – say a Communist – or strange as in mad but not mad enough to be locked up. Just mad enough to give her very young son strange ideas about existence, values, what's right and wrong.' She then continued with her list describing Bible John.

'Sexually abused – probably by someone outside the home and probably a man. Has homosexual feelings now but may not act on them. Could be impotent.'

Beattie frowned and interrupted, 'But what if we can prove he wasn't impotent?'

'Are you so sure? Are you sure that this proof definitely comes from him?'

Joe Beattie was thrown as if something had occurred to him for the first time.

'Can I come back to that later, please?'

He nodded his head and Ruth went on.

'He can't relate to women on a day-to-day basis. Part of him wants to be a woman – wants to change sex. He may dress in women's clothes at home – maybe even his victims' clothes – or have cut his genitals – not off but disfigured them, scarred them. When he goes killing, he sees himself as having some special role – like a messenger of God, maybe.'

Beattie was nodding.

'But not necessarily God as the recognised religions mean. His God could be almost anything. Could be closer to what we call the Devil. Or someone special in his life but not his mother. The man who abused him, his father, an uncle – definitely a male. He's possibly a member of all-male clubs and organisations. The Freemasons would fit with his belief in God.'

'Aye, we've been down that road,' said Beattie. 'Nothing.'

'But he'll not be an active or prominent member,' said Ruth. 'You need to be able to tolerate the company of people to do that. He may have just joined and never appeared again but still feels proud that he's a member. Mind you, it could also be Corpus Dei though the Freemasons are more likely.'

'Why?'

'The Freemasons don't tell you what God to believe in. So Christians, even Catholics if they don't tell their priest, Jews, Sikhs – all these people can join if they believe in one all-powerful God. But I say it's most likely the Freemasons because they are all men.'

Beattie was nodding and thinking to himself that maybe he hadn't been too far off the mark after all.

'He has money. Money he hasn't earned but money he feels reflects his worth – that was his by right. So he's mean, tight with the cash, and he despises poor people – thinks that his

God hasn't favoured them. If he has ever worked, it will have been in a clean job where he can wear a suit like an office job but more likely something that some men see as effeminate – a tailor's, selling furniture, soft goods in a big store. But he won't have lasted long because he can't get on with people. The killings make him feel strong. The killings may make him potent.'

'I thought you said he was impotent?' said Beattie.

'I said he could be impotent,' said Ruth, 'but, if he is, the killings return his potency. He masturbates a lot afterwards. Probably recalling the killings. Maybe thinking of his mother. Maybe even in public. Have you checked the records of known flashers for suspects?'

Beattie nodded wearily, thinking that there couldn't be one file, one group, one name or bit of paper in the whole of Glasgow Police's possession that they hadn't examined and Ruth noticed how tired he looked. He was a strong-featured man but, up close, she could see his bloodshot eyes and that his lined face was a grey colour and there was a puffy, pasty texture to his jowls. The poor man must be exhausted, she thought.

Ruth continued.

'He may or may not kill again.'

'You mean you're not sure,' he said with a smile, like a teacher catching out the bright kid.

Ruth wondered if he thought she was arrogant – a young upstart waltzing into the cop shop and telling the experienced detective all about the man he had been chasing night and day for nine months.

'Why no'?'

'It depends on his mission and we won't know that till we get the man – get inside his head.'

'Might be too late by then,' he said.

'I know but don't make the mistake of thinking thrill kill-ers keep killing – especially not Bible John. He'll do what he

307

believes he is being ordered to do and then he'll stop. But, then again, he might never be ordered to stop . . .' She shrugged, 'There's a limit to every science and this is one kind of study we've only just started on. Besides, I'll only tell you what I'm sure of.'

'Fair comment,' he conceded and then he looked at his watch.

Ruth took the hint and moved on to her final point – an important point.

'He acts alone but may not be alone.'

'Now that you'll have to explain, Ruth.' Beattie moved forward in his seat again and sipped at his teacup, before realising it was empty.

'Are you familiar with the phrase "If America sneezes, Britain catches a cold"?'

Beattie nodded.

'The same is true in crime – as you know. Over there, the new freedoms people have are bringing out people's deadlier sides – more sex offenders, more thrill killers, more opportunity.'

So far Joe Beattie didn't disagree with anything.

'We are also learning that some sex offenders and sex killers tune in to each other, copy each other, follow each other.'

'You think this might be true here?' Beattie asked.

'Well, Bible John only ever hunted in The Barrowland, right?'

Beattie gave a nod of confirmation.

'Having been there a few times on Thursday nights . . . Strictly work, you understand – research . . .' It was Ruth's turn to smile. 'I've seen that it's a perfect hunting ground for sex killers.'

'No disagreement there,' Beattie said.

'A city the size of Glasgow must house hundreds of predatory rapists and maybe three to five sex killers at any time. Maybe more?'

'Aye.' He rubbed his face with a big hand – a tired man facing up to an unpalatable fact.

'If you were a sex killer, where would you go for easy targets?'

'The Barrowland would be on my list of top five venues, right enough,' he said, 'though that's changing with all the discos opening and every night seems to be party night now.'

'They're not Bible John's scene, though, are they?'

'Doesn't seem like it but, as things change, he might change his ways too?'

Ruth was shaking her head in disagreement. 'If I'm even half right, he won't change his ways – he'll just get older and maybe burn out.'

'Burn out?'

'Yeah – the way some schizophrenics burn out. They're ill most of their lives and then suddenly they're not.'

'Interesting and let's hope sooner rather than later.' He looked at his watch again. 'I'm sorry, I'm afraid we'll have to finish up now.'

'OK, thanks for your time.' Ruth stood up as Beattie did.

'No problem but tell me something.' Beattie was wide awake now and had moved up close to her, looking intently into Ruth's eyes. 'Do you know he wasn't alone? I mean really know?'

Ruth believed that the best detectives had some things in common with crazy hero soldiers, cold contract killers and incurable psychopaths. She believed they were all detached from the world around them, treating it all with suspicion, seeing all people as worthy of doubt. Some may disagree with her point of view but at least it meant one thing – she was ready for that question.

'I'm certain he wasn't alone.' She held his eyes for a second that seemed to last forever. She was telling him she had nothing to hide.

'How?' His word hit the air like a single sharp slug from a rifle.

'Trust me . . .' She smiled and handed him her report on Bible John. 'I'm a psychologist.'

As she walked slowly to the office door, she thought of Senga and the beautiful silent Maggie and how saying anything about what they had seen that night would be betraying a confidence – would land them in big trouble. She couldn't do that.

She stepped out of the police station door into a sunny Saltmarket. She looked up to the mass of a church directly opposite. It was looking down on her, judging her, but Ruth didn't care. She turned round to where Joe Beattie was still standing in the open doorway. 'And, if you can't trust psychologists yet, just mark it down as woman's intuition.'

Beattie watched her stride away. A good-looking blonde woman with long legs, in a short skirt, she held the key to knowledge he wished he'd had on his first day as a cop, never mind the day after Pat Docker was killed.

'Your time is coming, young Ruth,' he thought to himself. 'Shame I'll not be around to see it.'

Walking through the ancient quarter of the city that is Saltmarket, Ruth marvelled at how much the Bible John story had centred there – as had many tales of murder and horror for centuries. She thought about how they used to hang people publicly there in the hope of sending out a message of fear to future wrongdoers – a message that had often gone unheard because of the lure of the proceeds of vice from brothels. Then it was enslaved women and now it was slaughtered women. Some things change but how come it was always the women who paid? Would any more pay the ultimate price?

Wednesday, 12 August 1970

I am at peace. Me and my girls, we spend some evenings together reminiscing. Some nights I'll tell them Helen's story, other nights it's Jemima and always my special, my first, Patricia. They ask me if new friends are to join us and I ask them to be patient. If my Father calls I will go.

Laugh! Some nights, I weep tears of joy remembering the fools we used to walk among. The two thick cops who stopped me and questioned me to see if I was Me. My girls like it when I say it that way. Of course they couldn't see me. I was wearing my badge, my special badge of protection. I wear it now – my compass through Devils and Life's Trials and Tribulations – wear it always. They will never see that I am me.

How it first raised fury in me that they were calling me a rapist. Me a rapist??? But then I saw my Father's way. If the fools thought they were looking for a rapist, then they'd search for a Devil. Not me.

Best of all, I laugh at how I left them clues but, of course, they did not listen. The night I cleansed my Helen, her sister, Jeannie, asked me my name. I told her. Twice I told her my chosen name and twice she never heard. Too busy looking over my shoulder.

John Templeton, I said. Templeton. All they had to do was hear and think. It means Knight Templar. It means I fight a Holy War. It means I belong to the Brotherhood. A Brotherhood but not of this world. It means I retreat to take stock for they will never understand me. Just my Father knows.

He knows and leads me back here to the place of my Trials. The soft countryside, away from my city. It was the house of my mother. It is now the house of my Father. Her voice is still. Some nights, when the Seed is in me, I dare her to return. She never does.

Here I have visitors. The best kind of visitors who only visit when I ask them to. Kindly people who ask how I am but never why I am how I am. I have seen what they write. A recluse, they call me, with mild personality disorders. Such good people who write me down in their files as if I have never been away. In some ways, they are right.

Call us again if you need us, they say, and I do when I return from my place, my city, my She, Glasgow. Then they visit again and give me pills and ask how I am and so it goes on. They are the only nice people I have ever met. They are more than that. In the land of the Devils, they are my alibi.

My Father sent them to me.

My Father will call on me again.

'How many men do you need to give you a hand, Tom?' Joe Beattie stood in the room in The Marine where Detective Superintendent Tom Valentine had spent almost every waking hour for the previous eleven months.

'Just a couple, Joe, but those two lassies who help me are the best of all. Better than any of the men.'

'Lassies?' Beattie rolled his eyes in mock shock. 'Changed days, eh?'

'Aye, thank God,' said Valentine, meaning every sentiment.

He should've been a happy man. The powers that be had decided to transfer him back to normal duties in charge of a division. Proper police work, most cops would call it, but Valentine knew that the handling of information was just as important as any kind of cop work in catching a killer. It would be good to return to normal duties, though, but first he had to coordinate the shipping of all the evidence he had collated to the Central Police Office. More evidence than he had ever handled before – more evidence than Glasgow Police Force, one of the biggest and the oldest police force in Britain, had ever collected before. It was such a shame that all their efforts hadn't snared Bible John.

'How are you feeling about this, Joe?' Beattie was to stand down and soon would be transferred to Tulliallan Police College where cops from all over Scotland would be trained. As Deputy Commandant he'd be influential in shaping the future skills of a generation of cops. It was a compliment to one of Glasgow's best-ever detectives but Tom was wondering if Joe saw it that way.

'Me? I'm just glad I'm no' shifting these boxes of files.'

'Aye, we'd never get sorted then, eh? But that's no' what I meant.'

'Failure always leaves a bad taste in my mouth, Tom,' Beattie said with a shrug. 'And that's the way it should be for cops.'

'We gave it our best shot, Joe.'

'Best wasn't good enough, though.' Joe Beattie wasn't about to be appeased. He never had been and never would be – not when some killer he had set out to catch remained free.

'I've been doing a bit of tallying up on this investigation,' said Valentine.

This didn't surprise Joe Beattie one bit – it was a mark of the man's thoroughness.

'Want to see what we've done?'

'Go on then, depress me.'

Valentine handed him a sheet of paper that declared:

```
HELEN PUTTOCK MURDER INQUIRY
30.10.69 to 23.9.70
TIPS: 4,586
LEADS FOLLOWED UP: 4,313
STATEMENTS TAKEN: 51,646
ID PARADES: 253
TAILORS CHECKED: 246
HAIRDRESSERS CHECKED: 453
```

'I've not completed it yet,' said Valentine when Joe Beattie had finished reading the short list.

'Aye, you might as well add "Suspects: None".'

'I was thinking more about the surveillance operations at The Barrowland, the hundred of guys we must have pulled in because they had one front tooth overlapping the other, the bloody Freemasons we upset . . .'

'"BALDY DOGS 1"!'

'Aye!' Valentine laughed, pleased to hear his colleague cracking a joke. 'The poor mutt with the right hair colour.'

But he had a sense of how Beattie was feeling. Men like Tom Valentine didn't like to fail either. In this case, he'd dread the phone ringing in case he'd hear that another young woman had been strangled, a young woman who was menstruating. He'd dread that till the day the killer was caught or the day he died, whichever came sooner.

'"WEANS WITHOUT MAMMIES 6".' Joe Beattie had hit a mark below the belt. Any cop worth their salt hated the thought of children suffering. They were in the job to stop children suffering – otherwise what was the point?

'But at least there's been no more murders,' Valentine said, thinking that no more children had lost their mothers at the hands of Bible John.

'No, not yet but it was eighteen months between Pat Docker and Mima McDonald.'

'But did that lassie that gave you the report – you know, the psychologist – did she no' say that he might not kill again?'

'Aye but, then again, she said he might. We couldn't tell till we got hold of him and unravelled his brains.'

'Hmm, aye, I remember now but what about that psychiatrist from the Douglas Inch Clinic – Robert P. Brittain – was he no' saying that Bible John would work out his killing style, get faster and then go at it till he was sated, finished. Eleven months since Helen Puttock – not exactly fast killing, is it?'

'Assuming that he'll do all his killing in Glasgow.'

'Aye, right enough.'

'But the lassie, as you call her,' Beattie was smiling at his mate, 'she phoned me when that psychiatrist went public – said he wasn't describing Bible John. He wasn't even describing serial killers. It was what they call sadistic murderers that he was on about. A different kettle of killer it seems.'

'She should know, eh?'

'Aye, she's a bright one, that.'

'That's where we win, Joe.' Tom Valentine was fitting big bundles of A4 paper, scarred black with print, into a grey box file.

'How?'

'Patience and talent. Patience and talent.'

Having filled the grey box file, Valentine placed it in a large cardboard box on top of others that looked identical but he knew different – it was all in the contents.

Turning to Beattie he went on, 'The polis will always be here waiting even if we're no'. Then you'll get new faces, new skills – like that lassie – and folk learning new tricks all the time.'

'Aye, policing is changing and fast, that's for sure.'

'Patience and talent, Joe. If he's still out there, we'll get Bible John.'

'Well, hello, stranger,' Ruth said with a smile as she walked over to Peter who was sitting at a table in The Curlers bar.

'Hello, yourself,' he replied, standing up and coming round the table to give her a hug and a peck on the cheek.

She realised that he had grown up so much since they'd first met almost two years before. Broader, he was still strong but more relaxed and confident in how he handled himself.

'I thought madam would wish to sit at our special table.'

'So it is,' she said, almost squealing as she remembered he was right. 'Aw, the first night we met – you romantic sod, you.'

'One does one's best,' he joked.

'You'll make some woman very happy one day,' she said and they both smiled with their eyes, acknowledging their friendship would stay just that.

'Hopefully sooner rather than later.'

'Are you winching?'

'Winching? Winching? You've been in Glasgow too long, Ruth, you're beginning to speak like the natives and that's not a good sound, not a good sound at all, so it's no'.'

'Ha, snob. Answer the question.'

Over the sound system, Jimi Hendrix was making love to his guitar and 'Voodoo Chile' filled the air.

'Yeah, I'm going steady!' Peter was grinning and his cheeks were red. He hadn't matured so much that he no longer blushed.

'One of these modern policewomen, is she?'

'No, she is certainly not.' He shook his head as if that was a fate worse than death. 'Mary's a social worker.'

'Ah, one of those soft-soaping liberal hippies! Is it a case of opposites attracting?'

'Not as much as you think.'

Ruth sat and listened to Peter explain that he was disillusioned by being a policeman. As he spoke, she looked around the bar at everyone with long hair, the men in brightly coloured loon pants with huge flares, the women in long, low-cut, floral gypsy dresses that swung as they moved. Here and there people passed round joints, something that the bar staff totally ignored.

When the door sprang open, she thought back to that first night when the Teddy Boys had pranced in looking for a fight. This time it was three young men, wearing faded ex-army fatigues with little red badges of Trotsky, bigger Ban the Bomb symbols and neat wee red and black stars. The decorations were good looking enough to be jewellery but they were much more than that. One carried a bundle of newspapers under an arm. Ruth craned her head to read what was below the red banner top which declared itself as 'Red Mole'. They were politicos and the only trouble they intended to cause was to Ted Heath's Tory government.

As usual, she was aware of everything that was going on around her. One thing that didn't escape her attention was that everyone smelled good – sometimes it was the strong suffocating smell of too much patchouli but good nevertheless. And she couldn't help thinking how much people had changed in two years. Or had they?

'The Bible John case,' Peter was saying, 'at first I thought it was such an opportunity. Even being involved in the slog of the routine work . . . being involved in one of the biggest manhunts in history as a young cop. Well . . .' He didn't finish his sentence but picked up his pint glass and stared into it.

'Peter, it must have been a great opportunity but you're obviously feeling down. What's wrong? Because it still isn't solved?'

He shook his head. 'It's not that though it would've been great to catch the bastard. It's how some of the cops went about their business.' He reached out for his cigarettes. 'Sometimes I got to believe that all you had to do in Glasgow was be a young, slim bloke with reddish hair to have the cops beat you up.' He turned and looked at Ruth square on, his eyes glistening with emotion. 'I'm serious, Ruth.'

'Not Joe Beattie and Dalglish and . . .'

'No, no, not them – they're top men. But the troops – some of the troops . . . It's like brutality is all they know. Joe Beattie gets knocked back by the lawyers from using a hypnotist on Jeannie Williams in case it jeopardises the case and these fucking wallies are kicking the shit out of suspects and possible witnesses. Word got out about that and maybe . . . well, just maybe some useful witnesses were scared away. Talk about stupid.'

'But, Peter, you don't need to be like them.'

Ruth didn't need to be told about police brutality and had long ago made her mind up about bad cops and good cops. She reckoned all such male organisations would always produce some men who resorted to violence. That didn't mean they were all bad.

'You can be one of the good guys.'

'Aye, of course, but I don't think I want to be associated with the violence at all. Can't stand it, Ruth. I'm beginning to think the peace and love mob are right.' He nodded in the direction of the bar where a man with long hair tied back with a bandana stood drinking, an acoustic guitar draped over his back. On the front of the guitar was a sticker saying, 'U.N.O. WE WANT PEACE'.

'Have you thought of what you're going to do, Peter?'

'I'm going to leave – that much I've decided – but, as for the rest . . .' He shrugged. 'There was something Joe Beattie said to me about the job not just being about the killer but about victims and their families.'

319

'What about it?'

'I don't know yet but it stuck in my mind.'

Over the sound system, the sweet tones of Matthews Southern Comfort's song about the festival at Woodstock started out.

'Did you realise,' asked Ruth, 'that the love-in at Woodstock was happening at the same time as the night Mima McDonald was murdered?'

'No. Really? That's Glasgow for you. Bible John's second murder, eh?'

More than that, it's possible that Canned Heat were on stage at the time, playing "Let's Work Together".'

'When?'

'When Jemima was being murdered by him – when Mima was being killed by Bible John.'

'You sure it wasn't Janis Joplin singing "To Love Somebody"?'

'Maybe!' Ruth looked at him with a rueful grin that said she understood his dark humour. 'But I prefer to think of "Let's Work Together".'

'Ah, does the hard-headed psychologist think there might be a message in that then?'

'Well, sitting here with a friend, she does like to think so. And, even if there isn't, it *is* the only way we'll catch the killer – by working together.'

'Too true. But are you still convinced all three murders were down to the same man?'

'I think so. In fact, I'm sure of it.'

'So am I. The question is will Bible John kill again?'

She shrugged. 'Now we'll just have to wait and see.'

The scream echoed through the black of night – one howling, piercing, agonised scream. A woman was in serious trouble but no one – almost no one – was listening.

They found her there the next day lying in a field of broken glass, used condoms and rusting empty lager cans. She had died on waste ground, her pleas for help unheard, except by her killer. It was November 1978, eight years since the city of Glasgow trembled in horror at the spectre of Bible John. Cops attending this murder scene took one look and asked the question, 'Has Bible John returned?'

Mary Gallacher was only seventeen years old, full of energy and hope for the future. That night she was only going a short distance from her home in Springburn to visit a pal – a short distance that took her close to Foresthall, an ancient old building that used to be a poorhouse where folk without any money were locked up to live out their days in misery with little to eat but thin porridge. In the night, the spires and arches of Foresthall were frightening, spooky. There were those who said it was haunted but that's not what Mary should have been scared of that night.

Out of the dark, he came for her – grabbed her from the road by force. She struggled and kicked but he was too strong. Taking her from Edgefauld Road that passed by Foresthall, he dragged her down near Barnhill Railway Station, which was deserted at night, and out on to waste ground where no one dared go, not even the stray dogs. They found her there the next day.

Mary was lying on her back, naked from the waist down, her throat had been slashed and her denims were wrapped tightly round her neck. Experienced cops looked down and wondered if Mary had been menstruating. It was difficult to tell. Those denims didn't kill her – her slashed throat was testament to that – but were they symbolic? Did they replace stockings? How many women wore stockings in 1978? Had Bible John changed with the changing times?

Glasgow cops had already asked the question whether the city's most infamous serial killer was back and killing the year before, in August 1977, when twenty-year-old Anna Kenny had gone for a night out at the Hurdy Gurdy pub in Townhead and was last seen alive going to look for a taxi home. She never arrived home. Officially, she was treated as a missing person but the cops were worried and with good reason.

Two men had been driving around Glasgow, late at night, preying on young women out on their own. They'd force them into the vehicle, drive to an isolated spot and brutally rape them. While those men were at liberty, the police expected a sex killing to happen. Had Anna Kenny fought back too fiercely? Had she become a victim? They would find the answer but not yet.

On 1 October 1977, thirty-six-year-old Hilda McAulay went to the dancing at the Plaza Ballroom in Glasgow's southside. Two days later, her body was found in a leafy lovers' lane in Langbank, a village on the city's outskirts. Hilda was naked from the waist down. She'd been badly beaten and she'd been raped.

The cops didn't like the idea of her last night having been spent at the dancing – albeit she'd gone to the Plaza and not The Barrowland. Detective Superintendent Douglas Meldrum was in charge of the case and he had learned the lessons of history from the Bible John case.

Keeping the murder from the public, he sent undercover female detectives, dressed up to the nines, into the Plaza. The Glasgow cops soon gave the brave women a name

– 'Meldrum's Angels'. Daring as they were, Meldrum's Angels didn't snare Hilda McAulay's killer.

Then the cops had a breakthrough. They arrested the two men who had been trawling the city, brutally raping women. They managed to pin thirteen vicious assaults on the sex perverts but no murders. So, now the police were really worried – there was another sex killer on the loose.

On 2 December 1977, twenty-three-year-old Agnes Cooney went for a drink at the Clada Social Club, a few minutes' walk from the Plaza Ballroom. Two days later, she was found dead on a lonely moor out in Caldercruix near the town of Airdrie, fifteen miles from Glasgow. She too was naked from the waist down but hadn't been raped. She had fought so hard her attacker had battered her black and blue and stabbed her twenty-six times. When he went to formally identify her body, her poor father couldn't recognise his own daughter.

Across in Edinburgh some cops were beginning to wonder if Bible John had paid them a visit. When a pair of seventeen-year-olds, Christine Eadie and Helen Scott, went to The World's End pub on the Royal Mile on 15 October 1977, they were looking forward to a good night out. By all accounts, they had a pleasant time and were chatted up by two guys they seemed to be getting on well with – two guys in well-cut suits, wearing collars and ties and with short, neat haircuts.

The next day, at two separate isolated locations, Christine and Helen were found dead. Both were naked from the waist down. They'd both been raped and strangled with their tights. After a thorough search of the scene, the police discovered some things were missing – they couldn't find the young women's handbags.

The World's End murders sparked the biggest manhunt in Edinburgh's history. As Hogmanay approached and, with it, a new year, the investigation had made no progress. As 1978 went on, the police were still no nearer catching the killer but the name on many Edinburgh cops' lips was well known – Bible John.

Much had been learned about serial killers since 1969 and the murder of Helen Puttock. That was thanks to a new breed of practitioner – criminal psychologists. The police no longer thought of psychologists as shrinks or nutters' doctors but as colleagues who could provide crucial information on thrill killers.

They knew that, while a serial killer is likely to develop a certain ritual of murder, he is also likely to change and develop it. So, not all the victims of 1977 and 1978 were menstruating but some were. So, not all of them were strangled with tights or stockings but some were and not all women wore such items by 1977. So, handbags weren't always taken from the scene but were all the investigating teams looking for such clues? So, a knife was used in most killings – had Bible John's inner voice told him to use a blade with certain women? So, not all of the victims had been to the dancing but hadn't it become playtime in whole cities every night of the week? Dens of iniquity were now everywhere. So, what if he did kill in Edinburgh? Doesn't such a man do as he is told? So, what if he had a partner in the World's End killings? Didn't some psychologist say back in 1970 that Bible John acted alone but wasn't alone?

Glasgow and Edinburgh cops fell out in private. Edinburgh police said there should be a joint investigation. Glasgow police said there was no need since there were several killers.

Then two shepherds took a walk in Argyll and they changed their minds.

With its purple heather, miles of silver rock and sea stretching all the way to Ireland, Skipness is a place of beauty. A peaceful place. An idyll. Then they saw the bones sticking out of the earth.

Men of the land know about life and death. The two shepherds knew instantly that the bones weren't animal bones.

When the cops appeared they found a human skeleton buried in a shallow grave. Around the neck was wrapped some material, red and white, and at the ankles too. It was 23 April 1979 and the local minister immediately went public, saying a witches' coven practised in the area and this was one of their human sacrifices. Symbols that had been placed around the grave supported the view – ancient symbols that looked like witches' symbols. Or were they Masonic?

With the skeleton transferred to Glasgow for full forensic tests, the doctors used what little identifying evidence they had – the teeth. When a match came back a puzzle was solved. Now the police knew what had happened to Anna Kenny after she disappeared twenty-odd months before, after a night out at the Hurdy Gurdy pub.

Anna had been wearing a red and white blouse. The killer had used her own clothing to bind her feet and to strangle her. Glasgow cops announced they had a serial killer on their hands and older cops had only one name on their minds – Bible John – but now they also believed they knew the real identity of the man who had haunted Glasgow for so long. What they didn't know was that his time was about to come.

'Just my usual please, Margaret.' Having served him almost every day for years, the barmaid in the Old Ship Inn, Stonehouse, knew fine well what the customer wanted. She pulled a half-pint of beer, measured a whisky from the optic on the gantry, laid them on the bar and stepped back. Sometimes she'd stand and chat with John but not that day – that day, he looked as if the worries of the world were heavy on his shoulders. The barmaid wasn't wrong.

'What's wrong with Bible John?' another regular asked quietly. 'No Bible quotes today?'

'It looks like there'll be no quotes about anything,' said his drinking partner.

Everyone in Stonehouse knew John McInnes – knew him for the strange man he was. And they called him Bible John for good reasons. He'd been brought up locally by his parents who were strict adherents to the Brethren faith – although some would even describe it more as a cult than a religion. The Brethren believe that the whole world is wicked and so they tend to keep apart from other people, including other Christians. Male members in particular are warned about the evil ways of non-Brethren women. Through his puberty and early adulthood, the teaching of the faith was left mainly to his mother as McInnes's father died when his son had just passed his sixteenth birthday.

Everything in Brethren lives is governed by strict reference to the Bible and often it's the Old rather than the New Testament. So, John McInnes could quote the Bible all night and often did – something that won him no friends, especially among non-believers.

As a teenager, McInnes was called up for national service and non-Brethren locals hoped that his time away among ordinary men, when he'd meet other people, including women, would help him break away from the religion of his childhood. It did change him but in a way that saw him return with a bad habit – heavy drinking. His soldier mates thought he was lazy and a very poor team player. He'd disappear to the pubs on his own and didn't seem to mind the consequences. They thought of him as Strange John.

Back in Stonehouse, McInnes got a job in a furniture shop and met and married a young woman, Ella Russell. They had two children but soon the marriage failed and he returned to live with his mother at 26 Queen Street. By then, he had become a regular drinker but still kept it a secret from his elderly mother, wanting her to believe he was still true to the Brethren faith. Locals laughed at him for thinking he could keep anything secret from anyone in that small town.

Army life had also given John McInnes other tastes – for smart suits. In Stonehouse, where most men would go drinking in their work clothes of dungarees and heavy boots, he'd turn up at the pub in a smart Italian-style suit, usually brown or blue, with a crisp shirt and often his regimental striped tie.

McInnes had another taste that the Brethren wouldn't approve of – dancing. Not jut any dancing but dancing at The Barrowland Ballroom and not just any night but Palais Nights – Thursday nights.

So keen was he on his weekly trip to The Barrowland that he lost at least one job by choosing his entertainment over business conferences. All of this went on during the final years of the 1960s. No wonder then he was hauled in as an early suspect in the Bible John murders.

Helen Puttock's sister didn't recognise John McInnes at that first ID parade. She'd see him again a few times as the cops persisted, pulling him in along with other Bible John lookalikes. On one occasion, Glasgow cops even travelled to the south of England to bring McInnes back from a holiday for an ID parade. Helen's sister Jeannie had once said that she understood why they had chosen him – she'd said there was 'a sixty per cent likeness' but he was not the man she knew as Strange John.

Most men caught up in the hunt for Bible John either kept it quiet or spoke out in outraged anger. McInnes, however, boasted about it. When locals found out, they soon started calling him Bible John and did so for years. McInnes just laughed and seemed to enjoy the notoriety.

When the Bible John investigation petered out, John McInnes continued his life as usual – going to The Barrowland and sneaking to the pub. At the Old Ship Inn, he'd join the old men playing dominoes. He was known to play badly yet he preferred that to keeping company with men his own age and seemed incapable of holding a conversation with any woman – he even found small talk with Margaret the barmaid difficult. Sometimes he'd be moody and sit on his own. He'd just have a couple of drinks and leave without saying anything. Locals knew he was a troubled soul but not exactly how troubled.

At one point he ran a small sweet shop in Stonehouse. It was a well-run, happy shop till, one day, customers walked in and there was no John McInnes. Locals wondered what had happened but did nothing till a neighbouring shopkeeper took matters into his own hands. He went through the shop to the storeroom at the back and there he found John McInnes on the floor with a broken noose around his neck. He had tried to hang himself and failed.

John McInnes attempted suicide on three occasions so there was no doubt that he was a troubled man – all the locals knew that. But what was troubling him?

'Just my usual please, Margaret,' he said to the barmaid at the Old Ship Inn that day on 29 April 1980. She served him his usual half-pint and whisky and left him alone. There was no good talking to John McInnes when he was depressed.

McInnes, now forty-one, drank his two drinks, turned and left the pub without as much as a farewell, which wasn't unusual when he was in one of his moods. He walked the short distance to his mother's house at 26 Queen Street, climbed into the small, cramped loft, took off his jacket and slashed himself.

The next day John McInnes was found dead. The man that many Glasgow cops believed was Bible John. The same man who many believed had returned to a murderous rampage. The man some Edinburgh detectives believed responsible for the World's End murders. John McInnes cheated them all through death.

When word reached Glasgow Police, some officers were relieved. At least the recent spate of murders would stop, they reasoned. Others pooh-poohed the idea that McInnes had been involved at all and some were too new in the job to remember the details of the Bible John killings. Others knew about McInnes's background and remembered the real concern there had been that some type of religious fanatic was behind the killings. Some had even been involved on the raids on churches to lift suspects – one time even from a Salvation Army hall. Then one detective made a phone call to colleagues out in Stonehouse.

'Does anyone remember the details of the Helen Puttock murder?' he asked his cop colleagues after the phone call. Around the room, he received a few affirmative nods in reply. 'Remember where they found her sanitary towel?'

'Sure, placed neatly under her arm,' one replied. 'So?'

'So, John McInnes killed himself by slicing an artery under his arm.'

Silence filled the room. They had dealt with almost every type of self-harm and suicide imaginable but that was a first.

'I think some families deserve justice,' he went on. 'I think it's time we identified Bible John.'

'Are all you forensic-type women good-looking blondes?' Peter stood at the bottom of the steep stairs leading down into his office, watching Ruth descend.

'You still know how to make a woman feel good about herself, Peter,' she laughed, 'but who is the competition?'

As she reached the last step his big arms came out and wrapped round her, almost lifting her off her feet. It was 1996 and a lot of years had passed since she had first met that tall, slim young man back at The Curlers pub. His hair had grown grey, almost silver, and he had a bit of a belly – not fat, just a comfortable girth.

'Oh, I'll show you in a minute,' he said, slowly letting her down to her feet. 'But, my, you're keeping well, Ruth.'

He was right. Her blonde hair had stayed blonde in spite of her having passed her half-century earlier that year. Lucky genetics meant she could eat and drink what she wanted and still keep her figure – that and the fact that she'd taken to walking over the years. Not rambling in the country but moving around cities as she sussed out some crime scene or followed some series of events.

'Come on through,' Peter said, pushing open heavy glass doors.

Not for the first time, the comfortable waiting room took Ruth by surprise. There just above their heads out on the pavement she had been walking through one of the roughest parts of Saltmarket past cleared sites and semi-demolished buildings, skirting the edge of the Barras flea market which was mostly shuttered and closed that early on a weekday. Up on top the vista was urban decay but down below Peter's office was warm, welcoming and plush.

Peter had been true to his word and left the police. After years of mature study and a few years doing his apprenticeship with one of Glasgow's biggest firms, he had emerged here, a practising lawyer with only one colleague, Sadie, his ever-efficient secretary, client counsellor, tissue-hander-out, tea lady and everything else that needed to be done apart from the legal work. There was method in his choice of office location, being situated, as it was, on the edge of Glasgow's east-end badlands. Peter had left the cops but not crime.

Ruth had stuck to her guns. Now the world recognised forensic psychology as an invaluable tool in solving crime and she was acknowledged as one of its most eminent practitioners. When appearing as a guest lecturer in some university or, often, to a police force and introduced as such, she'd always start off by saying, 'Not so much eminent – more just a case of early.'

Professor Pickford, her old psychology tutor at Glasgow University, had taken a risk on her after she'd completed her PhD and created a lecturer's post just for her and her forensic psychology. All these years later and she was still doing that same job except now she was an associate professor at the university, a consultant at the Douglas Inch Clinic at Glasgow's Charing Cross, on the international conference circuit as a speaker, called in frequently by police forces all over Europe, the author of three books and, increasingly, a face on the TV.

'But only BBC2,' she'd scoff, 'and even then only late at night.'

Ruth and Peter were very satisfied with how their lives had turned out.

'How's Mary?' Ruth asked.

'Doing very well,' he smiled, 'but still the bloody social worker lecturing me about inequality and poverty, you'll be glad to hear.'

'Good woman. And the kids?' Peter's children had long since qualified to be called young adults.

'Oooh, I'm having real problems with the lassie.'

'That's women for you,' said Ruth, knowing by Peter's tone it wasn't something serious like drug addiction or sensitive like unplanned pregnancy.

'Well, this harpy wants to be a cop.'

Ruth laughed out loud.

'Keeps telling me that she could contribute to the well-being of society.'

'Now where have I heard *that* before? Mmm?'

'Aye, all right, and then she tells me that it's all changed since my day.'

'She might be right.'

'I'm not so sure.' Peter had a reputation for fighting cases of unjust conviction – fighting and winning. 'Besides, if the boys hear my daughter's a polis my business will be ruined.' As an ex-policeman turned lawyer, Peter was very popular with the criminal classes of Glasgow. 'Anyway, enough of my grief. How's your better half?'

'She's fine. Still trying to convince me we should move to Venice.' Ruth rolled her eyes, not needing to explain to Peter that it was just what you should expect if you chose to live with a lecturer in Italian.

Peter laughed. 'How long have you two been together now? I mean lived together?'

'About sixteen years.'

'That's an old married couple these days, eh?'

Ruth smiled.

'Yet, every time I think of the pair of you, I blush a wee bit thinking of that skinny kid who asked you to pass me the ashtray in The Curlers. How naive, eh?'

'You mean you had an ulterior motive, Peter?' Her voice was full of mock indignation. 'They were more innocent times in so many ways.'

'Aye and no, Ruth, aye and no. I've been thinking a bit of an old pal of ours lately.' Peter pushed a thick buff file towards her across his desk. 'Think you'll be interested in this lot. A fried of mine who works for a broadsheet passed them to me – unofficial, of course.'

As Sadie, quiet and efficient as ever, placed a tray with a cafetière of coffee, mugs and some biscuits on the desk, Ruth opened the file and started leafing through. Inside were pictures all taken in the same graveyard. The first few showed a group of policemen, other official-looking types, a hearse and some undertakers standing around. As she went through them, the pictures slowly unveiled the action. Lengthy poles were stuck into the ground and canvas screens were draped from them to shelter one grave. Men in black overalls were digging at the grave with shiny spades and then someone significant appeared into a shot.

'Ah, Dr Marie Cassidy – the good-looking blonde,' said Ruth.

Cassidy was one of Scotland's top pathologists. She had handled many complex cases and provided effective expert evidence. She was so good media people had used her as a consultant of the TV series *Taggart* and based an entire television drama series, *Silent Witness*, on her. She was also, as Peter and Ruth both acknowledged, good looking.

'Who's the lucky person getting Marie's attention?'

'John McInnes,' Peter replied, knowing that further explanation wasn't required.

'Bible John, eh?' Ruth continued flicking through the photographs.

'Many people think so.'

Since 1990, ten years after McInnes's suicide, the police had been trying to get permission to exhume his body. They argued that new developments in DNA, which allowed tests for a match between single cells, could now be used to test his DNA against a small amount of semen found on Helen Puttock's clothes. The cops had received a great deal of resistance to the exhumation and some politicians had even got caught up in the wrangling. For the past six years, the cops had taken samples from some of McInnes's belongings, his brother and other family members but none of that worked. So, finally, they had won permission to dig up John McInnes's body but were told to keep a low profile, to keep it out of the public domain, in order to protect his surviving family members.

'Well, McInnes's background matches a lot of Bible John's psychological profile,' said Ruth. 'A lot but not enough.'

'If you were a betting woman,' said Peter, 'would you put your money on McInnes being Bible John?'

'Bible John as in the man who actually strangled and murdered Pat Docker, Mima McDonald and Helen Puttock?'

A lot had happened in the intervening years. Many more women had been murdered and the name Bible John was often put in the ring so it was reasonable of her to seek clarification.

'That's who I mean,' Peter replied.

'Then McInnes is more likely to be the mysterious Castlemilk John.'

'The guy they never traced?' Peter was shocked. 'You serious?'

'No,' she giggled at him. 'Not at all, I think Castlemilk John is of no importance at all – a red herring.'

'Thank God, Ruth, I thought you'd lost it there. So what about Bible John? Is McInnes Bible John?'

'Absolutely not.'

'Shame you're not a betting woman, Ruth,' he smiled. 'One of my police contacts has whispered to me that they're about to announce there's no conclusive link between John McInnes and the forensic evidence from Helen Puttock.'

'You mean admit that he's not Bible John?'

'Aye but whenever did the cops just come out and say something straight?'

'Well, I do remember meeting this fresh-faced polis rookie one time . . .' She smiled, enjoying the fact that she could still tease him.

'There's something else, though.'

He sipped his coffee and waved a refusal to a cigarette offered by Ruth. He was desperate for a smoke. Had been every day for the past two years since he quit.

'They won't tell me who, not even off the record, but . . .' Peter hesitated and breathed in the second-hand blue fumes from Ruth's cigarette. 'They're going after someone else.'

'Interesting,' said Ruth, 'after all these years as well.'

'This one's still alive.'

'They think Bible John's still alive? Who the hell are they going after?'

The judge moved into the court, his gown flowing behind him, his wig perched on his head. Everyone stood but the last to get to his feet was the man in the dock. What did he care about respect? What did he care if he got into trouble? He was in the worst kind of trouble already.

'M'lord, the accused stands accused of, on 15 October 1977, along with another now deceased, murdering Christine Eadie and Helen Scott, both aged seventeen years.'

It was 30 October 2006 in the High Court, Edinburgh, and a man was being accused of the World's End Murders twenty-nine years previously. The sixty-one-year-old man looked ordinary and weak. His appearance gave no hint as to his background. He was no stranger to the court, having been convicted of the culpable homicide of a seven-year-old girl in 1961, when he was only sixteen years old. When freed, he became embroiled in a series of rapes and sexual attacks until he was eventually jailed for life in 1982.

The police knew Angus Sinclair was capable of sexual perversion, rape and extreme violence but it would take another nineteen years before they began to get the true measure of the man. Whiling away his time in the sex offenders unit up in Peterhead Prison, Sinclair didn't know it but the cops were coming to get him.

Following the failed DNA tests on John McInnes in 1996, Glasgow cops had quietly gone about their work. They had unfinished business to attend to. The families of some murdered women were still waiting for answers.

Mary Gallacher had died a lonely death on waste ground in the north of Glasgow. The killer had stripped her from the waist down and brutally raped her before slashing her throat and strangling her with her denims. He had been so careful but not careful enough. One speck of semen had been found and retained. The same developments in DNA they had hoped would prove John McInnes was Bible John were now applied to Mary's case. On 14 June 2001, Angus Sinclair was finally found guilty of raping and murdering young Mary Gallacher.

Behind closed doors, a team of cops was set up to look at Sinclair's life. The man was now proven to be capable of the most horrendous violence yet he had been free for many long years. What else had he got up to?

They dusted down every unsolved sex killing and asked themselves a question. Could Angus Sinclair have been the killer? Old arguments between Glasgow and Edinburgh cops were long dead. Just as well – after Mary Gallacher, the next positive findings came up for the World's End Murders in the capital. And that's how Sinclair found himself in the High Court in 2006, accused of the double killing along with his much younger brother-in-law, Gordon Hamilton. But Hamilton wasn't in the court for a very good reason – he was dead.

Sinclair had hired one of the best lawyers in Scotland, Edgar Prais QC. Prais argued that certain pre-trial publicity might have prejudiced the case and was allocated extra time to hold these arguments and trial was planned for spring 2007. It was OK for the wheels of justice to turn a little slower in this instance – Angus Sinclair was going nowhere except back to prison.

Meanwhile, Glasgow cops had brought a team of detectives out of retirement. Without having the pressure of any other work, their job was to re-examine unsolved cases that had gone cold. Publicly they announced that Sinclair was the prime suspect in the murders of Anna Kenny, Hilda McAulay and Agnes Cooney – all murdered in 1977 and 1978 and all suspected of being murdered by Bible John.

It didn't take Sherlock Holmes to work out something about Angus Sinclair. He was around Glasgow at the time of the Bible John murders.

Jailed for six years for culpable homicide in 1961, he was free and in the city by late 1967. Pat Docker, Bible John's first victim, was killed on 22 February 1968. And they knew something else about Sinclair – he liked the dancing. Like most young men, he was keen on sex and where better to meet women than at the jigging? Especially on Palais Nights – Thursday nights at The Barrowland Ballroom.

But such tastes were not exclusive to Sinclair – he was just one of many, many men who shared the same inclinations. The difference was that he was a known rapist and killer. With the benefit of modern forensics, the old cops began to look at Angus Sinclair in relation to the murders of Pat Docker, Mima McDonald and Helen Puttock.

Wary of the decision won by Edgar Prais QC at the High Court that certain pre-trial publicity might prejudice the case against Sinclair for the World's End Murders, the police couldn't go public.

'Can I meet you at the usual pub?' the familiar voice had said down the phone.

'Sure you can,' replied the journalist. 'The usual time?'

'Aye.'

Police and the media have exchanged information ever since they have existed. Sometimes it's for brown envelopes full of used banknotes and sometimes, as on this occasion, it is to serve justice.

'We can't name names, even here, but you know who we've been investigating.'

The journalist did.

'We've found a match, a DNA match with all three Bible John victims.'

'Fuck.' This was big news indeed. 'A hundred per cent match?'

'No, eighty per cent but enough to get it through court.'

'Get a conviction?'

'Oh, aye, a dead cert.'

'And you sure we can't even whisper a name.'

'No chance.' The cop was on his feet heading for the door. 'And let Bible John go free again?'

Thursday, 19 April 2007

My trials and tribulations are not over. Even from a distance they try to bleed me, try to malign me. But I'm stronger than they are. I am free.

Devils have haunted me through my life. My cold-hearted mother. The torments of children. Those men who would sex me. They were but the beginning. Then came the Devils who followed me. The Devils who copied me. Now those who say they have caught me. They have snared a Devil.

I am free.

I sit here with my girls and my Father. I am at peace.

Some days we return to my city – She who fed me. I walk the familiar streets and weep for the change. But still She is my place and I will return to Her till the day I die.

Soon there will be a public spectacle in Caesar's court. Devils will punish the Devils. Those with sin will throw the first stones. Those with sins will punish those with sin. A sham. They will hold up a severed head and declare that I am dead.

I am alive. I am free.

Maybe my Father will call on me to teach them once more that I am free. Maybe He will need me to seek those with the Fire once more and cleanse them. Maybe.

Who will believe it is my severed head they hold up?

They know me as John and fear me still.